The Sovereign

Andrew Elias Colarusso

THE SOVEREIGN

DALKEY ARCHIVE PRESS

Library of Congress Cataloging-in-Publication Data
Names: Colarusso, Andrew Elias, author.
Title: The sovereign / by Andrew Elias Colarusso.
Description: First Dalkey Archive edition. | Victoria, TX : Dalkey
Archive Press, 2017.
Identifiers: LCCN 2017005008 | ISBN 9781943150106 (softcover :
acid-free paper)
Subjects: LCSH: Puerto Rico--Politics and government--Fiction. |
Puerto Ricans--Fiction.
Classification: LCC PS3603.O41235 S69 2017 | DDC 813/.6--dc23
LC record available at https://lccn.loc.gov/2017005008

www.dalkeyarchive.com
Victoria, TX / McLean, IL / Dublin

Dalkey Archive Press publications are, in part, made possible through
the support of the University of Houston-Victoria and its programs in
creative writing, publishing, and translation.

Printed on permanent/durable acid-free paper

Love you Mom
I win

"... ninguém é obrigado a ler o livro inteiro."

O Sumiço da Santa
–Jorge Amado

THE SOVEREIGN

CONTENTS

BOOK I: DEMESNE

Cordyceps
Remex & Rectrix
Inertia
Abendlanguage

BOOK II: SOLIFUGE

i.   Andante Moderato
ii.   The Austringer's Set
iii.   Sobras
iv.   Essay on the Uses of a Cowbell
v.   Orations [Redacted]
vi.   Poshlost
vii.   Music for the Law of Club and Fang by Jack
        London [Studio Sessions]
viii.   5CREENSTARS

BOOK III: THIGMOTAXIS

////\•/\\\\

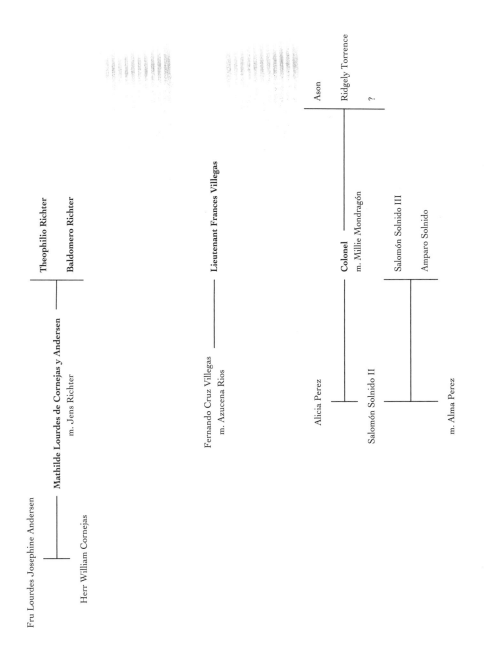

I.
DEMESNE

CORDYCEPS

WHAT COMPELS THE ANT to break from the rule of its social nature, enmeshed as we are, and ingest its own mettle in idealer atmospheres. Tarsal claws and mandible clutching and frozen at the foible of a tall blade of grass. The tallest in fact. A bright whit postured in a bare thread of sunlight, solemn and maddened, ready to expel the feverish multitude that bores through its muscular body. Only that morning had it revealed its supernumerary malfunction by stepping stepping finally out out of line to linger in the heat of a sun-glade. Then moving in staggered circles outside of the foraging pattern. For days the ant held fast against some vague ideation of a world beyond the dark walls of its colony. Like what is flight or the taste of sunlight. Then the ant slipped.

The fungus it harbors is an active life force within the ecosystem—a kind of parasitic flora which acts as a natural control for the unhealthy proliferation of social insects. The host [ant] as vessel is somatically compelled to satisfy the conditions necessary for the growth of the fungus. Spread of the fungus means catastrophe for the colony. Its presence like a ticking time bomb. As a result the infected ant is carried away, into the hinterlands, by a proximal worker tasked with the removal of its infected body.

If carried away from the colony in a timely manner the emissary worker returns to the colony unharmed. If too late, the worker risks spreading what illness festered in its comrade among the colony's healthy. This demonstrates that madness in the animal kingdom is communicable. If we can call this madness, this also

suggests that commonly observed and recorded abnormal behaviors within social creatures may be grounds for an operational definition of madness that would include human beings. If we
were to extrapolate this idea into some definitive understanding
of madness as manifested biologically among social creatures, we
might find ourselves at the essential nature of [mental] illness
and its propagation—in search of what compels the ant to break
from the rule of its social nature, enmeshed as we are, and ingest
its own mettle in the idealer atmospheres of ascent.

But beyond even this idea/question, which is not new, which is
in fact an obtuse reduction of a complex problem, we cannot
explain the marvelous spectacle of the ant as it exists beyond the
foraging pattern. Does the ant's life signify some revolution or
evolution in the collective consciousness? Is it merely regarded
as blight? Is it regarded at all—which is a question of the soul
and perceptive consciousness of a creature outside of our own
species. You have to admit: there is something remarkable about
the phenomenon, about the ecstasy of nature ejaculated from
the eye of an ant. As witness you recognize without recognizing
your awe at its violence as the ant, no longer suitable for life in
the colony, tumbles slowly upward.

For you who are solitary or singular and suffer, the host ant is
full of a pathos that mirrors your condition—a grade of spectacle that affirms your position and culture. Surrounded on all
sides by threat, tangible and intangible, each creature regarding
the ant must contend with and understand its own mortality
as prey within the kingdom. The tree frog. The wild cat. The
kingbird. Yet the host ant exists at an apex neither living nor
dead, but wholly submitted to forces that dictate the rise and
fall of generations and inspire palpable hope for the possibility
of what is meant by home. The ant is transformed and watching
as it burns is transformative.

This is important. Learn how not to rehearse the synapses of your traumata. Those stellar arcs and their astral projections. "The same tragedy lived over and over again by the great, and the ordinary."

You've seen it before flash in the pan. Learn how not to be confounded by your own mystery. The rest follows. "You'll never know why I'm laughing. Have a great day. Take a little time to enjoy *the view*."

There appears a Shanghai architecture in the panorama. The Tower at One Bryant Park by COOKFOX Architects. New York on Eight Spruce Street by Gehry, shimmering like a school of sardines beneath clouds the color of canned salmon. Skidmore, Owings & Merrill. One World Trade.

"Still in all we livin / Just dream about the get back" How many years and there remains the taste of rigor mortis in the rubble of Cortland St. as we pass in memoriam, our lips brittle with cold and submergent authority. This to rehearse the synapses of our traumata. This to corral the planets, to address the vast and bending. "Don't look down / It's an impossible view" Passing Cortland in memoriam northbound. Yesterday your older boy gave you Chaz Bundick. He said listen. He listens to Chaz Bundick nearly every morning with a breakfast pear passing Cortland in memoriam. "Don't forget / Don't forget" You skip Chaz Bundick. "We were on the same ship when the slaves were checked / I had to pull your card you was on the top deck / So I plotted my escape / I saw the thin line between love and hate" Dressing catastrophe in rhetoric and hope.

How you dreamed one day of fathering a girl. Her skin a tissue colored the muted bark of an ash. Lulled by the train rocking its way from side to side through the tunnel. Floating between one or the other side of a habitable moment. Now your older boy is learning to read and write these silences.

You remember that day, years ago, having nearly hit a man in a purple jumpsuit doing fifty through fog down Nostrand. Your older boy, then buckled in the back seat, hasn't touched anything purple since. An abstract aversion. You realize something of your conditioning. How conscious an effort it takes to parse from the milieu one's identity. Imagen. That color breathes meaning through memory. And this we call maturation. Dropping him off late, small and shaken, at the gates of his junior high school. You kissed him on the temple and gave him a gentle push, watching as he took his first nervous steps toward manhood.

Lucky you got a seat. Which is due neither to your belief in God nor your faith in Humanity.

On the way, you saw an elderly couple walking hand in hand in snow. You think of your father's gag, asking your mother from the driver's seat ¿A quién tu quieres más? ¿A mi o el Pastór? How they laughed in their age at their age. Your mother a bit demure. Your father a bit lightheaded. At the wheel. You un-buckled upside down in the backseat of the rundown Nova. The summer you learn of the Pastor's wandering eye. The summer you feel for the first time the electric ambiguity of touch. The soft sixty-pound sheet drawn over your closed eyes and the charm whispered into your ear.

Passing between fluorescent light and subterranean pitch every few minutes. Every few hundred feet blue light marks emergency stations; a phone, a fire extinguisher. Every few hundred feet from the third rail white-blue sparks blister the murk. God's own every day fall asleep in this light, are buried in this light.

The train slows to a stop in the darkness of the underground, descended from the Manhattan Bridge. The conductor announces that the train ahead of you is being held at the station. Due to a medical emergency there will be no train service through Montague Tunnel. Then the automated announcement. «We are delayed because of train traffic ahead of us. Please be patient» We will not be stopping at Prince or 8th. No blue light in the window. Our expressions betray a frustration with the selfishness of others. We want places to be. We are places to be. And returns to himself.

REMEX & RECTRIX

A SLAVE FOREVER DILUTES with dignity the fiction of love. The truth of this is spectacular. I was a liar and a righteous man. Destroyer and preserver waiting at the gates for order's lamentations. I have no language. I have no nation. I have my loyalties and they're few. I did what I did for you.

Remember that summer day. Remember your—our—younger boy running into the house for a plastic cup to fill with water. Head full of sun, you hear him burning up the front steps into the kitchen. A few moments later, from the same window, you watch him run back outside and attempt to pour slowly his water down the chute of an ant colony. On the lawn. He stares, squatting by the small hill, waiting, listening perhaps for a sound. Every morning together I chance, my hand over your kicking womb, that beauty is the perpetuation of this third language.

A young man at the opposite end of the car vomits a nickel-yellow puddle between his black penny loafers. One nearest him jumps from her seat startled, almost caught in the blast radius. There begins an exodus. Eyes and thumbs parting slowly from personal devices. A boy, anxious and titillated, watching a film about a freedman turned assassin on his smartphone. An older woman engrossed in a colorful match-three puzzle game, silenced so as not to disturb other passengers. Three tweens scrolling through social media photos from their last-night-was-mad-trill event. All get up and move or leave the car entirely. Disgusted. Reminded.

The sick young man is wearing a black leather jacket and black trousers. Nodding next to consciousness. His crewcut hides nothing of his embarrassment. Wanness with eyes closed and hunched over, his elbows atop his knees to keep from falling over. A precarious balancing act. A silvery string of dribble hanging from his open mouth, distended by gravity, finally snaps back to his lip. Then the smell. Slightly more of vodka than bile. He retches there, sitting alone on the glossy slate-gray bench, leaning slightly against the brushed-steel rail in bright fluorescent-white light beneath advertisements for Skin.

We are still sitting impatiently in the dark. Those of us who have not left the car, cooperating with the odor and the blinding white and mirrored surfaces of our holding pen. Fascinated with ourselves, reflections cascading *mis-en-abime* between the angled double panes at each end of the car.

Things on the train settle into tepid equilibrium. The sick young man is hard to ignore. The smell of his vomit is harder to ignore. Across the car, etch on the pane of an etch-proof window reads: *er schreibt es und tritt vor das Haus und es blitzen die Sterne er.* What Heidegger was unable to say. The naked thought he could only suggest. To us who are eyebright and arnica sitting impatiently in the dark. Those of us who have not left the car, cooperating with the odor.

INERTIA

HE IS NOTABLE FIRST for the way he holds his paper, a broadsheet spread brazenly from cover to cover so that none within eyeshot need purchase a paper of their own. Headlines are in plain view. Practically a public service. The arts and business sections lie folded neatly in his lap while he, comically wide-eyed behind thick prescription lenses, scans each page. Likely not reading everything, but poring over the characters for some sign or signs that pique his interest. A word like *alveolar* or *agathist* or the unusual digital misalignment of columns and letters. Perhaps what really makes him notable is his complete lack of interest in the spectacle of a boy vomiting. He seems entirely unfazed by the smell, completely wrapt in what may have been his regular commuter's ritual. Accustomed to thinking perhaps that news as printed is the only news. And the rest, or what could be called news, is not news unless he reads about it in tomorrow's paper. If, for example, tomorrow's headline reads, YOUNG MAN FOUND DEAD OF DEHYDRATION IN TRAIN CAR, will he or any of us recognize?

The car is quiet, but agitated. If you knew what you were saying, a middle-aged woman says to the boy next to her breaking the textured silence. He is smiling impishly. A visitor's pass is stuck to the plaid hoodie beneath his unzipped goose-down. If you could hear yourself, I mean. No—actually. If you knew what you were saying . . . The last thing she says before she becomes suddenly self-aware, at which point she stops trying to say anything, or perhaps tries to say it all by staring into the boy's face. Imparting a sense that the boy, likely her son, was a miracle he could not yet understand. The circumstances of his birth and the fragility of the world in which he grew up. A world complicit in the fluxuating valuation of his invaluable life. The miracle even of the train that carried them, maybe home, maybe somewhere else. If you knew that sound of catastrophe is the blue midday. Maybe you're too young. So young, but . . . How many at any given moment are above and beneath you is the sound of blue collapsed in a contact shoe touching the third rail. She looks away. Hurt. Disappointed. Remembering. He stops smiling.

29 Wells Ave. Building 4. A Kawasaki plant in Yonkers. Kawasaki Heavy Industries Limited—Tokyo-owned, Yonkers-operated, in a building that once housed an Otis Elevator Plant. Operating under United Technologies Corporation, the plant was closed in 1982. $16 million in taxpayer grist spent as investment of good faith in the modernization of Otis Elevators. It is now Kawasaki Rail Car Inc. Tokyo-owned, Yonkers-operated makers of the brushed steel R160B rapid transit. Where we sit unaware of the hand of Yonkers. Wearing safety goggles. With soot in bed and sinus of nail. Laborers disappearing entirely in a show of embers and the grooming machinations of an assembly line. Riveting America.

The factory façade is built of distinguished red brick. A red-brick smokestack projecting white emulsions into the blue midday. Where Salomón Solnido III, for four years, worked as a heavy-crane operator. In his fifth year with Otis he was assigned to overseeing elevator repair-part production. Never lacking in ambition per se, but dutiful.

I was twelve when the Second died and my brother never complained. The spitting image of Salomón Solnido II, but the Third had a softness of character that the Second kept hidden. There was surely tenderness in the Second, our father, but it was a well-kept secret, an uncommon response to a given situation.

Once when I was in elementary school he watched as I fought a boy twice my size. He just watched. We were in the schoolyard. P.S. 139. And when it was clearly done he walked over slow and stately and dispersed the crowd. He said nothing to me. I remember crying. Tears were running down my face. He held my hand, which fit cleanly in his palm as I recall, and we walked to the corner store. He bought me a creamsicle. Orange was my favorite color. I'll never forget it. Funny the fights bone and muscle can forget. The scars though. And that was often his intention. We learned. We ate fear behind.

Our father, not long after that fight, found a pack of Winstons in my brother's bedroom. He dragged the whole Solnido family out—Mami, Mom, and our sister Payín, into the living room around midnight. The pack of Winstons sat suspect in the dim lamplight of the coffee table. His lawyer lamp we called it, with a green glass shade over the bulb and a brass stem. Our father opened the pack and handed my brother a Winston. The old man gave him a light, then stepped back a mile into the dark while my brother in the catbird seat took nervous drags. Where are you going to put it out? my father asked from beyond the glow of the lamp, his eyes hollowed sockets in the unlit expanse of the living room. My brother at the end of his seat, at the edge of his seat. The women stood shoulder to shoulder watching like dispassionate attendants at an execution. The Second stepped closer to my brother, who looked starved for air, trembling. His hand reaching up toward the approaching Second with the smoldering butt between his thumb and index finger. One last gesture for mercy. Then in the light said Second to Third: Open your mouth.

No hay nada mejor. The Third, my brother, his eyes always on the prize, gleaning his small seeds. He changed after our father died. Coming home after dark. Mouthing James Brown in the

kitchen. Eating lukewarm leftovers earlier prepared by Veronica
or Mami or Mom. Sometimes I'd sit with him. Just listen to him
sing or hum or tap a beat. Wait for him to look up from the plate
and grin my way. A lovely, feral grin. A fatigued grin. I was in
my middle teens when in the early months of 1983 Veronica left
him for Willy Detroit Wallace and Detroit. Took his son, my
nephew. The custody hearing lasted into spring of the following
year with Veronica flying in at regular intervals, late and sloppy.
His son, legally bound to visit, would not return to Brooklyn
without his mother for another sixteen years. The morning of
the decision I remember lifting *Batman and the Outsiders* #10
from the corner store.

THE

KILLING

OF

BLACK

LIGHTNING!

I saw Black Lightning strapped to St. Andrew's cross, broken
and on the verge of death. It was raining. I cried quietly. Like
a man I thought. You couldn't see my tears. And my brother,
having driven home our father's old Nova for the last time, was
gone by morning from our house on Stratford. I should've said
something. I knew how neglected she felt. Always waking alone
with the child. Nursing alone. Bitter about the accidental body
of her infant son.

So unraveled the promise of his prize. His promise. A broken
bower.

And I.

"It's getting late." The vomiteer is breathing softer now, pulling air thinly through the narrow opening between his lips. The muscles of his back are tensed to regulate respiration—shallow breathing to keep from further upsetting his stomach in the car that is spinning uncontrollably around him. He shudders and heaves once, but manages to keep his newfound and fragile composure. He leans his flushed cheek against the cool brushed steel rail. The air still thick with malhumor.

At my right sits an adolescent and beside him his mother. As goes the smell of his youth mingled with malhumor: shit and fresh laundry. Fidgety laundry and fresh shit and malhumor. At my left are three teenage girls from middle America clustered together, wearing pajamas, carrying blankets and luggage from Wal-Mart. Leaning, almost huddled, over the girl seated at the center of the troika discussing their lateness in a mistaken volume. The girl closest to me turns and asks—Does this train stop at 23rd Street? Her young breast exposed beneath the deep neckline of her tanktop, cleaving the light between us. Certain taboos through sleeplessness trespass like rapture. She repeats her question softer now, friendlier—Does this train stop at 23rd Street? Yes, I think so. Or at least it will after 14th. She nods her thanks and turns away. They discuss their lateness, their waiting, waiting. I am watching the dark window. In the window she is watching me. Her friends have moved on to a new topic of conversation. «running express to 14th Street—Union Square» I know what she wants to know from me.

After the Second's death. In the absence of the Third. Skipped by the numeral assignation of my birth. I am First. The last mile is squealing before movement in four slotted tones up and one tone down. We're moving now. And that's it.

y sigo mi vida
     con risas y penas
          con ratos amargos
               y con cosas buenas

     yo soy el cantante,

ABENDLANGUAGE

Its left eye, left open wide skyward,

II.
SOLIFUGE

i. Andante Moderato

reflects fully the light, shrunken obsidian, of what little sky is visible having fallen from such ceiling.

Unfree so long they imagine no future without unfreedom. Always elsewhere, it seems, when it begins to rain and in those moments before become slim and slip lightly, ground glass through the keyholes and cracks. The sidewalk quivers. Concrete-jeweled calcite under the sodium lamps show for the shoe-gazer what smells like rain. The New York of this vatic odor owing in part its shape to the gilded imaginations of McKim, Mead, and White—their vision of a city without shadow, drafting through the turn of the century and well into the blushing progressive presidency of Teddy Roosevelt a metropolis measured in caryatid limbs and clean lines, the sun in every foyer stretching its brass beams over marble, a neo-Georgian concern for classical symmetry in every portico, every Corinthian colonnade littered with the discarded paper-voice of yesterday's peopling—the *Times*, the *Journal*, the ragsheets, the flyers—and the sandstone and limestone abiding the excesses of corporeal being. All of the courts and halls, the parks, the squares and docks of the new city. From the parapets acanthus and no sound left unarrested between sentencing, no sign otherwise. It smells like rain settling on the brick and verdigris, the sidewalks, and with it a spoor neither human nor animal, but somehow both. And if both, if this is his home, the place he's known too long to discard without excoriating his insides, then this scent in his nostrils and down his throat, settled on his palate, is also his

troubled joy, his troubled water. It smells like home where den-
sities greater than water fall from the sky and mean to make one
look. Like birds might fall or throw themselves, failed to fledge,
dead as dead to the ground—but *this* bird, this unattended body.
Street light, orange over the bird's bull eye, and flourescent light
from the Food Emporium pouring over the mica-gray sheen of
its feathers suggests a natural death—its dark eye skyward, its
left wing splayed over its own body in no pool of its own blood,
as if the bird attempted flight, but found instead its final ceiling
in the gorselight of Zeckendorf Towers. 1 Irving Place. Unim-
pressively contemporary by Davis, Brody, and Associates,
hinting at the gilded neo-classicism of McKim, Mead, and
White, the palatial steel frame vested in brick and plexiglass,
each of its four pyramidal spires illuminated and adorning the
skyline over Union Square. Completed in 1988, its lack of or-
namental nuance gives it the thrown-up appearance of an
upscale project building, designed and erected for expedience
and utilitarian or politically motivated urban design—an imper-
sonal and self-sufficient full-block complex perhaps intended to
raise property value in efforts to purge Union Square of its nineteen-eighties New York City demographic. A nighttime demographic which catered to the Palladium set. Then a club just
across the street operated by Steve Rubell and Ian Schrager of
Studio 54 fame, the Palladium saw its fair share of storied New
York City transformations. By the mid-nineties the party scene
had cooled considerably and in 1997 the property was purchased by New York University. Witness to the demolition of
the Palladium, the Zeckendorf Towers stood as if waiting for
Union Square to find its *renaissance*, as if waiting to claim its
place in the new millennium. The towers stand today like anything else in the general commerce. Quietly proud of itself. The
development's green-railed terraces create the illusion of verdant
exclusivity, despite in actuality being incredibly drab and disap-
pointing. As of 2006, Davis, Brody, and Associates is now Davis

Brody Bond LLP, a major constituent firm of the international Aedas Group—a purportedly global network whose task it is to build upon the world reflecting absence, extinguishing iterations of the chaotic in poetic geometries. Steven M. Davis, FAIA, of Davis Brody Bond Aedas, is an active director on the global board at Aedas and was selected as associate architect, architect of record, for Michael Arad's *Reflecting Absence*—the National September 11th Memorial. The memorial, while not Davis's design, in some sense now bears his name. What to do with the question of meaningfully arranging the names of the dead? The trees are lined arbitrarily along an armature of paving extended longitudinally around the original sites of the towers—described by the primary designer and architect, Michael Arad, as an arrangement of beads along an abacus, as long allées. Among the panelists who'd selected this design in the winter of 2003 were the craftsman/carpenter Martin Puryear and the architect Maya Lin. Of interest: Zeckendorf Towers remain unlisted among the major works of Steven M. Davis, FAIA. Like Stanford White, Davis is now internationally recognized. But, unlike White before him or even Wright, Davis wears no discernable persona— is no true poet, no visionary. Again, this can be argued. It could be that White, shot by a billionaire for the affections of Ms. Evelyn Nesbit on the roof of his own terra-cotta palace, Madison Square Garden, has imbued this New York City with his spirit and survives the veneer. It is as well interesting to note that Zeckendorf Towers remains unlisted among the major works of Steven M. Davis, FAIA. Then again, what architect can include on her credentials every residence to which she has lent her name? It smells like rain. At the corner of Irving Place and E14th, on the northwest corner, there is a popular café. In the window, seated on a high stool, is a small woman eating soup. She's engaged in the delicate process of breaking crackers behind the pane that sits between them. On the table before her is a recent issue of *Scientific American* opened to an article on the projected prevalence of thyroid dysfunction in eastern and central Asia. She rubs the tip of her index finger in ginger circles about the flat of her thumb, her left, in a way that suggests she enjoys receiving oral sex and clitoral stimulation (expert clitoral stimulation). But her hair, its almost unkempt helical beauty, suggests she is disdainful of men who lay genuflect in the airs of her clerestory. She looks up at him through lightly fogged glass and then casually turns her attentions to the article, simultaneously lading her black plastic tablespoon with soup and broken crackers. She blues, not having seen the bird. Beneath the hum of the Towers, everywhere in the sound, there is life returning and the traffic is, as a matter of Wednesday, caustic to the flaneur sensibilities of one who prefers to, or is bound to, walk through the windswept channels of the designscape. Emboldened by the change of light at Irving and 14th a livery cab jumps the curb in a blur of black fiberglass and aluminum. Its struts smash against the body and chassis, vaulting the Crown Victoria three feet into the air. The natives, each holding a practiced glaze against an ever-present nihil, flake from their nostrils in impossible increments the reverential zeal of youth. Hardly a hitch in the strides of each, these natives, beneath the shadow of a flying Crown Victoria. Everywhere is there life returning as the vermiform distension of enveloping space. This New York City is super-saturated with expectations of the divine universe and made manifest in that righteously brutalizing spirit of enlightenment and gilded grandeur present in the water through the turn of the century. In short: these are they that would die happy. For, and despite, the architecture. This is the only gauge of cosmopolitan nativity. Scuse me brotha, you read the Bible? The light changes and, stepping off the curb looking both ways, he realizes the speaking stranger has taken it upon himself to follow him across the street. Eyeing the sky he thinks, why me Lord—all the people in this city and it's me, every time? Immediately following his existential query he wonders why he is wont to gaze up into the sky at all. It's not like God is sitting on a cloud—although, once upon a time he believed whole-heartedly in the idea of the divine being enthroned on the cottony backs of mares' tails. It could be that, consistently staring into the speechless ether, he leaves himself open to all manner of terrestrial speech—drawing him, his eyes, his ears and mouth, his nose, back to street-view. You look like you read the Bible. You got a full sense of peacefulness about you. But lemme ask you, do you derive your strength from the Bible? From the so-called Word of God? This native sounds like creatine and smells of misgiving, fading in and out of the white lights hanging beneath the scaffolding. No, right? The translation is all wrong. Why would you or anyone let a man, under the authority of another man we call King James, derive the word of God in a fallen language? The zealous stranger suddenly sucks his teeth and wags his head in mock disappointment. I haven't even introduced myself. Gideon Schwartz, son of Ham. Gideon extends a burly right hand in greeting. As I was saying, what can man preserve of divinity in translating the Word, the message of God? Nothing, right? It's just not possible. You follow? So what are we reading in the Bible? What's been written? There's something there and it's our responsibility to find out. Revision is important. The New Testament for example was written in Koine Greek—a common dialect used throughout the late Roman Empire. You see what I'm getting at God? Anyway, that was just a little exposition. I said all that, to say the Truth, God, is not the book. It smells like rain. A black squirrel stands on the precipice of a half-lidded, aluminum-ribbed, municipal trash receptacle fitted with a lemon-scented trash bag, on the corner of 3rd and 14th. It dips its head into the abyssal mouth, then its upper body, and frantically falls in kicking and scratching. Seconds later, and not without a small encampment of concerned spectators, the squirrel jumps out of the trash in one swift leap with a piece of bread clenched between its teeth. A few of the spectators jump back in shock and relief as the squirrel tears off in a sprint, headed for the scaffolding between 3rd and Irving. They cross the street. It's an old saying where I come from—a child has eyes, but only an adult has ears. Where you headed man? This thought occurs: licking the undersides of hinged doors in public places and the yellowed undersides of bowls in public restrooms. Gideon is tall with the narrow arrogance and pale ineptitude of a self-employed royal. Hey Gideon listen I'm on my way to Beth Isr— Oh yeah, my fault. Let me give you my card. I'm a cab driver. He pulls an off-white, slightly creased card from his back pocket and hands it over. Wait a minute! Gideon drops a heavy mitt on his right shoulder, stopping him cold and ripping blustery through the sated nonpermanence of their propinquity. You look familiar. Gideon's voice has dropped. This thought occurs: that a man desperate enough to identify a stranger as familiar is perhaps a danger—an inhuman gesture (or an all too human gesture in the biblical sense) motivated by some arcana of the soul. Even now, as he responds paralinguistically to Gideon's intrusive observation, he can hear her saying—*you been here this long and you still ain't figure it out?* Then Gideon says it. I used to know this cat named Solomon. The shock of the name despite its anglicization (made worse by its anglicization) is enough to make him experience the swift heat of embarrassment and vulnerability, the sort of vulnerability that forces one to become defensive, even dangerous. In the scant window-light of Duane Reade they stand facing each other, piecing out the features of the other's face, absorbing the other's scent, scaling the heights and abysses, every store of memory, for some trace. It begins to rain. I take it by your silence you know who I'm talking about. You're his younger brother, aren't you? He straightens himself to full, imposing height in the downpour. I know all about you son. I know all about your brother. We were boys. Gideon seems to sink having admitted as much. It is impossible to tell at what point in their conversation the sky peeled open. Water, gathering weight, slaps against Gideon's high forehead, trickles seen into the cracks at the corners of what look to be heterochromic eyes, one the color of a deer's ass. Drops of gray rain sliding farther down Gideon's razor-burned cheeks settle at the corners of his mouth and dissipate like mercury between the bluish transhuman transparency of his lips, through which are visible all of his teeth, his incisors—the sharpness of them unnerving. With dramatic overtones of Bogart, Gideon flips up the collar of his leather jacket, pulling it tight around his neck, lifting with it the heavy scent of wet, tanned cowhide. You *are* his brother. Gideon cocks his head slightly to the right and squints, staring deeper into his face. Strange. Hey listen man, I know you're on your way to the hospital. I don't wanna keep you long. You got my card. Call sometime. Or if you need a cab, gimme a call. You're almost like fam. Gideon finally releases his shoulder and in the hot rain takes leave, moving jetways toward Union trailing an odor of wet leather and Pall Malls. Left bluing in the loud silence and low visibility of a mucus rainfall, his questions left malformed and unpronounced—the streets nearly emptied and traffic unusually lean. Each wet vessel of this New York City, vacated before the god-spit downpour by the sound of billions of distended beads percussing against concrete, comes apart under fatigued requests for taxis hydroplaning in and out of the deepgroovechannel where the avenue and sidewalk meet, kicking up jagged tidal waves, like rusted blades, into pedestrian space. All of their off-duty lights on. After a while it almost appears as though the rains are falling up, exploding upward from the thin sea formed to the face of the city. Had Gideon really known the Third? He couldn't recognize Gideon in any capacity, but could feel the heavy print of his mitt still etched into his shoulder. Bluing from the scent of wet leather and Pall Mall in falling water—thrown by Gideon's presence, the directness of his speech and his insistent claim to knowledge of the pro-nounced-dead. An approaching M14AD headed west hovers lethargically with half of its heavy body leaning in the deep-groovechannel; its fogged windows glow with the warm yellow light of its coachwork. Come to a complete stop at the red, the M14AD seems to lurch forward in exhaustion and then, when the light turns green, grinds lethargically away, blind and glowing through a veil of heavy rain. In its wake, the gutter-tongue of the deepgroovechannel reacts lapping the sidewalk under the torque and horsepower of the westerly M14AD. Wading toward 2nd Avenue, his monk-strap shoes by John Lobb—bespoke shoe and bootmakers—are essentially ruined. He contemplates the possibility that his brother is somewhere alive. And if he's been alive all this time, why hadn't he come home? Why now the mad impossibility of a strange herald? He would have to reassure himself (another repressive madness) that this New York City is filled with hustlers and conmen looking for quick money. Gideon Schwartz, son of Ham. He checks his pockets. His wallet in his back-right. His phone in his front-right. His keys in his front-left. His watch on his right wrist. The lanyard on his left wrist. Everything seems in order. So what? What was that all about? Fuck that guy. Just another con man. Gideon Schwartz, son of Ham. Just another crooked piece-of-shit-cabbie washed up in the rain. Heavy rain. It never occurred to him, leaving the house, that he should bring an umbrella despite the light snow, the dark nimbus clouds, the thunder. All the signs. But the deluge soon ebbs into a soft patter over the rushing sound of waters pooled to rivers along the deep-groovechannel as he wades onward to the corner of 2nd and 14th. He wipes the water from his face, but can't shake the uncomfortable feeling of having met Gideon. In the sweeping hush he returns to her, her promise, young and nilotic in a form-fitting neon blue one-piece trimmed in yellow. *How often do you think about coming?* All the time. *Come to me. Come for me.* Extended play beneath her green moan, orchestrated in pink nail polish and fingers glossy with her own silk. Arching her back; her small, firm breasts weathervane to pleasure. Small nipples swollen and excited. Two fingers deeply probing and wet, the wet south of her body, her long legs, her breath doled in sspassmodic cupfuls into his nostrils and down his throat, so he'd taste it. Breath electric and entirely imagined, but he'd taste it. Her eyes closed and lips pursed, panting and gasping. Calling and recalling the curiosity less for its sex, so much as a need to quell the mad ape on his back. For a while she stares, the present contaminated by what bitter magic was hers before he terminated the feed and reached for the towel. *I want to play with you—make your mind all mine.* 2nd Avenue is bare. *You'll always be mine.* 2nd Avenue is bare. *Your mind all mine.* 2nd Avenue is bare, a spectacular obsidian and gold show beneath the sodium lamps. Light sliding playfully over wet asphalt with just enough mist in the air to suspend the prismatic glare. As though he were the last small man strolling by the emptied kiosks in a carnival of light. The last breathing being caught in the membrane. Water falls perpetually, rain or not, from the high places of this New York City. Air conditioners and exhaust vents drizzle their discharge in all seasons, at all hours. To look up is a hazard rarely ever worth it. One might drown or swallow some chemical death. He remembers a myth about the turkey being so dumb it can drown in the rain and wonders if it's true. Only men die this way. From the corner of his eye he catches a shadow. It draws quickly across his step. A mouse or rat likely. Then it stops, hidden in the dark not far in front of him. Out of curiosity he stoops over to get a better look. What he thought was a rodent is only, after appraisal, a fallen leaf. When it fell it must have passed through light overhead and cast an exaggerated shadow. Ever since the fall of the province his vision has been slowly deteriorating and with it his depth perception, his sense of scale. It bothers him how excitable he's become since the fall. His eyes meet decapitated St. George, its stone façade blushing deep red from the rain and humming over the western flora of Stuy Square. Stuyvesant Square is a quick study in partitions and striations. Each half of the park, bisected by 2nd Avenue and quartered by 16th, is enclosed in cast iron. Robinson Iron, established in the 1950's by Sara and Joe Robinson, recast the iron perimeter paying close attention to its nautical detailing. Palisading lances adorned in a procession of helms, perhaps in honor of the exploratory pegleg for whom the park was named, painted in black Tnemec. Once clear of the gate the eye is drawn to the east-side fountain. Its bluestone coping, well carved and wide, lends the park an air of age and plenitude. Surrounding the wide fountain is a railhead formed of red flowers nearly in bloom holding holy communion with petaled cupfuls of newly gathered dew. Top-heavy heads full and swaying from side to side. From the center of the fountain, usually during spring and summer months, there spouts a single unimpressive jet of water. The spout is turned off at night and the fountain is still, a pool of sitting water visited by insects and roiled by April showers for a marvelous demonstration of Newton's Third Law—beads of black water jumping upward, raining in reverse from the surface before falling into brilliant rippling waves across the glassy plane. Between all of this is the sound of air escaping and a gentle human rustle beside him. Sitting on one of the near park benches is an old man; his face hidden beneath an umbrella. The old man's dog, a dirty bichon frisé, stands at attention. Fur clings in mangy wet tufts to its small body, making it look more like a wet cat than any kind of dog. Where you headed in such a hurry boy? The old man's face is just visible beneath the gores of his large umbrella and it's clear that his torso is bare by the sallow paunch hanging over the elastic band of his basketball shorts. His legs, frighteningly thin, are crossed leisurely at the ankles. Nylon socks and sandals. I'm headed to the hospital. My wife is— The old man interrupts him to ask, Is it still raining? No, I don't think so. He holds out his palm to check. No. Right, replies the old man, right right. The old man pulls back the umbrella to reveal a left eye glowing

like illumined jade and the rippling flesh of a scar beneath it.
The eye is green, without pupil or iris, and covered in a cloudy
film. Lights strobe across the prosthetic cell matrix as it receives
visual stimuli, reason for the eye's glow—an optic circuitry snapping synaptic signals to encourage development of lost or
damaged retinal ganglia. Lemme ask you something. The old
man growls over a glut of phlegm, then winks with his left eye,
lucent green. You were there for the fall of the provinces, am I
right? There for the massacre?

I'm late. I have to go. My wife is—

Oh that's right son someone waiting for you. The old man sucks
his teeth loudly and points to the hospital. But you know what?
I'll see you later.

The old man's jadeite gaze lingers in the haze behind him. One
jarring node of regeneration waylaying the common transit of
the future.

And then his green gaze disappeared entirely within the mist. I
was once an Evangelist. He thought he heard him say. Paradise
began with unction. He thought he heard him say. You were not
the first; you won't be the last. He thought he heard him say.

13 OCTOBER XXOI [AIBONITO] Then they were each, each breath, manifestations of a timid wind. Each more unsatisfying than the last. In the thought that even his breath spent itself breathing, shuddering in his chest, was a kernel of breathlessness.

She keyed poorly by candlelight the right hand of Stravinsky's *Shrovetide Fair*. Fair enough to preserve the melody, but they both knew. It was the only piece, after learning the basics, that she wanted at her fingertips and so devoted the better part of six years to its mastery. Still, midway through the *Fair* and without fail she fell apart, not yet capable of riding the ecstatic nerve necessary to match Stravinsky at his game.

"Is *Petrushka* your favorite?" he asked, though he already knew what she'd say in response.

"You already know."

"Why is it your favorite?"

She stopped playing altogether, resting her hands in her lap to take a deep, natural breath before deciding on an answer.

"It's about a frustrated puppet. What's not to love about a frustrated puppet?"

"Can you even?" he added.

"Can you even what?" she intoned with a hint of exasperation.

". . . love a frustrated puppet."

He leaned over the edge of the piano as she began to play again, from the top. "You know Coronel—" she began to say, stroking a muddy C before he interrupted.

"I wish you would play something else, Lieutenant."

She looked up at him. He was a head shorter than most men, unshaven and dark, leaning over the piano on his elbows. He was struggling for breath and doing his best not to appear so, breathing from his nose to keep from audibly wheezing. His face was strained, like the face of a child straining against its own body, half-hidden in the darkest corner of the family room. From this shortness of breath, a residual ailment some speculated as having developed from childhood bronchitis, he had a barrel chest and a hardened expression that struck awe among the ranks of the tercios and guerillas. Few suspected him of being one stray shell away from swooning. He had arrived just hours earlier in full disguise from the growing underground in xxx xxxx. He was forced to depart for Aibonito when news of police recovering the torpedo in Quebradillas hit American presses. The riots that followed many now consider apocrypha of the new natural canon.

The Lieutenant started playing again, from the top. "This is my song, Coronel. It brings me joy even if I don't play well by your standards."

Lieutenant Frances Villegas played what she knew of the three-piece suite from memory. The music, every note, she kept entirely in her head and in the muscle memory of her hands and wrists. She studied religiously a VHS recording of Alexis Weissenberg playing each of the three movements, alternately expert and empassioned, then emotive and tender. Lieutenant Villegas rarely if ever mentioned that she never read or even learned to read Stravinsky's sheet music. She played mostly by ear, imitating what she could hear and see in recordings.

Colonel lifted himself from the glossy black hood of the piano and walked to the window, pulling back the curtain to look over a small swath of cultivated acreage in Aibonito. Casa Villegas sat on a high leeward shelf in the cordillera central, well hidden under the trees, the occasional maga taken from Luquillo and planted by her great-grandfather over a century prior.

The slope by day was speckled red-orange from a proliferation of June-blossoming flamboyant, all among the older and larger maga. It was a quaint two-story cottage and the only remaining demesne of the once powerful Villegas coffee hacienda. Roofed in weathered Spanish terra-cotta tiles with its walls solidly built over a concrete foundation and painted in soft yellow, la Casa garnished the high blushing shelf with more than a touch of the old world. For most of the 19th century the cottage had been a slave quarter, housing three families. By 1873, following *Ley Moret*, two of the three families had already attained freedom by stipulations of the 1815 Decree of Graces, but stayed in the house working the land. The last family escaped. Cimarrones expunged from a lost ledger.

The landscape changed dramatically at the turn of the twentieth century. The Spanish-American War was quickly deciding the future of the country. Neighboring Coamo had fallen to American ground forces while Asomante held. In vain. All that remained to commemorate the last futile stand of Spanish colonial rule was a plaque atop a white marble plinth behind a private plot of land owned by Don Ramón Rivera.

TRINCHERAS DEL ASOMANTE

EN ESTE LUGAR SE DETUVO EL AVANCE
DE LAS TROPAS AMERICANAS EL
12 DE AGOSTO DE 1898
AL LIBRASE LO QUE CONSTITUYO
EL ULTIMO COMBATE ENTRE LAS
TROPAS AMERICANAS Y ESPAÑOLAS
(GUERRA HISPANOAMERICANA)

ADMINSITRACION MUNICIPAL DE AIBONITO
HON. JOSE ALBERTO DIAZ ROBLES
ALCALDE
1998

Don Ramón was a gentleman, schooled in the old ways of the mountain with white hair, blue eyes, and a noble face. He worked with his hands and freely allowed passage to visitors who expressed a vested interest in the history of the Spanish-American War. When American commanding officers had chosen to deploy Troop C, a section of the New York Volunteer Cavalry from Brooklyn, for that last leg of the war, Don Ramón's grandfather was a militiaman who quartered soldiers conscripted to fight for Spain against American forces.

As a descendant, Don Ramón dutifully escorted visitors behind a jagged man-made fissure in a chainlink fence down the wild-flowered slope of the trinchera, and allowed them to participate in the solemn memory of a drawn out battle—creole ghosts still on patrol and waiting to act on orders. The trinchera with its spectacular vantage point provided a natural bulwark against artillery and the threat of pincer flanking in the context of late 19th / early 20th century warfare. It was a securely fortified position for a lost cause and the last battle of an already lost war.

"I was going to say—Petrushka comes alive in the finale."

"Like Pinocchio." intoned Colonel.

"Not quite," responded Lieutenant Villegas. "Get away from the window. Drones have been making rounds over the fields at odd times."

"Have they started dusting the fields?"

"No sign yet. Intelligence indicates some plans to target patches of land near metropolitan areas, but these fields they've so far deemed inconsequential."

"That would kill the farmers. If they don't know we're here, we need to be certain."

"It seems they don't know, but U.S. intelligence can't be that blind. We have to assume they know your whereabouts at all times. Second and third tercios have been notified and broken into smaller guerilla units. All of the commanding officers are at risk of assassination."

He drew shut the curtain and moved back toward Lieutenant Villegas, who was still sitting attentively at the piano. "So why are you staying here?" he asked her.

"This is my home. I'm not leaving my home. I'm not leaving my piano. They're going to have to kill me before I let go. Presently we have two covert patrols on our station." She pulled her sidearm from its holster and laid it on the keys, releasing a pained pang from the piano. "I'm prepared."

"Quartering status on tercios and guerillas."

"They're being housed in private, consenting quarters in the outskirts and neighboring cities of xxx xxxx. They're prepared to move on my order."

"How is progress on anti-air and artillery stations?"

"Production has started. Trying to vacate the Pfizer and GlaxoSmithKline plants has proven a challenge, but not impossible. We are doing a pretty good job of winning converts among the pueblos. At least Pfizer has made it easy with their tanking stocks, expired patents, and growing distrust from shareholders—although I should warn you that Ireland's growing command of American pharmaceutical interest will mitigate the effects of our demonstration."

Colonel furrowed his brow in disapproval. Lieutenant continued.

"Regardless. Our physical position is being fortified as we speak, under cover of night, along with the construction of low-yield electromagnetic pulse stations."

"Good. That's what I want to hear."

"When are we moving on xxx xxxx?"

"Soon," he said curtly. "Have Baldomero dispatch the captive."

She radioed the order then holstered her sidearm and returned to the slightly-out-of-tune, slightly-out-of-time Steinway. Colonel slid into the wing chair by the window trying to return his anxious breath to its resting rhythm.

The Lieutenant looked dolefully on the keys of the piano. Her rounded moriscana face and thick black mane bore traces of southern Iberian heritage and several centuries perhaps of clandestine miscegenation. She had small elfin ears barely lobed and her eyebrows were plucked into narrow black lines above her bright green eyes. She had the shoulders and long torso of an Olympic swimmer, seated slightly hunched over the keys.

Colonel enjoyed watching her filter into the *Fair*'s ipseity. She was, he had to admit, attractive in her way. Whenever she played, all of her upper body swayed with the graceful restraint of a master pianist. Her arms and fingers moved in fluid if poorly timed arcs even when hitting the wrong keys. A deafened man could barely tell the difference, save the out of place vibrations that dangled in the atmosphere, or her finger placements (if he were to observe carefully). For Frances, playing the piano was more dance than audile performance. And Frances loved to dance. She would and could dance almost any step with ease, but refused to dance bachata on principle. Bachata was a dance considered by Frances unromantic, saccharine overcompensation for misogynistic impulses. And merengue she thought of as an artless, dressed-down, and shameless appropriation of a Haitian tradition. Samba too she considered a dance of the favela, appropriated by whites with unseemly import. She felt it beneath her. Colonel knew better than to ask.

A light foehn carried down the mountain, venting the cottage with warm, sweet air. The second floor was a relatively open and unobstructed square space. The upper floor measured approximately forty square feet by twelve feet high. Attached was a small washroom, for the convenience and privacy of visitors, and toward the west wall was an old, but functional, gas stove. Frances used to culture artisanal queso blanco on the stove. There was room enough for her Steinway, an armchair, a large trunk, and some old furniture—antiques mostly. At center, laid out between the armchair and the Steinway, was a turn-of-the-century broadloom Qaraajeh carpet. Its edges were warped and frayed from age, but it held together nicely. Maroon red medallions arranged over a warp and weft foundation of midnight blue; the largest of these medallions, in the middle of the carpet, had at its center an unusual almost three-dimensional tetrahedron. Along the border were rich greens, orange, and pastel yellow in a floral pattern with bright flowerheads and petals drawn beside their leafy stems. Her grandfather acquired the piece from a Sotheby's auction in London, 1946.

Farther down the mountain was a thriving three-acre cattle ranch cordoned off by barbed wire. Don Emeterio Froylan, the owner of the ranch, once every two months allowed her to milk the eldest cow for her own supply. To make the queso blanco she'd get the milk boiling, at which point she would add a light brine comprised mostly of vinegar. Just before it curdled she threw in a mixture of crushed black cardamom, brown sugar and dried orange zest. She let it drain, wrapped, hung, and dripping from the cellar ceiling in small bulging sacks of cheesecloth.

Now it seemed the stove saw little use aside from the occasional pot of coffee. It bore no splatter marks or other evidence of epicurean experiment. Like so much else in la Casa, the stove was coated in a thin, but noticeable layer of dust. Much of the upper floor, upon close inspection, appeared to be decaying beneath the ownerly neglect and military preoccupation of the Lieutenant. Creatures and cobwebs settled in the corners of the room. Blood-soaked slacks were left straddled like a hammock between the backs of two small chairs. Trash had not been disposed of in nearly a month and a severe black mold was growing in the bathroom. There were parts of that bungalow that once seemed so alive with the magic of the land and the bright cosmopolitanism of its caretaker. So much now seemed closed off or occupied, if not by arms and provisions, then by the sad burden of empty space. Access to the balcony on the upper floor, for example, was restricted.

The balcony, on a clear day, afforded a view miles deep into the heart of la cordillera central. Cantilevered above the entrance to Casa Villegas, the balcony was large enough to hold comfortably two teak armchairs and a small coffee table. With good reason the Lieutenant deemed the balcony a liability. She left the door to the balcony bolt-locked and had it reinforced with a bullet-resistant composite—a level 8 protection rating by UL 752 standards. The windows too, left open for the evening, were screened and paned in a composite, bullet-resistant material. Strapped almost decoratively beneath each window was a fully loaded Glock 19, custom-made. So much had changed so quickly.

La Casa was once a place filled with things she loved, gifts given by people who loved her. Original oils by Pou and Campeche— gifts from her uncle in Río Piedras. An original portrait of Hacienda Villegas at the height of its power by Francisco Oller, the realist-impressionist master who instructed and inspired Paul Cézanne. A tableau by Pío Casimiro Bacener, of questionable origin. Ponceño vejigante masks handsomely hanging in a row. All sold. All gone. What remained on her wall was of little or no market value. Staring down at Colonel from the wall, just above the piano, was an old reproduction of Rafael Tufiño's *Goyita*, which the Lieutenant purchased from El Museo del Barrio. Goyita's black gaze, bronzed by birth and wrinkled from labor, took him back to the torpid domesticity of his youth and the watchful eye of the matriarch who blessed him and burned him with bendición every night before sleep. He suppressed a shiver.

Another familiar oddity of Frances' pre-war persona remained tucked between volumes of Eugenio Maria de Hostos, Rosario Ferré, *Sin Nombre*, and other dog-eared tomes of cultural in-surrection—notwithstanding the marked absence of Giannina Braschi, an aversion she vowed to take with her to the grave. There, Frances maintained a small aquarium. In the aquarium were several entwined ferns, hair grass, and hornwort swaying softly—and one, always and only *one*, diving bell spider. This one she'd named Frank. Colonel stared into the aquarium looking for Frank and his silvered abdomen. Had Frank been suspended behind a fern, it would have been impossible for the Colonel to see him; but, in the glim light the spider looked like a small jewel bobbing in and out of the water, building its bell which grew larger with every mercurial orb pulled from the surface and pinched from its spinnerets. Frances fed Frank small insects that she'd trapped on tape left along the windowsills. But Frank, who matured to nearly two full centimeters under the Lieutenant's care, was uninterested in consuming docile prey. The mayflies no longer satisfied his aggressive impulses. Frank had grown accus-tomed to a steady diet of finicky guppy fries which he caught as they jumped the surface and dragged back to his bell. Colonel shut his eyes for a moment, his focus washed out. He was tired, but didn't want to fall asleep in front of the Lieutenant. He tried to focus his attentions again on the aquarium, where the mercu-ry-clad predator had disappeared in a fray of greenery.

A half-year prior Frances began introducing larger schools of guppy fry, ten to fifteen at a time, and watched as the spider attempted to take each of them down before they could reach full maturity. Of the two that survived to maturity, only one remained. From the bottom of the aquarium the last guppy came swimming toward the surface looking to rest in the fronds of the tallest shoots. Suddenly the guppy, obscured in a green mess of hornwort, began to convulse. Colonel watched as its body went tonic, struggling to free itself from the concealed spider's pincer-grip before going completely numb from its venomous bite. In the ensuing struggle both fell to the bottom of the tank and landed in a tangle of hair grass.

Casa Villegas was an intimate part of the Lieutenant's mythos, but she entertained no illusion of proprietary joy in the afterlife. Though they were almost entirely off the grid she tried not to indulge in the fantasy of completely safeguarding the old shack. There are defense measures in times of war, she famously conceded, and then there is fear and cowardice. If the U.S. government wanted the plot of land under which she intended to be buried, they would have tried to take it. And finding they could not take it, they would have destroyed it. The Lieutenant was all too familiar with American foreign policy. Colonel on the other hand preserved an optimism bordering on naïveté—a tragic's naïveté proven visionary or fatal only once the din has died down and the smoke has cleared. The Lieutenant's place seemed to him the last bastion of safety since the xxxx referendum. Strange, what was once part of a coffee plantation for them bore the promise of freedom and all the risk of being real.

The Brothers, Baldomero and Theophilio Richter, were on sentry duty for the night. Baldomero sat at the foot of the steps, just out of earshot, guarding the first-floor entrance and armed with an array of defensive and interceptive weapons, while Theophilio made stealthy rounds over the hacienda grounds under cover of night. He was flanked by a small task force of Evangelist operatives, all of them trained to survey, detect and dispatch threats. Theophilio was the elder brother (by thirty seconds the elder) and Baldomero the younger. They were identical twins born to Mathilde Lourdes de Cornejas y Andersen, a seamstress whose family emigrated from St. Croix, and Jens Richter, a Danish-German architect who would work closely with Henry Klumb (a student of Frank Lloyd Wright) and inspire Leon Krier's later nineteen-eighties work on the modernization and completion of Santurce. Richter's family fled Berlin not long after turmoil began in the Weimar Republic, following the Kapp-Lüttwitz Putsch in 1920. Jens was two. Mathilde was born three years later, November 16th 1923, in Santurce. By the time Mathilde was born her parents had already established their humble sastreria in Santurce.

Following World War I, American imports of embroidered cloth and drawn linens from France and Belgium ceased almost entirely. With U.S. incentives, home needlework in Puerto Rico was thriving, second only in numbers to the sugar industry during zafra. With one treadle-operated Singer sewing machine the Cornejas family managed to build a respectable and thriving business. Their clientele grew over the years as their technique was prized and their consistency sought after by the well-to-do and the pobre alike. They were not opposed to making pro-bono mends for some of the poorer families in the community. And they weren't too proud to accept large tips from the rich for keeping bochinches from the very same community. It was in this context that Mathilde grew up. And it was in this context, as young heiress to one of Santurce's more important community hubs, that she would meet and fall in love with two unusual young men from the neighborhood.

By November of 1923, Herr William Cornejas was expecting

the arrival of a boy. His wife, Fru Lourdes Josephine (née Andersen) was carrying low and wide with no apparent sign of complications and no indications of premature delivery or stillbirth. Because the Cornejas line was long in the business of tending Cane, as slaves and as freemen, it appeared to William that Josephine was carrying another strong-backed, long-limbed Cornejas. He'd elected to name the boy after his father, Mikkel. Josephine, meanwhile, would steal away from their marriage bed after William was fast asleep, to chew and suck on the heads of some cut sugarcane she kept hidden in a small box behind the caserío. She knew what was coming, by virtue of her clandestine craving for sweetness, and didn't have the heart to tell William that the baby boy Mikkel was actually a baby girl, Mathilde. Then too, on the night they'd conceived, Josephine came first—a fact that William would die without learning. William was the type of man who casually threw blame for his shortcomings on others and that blame fell frequently on his wife. Josephine, for better or worse, learned to tolerate his occasionally cavalier tongue. Even still, he was never a physically violent man. More often than not he was remembered as tender. After all, he was a tailor and Josephine was well acquainted with the eternal boy in his adult soul.

In the late hours of November 15th, on what was to be Josephine's last midnight sugarcane jaunt, her water broke. She hadn't quite noticed until she felt it pooling around her bare feet, making the earth beneath her soft and muddy. At first she thought she'd peed on herself. Then she felt a sharp pain.

Before alerting her deep sleeper of a husband she threw the chewed husk of a sugarcane over the yard fence. If it wasn't for the water, she would have crept back upstairs, but William wasn't so dense and after the birth he would have inquired about what she was doing in the backyard—*when she should have been in bed.* In any event, the time had come. She slowly waddled her way through each contraction onto the hammock in the veranda.

It was an hour of moaning and calling over the noise of nature at night, with contractions becoming gradually more intense and painful, before William discovered his wife in labor. Upon finding her, spread-eagle and floating over the darkness of the veranda, the color drained from his face. Over the side of the hammock she reached toward him. It took him a moment to realize that this was the real thing, that his wife was giving birth in the open air and he was the only one around to attend. The midwife was gone for the evening and it would be bad form to wake the neighbors—if they hadn't already heard.

Like a boy who'd walked in on something decidedly adult, William scrambled back into the caserío. She held tight the sides of the hammock, held her breath and pushed the heaving mass as hard as she could before gasping in dizzy fatigue and frustration. She felt weak and William, apparently, was not there to help her. The humidity made it hard to breathe, there was certainly rain in the air, but a cooling breeze came sweeping in over her skin, almost in unison with her every contraction.

Inside the caserío William lit the stove to warm some water while Josephine's contractions intensified and her pained cry turned into heavy moaning. He lit a lantern and grabbed a red cloth from the kitchen to wipe her forehead.

William returned, to her relief, the light of the lantern gleaming on her skin. Josephine was trembling. Hyper-ventilating. Doe-eyed, he kneeled beside her and wiped off the excess sweat which hung precariously from her brow. He reached for her left hand, which clamped down on his with a strength and ferocity that took him by surprise. Then, still holding her hand, he stood up and went around to examine her vagina. Fluids in various hues were dripping from her swollen parts, slowly soaking through the hammock cloth. It was wet like he'd never seen and stretched, like it'd been beaten, but no sign of the boy's head. Nothing yet. How they'd have sex again, he couldn't fathom. Even the thought of sleeping in their bed, soon to bear witness to full birth, seemed foul, but such concerns in matters of life and death took little precedence.

He kissed her forehead and unpeeled her hand from his own. Sliding his arms beneath her back and under her knees he managed to lift her from the hammock. She winced in pain and wrapped her left arm around the back of his neck for more leverage. The sheer torque of her arm's hold around his neck nearly toppled them both. But their line was long in the business of tending cane, as slaves and as freemen, new settlers though they were among older cangrejeros. With some effort he reared back, redistributing the full weight of the two human beings he carried in his arms.

The bedroom was warm. William set his wife and child down on the mattress and opened the louvered windows, cooling the room with a small cross-draft. Her chest was heaving and the frock she wore was drenched in sweat. By now the water on the stove must've been boiling or near boiling, but before leaving her to retrieve the heated water from the kitchen he pressed his right hand over her chest and muttered a prayer. Then he began to unbutton her frock, from the top, with a tailor's steadiness and an expectant father's circumspection. He noticed relief pass briefly through her face when finally her breasts and rollicking stomach were exposed to fresh air. But her relief was indeed brief as she began howling again in pain and pushed as William again stepped out, leaving her alone with the boy.

There was no moonlight in the kitchen window leaving him to navigate by the flickering light of the stove. He took the water off the fire and poured it into an aluminum pan. While in the kitchen he also grabbed a bottle of unrefined caña, a knife, and a segment of sugarcane he kept wrapped in six layers of butcher paper, hidden in the topmost corner of the pantry where Jo couldn't reach. Chewing sugarcane was his only vice. Now, he thought, the sugarcane might serve a purpose beyond sating his secret sweet-tooth. Josephine, whose teeth were gritted dangerously with every contraction, could instead bite down on the sweet, scored cane.

When he returned to the bedroom, to the sight of Josephine covered in blood, he felt suddenly lightheaded. This was not a blood like was deflowered from their first sex—their hungry play for each other in the fields when they were still so young in Sankt Croix. Then, when he'd penetrated her, the blood came barely, spotting the dry yellow grass in the canebrake beneath them. Her blood slid out slowly then, bright red and thin, twisting down the length of his shaft, settling like cool rubies in his matted pubis. She'd dug her fingers into the green muscles of his back, urging him to breach slowly. So he did, moving with great care to the bleating tensions of her new body.

But this, before the birth of his son, was different blood. The air in the bedroom was thick with the scent of her insides which, for nine months, carried the new male Cornejas. He put the pan at the foot of the bed while muttering prayers. To give her some leverage he slowly lifted her upper back and placed some pillows beneath her. Then, with his wife propped up, he grabbed a small towel and poured over it a tablespoon of cane alcohol. He rushed to her side and began to wipe the sweat from her skin with the wet towel, invoking Yemayá and San Lázaro repeatedly, almost singing, to save his wife.

She felt him beside her, urging her on with dramatic invoca-
tions steeped in the cool, strong scent of cane alcohol. She could
tell that he was afraid to touch the blood. But what came next
would for a long time remain a mystery; it shocked her into a
heightened state of self-awareness. William crudely placed at
her lips a stick of scored sugarcane. She almost cried. *Where did
he find the sugarcane? And how in hell did he find out?* He didn't
look mad, just helpless; in fact, he seemed to be offering her the
damn thing. By the way he was nearly shoving the sharp cane
into her lips this was either some odd form of punishment or a
concession. *Why now? Was he looking for a confession?* And if she
was to admit that this, *this girl*, was her fault, would he stop the
birthing right there? No . . . She'd kill him before he could try
anything. Was she supposed to—

At that moment another sharp pain came sweeping through
her, rushing from her pelvis through the small of her back into
her teeth, then her eyes. William dropped the sugarcane and
the idea of the sugarcane, which seemed suddenly simple and
inappropriate. He could see her gripped with pain, arching her
spine, unable even to scream. She felt like she was being throt-
tled repeatedly over the head. Now was the time, she knew.
Her body was sending her signals and if she didn't react one or
both of them would die. She reached toward William, groping
his person for some hold, his hand, anything to grasp tightly
for the next push. Within seconds she found a piece of her
husband and, with the strength of five men, clamped down in
preparation. William gave out a high-pitched wail and jumped
backward, clutching his mid-section. Josephine had found his
sugarcane. Apparently William also brought a pair of radishes,
which Josephine seemed to get hold of.

As William staggered back toward the foot of the bed, Josephine gave another strong, empty-handed push. Something in William had been awakened then because he had sense enough to stirrup her feet against his shoulders. Between the pain radiating into his stomach and the odor emanating from his woman's gaping birth maw, the strong-willed, strong-backed Cornejas wanted to vomit. But kneeling at the foot of the bed, he could see his son's head. Tiny obsidian curls peering out from her stretched lips, covered in blood and fluid. Josephine gave a final push followed by a cry of relief and a gush of alien fluid. He pulled it out by the head, tugging loose its girth.

She looked down colored by fatigue, crying and grinning because she knew it was done. She watched as its small limp legs were pulled from her body.

The proud father held the crying little boy in his left arm and with his right reached for his favorite shears. He spilled the remaining cane alcohol over the shears, then dipped them in the boiled water.

Just before he snipped the cord William performed an obstetrician-tailor's examination. He gave little Mikkel the once-over. Then the twice-over. Doe-eyed, he scanned the length of the infant body, weighing its new life in his forearms until he failed to recognize the part that typically distinguished a newborn boy. A few inches beneath the cord was a loamy little slit and no sign whatsoever of a penis. William's tremendous post-examination chagrin found repressed expression in the sudden twitching of his upper lip. With the shears in his left hand he stared down at the newborn whose eyes were shut tight and whose little mouth stretched into the universe as she cried aloud to be cleaned and clothed. Josephine lost blood, but for the moment, beaming down at William, who'd just finished cutting the cord, she seemed well. Well enough. She held out a trembling arm for her baby girl.

Mathilde in her mother's arms stopped crying. William stooped over Josephine's shoulder. They both stared down at the new girl. Gowned in white vernix and wrapped in a small red cloth, her puffy new eyes opened and peered into the puffy old eyes of the man she would one day call her father. He uncurled the tiny fingers of her doughy fist, pressing her palm into his own, and wept.

////\•/\\\\

Mathilde Lourdes de Cornejas y Andersen (called Malou) grew and learned quickly. At home she always involved herself in adult business. By age four she was rummaging through her mother's drawers, trying on her clothes, and searching for her father's illicit sugarcane segments, which he scattered and hid throughout the small house with squirrelly fervor.

As soon as she learned to speak the language Malou was an unmanageable ball of energy and youthful curiosity. Her partner in crime was her imaginary older sister named Awilda. The origin of Awilda's mother was a point of contention between the sisters. Malou insisted that Josephine was rightful mother to them both, but Awilda was less than convinced. If Josephine was her mother, she reasoned, then why was she so dismissive? It was like Josephine couldn't see her. This embarrassed Malou.

Awilda was a light sleeper and if disturbed, or provoked, she was prepared to argue, which made her difficult to get along with, but loveable just the same.

Malou wasn't shy about her relationship with Awilda, which prompted her mother to call the neighborhood bruja, who nearly performed an exorcism. Fortunately for Mathilde, who remained aloof to the small controversy, the church intervened and declared the exorcism barbarous. William carefully reminded Josephine of the hours they'd spent as children traipsing through the cane fields, making up all sorts of stories as they went. Josephine had no recollection. Fortunately or unfortunately Awilda ran away. Awilda was constantly telling Malou stories about the sea. So she escaped the hostile environment as a stowaway on a merchant marine ship headed for Martinique. She wrote to Malou monthly. Awilda loved the experience of the sea so much that she ended up traveling around most of South America before settling in Brasil with her new sister Ervilha Linda. Malou never heard from her again. In a way Malou was happy for her sister, the black sheep of the family, but Awilda's sudden departure left her feeling unnaturally sober.

Josephine enrolled her at a school run by well-meaning American transplants after she noticed a difference in her daughter, the only daughter she officially recognized. Often she found little Malou swinging restlessly in the hammock during the afternoons. Josephine, without realizing, had grown accustomed to her little girl walking around the house chatting and smiling and playing. Her new silences were disheartening. Imaginary sister or not, little Malou had grown unusually stoic.

Despite the fact that the school year had already started and the classes formed, Josephine and William decided that school would be best for her. Learning in school would feed her insatiable curiosity for the world by keeping her engaged and social with decidedly *real* children her own age. Up until this point she had been home-schooled by her mother, who taught her how to read, write and work basic arithmetic.

At the same time her father taught her the basics of his trade.

She grew into every seam that needed mending. Herr William took it upon himself to teach her the fundamental techniques every tailor should know. Soon her mother and father relied on her to piece together sports jackets and mend the torn knees and ripped inseams of children's trousers. But it wasn't enough. She passed through the house sighing like a ghost in apparent loneliness.

So Herr William walked his nervous little daughter to the Padre Rufo School on Pda 23 for what was to be her first day. There they were greeted at the door by Ms. Panaini, the teacher. She lived in San Juan on American tolerance sums.

Several boys and girls of various heights and ages with their books strapped in tow were running up the steps in a hurry to reach their desks before the cowbell, which hung upside down from a belt around Ms. Panaini's high-hiked mauve skirt. A few of the students clung to the doorway, staring with wide eyes at the new girl. Ms. Panaini was a woman in her thirties with crow's feet stretching from the corners of her eyes. She wore a warm, weathered expression and bowed slightly to greet Malou. Malou slunk sheepishly into her father's shadow. Ms. Panaini straightened herself and smiled stretching her painted lips over what appeared to Malou as several rows of sharpened, yellow teeth. Herr William reached around his back for the trembling parcel that was his daughter and pulled her forward. He gave her a light pat on the rear and sent her on her way. She only managed to look back twice before Ms. Panaini, still smiling, grabbed her by the hand and took it upon herself to escort the young heiress of the Singer of Santurce into the schoolhouse.

It was a spartan red building with two classrooms separated by a hallway which led to the latrines in the backyard. Ms. Panaini led Malou into the classroom on the left. When finally Ms. Panaini let go, Malou felt the air rush out of her lungs. She took a moment to glance around the room. Several students from the other classroom were peeking inside to get a look at her. She felt panicked and unwelcome. She also, admittedly, felt slightly spectacular. Almost special. ¡Oye tú! someone behind her hailed. She turned and there he was, wearing the polished shoes of a boy twice his age, staring boldly back at her. He grinned at her and then strolled off across the hall toward the other classroom. The air, what little she had left, rushed again out of her lungs, a weight on her chest, and everything felt light and everything and everything felt and everyone went white.

...

The first thing she saw when she came back around was Ms. Panaini's freckled neck beaded in sweat. She could feel Ms. Panaini passing a cool towel around the top of her back, at the nape of her neck, which left her feeling, among other things, exposed. It was mostly quiet inside of the nondescript murmur that seemed to surround them both. Ms. Panaini's neck was close enough to her now that she could feel her heat radiating in sticky waves; she could smell the woman's hot-rot and it nauseated her. Despite the concerted effort of her doting teacher it wasn't the first time Malou had passed out. She hated the attention. Her lack of control over the attacks frustrated her most.

It was something she'd seen in her mother. Thank God they were at the shop when it happened. When Josephine, her eyes, unprovoked, went wide and blank and she fell like dead weight to the floor. She was sweating, leaning over the sewing station. Her posture didn't seem unusual. That kind of heat exhausted everyone. She was breathlessly commanding Herr William to fill orders which, again, everyone attributed to the heat (and his general lack of hurry). Then it happened. Malou saw this from the back room and thought the worst. An unusual heat pulsed through her young body. Frozen in place, she felt dread creep up from the pit of her stomach and the thought that her mother had just entered the everlasting arms spilled from her mouth in a cold whimper. Herr William vaulted the table, knocking over a stack of starchy white shirts, and kneeled beside her. He called her name frantically as he shook her, trying instinctively to revive her. And there, in the back, stood Malou frozen with fear. By the time the doctor arrived, Josephine was awake.

They all had questions. What caused her passing out so suddenly? Was it potentially fatal? Malou had been excluded from these adult conversations. Perhaps now, she thought, it was time to find out about this matrilineal curse.

All she knew for certain was that she wanted to go home and wash away the embarrassment that dripped like mercury all over her body.

Her heart was finally coming down from its Paso Fino trot around the universe when one of the students shouted "Her eyes are open!" and Ms. Panaini's neck snapped back to look Malou in the face, grasping her with unintentional force by the shoulders. "¿Estás bien mija?" Ms. Panaini leaned in closer, appearing alarmed and nearly pressing her mouth to Malou's ear. "You had a little accident." Malou hadn't realized. What she thought was sweat trickling down her thigh—She turned to see what'd happened and became suddenly conscious of her audience gawking at her from behind. To her chagrin, there by the doorway where she entered and fell, soaking into the wood, was a puddle of Malou's own urine.

A tall boy with a blue pail of sudsy water and a scrubbing brush stood beside the dark spot, hesitant to get busy with what appeared to be his custodial duties. He was fair, trigueño, with red hair. He wore an unforgettable grimace, but even grimacing he was notably handsome. His name, she later learned, was Baldomero.

Aside from the obvious discomforts of her vasovagal condition and an acquired incontinence, an unfamiliar feeling spun up from her stomach, searing her chest on its way, and lodged itself in her throat. She was curious to know about that boy—the one who called out so frankly to see her. Her body itched wondering what he must have thought of her. What could he have wanted? He carried himself with a highborn easiness. His grin was like music. He sat quietly a few rows ahead, uninterested in what was happening behind him.

The tall boy with the blue pail finally began to clean the spill and Ms. Panaini assumed her position at the front of the room. Class started with arithmetic, then moved into composition and language. After language they broke for lunch and recess.

In light of the day's circustances Malou decided she'd stay inside and save face. It was unlikely that she'd be met with a warm reception. Girls are not quick to forgive or forget. And boys love the scent of fresh meat, even if the meat in question is covered in displeasing bodily fluids. These two things she'd learned over the years while observing customers and their habits at the sastreria, eavesdropping from the backroom or seated unassumingly beside the elders. Then too there were Josephine's bochinches, which often came in parable form and imbued in Malou a sense of her own personhood. One such story involved two strange men fighting over one woman who was married to a fishmonger from Carolina and also sleeping with the mistress of a landowner in Vega Baja. The moral of the story, which was always somewhat arcane and somewhat over her head, had long been forgotten. But the horror of the story, which she would never forget, was enough to engender some relational caution in Malou. Other such parables held less ontological sway, but seemed somehow to be epistemologically relevant. *El que come cebolla, se le para la polla.*

Ms. Panaini had no objection to her staying inside, eating a solitary lunch. Malou was content to listen to the children all making their playground music from the safety of the classroom. She tried to piece together names and characters by their insouciant outbursts over a small cup of leftover sancocho. She scanned the room, tracing afternoon sunlight through the sooty panes of two large windows. That warm almost friendly light seemed to pour in over the rugged gray grain of the floorboards, into small knotholes and cracks from which dust swirled in some divine, indecipherable pattern. Their desks were arranged in rows and nailed to the floor with a small drawer above the lap where they stowed their books. At the front of the room was Ms. Panaini's desk. It was painted white. On top of her desk sat three notebooks, two of which were closed and each corresponding to a different subject. Ms. Panaini reclined, legs crossed, in her wooden chair behind the desk with the day's print of *El Imparcial.* Light threw the long shadow of the window mullion across Ms. Panaini's blouse. She pulled a cigarette and a matchbox from the drawer. She lit the cigarette with a match and soon the room was filled with volutes of burning blonde tobacco. Malou tried not to stare.

Behind the desk was a dark green chalkboard over which hung the holy cross. Half of the board was devoted to arithmetic while the other half was covered in verb conjugations. I run. You run. He/She/It runs. We run. They run. The English language, she thought, was remarkable for its lack of formal address. America must be a radically different place, she thought. A place where everyone, at least on the level of language, saw themselves as equals. Ms. Panaini mentioned that their study of conjugations was in preparation for an American book about a boy and a girl whose names Malou couldn't remember.

The spot now where she peed was beginning to fade and beneath the smoke was the faintest odor of soap used by that tall boy to clean it up. She began thinking of ways to thank him as an ameliorative and diplomatic measure. She might have struck out with an awkward first impression, but she wouldn't live with the reputation. She knew she was better than that, she was raised better than that, and her classmates (and Ms. Panaini) needed to know that the Cornejas line was one of good stock and superior breeding. In fact, many of the students she recognized as clients of the sastreria. She knew their parents. She knew their bochinches (some of which even their children could not have been privy to). Maybe she could parley some deal for the students as an information broker. She liked the idea of being a dangerous liaison, but she knew it wouldn't be wise to get on this woman's bad side. Not so soon.

Between the windows and the chalkboard, leaning tall and splintered in the corner, was Ms. Panaini's ferule. A foreboding switch that appeared to Malou stained and encrusted with the blood and flesh of obstinate juventud and academic insolence. It was slightly bent at center, which must have meant that Ms. Panaini folded it in half before taking it to the exposed asses of her students. She couldn't imagine the whole affair, how it happened, how she could take students twice her size and in their teenage years over her knee.

Malou kept her eyes down when the kids came steaming back in. She didn't want to catch any more untoward attention, at least not until she had a chance to make a new impression on them. For the rest of her first day at school she kept quiet, barely moving even in her seat.

////\•/\\\\

By dismissal Malou found herself thoroughly fatigued by the consuming distress of self-consciousness and embarrassment. She was last to leave with Ms. Panaini close behind her smiling and ready to greet Herr William, who stood, arms crossed, tall and proud at the curb waiting to greet his little blackbird. Unfortunately Ms. Panaini managed to make it to her father first. The American pulled him aside where in the shade of a tree she muttered something grave and inaudible. Malou couldn't feel any smaller. The adults parted cordially, Ms. Panaini returning

to the schoolhouse and Herr William walking slowly toward
Malou.

He stood in front of her. She looked up at him, impossibly tall,
dark, and glowering. Invincible. He was well dressed, perhaps
overdressed for the occasion, sporting a tailored suit and tie that
Josephine undoubtedly took the measurements for.

When Herr William smiled at his baby girl, who might have
been a baby boy, Malou couldn't help smiling in response.
Always the gentleman, Herr William extended his large hand
for the young lady and, to his delight, Malou placed her little
hand in his own. They walked home hand in hand.

////\•/\\\\

The first thing Malou noticed when they got home was not how
well dressed her mother was, or the 8x10 Deardorff perched and
waiting patiently on its tripod beside a spotlight, or the photographer grinning awkwardly at the arrival of the young lady, or
the new and thoughtfully stocked library. Malou first noticed
the girl-sized dress, perfectly tailored to her dimensions. She
looked up at her mother, who, with smiling eyes, nodded once
in confirmation. It was all hers. Malou pulled it down slowly
and delicately from the hanger. She savored the texture of the
fabric between her fingers, a light cotton blend she loved for
its breeziness. It was a navy blue darling-collared dress tapered
at the waist with a thin white sash tied in the front. The skirt
was finished with a pleated white lace hem. Perfect little white
buttons up the back. She'd never seen anything like it. A fresh
new look. She wanted to wear it to school with her white patent
leather shoes, but she knew her parents wouldn't allow it.

With her hair up and the white collar of the dark dress accentuating her neckline, the possibilities were endless. She had to admit, the day started off in an odd way, but it was getting so much better. Josephine escorted her daughter to the backroom, where she dressed her and fixed her hair.

Thirty minutes later the Cornejas women emerged ready for the family photo. Herr William sat waiting and chatting in Danish with the photographer over coffee. The gentlemen stopped mid-conversation and looked up at the ladies primped and primed for posterity. Malou felt like royalty, a princess strolling into the living room alongside the queen. In proper Danish the photographer directed the family to stand in front of the library which Josephine and William bought as a gift for Malou's first day at school. Following the directions of the photographer, and Malou following her parents, the family gathered neatly in front of the bookshelf. Herr William stood with his arm behind Fru Josephine and Malou in her beautiful new dress stood in the foreground between them. Cleanly shaven and with his hair slicked back doe-eyed Herr William had the pugilistic intensity of the Cocoa Kid. Fru Josephine was a head shorter than her tall husband, even in her black strap high heels, and stood beside him in travertine elegance wearing a sleek and dark dress with broad padded shoulders, a notched lapel, and belt. She admired the style of young journalist Julia de Burgos, whom she found a picture of in the gazette. Using Julia's style as template she tailored the dress to drape her curved hips and fall cleanly mid-calf. Her hair was parted down the middle, pulled into a tight and lustrous bun at the nape of her neck and she was wearing the most brilliant red lipstick. She was dazzling and forever thereafter Malou's model of beauty and dignity.

The photographer was a young man. He couldn't have been much older than Malou, a head taller with a long pale face and icy blue eyes. Mock-framing the Cornejas family between his thumb and index finger, tilting his head to the side and scrunching closed his left eye, the young photographer nodded once in approval and flashed a smile quickly before ducking his head beneath the shroud of the Deardorff viewfinder. The light flashed. The camera snapped. And the photo was done. Their postures immediately relaxed into comfortable slouches.

Herr William knew the boy from the Richter account. They were a fairly well off family from Germany. Fru Johanne Richter was of Danish origin and they both spoke Danish as their primary language. Herr Martin Richter was vice president of an insurance company. The Richter family had somewhat settled in Condado.

Herr William and Fru Josephine became trusted confidants for the Richter family. Not only were they tailoring and occasionally cleaning their clothes, but advising them on their personal tribulations over coffee. Herr Martin, Josephine would learn from Johanne, couldn't maintain his erections without flagellation. Part of the reason they were so loved and trusted in the neighborhood was because they never betrayed confidences.

During one of their typical conversations over coffee it came out that Martin's son, Jens, was an amateur photographer and draftsman, five years older than Malou.

She heard oblique talk of the Richter boy even before meeting him. He wasn't quite what she had expected.

With the photo taken and the heavy wooden camera packed up, young Jens excused himself, promising to have it developed in a week. He bowed for Fru Josephine and shook Herr William's sturdy hand. When he approached Malou, who was staring, he took her hand gently in his and bowed awkwardly to kiss it. She wanted to pull her hand away, embarrassed by his forwardness before her mother and father. She noticed unseemly sweat on his brow, and how his hair seemed to stick to his glossy skin like the loose threads of an unfinished seam. She noticed how quickly and easily he flushed. The moment went on too long for Malou, with too strong a gaze into each other's sheepish eyes, and she withdrew her hand from young Jens' grasp. He righted himself, nodded once in the general direction of the family, turned quickly on his heel with his heavy equipment, and left. Malou looked first at her mother, who, with eyebrows raised, looked back at her baby blackbird with bemusement. She looked to her father, who only smiled and shrugged. He quickly changed the subject by directing her attention to her new library.

Clearly the girl was an advanced reader with a passion for learning and while both Josephine and William knew how to read, they hadn't the time or patience to sit and read for pleasure. These books, they thought, would serve her well moving forward as a worldly scholar with a trade. They sought out classics, texts that would instill in her a sense of individuality and historical progress. The works of de Hostos, Bibiana Benítez and her niece Benítez de Gautier, Lola Rodríguez de Tió, Lloréns Torres, Virgilio Dávila. Texts on the history of the island and its relation to the United States of America. Betances and his translation of Wendell Phillips's *Toussaint L'Ouverture*, his essay on Alexandre Pétion, as well as some fragments of his Masonic orations on revolution and the sovereignty of nations. The poetry of Garcilaso de la Vega, Góngora, Quevedo, José de Diego, El Mio Cid. But perhaps her favorite set of books, and the shelf she would spend most of her time with, was entirely devoted to the works of Hans Christian Andersen. His fairytales captivated her imagination and reinforced the divine romantic in her. Herr William read a new tale to her each night in Danish, a language imprinted in her from birth.

Danish was her native ear. It was the first language she heard spoken intimately between her parents, despite their speaking to her conscientiously and almost exclusively in Spanish. When irritated with her their Spanish would lapse into heated commands in Dansk, and although Herr William and Fru Josephine would do their best to teach her *their* native tongue, Malou's native tongue would always be Puerto Rican. They preferred it this way.

Malou pulled a clothbound copy of the *Little Mermaid* from the shelf. Its pages hadn't yet been cut. Josephine and William intended the bookshelf to be a coming-of-age gift. They wanted to encourage her studiousness and vivid imagination. It was a gift she would always treasure, instilling in her the importance of literature and poetry. A precedent she would set for her own children so many years later.

///\•/\\\

13 OCTOBER XXOI [AIBONITO; CASA VILLEGAS] General T. Michael Moseley, former Chief of Staff of the United States Air Force, former F-15 Eagle pilot: "We've moved from using UAVs primarily in intelligence, surveillance, and reconnaissance roles before Operation Iraqi Freedom, to a true hunter-killer role with the Reaper." When the world again realized that destructive imagination had surpassed creative imagination, that military technology had advanced beyond healing and social technology, there was reason for the rise of individuals like the Brothers. War was no longer a matter of crossing the Maginot. Tacticians no longer had need to leave the war room, virtually mediating their weaponry with precision enough to headshot a rabbit mid-flight. The rules of the hunt had changed. The age of the punitive strike had arrived finally with a new ascription of moral

authority. Little Boy and Fat Man, but quicker and cleaner and quieter. Punitive measures for past, present, and future crimes.

Baldomero Richter sat in the relative darkness of the first floor readied for infiltration by DEVGRU, Delta Force, or 24ᵗʰ Special. The Lieutenant's property was rigged a mile around with radar to detect an alien presence, this included airspace whose traffic they had monitored. Beyond this one-mile radius Theophilio's task force patrolled the perimeter. Had U.S. Intelligence identified this small safehouse as the most recent iteration of their command and control center, they could have easily ordered an accurate and effective Reaper strike—but their objective was not immediate neutralization. Each "Evangelist" identified within the organization was classified as precious cargo, in a sense, and needed to be handled as such. The fact was that the U.S. had not been able to apprehend any of the top commanding officers within the organization, which gave all of them, from Arjún to Frances and farther down the chain of command, the foreboding impression that the world's foremost military power was biding its time.

The body writhing and shivering on the floor at his feet attested to as much, laid on its right side, hog-tied, blindfolded, denuded, and gagged. Its face bruised and swollen. Cyanotic and completely shaven from head to toe. Blood caked and separated around the cauterized wound where once was its left ear. A tracking device was removed from a cochlear implant and attached to the ankle of a carrier pigeon that they sent westward as a decoy. Only an hour ago had the captive stopped moaning. They sat together in silence, he like an angler at dawn beside his bait. His catch.

His engagement with the captive body, deprived and on the precipice of disaster, kept him awake. In the past forty-eight hours he managed only eight hours of sleep, just enough to keep him vigilant while on duty. He was quiet, quieter than his brother though they shared the same temperamental disposition. Then in their mid-fifties. He was tall, six foot three, two-forty pounds, and tattooed from his collarbone to his ankles in the ornaments of his undocumented life. A frenzy of images and text like the gray matter of a brain wound economically upon itself. The piece started on his back at sixteen. The first object of his tattooed undocumentation was the nationalist flag. It was gradually surrounded in italicized gothic font by the text of de Hostos' essay *Armonías*. It was a favorite text of his mother, who made him read it several times as a teenager . . . *Encerrar en un espacio limitado lo que no tiene límites; comprender lo infinito en lo finito; encarcelar la inmensidad, es someterse en suplicio.* The opening paragraph of the essay wound around the black square at the center of his back and its distinctive white cross potent hung along the disks of his spine.

They called him the Shepherd. He had graying hair and a rabbet of a scar curved from the inside of his right eye around the cheekbone toward his ear. What appeared to be a tear tarried permanently there in the corner of his right eye. His way was abiding, if ultimately unforgiving, and his unwavering sense of loyalty made him the ideal enforcer. He was a boxer said to have gone toe-to-toe with Miguel Cotto for several rounds before the old champ conceded defeat—local lore he neither confirmed nor denied. For two years he pursued a degree in psychology at La IUPI before dropping out and this, paired with an affinity for and skill with blades in close quarters combat, made him an effective intelligence operative. *We're in the middle of nowhere. On an island.* His favored mode of information extraction followed the cartesian logic that the captive would be at first uncooperative, then convinced that compliance would be easiest.

On an island. Just us two. Just me and you. And no one is coming. And no one knows.

Baldo stood up slowly, unsheathing a knife from his vest. He cut loose the body, which had curled instinctively into a fetal position on the concrete. He pressed his right knee into the throat of the captive who, blindfolded and gagged, barely recognized what was happening and could only struggle feebly against the pressure before it suffocated him completely. Baldo radioed the Lieutenant before pulling a small calfbound edition of the Psalms from his back pocket. He turned to chapter 94 and scratched an itch on his neck where once he wore a beaded necklace.

A mile and a half away Theophilio, whom they called the Hunter, crept like a cat across the earth's shadow to survey the mountain. He stood at the edge of the woods, at the edge of a cliff, clinging to the trunk of a tree to project a brief radio sweep. The sweep yielded an eerie emptiness. Animal blips, nothing significant. Nothing worth noting. He attached to the tree a small electromagnetic pulse which could be remotely detonated in the event of a drone strike.

The Lieutenant's cabin occupied one of the most fortified positions against land and artillery, but an ordered air strike or special task force drop, the U.S.'s preferred military tactic since the Gulf War, would destroy them.

The Lieutenant, shortly before the events of xxxx, had the land beneath la Casa carved with a circuitry of foxholes which, since Vietnam, presented some challenge for U.S. intelligence. It was near impossible for surveillance to detect a heat signature from the depths to which the tunnels had been carved. Such rudimentary technology always seemed to elude modernity in its primitive effectiveness. The only risk was having the tunnels discovered. Once found they were easily dispatched, handled the way a child would pouring hot water down the chute of an ant colony.

Theophilio paused there to drink from his canteen. He took a swift swig of warm water and felt it wend its way through the dryness of his throat, cool in his chest, and into his belly. The humidity of the jungle, his black fatigues, and all of the equipment he carried had him sweating and exhausted. A welcome breeze passed across the edge of the earth where he stood overlooking a black tarn. The tarn reflected the brilliant clarity of the night sky, which he couldn't see if he looked up for the denseness of the canopy. The perfect reflection of the cosmos in the mirror stillness of the tarn's surface broke so suddenly into small rippling waves that he flinched. He recognized Orion's shield, which he'd always considered a bow, and Orion's sword hanging from the asterism of the Belt which pointed toward the bright redness of Aldebaran, and Sirius in the opposite direction—all backward, all mimed and reflected in the black pool some fifty feet below. Starsprent clusters enswathed in a vastness of nebulae burning astral plasma older than mystery itself; what about this ancient relationship between men and stars, polluted by ambient light, was lost. The Milky Way spread like a gash across the belly of the night in the city would have been obscured. The visible light of the universe itself rippled across the surface of the tarn, as though it were laughing, or being laughed at.

He was called the Hunter not because he was a capable hunter, though he was; his father had taken him, the elder brother, hunting late summers in Aibonito ever since he was thirteen. They called him the Hunter because he was able to track and neutralize foreign surveillance, human and otherwise. He was an invaluable resource for countermeasures and preemptive strikes and carried an AR-15 on every perimeter check. His was a pre-ternatural sense of game.

His involvement in the movement came at the behest of his mother, who encouraged him to meet a "very interesting young woman." Theophilio had just finished a semester teaching abroad and returned home to find divorce papers readied by his wife, an actress from Guayama and former Miss Borinquen Teen, Diosa Monroig. They met while she was studying for a Communications degree at la Universidad del Sagrado Corazón and he was finishing his Eng.D in Mayagüez.

For a supplementary income while he finished school Theophilio was a freelance photographer. His father had several pieces of old photographic equipment and encouraged him to pursue the craft. He loved cameras, the old Deardorff and the handheld Leicas, as manipulable machines, as objects of beauty intended to capture light and image. So he spent much of his free time after classes in his father's darkroom.

While a junior in college, Diosa, whose real name was Juana de Dios Monroig, contacted Theophilio through a friend of a friend to request headshots. It wasn't long before they became a couple. They married each other at the tail end of one year together. It was quick and ill-advised, his mother took every opportunity to remind him. She disliked what she perceived as superficiality in the young, beautiful actress. She instead knew, preferred, and often conversed with a certain alumna of Perpetuo Socorro whose family regularly and dutifully patronized the local landmark, *Sastreria Cornejas*.

This "very interesting young woman" who, according to his mother, was an alumna of Perpetuo Socorro and loved to dance, could be found Monday nights behind the bar at La Respuesta in Santurce. His mother strongly encouraged him to be there, at 1600 Ave. Fernandez Juncos and Calle del Parque. She was, according to his mother, an Andalusian-looking alumna of Perpetuo Socorro whose love for dance somehow belied an engagement with contemporary international politics as they related to the socio-economic well-being of the island and its inhabitants. That's all she was willing to say about the "very interesting young woman," alumna of Perpetuo Socorro who loved to dance.

He arrived at La Respuesta smartly dressed the following Monday night and was waved to the front of the line. Inside he saw her behind the bar mixing what looked like a gin and tonic with a twist of lime for an impatient American twenty-something. Navigating awkwardly through the crowd at the back of the club he walked up to a narrow opening at the bar and waited to catch her attention.

She gradually worked her way down the bar bathed in the bluish discharge of argon lamps and approached the stranger.

"It's likely that we're not what we call ourselves. Warm blooded. We display tendencies of cold-bloodedness, purely speaking on a somatic level . . ."

She glanced from left to right and back, speaking loudly over the din. He noticed a band-aid over her throat. DJ Adam was spinning dancehall. Someone at the other end of the bar was calling for her attention, waving a ten-dollar bill. She continued, leaning in.

"My father in his forties regulated his body temperature by swimming at dawn in freshwater ponds. He followed up his swim with a hot twenty-minute shower. I mean *steaming hot* Hollywood showers. And that was his routine. He needed it to keep himself at even keel."

Theo's vacant expression betrayed the expectation that there was more to her story. But he was pleasantly surprised by her gregariousness.

"He committed suicide." She said bluntly.
"I'm sorry. I didn't get your name."
She hesitated before answering. "Frances."

Without announce she took his large hand in her own. He felt slightly embarrassed by the unkempt nature of his hands. They were dry and his nails were longer than was acceptable for a man, but he didn't resist. In fact, he was amused by her spontaneity and titillated by her familiarity. She took a red felt pen out of her pocket, uncapped it with her teeth, and wrote her name and number in neat little strokes across his wide palm. Then she returned to the bar. He left wondering if life every day thereafter could be such a dream.

A meteor shot across the surface of the tarn. A shooting star. A fallen star. He turned from the prospect of the universe and readied himself for return and their move on xxx xxxx. He readied himself to crawl on hands and knees through the uncertainty of perfect subterranean darkness. He readied himself for whatever he'd find on the other side of the foxhole. Then he disappeared like a phantasm into the earth. He thought of her.

////\•/\\\\

"The captive has been dispatched, Colonel."
"Good."

Seated on the piano bench, a hair taller than the Colonel, with early indications of marionette lines at the corners of her wide mouth, the Lieutenant, it seemed, had her fill of the piano for the evening. When finally she stopped the sound of the cordillera central filled the new silence of the room. The island's lost children chirped in concert, *co-quí, co-quí,* calling for the wistful comfort and company of each other. The curtains, opaque muslin, flew with a stray wind high enough to let enter the light of a moorish moon which fell slantwise over an inelegant hand-hewn teak shelving unit, coloring the thing white before the curtain settled and left the room flickering again in medieval light.

"You're a natural phlegmatic." Colonel said with a certitude that took her by surprise.

"Only lesbians are naturally phlegmatic. What are you trying to say, Coronel?"

"I'm phlegmatic. I think."

"But that's impossible. You're not a lesbian."

"But," he paused, "you *are* all of a whole sudden?"

"No." She grinned.

"What about dykes? Different?"

"Melancholic-choleric," she said. "All of them. Everyone knows the dyke archetype. ISTJ."

"But I'm like a melancholic-choleric. What's *me* on the Myers-Briggs?"

She squinted, cocked her head to the side and decided, "Well, you tend to stare."

"What?"

"Staring—it's a dykey thing," she said, then paused to gather her thoughts. "I don't know. I've been reading this book, *People of the Plain,* by David Gilmore. It's an ethnographic or . . . ehm . . . *sociólogico, él?*—*sociological* study of rural life in the south of Spain after Franco. He writes about *la mirada fuerte*—the cultural weight attached to the male gaze. The gaze is central to macho-relational politics—to the point that looking at another man's woman, or eyeing a kept woman on the street, might be treated as rape. What's funny to me is the ubiquity of la mirada fuerte después de la propagación de la leyenda negra, cómo cambia contra la psique colonial. This is basic barrio politics all over Latino América. Obviamente esa cosa que se llama la mirada fuerte is not exclusive to Andalusian culture, but—you know, lately I've been thinking about love at first sight and the gaze and light diffraction. If you can make direct eye contact with another person from the *ideal* angle, something passes prismatic between you, something in the eyes. The experience of love at first sight is literally *witnessing a rainbow* of romantic and spiritual possibility and of course it all depends on temperature, humidity, wind resistance, and velocity. When it happens I think the connection is primal."

"I'm not a dyke. You've been watching *Maldeamores* on repeat again. You're fixating."

"¡Ay no chico! No vengas con esa bellaquería. You don't have to get defensive."

"Pue' tranquilízate Teniente." He leered and continued: "¿Cuándo llegará Arjún?"

"He's coming on foot from Lares."

"¿Pero a pie' de'de allá?"

"The highways are being patrolled and if not patrolled then monitored. He's due to arrive soon. That's all I can say."

"Why Lares?"

"Perdóname pero lo que ellos me habían dicho e' que el estaba 'sembrando yuca.'"

"What?"

"Como dicen en Carolina 'Cambiando aceite con una muchach' allí.'"

"Seriously? Pero 'chacho, se me olvidó que'l siempre fue un bellaco. Ese hombe." He grinned like an incredulous pre-teen and shook his head. "Have you kept up with him?"

"Cully arrived earlier today with a note in his jesses. He's close."

"Good."

"We've also been using code from disparate nodes, hacked IP addresses registered across the pond. It wouldn't be difficult for U.S. Intelligence to get a bead on location, but it's unlikely they'd be tipped to follow our accounts. As it stands Twitter is a highly censured media outlet. Internet has been crucial. I'd wager that 60% of our guerilla operation is situated in the virtual. So as not to trigger any alarms we've relied heavily on code—as I understand it, a mixture of American vernacular, pop culture hype, trending topics and the occasional quote from *The Quiet American.*"

"Do you have access to the codes, the chatrooms, any of the Twitter accounts?"

"Not explicitly."

"What does that mean?"

"He's kept the code to himself. I do my best to stay off the grid here. I've received his signal through other means. Cully mostly."

Colonel said nothing.

A few loud coos and a dusty flapping of wings rattled the pigeon coop outside. Anxiously they both turned to the window and waited for a moment solemn in silence, like expectant deer, for some sign of a Reaper before resuming their conversation.

"*The Quiet American?*"

"Arjún loves the book. He knows it inside and out."

"Pues 'tá bien." Colonel gazed into the aquarium. "It's getting late. Play something sweet. Miguel Zenón."

The Lieutenant paused to weigh her words, then announced, "Honestly, Coronel, I thought you had access to the codes. I was going to ask you."

"I don't, Lieutenant. Is there something else you want to ask me?" He shot her a look.

"We can't afford to make any mistakes. That's all I mean

to say," responded the Lieutenant gravely, shuffling through a stack of CDs on the shelf above the aquarium. "One mistake and this will all come crashing down around us. The stakes are high. Don't forget how they did Ríos."

"I can't believe you bringing up this shit now. Frances, we passed that point. We know our history and we know what and who we're dealing with. Ríos didn't do anything worth shit. He was loved locally, but you know that's not enough. He spent his life running. After Wells Fargo it was impossible for the Macheteros to make any progress on liberation or even populist concessions. After Wells Fargo they were labeled *terrorists*. Operating under false assumptions. Running around like little girls mad at daddy, doing *bad* things. If we're going to break the chains, we have to first expose the chains. Follow? Once we've exposed the chains, once the world bears witness, we won't have to worry about finding a sledgehammer to break the chains. We'll have won the key. It's obvious we can't win a gunfight with the world's greatest military power. Not without sustaining serious casualties. We have to play the politics game and we've successfully managed it so far. We have to appeal to an international theater. Arjún is our guy. His nose is clean and he's got the ideas. He's read the books. He loves our people. This isn't about demagogues anymore. This is attrition. ¿Tu m'entiendes?"

She sat quietly at the piano, arms folded in expectation of the Colonel's peroration.

"Who are we, Lieutenant?"

"The Evangelists."

"No. No. *No*. That's what *they* call us. Who are we?"

The Lieutenant wasn't following, but she had a feeling he was ready to enlighten her.

"We are the music makers, Lieutenant." He paused to cross his legs, then his arms. His breath became shallow and his expression hardened again. "*We are the dreamers of the dreams.*

And when all is said and done we will have been the founders of a new society—one apart from the stale rhetoric of the so-called American creed. Apart from its veiled brutality and militarism. We'll stand apart from the pyrrhic romanticism of the empire that's impounded us. Why? Because it's time. *Now is the eve of our liberation.*"

She nodded once. "Voy hacer café."

Sheathed at her waist opposite her gun was a knife with a handle she'd carved from maga wood. Her father taught her how to craft a knife from scratch and this was their first and finest collaboration. It bounced against her hip walking to the stove, where she poured two cups of coffee. She reached for a small sack of sugar in the cabinet over the stove. The cabinet was lined with small brown glass flasks, most of them emptied and each topped with a rubber dropper. She removed one. She put a drop of laudanum in her coffee.

"God is on our side," Colonel added, his eyes getting heavy again a few minutes into *Leyenda.*

Open your mouth he said. And in the dark came down his fist aglow with the Winston's cherry. He hit him once against the temple, blunt force, which made the Third's head snap to one side, followed then by his shoulders and torso, which were caught in the undertow of his father's rage. Thrown like a ragdoll. The cigarette was crushed into the side of his head. A violent show of red-orange embers, welded immediately into the deepest parts of his psyche. He lay thrown over the arm of the sofa with his eyes open and glassy shuddering for air. Like clay if it could shudder. He just lay there. In shock. Beneath his father, who stood with fist cocked again above his eldest son. Salomón. Salomón. Solomon. Advancements in contemporary prosthetics had opened a world of possibility in regenerative healing through the advent of neural silicate therapy. AARMs (an extension of Genetics, Nanotechnology and Robotics: Acutely Aware Replacement Modules) had successfully restored the functionality of lost limbs, arms, legs, internal organs—all with the potential to mold and conform to any segment of the human form that had been atrophied, amputated, or broken by the unsentimental march of time. It was developed as a hybrid technology based in parts on gene splicing and stem cell modification, engineering, fiber optics, and geology. The cyanotic silicate in Gideon's lip was a recognizable, and perhaps the cheapest, measure of fiber replacement granted to low-income or menial Veterans. When newly applied this breed of silicate was of a bluish transparency that, as the body began to accept its alien chemistry, turned gradually red with capillarity and cell-confluency and became finally flesh toned—ultimately assuming the density and composition of the individual's original makeup. Axon terminals and myelin sheathes fused to the implanted neural fibers and formed newer, stronger nerve tissue. Feeling returned gradually. But in some instances individual immunities would reject the transplant, which left the original trauma festering. In these cases, the skin would blister reddish-purple at the seam where it met the cyanotic silicate. It produced an unpleasant odor and a puss akin to battery acid that, if left unchecked, could harm and scar the healthy flesh around it. If caught in time the transplant could be modified and replaced, although this could take up to two weeks. When enduring such a period of waiting, because of the delicate and highly individualized process of molding these AARMs, individuals ran an increased 0.47% chance of fatality. He pulls a hair from the tip of his tongue with his index finger and thumb. It slides from his soft pink, coiling quickly in the black air between his pincered digits. He flicks the hair into a rill of rain escaping into the drain. The controversy of rebuilding soldiers who'd lost their limbs in battle was secondary to popular civilian demand for the technology. Loss of a limb or severe trauma was no longer grounds for the discharge of a soldier if she/he/they was mentally fit for the field. But the merits of the soldier, in a general sense, were limited. The field of battle had been digitized and the soldier supplanted by hub-operated drone technology independently capable of comparable intelligence quotients if disconnected from the operator. Drone technology had become painfully familiar, popularized by national artists—artists invested in the inevitable strange-loving of the military apparatus—and, after a brief period of curious upheaval, accepted as tools in the insurance of American puissance. Minority opposition was fond of tracking the correlation between drone operations and the preponderance of "Terrorist" as a vehicle for wide media coverage of all alien and local conflicts even remotely tied to American interests. There was some truth in these assertions, but not nearly enough to break the hold that such an assertion can only be made from a place of power and comfortable sovereignty. Whether explicitly or in protest the need for drones in the Holy Roman Empire was acknowledged as necessity. It vibrates in his pocket. Departing through the nautical gates of Stuy park, on the windward side of the hospital, in the still smuggling laughter of the old jade-eyed vagrant and a receding mist, he reaches for the phone in his front-right and then decides not to. He breaks into a brisk trot, crossing the street in four wide strides splashing through two puddles deeper than he'd anticipated. At his back dopplers within inches a hurried ambulance making the sharp right then left toward the maw of the docking bay into which it disappears. It whips up a whirl of wet wind which pulls against the skin of his face, the fur on his neck. A gurney is unloaded, its aluminum frame and the body it carries, its feet exposed, pushed quickly back into the maw up the ramp toward the emergency room. His lungs and passages have tightened and the moisture in the air makes it difficult for him to breathe. He slows and crosses the street to enter Beth Israel through triage, evading the desultory gait of a painted prostitute coming down the ramp with her heels dangling from her right hand. Barefoot and underbrightened. A black bruise on her cheek swollen beneath an excess of mascara and sweat-smudged blue eye shadow. Passing in her wake he gets a whiff of her perfume. Inside the hospital the air is drier and denser. The clime does nothing to ease his hyperventilation. Sitting behind the podium is an old Dougla security guard with curly white hair staring dumbly at the door. A passive observer of traffic. Their eyes meet and the Dougla security guard directs him to the fourth floor. Without stopping he heads for the elevator, acknowledging the guard with a nod. He considers the stairs, down the hall and to the right, but the elevator doors are open and waiting and despite all of the evening traffic and the after-dinner jeopardies, the elevator is empty. Its doors draw shut leaving him to the hum of the shaft, the winding of wire rope, and littered on the floor is the hot-pink wrapper of a protein bar branded with a kind of toucan. He presses for 4 and the screen lights up red behind the tip of his index finger. Now in another sort of mechanized waiting, he checks his cell phone. His fingertips still wet with sweat and mist, it's hard for him to toy with the face of his smartphone. His

thumb streaks oil and sweat across the screen, unlocking it to
open the call log. It makes him feel old to remember the tactility
of buttons, the key travels numbers and symbols on keyboards,
all of which for him meant a sort of music in the mundanity of
things. On screen are displayed three missed calls from the same
Manhattan landline and one voicemail. 0:00:39 seconds long.
+1 (212) 334 0711. The elevator has stopped on 4. The nurse
at the desk, before he has even stepped out of the elevator and
without asking his name, points him toward his wife's room.
Hers is first on the right. The halls are unusually quiet. Through
the window he can see his wife, her back to the door, just her feet
and ankles propped up and oddly still. He can't see her face, but
he knows it's her because he recognizes her knees. Small knees.
Like perfect little triangles capping her swollen thighs. The
nurses are orbiting her bed like the moons of a great planet. The
doctor, masked and standing at the foot of the bed, is mouthing
instructions. A tall male. Their eyes meet through the window
and the doctor waves him in. As he pushes into the delivery room
the nurses like meerkats stand at attention to observe him and
as quickly and briskly return to their stalking orbits, adjusting
intravenous measures and reaching for towels. Come in come in
says the doctor muffled by his blue mask. Two nurses proceed to
glove the doctor's upturned hands, presiding like Cristo Reden-
tor over the Rio of his wife. Baby? Millie asks for him extending
her hand over the right side of the bed. Her wrist limp. I thought
you wouldn't make it. No no I'm here baby I'm here he wheezes
back. Where's your mother? he asks. She couldn't come. He
reaches backward still holding her hand to draw the curtain
closed. Where is my son? She asks through gritted teeth. I left
him a message before I got on the train. The phone rang so he
must've had reception. I don't know, then tightens her grip. She's
crowning, says the doctor. Two of three nurses are wearing black
leather clogs. One of three nurses is wearing an oxblood variation of the same clog. The doctor is wearing Asics. The phone

in his pocket vibrates once, short and brisk, to indicate another voicemail. The room becomes a mustry snow-blind. Strange, the spider slinking down its mercurial skein from the ceiling in the coolest corner of the room. The spider is small. The spider is yellow. The spider is diligent in its descent. The semblance of its sac at the ceiling in the coolest corner of the room is unusual. Rarely do they construct their sacristy, these small yellows, in places of high traffic—air, light, noise. In January, in the bath, he flipped the light and happened on a newly hatched brood. The mother frozen on the ceiling above them as they began their flight to all corners of the room. He spent an hour and some minutes smashing each of those tiny yellows with Millie's left slipper. He counted thirty-two. The mother of the brood he carried outside in a blue pseudo-Athenian styled paper coffee cup that read WE ARE HAPPY TO SERVE YOU and deposited her in the neighbor's erica. The nurse in the oxblood clogs is some sort of West Indian. She leaves. The remaining two nurses are Pinay. Downstairs the young tenants of the house dream loudly. They make love on occasion and sometimes fuck loudly. Curious the sounds they make even as the mail is being delivered and from the window he can see the postman shake his head and grin. They are young and she is beautiful. He dreams occasionally that he pulls aside the cup of her black lingerie and sucks on her clitoris. At this she moans in a tone of adolescent ennui. Another woman joins them and grabs his hand asking him to feel how tender how soft how wet she's become. She pulls him inside of her. His tongue is occupied by the salinity of his tenant's box and the pleasure of this, his fingers in another sopping copse, is the pleasure of playing the only instrument. She can dance on his tongue until she's come and then he is ready. Then the other, removing herself from his left hand, anticipates the discharge of his mandragora and he wakes. What crawls up his tongue from the back of his throat and throbbing at his core. Desires that even in his age have not been extricated from the language of

his subconscious. Now these dreams simply are. He is grateful
to the young woman who's entertained his fancies online. She
is easy. She is creative. She knows how to play, how to toy and
yank with a youthful insouciance bordering on brutality. He is
grateful to these visions of the scores of women that come to him
in sleep and keep him at his paces. Still virile. Still an appetite for
pleasures. The last novel he read for pleasure was read sometime
before the war. It was a science-fiction thriller purchased at an
airport bookstore. He read it and threw it away. Novels how they
exist for the most part in obscurity are made of felled and sound-
less wood and born from an agon of aspiration to an economy of
idealism, which is the necessary acknowledgment of failure. Literature measures its worth in this way. There had been enough
literature in his life and a period when he imagined there'd be no
need again for such things. He dreams of drowning. He dreams
of laws. He dreams of undoing with hindsight what was done
and what he'd chosen and thought to be and wakes up startled
in his marital bed grasping for things against the nearness of
death. It hangs two feet from the ceiling observing blankly. The
small yellow thing, almost translucent, reminds him of how
quickly his vision is deteriorating. Unlike his father, he is not
hypertensive. Unlike his father, he is pre-asthmatic and strug-
gles at the slightest trigger to gather his breath. Ason's absence
is underscored by the woman's swelling. This is his mother. The
girl is born. Tan lejana. Her skin a tissue colored the muted bark
of an ash.

ii. The Austringer's Set

Arjún stuck the tip of the bowie knife into the body of a tick buried and engorging itself in the flesh over his left bicep. It sloughed from his skin and sat fatly between two dark beads of blood on the tip of the knife. He crushed it on the bark of the tree against which he sat and removed a flask from the inside pocket of his jacket. He took a grimacing swig and poured some over the awkward incision. He pulled a handkerchief from his pocket and tied it over his bicep to clot the bleeding. The moon was to his left through the canopy half-squandered in the cloying din of tree frogs and the occasional bleating of a wild goat. For the sake of removing just one tick he knew it unwise to sit too long nursing fatigue, but his feet were bleeding and raw at the balls. His toenails, long and jagged, cut into and began peeling upward through his socks against the inside of his brogans. From a lunar beam drifted a black moth which landed on the mistaken bark of his temple and he thought to swat it and he thought to move. Nodding out uneasily. Hallucinating in the lap of the tree, shifting in and out of sleep and sense. Cully, blind in his left eye, was gone. The hawk flew veering toward the first monocular red of dusk.

Arjún thought to move for an hour before he was actually able to move. His muscles were stiff, his limbs heavy. His bicep ached from the incision. He rolled down his sleeves and fastened rubber bands around both wrists. A ghost of gnats hovered around him clouding his line of sight. It was getting cooler and soon thick drops gathering mass on the leaves of the canopy began to fall until it was all and so suddenly sound-cracked and it could have been a drone or it could have been thunder. There was no flash of light to confirm either. The rain came down in torrents making the earth soft and quick. He kept walking, trudging eastward, over the hollowed logs that played host to termite colonies, under the elephantine leaves, the banana leaves, reeds of bamboo bent toward the sun. Things glistened. The soil black became abyssal black. This rain drumming the leaves in vitreous sheets rippling over bark and pooling in the interstices. His brogans came down tramping hard and heavy with fatigue with numbing between the cracks and soft crevices that opened for his passage.

Arjún was close now he knew. For three days and three nights he'd appealed to the breast of the wood for her favor and she would. With a mango, loose and wild and pulled from the road-sides, she fed him. She fed him with the meat of an ambling boar that he'd pounced on from a low tree branch and gutted with his bowie knife. Its flesh, even its cheeks, he'd cooked on a bamboo spit over a pit which took him hours to construct. He'd found garlic, which meant he'd stolen garlic, and wedged whole cloves in the flesh of the boar so that while slow roasting the cloves softened or melted entirely and infused their fragrant good-ness. He cracked its jaw and dislodged the small tusks from the carrion skull. He wanted to wear these, so he kept them in his pocket until he could string them together with Cully's creance. Then he buried the carcass and covered the pit so as not to be followed by man or beast. He'd washed in small streams on the way and half-slept sometimes in the high crotch of willing trees. Delirium crept on him now sauntering through the last wet leg of his journey to the Lieutenant's cottage. It was the presence of other presences that came with his heavy eyes and his perception blurred somewhere between memory and pure invention. He reached for falling mangoes in places barren of fruit. In his last sleep he'd chewed into his lip and woke up sucking the blood as though it were sweet sap. He'd start to speak incomplete and arcane clauses at arbitrary moments that, after coming to awareness with a small convulsion, were lost in the claustral ether. He couldn't recall what was said, only the kernel of its logic which was illogical. There were people speaking to him, familiar people bargaining for objects that he'd perhaps possessed in another time and place. There came the specter of a Reaper, which made him panic. *Black reapers with the sound of steel on stones.* He argued over the face on a medallion and its proprietor. It's not mine he said once and then remembered to forget.

No one died in these mountains without premeditation. These were no barrens, no frontiers that had not already been settled by jíbaros settlers centuries ago. But Arjún, who spent most of his life between cosmopolitan coteries, who'd been educated at Oxford, who was in contention for the Sakharov Prize, was wholly new to the heart-ranges of his home.

Stumbling over a black stone he fell hard on his right knee, which cracked against the bark of a tree and with sudden surcease of motion settled a heaviness in his limbs which threatened death. He clutched at his right knee. Gone numb. As had his foreleg, his calf muscle, his ankle and foot. His left leg began to cramp as the rain came down harder and rose in inches in the interstice. The earth was so sodden and getting softer and muddier by the moment, but he had no choice. He had to crawl his way into a drier, safer space or risk losing everything.

One handful at a time, clawing for a solid hold, a vine, anything fixed. For every six handfuls of mud he found a root that allowed him to drag his body for a cold meter, but it seemed endless— dragging his own corpse through an abyssal quick until his right arm locked and the muscles of his back seized painfully. The sky sparked its teeth illuminating his surroundings before darkness settled again and within seconds followed the boom of thunder which shook some dryness from the canopy. What shapes he could make out began to dim and the coolness of the earth came to greet his cheek in a way inviting. *Sálvame.* The sky sparked again and came another boom, which shook the walls of his chest and illuminated the space long enough for him to see. He lay in a clearing, facing a wall. Just one wall, four meters ahead, which in the dark looked like the last remaining wall of a small country house. It was weathered beyond repair. Its wooden beams were exposed to the sky and its plaster was half covered in vine. Its surface was riddled with holes, a deliberate smattering like the hail inflicted upon men under firing squad.

Then the sky sparked a bright white and a jagged beam of light came down parting the darkness, cracking upon the wall which split in half and lit on fire. The pure force and blinding power of the lightning so near his face lingered in his eye and vacated his bladder. He felt its heat affirm the density of his bones and hollow the earthen vessel of his body. It palmed the paces of his heart, which went beating again with fear and awe. He lay there in the warmth of the fire trembling and weeping—a weeping which turned to laughter, a laughter which turned to sleep.

////\•/\\\\

When he managed to open his eyes the white light of day cut into his pupils like hot knives and pain surged through the front of his skull. He found himself on the back of an oxcart, covered in hay and nearly deaf in his left ear which must have taken in an excess of water during the downpour. It felt like someone was cupping a hand against the left side of his head and he could barely move. The ache was extraordinary, radiating through all parts of his body, from his core to his extremities. He tried to get up and turn on his side, but his body—he felt himself shot through by the sharpened harms of Saint Sebastian. He lay there, a density tossed painfully in hay as the oxcart trundled up the rugged dirt road.

He could hear the beast, its grumblings, its laggard economy of movement in the sun-dust. He could hear the cast-iron chime of its bell. He could hear the wheels, worse, *feel* the wheels grinding up the road. His chest was exposed and he could see without feeling an army of ants crawling in all directions over his body. A tanager landed in the cart and hopped onto his chest, where it began anting. The ants scattered and what ants the tanager managed onto its wings began expectorating acid. Arjún groaned once and deeply, which startled the bird into flight. A few ants clung to his chest in agitation. They each began to sink their mandibles into his flesh, swinging their legs wildly. Another sank its mandibles into his cheek, transmitting a sharp, discomfiting heat, which made him groan again in exasperation.

Fingers, like the fingers of a child, which appeared over his body fragrant with earth and out of focus, picked the ants off of his chest one at a time and flung them over the side of the cart. With some hesitance the small hand reached for the ant flailing in Arjún's cheek and plucked it away. Arjún angled his head upward with some difficulty to see a girl leaning over the wooden edge of the oxcart. He squinted to see her in the flooding light. She brushed some hay over his exposed skin, over his face, then turned away and returned to the ox. She wore her pava cocked toward the sun, which left her neck and shoulders in shade and wreathed in a cloud of gnats. She was brown-skinned with long hair. Just visible beneath the fringe of her hair was the twine of a necklace which strung together what looked like small teeth. She was a petite thing sitting on wide hips. She wore a yellow tanktop.

Arjún was nauseous with hunger and his head felt as though it could burst at any moment. He closed his eyes again not entirely certain of his direction or the intentions of the driver, but armed with the confidence that he would, by and by, arrive at way-point. Nothing was ever lost in the heart of the country, which still longed for, which still stood as the exemplar of, a mode of unpracticed freedom.

He spent most of his time in Lares quartered in the attic of a guerilla garrison broadcasting his orations from a military radio and circulating texts on the potential economic future of the island—delineations of fiscal and political self-governance. American media, upon news of this new movement, branded them dissenters and *Evangelists* because of anonymously au-thored pamphlets recovered by the NSA and CIA. Arjún was their primary propagandist, so to speak. He attempted the launch of a media campaign to bomb various internet sites, hacking advertisement space, feeds, and major dailies like the *New York Times* and *Washington Post*. El Museo de Lares was kind enough to help transmit his work to various sympathizer radio stations across Puerto Rico. His time to work in Lares was limited. U.S. Intelligence needed relatively little time to track down a broadcasting dissident. Because of this he nightly varied his quarters within the municipality. The garrison, a tall house not far from the plaza, offered the most security in manpower and communicative freedom, but it was also a site at risk. They all knew, the guerillas and town sympathizers, that it would only take one drone flyby to violently disarm the entire operation.

But being people of Lares, people whose attachment to liberation engendered a revenant bravery, they believed in the Evangelist cause and the promise of independence. There was an undercur-rent of commitment to the notion of freedom and its nearness that circulated through the body of the town. They knew Arjún or they knew of him and they were proud of the native son and the work he'd already done to inspire the people and the world. Because of this none spoke his name. Know-Nothings. Arjún also knew that his presence in the small town, despite their hospitality and courage, was a liability to their safety. In fact he began to suspect U.S. Intelligence of closing in on his location. He left in the middle of the night, early morning, October 9, with Cully and few rations to take on his journey to Aibonito.

His suspicions were too soon confirmed. To his surprise police sat sentry one quarter of a mile down PR-111, leaving Lares. They were quicker than he had anticipated. Originally he had planned on following the interstate to waypoint in Aibonito, but it was too risky. Arjún, so near the road, could see and hear the officers making small talk, grunting, snorting, and complaining about the state of the country. They had German shepherds leashed and waiting to find and tear flesh on the trail of an unfortunate tailwind. Cully was getting impatient. He needed to spread his wings, but to do so on foot, so near the checkpoint, would endanger them both. Slowly he backed into the dark wood. In the morning they would take off over the mountain, carving a direct and grueling path to Aibonito. Once in range of waypoint he could send Cully to notify the commanding officers in advance of his arrival.

This strange detour, stranded and numb, was not part of the plan. Immobile on the oxcart his body called quietly to things in the trees, to the trees themselves which responded in turns alerting him to each of their names and more private cartographies. And the sun, from the same shores where once the natives retched spirits from their bowels in ritual, sat on what slivers of his skin remained exposed beneath the hay. The cart began to slow and they came to a shaded place where the wind spun upward in soft balmy circles brushing some of the hay from his face and chest. The rest of his body, his extremities, remained alien to him. His heart beat slowly, weighted in his chest as if on its last legs. Abiding. She unbridled the ox, which tipped the cart softly into the earth. His body slid forward. His heels nearly hit the ground. She came around and wrapped his arm around her shoulder, lifting him from the cart with surprising strength and command and slowly dragged him into a small wooden shack with a corrugated zinc roof—its front door left wide open. Two white rabbits hopped out insouciantly before they entered.

Scant light filtered in from the northern wall which overlooked a small blue-green charco. The ox was just visible on its bank. The windows, one square opening in each of three walls opposite the entrance, were covered only with sheer cloth and let in a gentle breeze. There was little separation between the domestic and the natural. The shack, clearly lived in and managed under a certain organic order, seemed the inheritance of some origin unknown to him. Some ancient order manifested in the diaphanous gradient between a world of men and a world of spirits. He felt self-conscious of the Gnostic poverty he carried into the place, which felt more shrine than shack, more noble than peasant.

She angled him delicately, all of his dead weight, onto a sturdy wooden chair without even a gasp for air or a grunt of exhaustion. She was possessed of an odd fortitude and density. Inside, the sounds of the surrounding jungle seemed to echo, augmented against the walls of the spartan abode which were covered in agrarian tools, jute rope, an assortment of fetishes and clothes, and a worn out cuatro. The varnish had long faded from the dark surface of the cuatro and the strings were tightly and awkwardly curled at its head.

She took off her pava and hung it on the wall. There was a small oven and stove powered by gas tank. She knelt at his feet, perched on her heels seiza style, and began to unlace his brogans. Her legs were long, thighs jutting from beneath the short, lean torso of a young woman. Her skin was dark, even in the cool obscurity of the shack. Her fingers took on an exceptional delicacy as she undid his laces, masterfully plucking open each of his knots. Dirt in the pink beds of her nails. Once the laces were undone she tugged the tongues and pulled each boot off from the heel. She straightened her torso before him, her dark nipples just visible through her tanktop, and caught a ray of sunlight across her face. Her eyes were like lake water in late summer. She undid the button of his pants. She tugged on the zipper, but found it stuck. She rose and at full height, in presence if presence could be measured, she was powerful.

An arable imposition. She turned on the gas and lit the stove with a match. She grabbed a large aluminum olla from beside the stove and went outside. As soon as she stepped out he tried to move, but he was still too heavy, still too numbed with exhaustion and overexertion. Fortunately his fingers and toes began to tingle near irritation with a faint prickling sensation. He needed to assess her intention, her person.

She returned shortly carrying against her chest the olla full of water. Floating in the olla was an orange, which she pulled out and placed on a roughly hewn table beside the stove. Then she put the olla on the lit stove and pulled the sartén from a hook on the wall. The sartén she placed on the second burner, then attended to the orange. She dug a thumbnail into the rind and the smell of citrus began to color the tenderness of air that soughed through the small house. In one long curl she unpeeled the orange, dropping its hide to the concrete, and took a raw bite of its flesh. A jet of crystalline fluid jumped from the place where her lips met the fruit, set on fire in a brief ribbon of sunlight before losing its arc to shadow.

From her mouth she pulled a segment and walked over to him, still slumped in the chair, to place the warmed orange at his lips, willing him to open his mouth and receive.

Then she stepped back. Sat across from him. Watched while she continued to weave.

///⋀•⋀\\\

He was outside in the sensation. It was like the uncanny warmth of sleepwetting that he felt bloom across his lower parts. The sensation of letting go with an accompaniment of relief. Abject relief. From his feet midway up his abdomen. And then her hand, which reached down beneath his right armpit from behind to softly scrub his bare chest with a tattered rag. His arms, draped along the rim of an aluminum tub, were coming through tedious needling toward full feeling. The nerves making their gradual return to normative function. His legs were in fact too long for the tub. All six foot of him. Still, he was comfortable, save his knees, which poked up above the surface of the water. He couldn't really feel them anyway. The tub had volume enough to hold him, all of his dead weight.

In the air hung the sweet smell of the humid country. Humming. The clime made for a perfect floral ménage. Just one sweet smell as thin breath from the breast of the mountain. A smell one could only know having been there. In it. Having walked backwoods Alabama in the dew of deep mourning. Having walked the pampas nearing home at twilight. This was that smell which hung in the air. Humming. Blown through by the spoor of an unidentified creature.

She breathed into his ear as she passed the rag over and over the length of his ribs, the water getting increasingly warm against his skin.

"¿Dónde'tamos?" he asked in a voice dry and cracking.
"Orocovix. Toro Negro." She replied.

Her response was final. Her voice, abrupt and more masculine than the delicacy of her face suggested. The rag jumped from his side down into the narrow space between the tub and his lower back. She inched the rag into the top of his ass and slowly made her way up his back to the nape of his neck, then along his shoulders. Massaging the stiff tissue, which made him wince with a welcome sort of pain. The water was hot now. Sweat began to bead along the ridges of his brow, which stung from sunburn. He lifted his right index finger. Up. Down. Then his middle finger. Up. Then down. His ring finger stalled, trembling to get lift. His pinky was unresponsive. He lifted his left index finger. Up. Down. Then his middle finger. Up. Then down. He lifted his left ring finger. Up and down. His left pinky was unresponsive. He could see his toes in the water, wedged against the tub, beginning to prune. They were gashed and discolored, but no longer bleeding, and his nails had been carefully trimmed. With some effort he could move the toes of his left foot, but the toes of his right foot seized with pain when he tried. A bone must have been dislodged from the joint. A ligament maybe.

In none of this could he rationalize her motivation. Why would she go to such lengths to care for a stranger? Unless she knew him? Or knew of him. Was she fatting a calf as offering for some bounty? Admittedly, what he felt was not the imminence of threat and, in any case, he couldn't escape in such poor physical condition. Invariably clear: he could not stay planted in one place for too long. Not now. Not so near the eve of a revolution that would bear his name.

From his shoulders she went down each of his arms, kneeling beside the tub, massaging against an accumulation of stiffness.

The sun in her face made her more marvel. Her lips were glossy. Her eyes trained on him, his muscle, as though he were the only thing in the world. But she was elsewhere, moving with mechanistic precision and impartiality. She reached down, elbow deep in the bath, discarding the rag to place her palm gently on the inside of his thigh. Her neck craned over the tub, over his body. It startled him, her touch, which lifted his pulse and quickened his breath. He could feel in his chest the heat which he tried to suppress, tried not to react with lightheadedness as she began to pet the top of his thigh, moving from his pelvis down to his knee and back again. Tensing as his blood rushed into an exposed rigidity. His testes triggered upward by cremasteric reflex. He hoped she couldn't see it in the murky water and perhaps she hadn't. She registered no response. She began to squeeze his thigh, gripping the flesh in her fingertips, tugging inadvertently on the hair along his thigh. He had to. Open his eyes. Her face enamored sun. Mouth agape and breathing heavily he watched as her nipples defined shape through the sheerness of her shirt, through her gaze which pierced him to boyhood, as though she were taking his body entirely across her own. She reached over to the left thigh, again petting gently, barely touching, up and down the long muscle. Arjún closed his eyes again.

Her wrist brushed up against his shaft, which made him gulp hard, nearly choking on his own spit. She stopped rubbing altogether and leered at him. With blood braying in his ear and then a throbbing at his temples, as though he'd been caught doing something wrong. He could only look away in disavowal. Until he felt her glide her fingers in beneath his excited testicles, cupping, rolling them in her palms. Then she applied pressure, squeezing tighter, without diverting her gaze. While she coddled his testes, Arjún's eyes roved between her nipples and her lips, which were pursed as though in disapproval. His head ballooned with blood.

A large mosquito floated into the corona of light around her face. It was the size of a silver dollar and it landed on her neck. With her left hand she swatted the mosquito, which streaked blood over her skin and left the fly twitching in her palm. Still cupping his testes, she dumped it in the tub breaking the surface to splash some of the hot water against her neck and rinse away the mosquito's residue. Beads of water suspended in air at the apex of their ascendance, fallen and dispersed on her neck, which she wiped off inelegantly. He imagined coming on her neck. On her cheek, a thick streak of pearlescent jism which would slide and hang from her jaw and chin. He imagined how she'd wipe it off. If she'd wipe it off. Then she stuck her hand back in.

He felt the fingers of her left hand wrap around the base of his shaft. With his right hand he clenched the side of the tub and straightened his posture, breath shallow and sharp. She'd gone from zero to sixty, slowly climbing his shaft while kneading his testes until she reached the head, circling the glans with her thumb. Gradually increasing tempo, she began to stroke his hard dick, twisting as she went, the sensation intensified by hot water. Up. Down. For Arjún things went from tedious needling to redness of flesh full of feeling and carnal healing. Up. Then down. Clenching in efforts to delay as the pleasure became more pronounced. Clenching to prolong. The stimulating friction, the masterful. Up and down. Her grip loosened around his testes as she slid the distal phalanx of her index finger slowly into his anus. First knuckle. He clenched. She went deeper, sliding in the thicker intermediate phalanx, second knuckle in his rectum tickling the hot bulb of his prostate. Up and down. She watched as he pinched his breath, almost asphyxiating with his mouth open and twitching to the visible pulsation of the veins in his temple and her fingering. Like an animal.

Evacuated, his body released from its erotic caging slumped forward throbbing with residual pressure and heat as she slipped her finger from his quivering sphincter. Out of breath and breathing now from the nose through an odd sense of shame and deadbrained fatigue he looked up at her, busy fishing his seed in threads and globules from the tub with her right hand. He watched as she slid her hand in softly beneath each coagulated pearl of hydrophobic semen stretched from the tip of his dick between his legs. Slowly she pulled the semen out of the tub, plucking it from his head, its volume cupped and wriggling in her palm. After examining it closely she brought her hands together, blade-side, angling his recovered ejaculate which slid like mercury from her right palm into her left palm until it was equally divided between both hands.

Everything, the innards of twilight, emptied over the tilled plain before him and the lake behind him glazed in blue rapprochement. Gripped in weak-kneed convalescence and reeling, he lay his head back over his shoulders closing his eyes for a moment before attempting to move his legs. He'd regained sensation in both arms, from fingertip to shoulder. His legs still felt gelatinous.

She watched him as he gripped the rim of the tub to lift himself up, enough so that he could establish a firm footing. For a few minutes he remained in the tub, visited by all manner of airborne blood-sucking insect while he managed to wiggle each of his toes and localize sensation at the balls of his feet and his heels. Then, with a deep breath, he pushed up against gravity and a painful sharpness in his knees brought him splashing back down.

"What is making you nervous?" she asked.
    "What's next. What happened."

The plain rolled downward along a hill that terminated in a bright red crest of flamboyant washed out in the dimming and the sudden deep utterance of the ox. Night over the peak so near and sometimes engulfed in cloud became juvenilia's wet echo chamber. War games played out in the grass, in the trees and mud, happened so small and so quickly transpired that they were impossible to witness at once. Sound in an orchestration of the sublime, which stands testament every night to what is risen and felled in the dark is the measure of what eludes measure. The day's last butterfly opened a veil, fluttered to the foot of the hill as the sun disappeared behind it and assumed the form of the flamboyant.

She stood still holding the semen in her hands.

"Párate," she said flatly.

He stared at her darkening above him, teeth laced around her neck, and when he didn't stand, couldn't stand, she neared the tub and settled down again beside it on her knees. Arjún opened his mouth and she fed him the left hand of his seed. It drifted in over his lips, slick and white over his tongue and down his throat. Then she got up and walked in the dark toward the bank of the lake where she deposited the right hand of his seed. She lit the lamp outside of the shack, which attracted the darting flight of several large moths and mosquitoes. She disappeared into the shack with the light. It shone from the windows.

His back began to ache from sitting so long in the tub, which was now full of cold water and floundering insects. He got out of the tub and hobbled on his left foot toward the light of the shack, where she sat waiting opposite the bed. Tall and nude, he walked into the shack, pausing to survey the space before deciding to lay down in the bed. She watched as a mosquito landed on his cheek. How the mosquito stilled in the flickering light of the lamp and the sullen numbness of its blood-feed, who hardly moved even to blink.

"¿Dónde pusi'te mi ropa?"

She didn't respond. He propped himself up on his elbow and stared at her with her back turned to him, her face concealed but haloed in the lamplight.

"¿Dónde pusi'te mi ropa?"

Again no answer. He rolled out of bed, left leg first onto the floor followed slowly by his ailing right foot, and hobbled toward her. He reached out to touch her shoulder, to make some connection or affirm some responsiveness. She felt cold and wouldn't turn when he pulled her, tried to turn her as if on a swivel to see her face.

"¿Dónde pusi'te mi ropa?"

He asked in her ear. He placed his calloused hands on her shoulders, shifting them over the grimy yellow straps of her tank top toward the nape of her neck and her unresponsiveness filled him with dread arousal, curious frustration. She lowered her head. He moved his right thumb in circles over the protuberance of her spinal vertebrae, three large hard bumps trailing down her back in reptilian crudeness. He let his right hand move higher along her thin neck, cradling her chin with his fingers, his thumb over the base of her skull, as though he were holding her skull which fit cleanly and quietly in his hand. In the fugue of the night she became so suddenly small and tender. He let his fingers slide in behind her ear, up into her hair, which she'd pulled into a bun atop her head. He undid her hair, which came

billowing down, dark, oily and musty. He stretched his fingers
in between the fibers of her scalp and took a handful of her hair.
It was soft and untenable.

"¿Dónde pusi'te mi ropa?"

Then he pulled so that it came out in thick tufts which he held
in his palm as she fell backward, skull cracked hard against the
floor. Fumbling over the rough hewn chair she scrambled to
her feet, head bleeding, and finally he could see her face bearing
the wild flash of severance from the wild, her eyes wide and
pupils dilated, her nostrils flared, and her body in a defensive
stance. Standing between her and the door, she broke toward
the window, diving in attempt to escape as Arjún grabbed her
ankle. She latched onto the curtain, which came down with her,
collapsed beneath his weight on top of her. She began to flail,
bite, and claw against the fleshweight of the man atop her who'd
forced her thighs open with his knees then punched her once
square against her temple and laid his arm against her windpipe.
He ripped the teeth from her neck, which flew scattered into the
air above them and fell clicking like chiclets around them. He
tore her yellow tank top from her chest exposing her breasts,
her nipples puffed and hardened into brown peaks. He seized
hold of her waistband and savaged the denim again and again
smashing up and down her pelvis against the floor until they
began to tear, until they tore entirely from her battered waist
and cracked tailbone. She went numb, her body flat, still and
still warm on the floor and he, submerged in forced entrance
the pain of having allowed what monster she would not allow
to forcibly enter what allowed his hands now on her shoulders
which felt as though like tissue they'd tear under the force iner-
tial of shame that shot up a lateral nerve between his eyes and
kept him surging for an hour more toward sputtering to stop
at sputtering the salve of his humiliation in the shallowest part.

She quifed and he pulled his dick out wet. Semen dripped thin and white from her bruised lips onto the floor. Then he saw her covered in sweat, sweat beaded around her eyes comingled with sweat, a streak of blood and scattered teeth. One eye red and swollen, the socket broken where he'd punched her. He passed out on top of her. Broken and weeping.

Their muscles flickered like horse haunches under the weight of a ghost.

////\•/\\\\

He woke face flat on the floor fully dressed. His head felt as though it had been smashed from behind with a brick and his neck, twisted to accommodate the awkward position of his face against the floor, went brittle with strain. His movements were truncated. Sharp pain surged through his upper parts. With difficulty he got to his feet, dusted himself off and stepped outside just as down the hill the day's first butterfly emerged from the red crest of the flamboyant to pull away the veil of dawn. Cully returned, now clutching a dead gray Kingbird between his talons.

On the near bank of the lake stood a black mare, which he rode bareback to waypoint in Aibonito.

iii. Sobras

14 OCTOBER XXOI [xxx xxxx] In the footage in the wake of the
bombings the deafening thread which went spinning behind her
eyes peripatetic. Her little sister stood her eyes down as though
she had misheard though she could hear nothing and moving
upward as if in slow motion to meet her sister. They were there
or how her hands how they got there upon her shoulders and
held her little sister just to for a second look at her and they
looked at each other two adults and they. There were bodies
rent of grace full of animal energy and pulling from the ruin
like moving convulsions all instinct. But her sister her body felt
tender under her palms which she could see but could not feel
so she saw to pull her sister away from the white well of smoke
the smell and they began they began to hobble together down
xxx xxxxxxxxx. Get to the car get away she thought and little
sister panicked and face blank for breath through a crack in her
book lungs followed this woman who when she was seven took
her limber made her cry and later brought her two una de china
y una de parcha in whose hands. The narrow cobblestone streets
were congested by cars from midday traffic emptying into the
sudden chaos against silent perturbation elsewhere in the old
city alerted to the noise but uncertain of what shook the coffee
in their glasses and began to rise over the hedera and the sisters
managed to tear away down an almost empty side street off
xxx xxxxxxxxx almost in awe together seeing without seeing
as the smoke thinned in the distance and slowly over the deafening thread the ringing came the slight and panic babbling of
exodus. Following another sequence of explosions tracer rounds

chained over their heads vying for space and then looked over
her shoulder at a mass of bodies swallowed as it rose with dust
to a pipe burst catapulting a hydrant and caved in a crumbling
roar the collapse of calle xxx xxxxxxxxx taken beneath the old
city beneath an ashen rain as though into the maw of a dragon
live in the belly of the old city. Entire buildings laid down into
nothing. Look away ahead she thought as the vitreous wake
of dust displaced and blinding climbed to colossal height and
roared toward them made her brace for impact cover her sister's
body before enveloping them both in a miasma of glass and
water which shimmered like powder snow in the light. Cover
her nose her mouth cover your mouth she thought. Hot light
tracer rounds through dust each alike arbiter carrying white
weight. Where. Down calle xxx xxxxxx. How and not in sev-
enty-six and seventy-four years could they have imagined but
how they had come from this walked away so far unscathed
and still moving at moments climbing and how over the half
tonnage of colonial pastels broken and hurtled into air before
them around the sisters. Two rounds passed so near her cheek
she felt their heat and nearly stumbled over unsure if they had
exploded from her chest. How they cracked and fragmented
into air cleaved and jagged pieces of a near stone wall and tile
the streets into her eyes and across her lashes to wince then
ducked and winced her teeth bared and felt herself hissing for
how long she couldn't have known. Her heel pressed into an
uncanny softness fragile and valuable like she had stepped into
a laugh which then like a foghorn blared in pain she pulled away
in fright from the body of a small man on his back black metal
wedged in beneath his left eye which bulged from its socket and
his mouth made sound as with his hands he tried to push the
eye back in hold it in against the hot metal that near cauterized
the wound and let so little blood come down his face until he
began tracing circles in the air and enveloping dust settled in a
thin layer upon him one leg seizing and his last mad utterance

the blackbirds feigned. Blackbirds whitegray with dust ambling in circles beneath the close roaring overhead of invisible things in flight. One shot high overhead and a man on fire standing like Christ on the cross on the precipice of a roof on xxxxxx and xxxxxxxxx. At the intersection of calle xxxxxxxxx in each channel writhing scores crawled hysterical with glacial weight down the hill toward the bus depot and the Governor's mansion like a dollhouse idyll at the edge of the earth at the top of the hill sleeping on the bay. Footage here distorted as behind the sisters calle xxxxxxxxx collapsed taking with it seventy-two people and still more injured some one hundred seventy total bodies accounted for in the chasm. Little sister almost eyes closed moved to her touch which she how was guiding toward still more air more vista more quiet a place where they could regroup and understand just keep moving as the babbling in her ear became through leavening deafness articulated noise a siren sirens car alarms alarms alarm. A queue of armed guards all in black peeling around the sisters as though they hadn't seen the women moving slowly away or they posed no threat she wondered something about their direction and what they intended to do with their weapons at the lip of the collapsed calle before she saw her sister stumble. She saw her little sister to her feet tripped and having come to a stop noticed how shell shocked she was eyes down and heaving for breath for air still wisps of smoke came in behind them with people panicked and running covered in soot directed by gravity and fear down the hill not stopping. Alone a little girl crying mutely against the light of the bay eyes shut and cindered mouth agape and mute nearly kneed and with malice by a bespectacled young man piss and vinegar in his face scrambling and resentful of the why now insolence of the lost thing in his way. Two armed guards shouting the flow of foot traffic down the hill. A woman on her knees crying out for forgiveness for absolution her prayers shrill with Catholic eschatology. Automobiles abandoned and streets emptying panicked

directed little sister up an alley away from the mass movement
to arrive at the air an odd mélange of burning industrials sea
hot and suffocating. She brought her little sister hobbled to sit
on the steps of a restaurant facing the bay it seemed safe enough
where thin smoke took on the orange hue of setting and drifted
down over the scent of meals which had earlier been cooked for
tourists.

And shouting which buzzed through the laser-cut fractals of
little sister's diamond wedding ring. It made her vaguely nauseous and to feel something like nausea which was after the
shock of the explosions the human warmth of fragility an odd
comfort. Beginning to feel a real heaviness rooted in the small
of her back behind the slow ebb of epinephrine. To see little
sister wearing it after so many years. Little sister it was often
said believed even more than Mamá in the commitments of Catholicism and what this meant for the harmony of the universe.
The little was by familial consensus the more conservative and
responsible. So they sat together little sister trembling and deaf
to the military commands being thrown from the center of the
old city coming to ruin. Near collapse. She could feel her hand
now on Alma's shoulder, sliding down her little sister's back to
console her. She sidled nearer Alma and whispered into her ear
as the sun set fully behind the smoky horizon. The sky went up
in a silent explosion of bent light and quickly cooled into the
sweeping periwinkle of dusk. Fires on the fringe of everything.
Alma nodded in agreement and they both, Alma quite slowly,
rose to their feet. The car was parked fortunately just outside
of the parking lot, which meant perhaps an easier escape from
the chaos. But Puerto Ricans in crisis, she knew, behaved like
sheep. Even on good days they drove like apes, at least in the
city, and she'd have to siphon two sets of old bones through the
bleating panic only to start the Tercel and find herself stuck. To
make matters more difficult, Alma was the catkin to her sister's

willow—a stiff wind could blow her emotional state to any of the four corners. Her little sister was sensitive to the slightest changes in the atmosphere and quickly internalized her frustration, manifesting itself in severe anxiety and a penchant for unexpected explosiveness. In fact, she was still trembling and hyperventilating while sheep trapped in the gridlock of the old city behind them were bleating, while the shepherds made noise among themselves from within the confusion clapping their sticks. She had to keep Alma from recognizing the fear that she herself was having difficulty managing. It wouldn't be long before they'd have to rejoin the miasma farther down the hill and there, she imagined, they'd be trapped in the urgent congestion of dumb bodies.

She turned Alma around and ushered her up the steps toward the restaurant. The door was still open, lights off and the din of the world outside settled in faded echoes through the space. She quickly locked the door behind Alma and gave the space a cursory survey. She'd never been to this restaurant, although she passed it several times on the way to the bookstore and recognized it as a site for pseudo-epicurean tourists. Standing at the entrance to the dining room among disheveled tables, untouched plates of patitas, and squirt bottles full of what looked like homemade mayo-ketchu, the sisters in synchrony shuffled over to the nearest table and pulled up two chairs.

The table nearest the entrance was visible through the glass door and she knew that if anyone were to pass by and see them it would be cause for some sort of scene. It was imperative that they hide away, but for now at least Alma could catch her breath. Clearly the restaurant had been evacuated within minutes of the first explosion. There was an eerie emptiness to it all. A full meal was left on the table—three plates of lukewarm rice, kidney beans, and chuletas. Alma reached for a glass half-full of water and trembling uncontrollably lifted the glass to her lips. Condensation on the glass rolled over Alma's bony fingertips. Much of the water went spilling down her chin and neck, prompting Alicia to reach out and stabilize her sister's hand. Their hands met and the glass, with renewed steadiness, met Alma's lips. Alma took three thirsty gulps without looking up at her sister and gestured to put the glass down.

True to form Alma still held, clutched at her side, her purse. Michael Kors. She loved it. She loved him. Nothing and no one could come between her and her Michael Kors. Alicia moved to wrap her right arm around Alma's shoulders in an effort to ease her tension, but Alma shrugged her older sister off with a surprisingly violent vigor. She glared at Alicia, projecting a familiar emeraldine contempt for her older sister before dropping the brown leather purse on the table. To Alma's chagrin, the purse was slammed down on the glass top with an unplanned inelegance. Out of habit she nearly excused herself. She hadn't yet regained full command of motor function, but her pridefulness returned all at once. Alicia recognized the purse as one she had purchased for her niece, Alma's daughter. Alma named her daughter Amparo, after their mother. At the age of twelve, on the cusp of so many things and quickly realizing the quid pro quo osmosis of adulthood, baby girl Amparo (Payín for short) asked Titi Ali (older sister Alicia) if she'd help buy a gift for her mother (little sister) Alma. Of course, Payín cautioned, it had to remain a secret—that meant neither Papi nor the brothers could know. It was a secret that excited Alicia, who had earlier resigned care of her only son to the father and his proper wife. She enjoyed the confidence of her niece, whom she liked to think of as goddaughter.

The chances of this being a full declaration of war seemed slim. Attacks like these, she reasoned, concentrated within the nation,

lacked sustainable infrastructure. Happening with wild frequen-
cy following the last decade of the twentieth century, these were
modern hit and run guerilla tactics. Terrorist cells, it seemed
to Alicia, with their limited resources and backward politics,
planned the execution of one reactionary happening for years
before regrouping. It would be best to wait it out in a low-pro-
file shelter, rather than be caught out in the sheepfold. But one
thing was certain: they needed to move away from the door and
into a private, well guarded space within the restaurant. The so-
diumlights came on suddenly, casting strange shadows across the
storefront glass. And against the chorus of sirens and panicked
exhortation, it was not safe to be seen idle. Looters were never
far from catastrophe. Here they would have enough food and
space to stay the night.

Alicia got up to browse for a store room, maybe in the kitchen
behind the bar. The till on the bar counter was opened and all
bills were taken. Change was conveniently left behind. Four
dollars worth of George Washington's bust and a handful of
Lincoln Memorials. It was an impressive bar—an old-timey
kind of heavy wooden bar with stools, stocked for any and all
foreign tastes. There was even a cheap brand of Absinthe, untouched, but waiting for some young derelicts with poor taste
and ridiculous appetites. Top sellers around these parts were
Bacardi and Don Q, followed closely by Johnny Walker Black.
The Piña Colada was probably the most requested mixed drink.
Some time ago, at a bar in Río Piedras, she spotted a new drink
on the scene apparently marketed to street urchins. It was called
Gasolina and it came in a colorful vacuum-sealed pouch, like
Capri Sun, which made it look like juice for children. The bartender explained that it was some crossbreed of cheap juice and
cheap vodka distributed in a million fashionable flavors and
with a straw for easy access. There was none of that here though.
None that she could see. In the grand scheme of her life Alicia

really had no reason to visit a place like this. The restaurant was fantastically themed in some romance of mestizaje where waitresses dressed like creole courtesans in white gowns with white head-wraps and waiters dressed like damned Jíbaros. Alicia had a pronounced distaste for such gaudy fantasy. Funny that fate would transpire to get her here. And more than that, force her to stay here in the middle of crisis.

Alma, left alone at the table, got up in a flutter to follow Alicia, who hadn't ventured more than ten feet away. She was still seizing occasionally, clonic spasms that made her shoulders contort and put an odd hitch in her typically practiced feminine gait. To Alma, who was making her awkward way to Alicia's position behind the bar, it looked as though her older sister was staring at her. Full-fledged staring, mouth agape, as though she had something on her face. She flushed. Alicia was in fact staring in Alma's direction, but it wasn't a look of repulsed fascination or pity, as Alma had interpreted it. Alicia had seen something on the other side of the glass at the entrance. Something with more light than shadow, more presence than ghost. It pressed its face to the glass, cupping its hands around its eyes to block peripheral light in order to peer inside. She could see its flesh mounted against the glass, discolored. Alicia held her breath as her sister continued to stagger closer. Suddenly then Alma stopped, frozen on the spot with naked awareness. She had realized that she left her bag on the table. Before she was able to turn around Alicia reached out for her shoulder to keep her sister from making the turn back, but it was too late. Again Alma pulled away from her sister's hand and turned back around to retrieve her purse.

What peered in from the other side of the glass seemed to catch Alma's faint movement back toward the table, and with revitalized interest began again peering inside. It wasn't until the door was yanked, shaken violently at its handle by this aggressive interloper, that Alma noticed she was being watched. She stopped in shock and saw its bare figure, both hands pulling on the door, head snapping dangerously backward with every sharp tug. Alicia motioned her sister to move backward slowly, but Alma's gaze was fixed on the fugitive movement of the wraith outside. Alicia stepped out from behind the bar and walked slowly toward her sister, grabbing her gently by the waist and arm so as not to startle her. Night had fallen without notice making it difficult to discern the sharp edges that comprised the inside of the restaurant. Alicia again found herself tasked with guiding her sister to safety, pulling her backward step by step, watching the door as the wraith's movement began showing signs of fatigue. Until it stopped. And ran away from the door with an alarming immediacy.

Alicia hadn't yet checked to see if the loading entrance was left open, or even if there was a back door this thing could creep inside of. Because the front door was left unlocked it was likely that those doors, at least the loading entrance into the kitchen, was also left unlocked. Immediately Alicia broke away from her shaken sister and moved, with as much quickness as she could muster, for the kitchen. She plunged through the swinging door into an immediate darkness and nearly crashed into a prep station, toppling several aluminum bowls which fell to the floor in an alarming cacophony. Feeling her way around the counter and over the bowls, which clanked against her shoes, she looked for a small thread of light at the foot of a door or a soft wind, even the scent of smoke from outside which she thought might be concentrated more acutely at an entrance. But she didn't need to search long. Suddenly there came a slow, barely audible manipulation of metal, the familiar chink of a latch being tampered with and, just like that, she could make the shape of the loading entrance leading to the rear of the restaurant just a couple of yards within reach. Something was trying to get inside. Alicia sprung to push against the door with her shoulder just as it was being opened from the other side. Whatever was attempting to get in managed to crack open the door just enough to slip in four mangled fingers. Light from outside filtered in through the pained opening to reveal its skin charred to the point of peeling and bloodied. She couldn't reach her hand down to loosen its grip without also losing her footing and she was starting to tire. Then, all of a sudden from the other side came a sound that nearly made Alicia lose her knees. A gurgle that turned into the suffering shriek of some otherworldly creature pierced not only her ears, but that place inside of her which allowed her earlier to keep moving after the bomb exploded. Heaving everything she had against the door, her eyes fell in resignation, and there, to her absolute surprise, stabbing at the flesh of the intruding fingers with a fork, was Alma. Alicia hadn't even noticed her sister come in, but it emboldened her enough to push harder. The fork, digging into the fingers of the intruder, its tines scraping the bone, weakened its hold enough for Alicia to slam the door shut and Alma, dropping the fork, scrambled in the dark to find and secure the heavy bolt lock on the loading entrance.

Alicia groped the walls for a light switch. She found it, not far from the door, and flipped it open. Wired on adrenaline she looked around in a panic to find Alma, still clutching her purse. She stood with a new resolve at the sink, about to wash the intruder's blood from her hands. She was again Alma. Austere. Dignified to a fault. Boldly perceptive and bitchy. Alma motioned Alicia to the dining room with her lips, a Taíno inheritance to be sure, while she finished meticulously washing the blood from her hands underneath the sink. Alicia took the hint, but before stepping out into the dining room she grabbed a meat cleaver from the prep station.

Things were quite still in the dining room. The echo of sirens was secondary now to the alarm of paramedic workers who struggled to retrieve bodies from the rubble and ash. It was a sign at least that the threat, whatever it was, had been summarily neutralized. Residual scents of comida criolla still hung in the air, although now secondary to the noxious odor of smoke and debris, remnants of the fallout. She could make out some of the odd nativist artifacts that lined the walls of the restaurant. This was their idea of décor? Palm fronds, petroglyphs, congas, and cemis? Now and again a shadow would pass across the windows, bodies in flight, a paramedic responding to a call or a cry. Alicia didn't want to turn any light on and risk alerting an alien body. She felt safer in the dark and she had enough light filtering in from outside to discern the landscape of strewn chairs and disheveled tables. There was what looked like an emergency exit opposite her on the back wall, which was most likely locked. She shuffled carefully forward, pending what forms came into focus before her, and gave the door a stiff push. Much to her relief, it didn't budge. It was secured and, according to fire safety codes, one shouldn't have access from the other side.

Now what? There were no entrances she could think of that an intruder with a mangled hand would have access to. What was so precious about this place? And what if another bomb were to explode in the vicinity? Questions she knew had no answer. No life is promised. Her doctor was sure to remind her. With high cholesterol and her pressure toeing the line she could have a stroke at any moment—which actually seemed to her the less appealing way to go, at this point. For now, and with cleaver in hand, it seemed safe enough to return to the kitchen and check in with Alma. She had a much easier time getting back, following the white fluorescent light from the porthole in the kitchen door.

In the kitchen Alma stood over a cutting board chopping an onion. She had prepared, in the minute or two that Alicia had stepped out, a mis en place of green peppers, recao, ají dulce, garlic, and pimiento for a basic sofrito. And the onions were nearly done. Alma, in the kitchen, always assumed commander-in-chef. Years of experience taught Alicia that it was wise to stay out of her little's way once she got going with knives. She took the cue and backed out of the kitchen into the dining room.

In the dimness of the dining room, behind the bar, she found a small light tucked beneath the bar-counter. She took comfort in her sister's new surety, so the prospect of being discovered frightened her less. She felt comfortable enough to flip on the small bar light and began looking for the goods to mix two drinks.

Her eyes passed first along the labels of the top shelf. And because she couldn't recognize most of the brands she figured it was well stocked, but nothing in the realm of the drink was more important than friendly familiarity. Stretching on tiptoes she grabbed a bottle of J&B. It wasn't anything her sister would touch, but this one was for the bartender. She uncapped the green bottle and took in its rich scent before pouring a shot, just short of full. Lifting the shot high over her head she closed her eyes, exhaled, and downed it in a breath. It felt right, burning on its way down, smoldering in her nasal passage as the din softened almost to dying with all semblance of natural light in the busy flux of recovery efforts. Three parts dry vermouth, one part coconut water, crushed mint and a dash of lemon with simple syrup over ice in a tall glass. She called it the Lolita, named for Lebrón whom Alicia grew up secretly admiring despite the generally unsavory opinion cultivated by those around her, including her mother and father. Her sister. Few women in history have had the distinction of firing on the U.S. Congress, and with a Luger no less. The irony was delicious.

When she really wanted to impress, instead of relying on the convenience of simple syrup she'd dissolve a sugar cube in the coconut water, before pouring in the vermouth. But this bar didn't seem to stock sugar cubes, and it had been nearly three decades since her little sister regarded her as anything like impressive. So she only had herself to impress.

She prepared two tall glasses, her mouth beginning to water at the tinny clink of ice cubes falling to the bottom of the glass. Eyeballing the proportions of the mixer, Alicia poured in the vermouth, the coconut water, a splash of lemon juice, and simple syrup. From the kitchen came the familiar aroma of achiote oil cooking over high heat.

After shaking the mix she put it to her lips for a taste and, finding it satisfactory, poured it over the ice. Like Lolita, the drink was strong, but touched by the coolness of the island. There was some wilting mint in the fridge. She broke off a few choice leaves and dropped them in. Using the back of a teaspoon she crushed the leaves against the ice, against the glass. Then she stirred the drinks with the spoon.

Admittedly, she was nervous to see her sister again, after so long. And now, both in their autumn and suspended in an overdue nostos. In the weeks leading up to their reunion she lived with pained reservation, spending hours, full days alone and silent in what she convinced herself was a period of spiritual preparation. It was such an unexpected request, after so many years apart. What would they talk about? Could they even? And speak affectionately? With all desire she wanted back what was lost and more, because finally Alma was everything of a life bygone. And so near the end of everything, *she could feel its nearness in her bones*, there was finally only the hope of rekindling the last blood bond of her youth. At least, in a perverse way, this bombing was a welcome icebreaker. The one she was hoping for. An odd godsend. She shut the light, grabbed the drinks, and backed into the kitchen, where Alma was peeling and cubing batatas.

Alicia set Alma's drink near the cutting board, out of her way, but still in her line of sight. She perched on a stool along the other side of the prep station. Watching her sister. Nursing her drink. She slipped her right hand into her pocket, palming a soft, small, gift-wrapped box. Surprised to know it was still there. A gift for her favorite niece, who must have been in her thirties by now. The drink was working on her empty stomach.

It caught her eye. The diamond perched on the platinum band of her little sister's wedding ring catching and refracting kitchen light over a slab of tocino. Alma stopped to sip with her back to Alicia. She paused with the drink to her lips, then nodded once her approval.

Something fluttered in Alicia's chest. Her little sister's hips and thighs were considerably wider than they were thirty years ago. Through her blouse, at the apex of her humped back, there was evidence of an abscess. Her black hair sat in a neat bob above her warm neck.

She watched as Alma cut into the pork, right hand pivoting from the wrist. Her left hand mediating placement. The slab of tocino in no time became a pound of perfect picaditos. Tongs at the ready to brown the meat. An olla over high heat. Alicia knew the dish. She knew Alma would need a braising wine. A Burgundy.

There was a wine rack for the chefs under the prep station. She pulled out a Burgundy. Alicia uncorked it and placed it by the cutting board, out of her little sister's way, but within reach. Like a ghost, she went right back to the stool. Back to the drink. The pork was beginning to brown at the bottom of the pot, its fat rendering. Alma threw in the roughly chopped sofrito and a can of whole, peeled tomatoes. She lowered the heat to a moderate flame. Salt. Pepper. No stranger to these professional burners. Alicia took another sip. There was no doubting the graceful matter-of-factness in the movements of her little sister. She still moved like the dancer she was in her twenties. Slightly bow-legged now as then. Now her feet were well worn by the damaging discipline of pointe work. Feet always noticeably angled obtusely away from the body.

With each successive sip of the drink came a subtle bloom of gratitude in Alicia. For the meal. For the silence and close circumstance. She felt loved. Felt light. In a new old way. Alma stirred the pot roughly, crushing the tomatoes which would eventually break down in the stewing process. She let it reduce for a moment, burning off the excess liquid before pouring in one cup, or thereabouts, of wine. She followed this with a half cup of water and lidded the pot. From here it would simmer, slowly cooking the pork down to a buttery tenderness. Alma stopped again for a sip of the drink and stood idle over the stove, hip cocked, with her back to her older sister. She would, in a moment, likely prepare a pot of white rice to accompany the cerdo.

Alicia stared down into her glass, which now only held a few melting ice cubes and a hardly recognizable streak of kelly green. It took her a moment to realize it was just mint and not goose shit—the kind she grew used to stepping over in the States. She was starting to see things. She considered making another drink, but she'd have to get up and go back into the dining room, behind the bar, with the meat cleaver in case she had to chop an hijueputa in half. She was already feeling light. Pretty light. Pretty loose and light. Maybe, she thought, she'd have water instead. Instead, for an indiscernible while, she stared at her little sister's ass. And her calves, just visible beneath a form-fitting white skirt, dusty white, tapered into black orthopedic shoes.

She watched as Alma ducked beneath the counter with the ease of a forty-year-old to grab another pot and some rice. Alma still had the better ass.

Alma was the owner of a small kiosk in Piñones which mostly served alcapurrias and coco fríos. Just on weekends. It was a passion project of hers and it supplemented her income. The income of a seventy-four-year-old dance instructor. Alma dropped the pot. Arthritis in her right hand. She bent over to pick it up and put it on the stove. There was a rice cooker, but she preferred the pot.

Alicia stepped down from her stool and toward the sink where she opened the faucet. It startled Alma, who looked over at her older sister, as if for the first time in thirty years, filling her glass with cold water. Alicia looked back into the green of her sister's eyes. Until her glass began to overflow, spilling over her fingers. She poured out the excess water, closed the faucet, and returned with some levity to her stool. Alma returned to the rice, which she began pouring into the small pot over a dab of canola oil. She filled it with lukewarm water. Filled to finger's width above the rice. Over high heat until the rice came to a rolling boil. Alma stirred the rice, folding it over in one pillowy white wave, then lowered the heat and placed the lid over the pot. She peeked at the cerdo, tilting open the lid, which released an aromatic cloud of pork-braised-in-Burgundy. Beneath it, the distinct scent of sofrito—the foundation of nearly every savory dish from the island. One could distinguish a chef, home chef or professional, by the flavor profile of their sofrito. Chefs seasoned in the art developed their own distinct blend. Still others inherited their sofrito so that one could taste the ancestors. Such was the case with Alma, who kept alive her mother's culinary legacy—the brilliance of this sortilege manifested in the faces of her diners. An odd delight crept across the brows of those who first tasted Mamá's sofrito and then Alma's, recognizing without recognizing the spirit of the old woman dancing on the palate.

Alicia's levity slid. The ring on her sister's finger. He'd have been eighty years old today.

Her eyes heavy, she almost dropped the glass startling her again into semi-lucidity. And there was her little sister, standing over the stove sliding cut batatas into the boiling pot. The rice was nearly done. Alicia took a sip of water and felt her body finally slow and heavy under the gravity of their precious ruin.

When the food was finished, Alma plated. Neither ate. Alicia lumbered to a seat on the naked floor against the pantry door, balling two aprons into pillows. Alma joined her on the claytile. She took off her ring, swallowing it in her palm. Alicia hadn't noticed.

"Ya tú sabes," said Alma, yawning, "si nos dormimos aquí, no nos vamos a levantar." Alicia could only manage a feeble laugh before passing out on her sister's shoulder.

iv. Essay on the Uses of a Cowbell

1933 [Santurce] Malou grew into the Cornejas library with
a semantic savvy that made her, from an early age, a commu-
nicator capable of contextualizing people and situations with
uncanny perceptiveness. Certain cultural idiosyncrasies were
immediately clear to her, both international and regional. She
could distinguish a person's origin by variance in dialect. She
could tell negros from Mayagüez apart from those of Loíza,
Fajardo, and Aguadilla. Beyond that she immersed herself in the
philosophies undergirding international politics. Locke. Rous-
seau. Declarations of war fascinated her. The military discourse
of every sovereign nation, she figured, could be parsed to the
significance of a foundational epic and a claim to divine right—
some need-based economy for insurrection, organized revolution, and then reformation. Homer. Virgil. Camões. Jefferson.
She began to contextualize Puerto Rico as an entity within an
international theater. She reckoned its significance had yet to
be defined as there was no canonical literature and no cohesive rhetoric to bind its largely heterogeneous population. Or
perhaps there was and something went missing in the fold. She
was almost finished reading every book on her shelf and had
started to develop coherent opinions on their construction, as
forms, as pictorial ideations.

She became conscious of widespread reliance on chiaroscuro.
Light and Dark. Good and Evil. The accompanying illustrations
for the tales of Hans Christian Andersen, their spines arranged
neatly along her shelves, were woodcuts which worked with

striking black and white contrasts. They were beautiful images, but clearly none of them resembled Malou. She wanted to be the Mermaid, a daughter of the air, but it didn't seem to fit. None of the fantasy fit and this dissonance sparked in her a marked confusion, which became dissonance, then resistance. She loved those books, those fairytales, but she recognized them as creations outside of herself from another place and time. They were not reflections of who she was or where she came from. Hers were lips full of divine convexity. Her hair was volunous, sometimes stubbornly strong-willed, curly and dark, ξ , as opposed to the tractable sea-locks of the mermaid.

There were no negritas in the illustrations of Andersen's world. In fact, the only thing prieta-esque was always to be read as the foil of goodness, a witch or some manifestation of pronounced evil. Still, she could recognize in the protagonist another girl like herself. A girl from the sea. A girl with feelings and aspirations, private fragilities. While she recognized Hans as a truly capable storyteller, maybe her favorite, the veneer of his fantastical mythology, which had as its muscle a sense of spiritual nuance, soon faded as Malou's interests turned to liberation literature—political and social critique. Something about being a dreamer alone felt irresponsible. She wanted also to be witness to the real and perhaps someday, its crier.

She took some joy in the idealism of de Hostos, who she felt was fairly representative of the island's culture. He was as near defining the lifeblood of the island as any cultural critic she'd read. Still, de Hostos could never accurately put his finger on the happening of a place like Santurce. It was a place that defied and defiled again and again his clear and clean logic—the anomaly and social survival of the diaspora was beyond the vast measure of his descriptive faculty. There was no rational explication or historical context for la Mesa Blanca, for Santería and the syncretic affectations of Brujeria, for cowrie shells, for strong coffee and song, for the joy and vigor of dance, for style and boasting and fits of laughter. It didn't have a place in the works of de Hostos. In his *Bayoán* de Hostos practically excludes the negropolis of Haiti from his united Antillean fantasy, its sovereignty subsumed in and consumed by the idea of Hispaniola, which bespoke his attachment to a sort of Colonial inheritance. Betances, on the other hand, was possessed of a more affected perspective on African syncretism. She enjoyed Betances because he was a Poe-like melancholic romantic, a doomed lover and a distinguished, if inadequate, healer. In so many ways Betances seemed to Malou a character right out of Andersen's imagination, whose ambitions, for their proper fulfillment, meant insurmountable sacrifice.

Rosendo Cintrón's insistence on formal grammar frustrated her. *Os*. Not because it was incomprehensible, but because it seemed affected again by certain Colonial inheritances. Despite this, Cintrón's almost darkly comedic, cynical and prophetic voice was intriguingly honest in later life and Puerto Rican in a way that the formality of his language belied.

Tomas Blanco's writings on Plena had just been collected and published in Madrid. Blanco was able to offer an interesting (and perhaps the prevailing) recipe for race in Puerto Rico through folk music. In no uncertain terms Blanco acknowledged blackness, but blackness as a sort of primitive ingredient in a salsa whose predominant flavor was Iberian, with a modest Native inheritance. Certainly imported African customs could not lay claim to the entirety of the culture, but it seemed equally backward to continue privileging the significance of the island's former colonizer. In any event this vacillation between and reckoning of roots was integral to fomenting a national self-image. The question then moving forward was what could a nation appropriate of its own history that allowed for its stable figuration in and as a national imagination? What could it disallow, disavow? This was the failure of theirs and succeeding generations. Cintrón knew it anticipating American citizenship and integration, his assessment largely conceptualized over African bodies and the history of African bodies in the Americas. *La Guachafita Fá.* In fact Cintrón could have been the poster boy for this characteristically untenable vacillation. *Es un perro, un buey, privilegiado en cuanto se le permite tener propiedad . . . Blanco,* on the other hand, and many of the cultural tastemakers of his generation, strung out on a kind of music, were not anticipating the cultural fugitivity inherent in the nation's origin as the nation's condition—*pero es un ciudadano cosa o es una cosa ciudadano; no es ciudadano*—as a port that has insisted on its sovereignty as a port, a point of arrival and departure. The tradition itself was not constituted by the object or the sound produced, but the means of production. Not the flag, but the use of the flag. Not the folkways of Bomba and Plena, but the figuration and reconfiguration of inclusive maroon hybridity. The national tradition allowed everything in consonant pageantry. *Lo Le Lo Lai. La Le Lo Lai.*

Schomburg provided an interesting alternative for her. His privary notion of African cosmopolitanism bordered on a fascinating sort of socio-cultural hoarder's neurosis. His writing was not particularly well articulated, but it carried the spark of true newness, which made it all the more exciting. Malou felt strongly that Schomburg was among the first in a procession of 20th-century players who would emerge as visionaries, whose ambitious vision would establish negro universality. But despite his radically prophetic notions of new negros finding an audience in North America, he was probably somewhere in New York, an old man pining for home, for alcapurrias and tamarindo—last her parents heard regarding his whereabouts.

Herr William and Fru Josephine never spoke about their experience in Saint Croix, but they openly admired Schomburg and his success in mainland America. In fact, they had known his mother, Fru Josefa. They were tight-lipped about certain members of the family lineage, those extended into the white recesses of slave labor, human capital, and propriety. Still, Herr William and Fru Josephine encouraged her to join in their discussions of current events and they taught her to read *through* the headlines. The paper was delivered to the house every morning and she would soak it up over breakfast before school.

She was cautious not to use her knowledge or flaunt the richness of love she received from her family in the space of the classroom, where she knew it would only serve to destabilize the group dynamic. Malou knew Ms. Panaini would feel immediately threatened and uncertain if she were to vocalize her deeper thoughts and opinions. The students of course would find her pretentious and ostracize her for it. In public she confined all talk to light talk, all thought to popular thought.

She'd managed to gradually build a sweet reputation by bringing ajonjolí to class, which she shared with everyone on the sneak during recess. Her classmates began to associate her quite literally with sweetness. But no matter what her intelligence allowed her to see through, or what her local largess allowed her to incorporate, there was the unresolved matter of that boy whose eyes carried every mysterious levity and whose smile wrested sweat from her palms.

Eliseo Sánchez had a charm and boyish grace that made him distinct from every other student in the classroom. She equated this to a sort of social intelligence that couldn't be learned in a book, or bought with honeyed seeds. He was funny without being obnoxious. Affable and handsome. He was neither tall nor short and commanded a certain presence in any and all circles he floated through. He ate his lunch rather quickly, chewing like a mad cow, and completely refrained from chatter during gustation—save perhaps a smile or a chuckle at the shenanigans of his less sophisticated cadre of boys.

Baldomero and Miguel followed him everywhere. They were bigger and louder than him, but they conceded always to his cool assessment, which they held in higher esteem than their own. So Eliseo always had the loyal protection and companionship of his boys who were, in their own right, popular and boyishly charming.

Today in class Ms. Panaini stopped abruptly in the middle of her lesson on Dick and Jane to sit despondently with her head in her hands. Miguel raised his hand and, without waiting for Ms. Panaini to call on him, inquired "¿Qué le pasa Ms. Panaini?" They were all thinking it, and it was partially for this reason that Miguel was a beloved classroom personality. He wasn't exactly shy. Ms. Panaini looked up at Miguel with a grimace and intoned in a voice none of them had ever heard "Tengo un dolor de cabeza." She sat back in her chair and pulled out a cigarette, which she lit so quickly it looked as though she had pulled it out already lit. The room was silent, save Miguel, whose loud and mischievous eyes were trained on the old American. After Ms. Panaini's admission of achiness, Baldomero, unrepentant sin vergüenza, got up from his desk and lumbered toward her. Standing six feet tall he was the tallest (and perhaps oldest) boy in the classroom. He towered over Ms. Panaini, who was reclining with her legs crossed under the table shuttling smoke from her nose. Baldomero, at the front of the room, looked at the class, smiled, then put his arm around Ms. Panaini's shoulders. Miguel had a wicked grin on his face. She looked up at

Baldomero with an eyebrow raised, moments away from scolding him, when suddenly Baldomero asked, loud enough for the class to hear "¿Teacher, a usted nunca le han dado una patá en los huevos?" He burst out laughing, and so too did the rest of the class. Miguel of course was the loudest, slapping his desk in raucous hysteria.

Ms. Panaini's raised eyebrow turned to a fury none of the students had ever seen. She banged hard once on her desk and all of the students went silent. She got up, grabbing Baldomero by the collar, then she grabbed the ferule and took that tall boy over her knee in front of the entire class with an unearthly and violent ease all at once tearing his shorts down to his ankles and whipping him until his high-yellow ass broke pink.

Malou couldn't look. The sound of him half-crying, half-laughing was enough. She couldn't block it out. She pulled from the desk her copy of the Elson Basic Readers book and began to interrogate the illustrations.

See Dick.
    See Dick run.

The girl, Jane, was a blonde.

Most of the kids in the class, in their early teens or pre-adolescent, were at this level of reading comprehension in English, and the rules of composition, grammar, and syntax were still relatively new and complicated for them.

The boy, Dick, was a brunet. Then there was Baby who Malou assumed was Jane's little sister. She was also blonde. It was an odd little book, entirely free of a narrative arc that would make it interesting for her or any reader. Malou wanted to scrutinize the ongoing relationship between Dick and Jane, but the more she did, the harder Baldo seemed to be whipped, and the more Dick and Jane appeared to be callously disinvested and perhaps involved in an incestuous relationship. Father and Mother made cameo appearances in the reader series, but whose mother and father were they? Is this what life was like for American children? All toys and leisure? No serious investigation into the nature of the world? It seemed so indecent and frivolous. The illustrations though, to their credit, were well colored. Bright in a way that made it all seem so idyll, so free of blue velvet and lynchings— which she read about in the papers.

Ms. Panaini dismissed Baldo from her knee, lifting his shorts back up over his raw hide and with that, sweat cresting along her forehead, she dismissed the class to lunch and recess. All except for Baldo, who tried to waddle out with the other kids before Ms. Panaini grabbed his arm, forbade him in English, and sent him to the Insolent Corner: a penitentiary/sanitarium of sorts she'd devised for the chronically misbehaved. He faced the wall in the grimiest, dustiest, darkest corner of the classroom for most of recess before [sitting] to eat some stewed chicken and yuca for lunch.

In the yard Malou kept her eyes on Eliseo. The kids called him El Caballo because, despite his size, he was among the fastest and most athletic boys in the class. She was planning on this moment, a tête-à-tête, and now that one of his loveable goons was indisposed it might be alright to give it a shot. She walked to within five feet of Eliseo, where he was sitting with a canister of soup, and then began to feel faint before . . .

In the anticipated best-case scenario she would have succeeded in catching his singular attention. In the dreaded worst-case scenario he would have seen her and walked (not even run) away in disgust. Actually, now that she thought about it, with her back flat on the earth, the worst-case scenario might have been his complete indifference. She peeked open one eye to see if Eliseo had taken notice.

"¿Are you faking?" He asked leaning over her corpse-posed frame.

He must have seen her open her eye. «Puñeta» «Don't panic» «Don't panic»

«cough» «cough»

"¿Oh my God, where am I? How long was I out?" she said feigning disorientation.
    "I saw you open your left eye . . ."
    "¿Oh, I feel so warm and delirious! Is that you Eliseo?"

She put the back of her palm to her forehead and immediately put it back down in fear that she was overdoing the performance. It had to be believable and right now Eliseo didn't seem to buy it, wearing a fox's incredulous grin.

"¿Are you ok? It was a pretty bad fall anyway."

He extended a hand to lift her from the dirt. She looked around and, to her surprise, they were alone. No one else seemed to care. She took his hand and rose to her feet before they both sat down in the shade.

"I'm ok. Thanks for rescuing me. Sometimes I just pass out for no reason." she fake-laughed. «jeje jeje»
    "Have some sancocho," he insisted.

He held to her lips a spoon laden with opaque orange-brown caldo and a piece of what looked like chorizo. She hesitated to take it because she only ate her mother's sancocho, but the gesture was so charming that she opened her mouth and swallowed down what happened to be a fine sancocho. It was still warm. Some of the caldo from the spoon trickled over her lower lip, sliding slowly down her chin toward her blouse. Eliseo reached up with both hands, lifting her chin with his right to wipe away the soup with his left thumb. He seemed to collect the whole thread of soup on the warm pad of his thumb, which made her feel like a doll. Then, with a quick swipe, he wiped his thumb dry on his own dirty white shirt. Their eyes roved toward each other, almost meeting in the middle. She wanted to thank him.

"¿So you're the tailor's daughter, right?"
"Yes."
"My mom thinks y'all are crooks."

She didn't know how to respond to this. No one had ever spoken to her that way. Her opinion of him was gradually beginning to change. Then he smiled.

"She also thinks he's handsome. Your father. She won't admit it though."

"¿Are you from Santurce?" she asked.
"216 Pesante. Parada 25."
"¿Really? You live that close?"
"Yeah." He nodded. "You've never seen me over there?"
She paused.
"¿You don't get out much do you?" he said flatly. "I always see you reading. ¿You like reading, right?"
"Yeah I do."

"I like reading too," he said with a grin.

The sun in the trees above them scattered between the leaves and they took turns glancing at each other in tattered light, their eyes almost meeting in the middle. The rest of the class was embroiled in a game of tag and hardly anyone seemed to miss them, hardly. Miguel, both boys of his cadre absent, the head and left-hand respectively, glanced over occasionally at the two seated tranquilly in the shade. He was only half invested in the game. The other half of his attention was engaged in the small theater that his best friend now found himself in. And the worst part for Miguel was that Eliseo, seated in the shade beside the priss, looked happy. Intrigued at least. It made him uncomfortable and self-conscious. Mildly envious.

Miguel's attention made Malou uncomfortably warm while Eliseo, focused entirely on her, began to look concerned. She could feel sweat beginning to seep from her pores, under her arms, and at her feet. Eliseo put his hand to her forehead to check her temperature, which startled her.

"You feel warm. And you look sudaíta. ¿Did you bring your lunch?"

"¿Aren't *you* hot?"

In fact he wasn't. He looked cooler than the other side of the pillow.

"It is hot, I suppose. Let me get you some water. Eat more sancocho. I'll be back."

She watched as he walked toward Miguel, conferring briefly before they both walked toward the schoolhouse. She eyed the sancocho beside her, which did smell good, but the thought of partaking felt somehow like a betrayal of her mother's cuisine. Most of these kids knew nothing about jerk chicken anyway. Or conk fritters. Or curried goat. Or pan-fried grunt fish. But criollo cuisine, between Saint Croix and Puerto Rico, was almost identical beyond its lexical difference. Bacalao and saltfish were the same thing and calalú was universally recognized, with slight variation, across the islands. Among island negros anyway.

She wondered about the difference between her mother's sancocho and his mother's sancocho. Whose was the more authentic? According to Josephine she had learned to make sancocho from one of the clients before Malou was born. Incidentally the client was called Madame Calalú, a practicing bruja from Santurce with roots in the Republic of Haiti. She was said to have worn a long purple shawl with a hood. This was true because Fru Josphine was often mending, hemming, and pressing them. Sometimes, it was said, she wore human bones around her neck.

She no longer lived in the neighborhood. Her whereabouts were unknown. But tales were still spun of her crawling Santurce's streets in the darkness beyond midnight for every full moon, ringing a cowbell at the front door of one chosen home, disappearing like a ghost before she could be seen. Legend had it that the ringing of the cowbell meant an impending death in the household.

When the cowbell was heard in the street hardly anyone had the courage to peek outside and see what the noise was about. Stories of Madame Calalú were told far and wide. While regarded with deference in the light of day, she was completely feared at night. Only a few had ever seen her saunter through the night streets dangling from her left hand the extra-large cowbell and lived to tell the tale. So the story went: Madame Calalú was at full moon the harbinger of death. A white herald. *How conve-*

nient, thought Malou.

In the day both Josephine and William could attest to her general pleasantness and prophetic wisdom. Madame Calalú was something of a touched beggar. The way they tell it, before Josephine was impregnated, Madame Calalú knew she'd be with child—and what's more, she knew it would be a girl. But Herr William wouldn't believe her and Fru Josephine thought it less and less important that she know the details of her daughter's arrival. Shortly after Malou's conception Madame Calalú disappeared entirely from Santurce, but not before ringing the bell at their doorstep.

Eliseo came strutting back to her with a cup of cool water. She took a sip and smiled at him graciously.

"¿How are you feeling, prieta?"

He called her prieta. She didn't mind it. The familiarity.

"I'm alright, Elí. Thank you for the water. ¿Do you mind if I call you Elí?"
    "No. I don't mind." He looked away bashfully.

Malou wanted to give herself a pat on the back. Turns out she had a few tricks up her sleeve after all.

Miguel had rejoined the game. A few of the children were starting to sideline and catch their breath, so it didn't appear unusual or pretentious that Malou and Eliseo were sitting it out together. In fact, the children had come to expect that she could faint at any moment so it would have been more unusual for her to play, running in the high sun, parched and near heatstroke.

"¿What happens when you pass out?"

"Well," she thought for a second, "I always see a bright light and then I hear a voice."

"¿What kind of voice?" he asked, genuinely intrigued and slightly mystified.

"I couldn't even describe it. It's like when Saul fell off his horse and became Paul. It's that kind of voice."

"¿Really?"

"Yep."

"Holy shit."

They both sat there, watching for a while as the children went barreling after one another. Ms. Panaini was watching them all from the schoolhouse window, reclined in the slim haze of her American cigarettes. They couldn't see Baldo from the window so he must have been [sitting] uncomfortably in the corner, pursing his lips and sucking his teeth in dissatisfaction and boredom, careful not to have his raw ass graze the seat of his pants.

While Malou was imagining the psychological state of tall, tragic-comic Baldomero, Eliseo began humming what sounded like a lovely little bolero. He was a young singer with an incredibly moving tenor vibrato, from what she'd heard. In fact he often sang to the girls in class—Dawila Mañach, for example, who had long legs, fair skin, and straightened hair. She was taller than Eliseo, but somehow that didn't matter when he opened his mouth to sing for her.

Malou liked Dawila. She was fairly quiet, polite and ladylike, which Malou appreciated. But Dawila also had a catty side, an acerbic wit which she only shared with people she felt comfortable with. Dawila liked Malou as well, although perhaps for superficial reasons. She had a not-so-secret sweet tooth, and she loved Malou's generosity with the ajonjolí she'd bring from home.

Fru Josephine knew the importance of bribery in securing the trust of strangers, so she was sure to outfit her baby girl with just enough ajonjolí to share with the class. It wasn't exactly hard for Malou to make friends, but she was reserved and introverted by nature. Fru Josephine also knew that this quality was what made her truly beautiful. She knew enough women forced into awkward sociability as girls so that in adulthood they would lose that wholly private mystique which made beauty and came from a place of healthy self-regard. Young women were conditioned to give so much that they rarely had anything left for themselves or worse, didn't know how to be wonderfully selfish. Women who through no fault of their own tarried in undifferentiated reality. These were rare and tragic husks of womanhood. Josephine didn't want that for her daughter. Thankfully, Malou's book-ishness was enough to keep her privately engaged and in awe of the world. She was never wont for unnecessary attention, or starved for affection (as some of the children secretly had been). She was curious, always motivated to learn and explore and, for good and bad, unwilling to concede to a thing she thought of as lesser or less than what she knew she deserved. In short, she was a strong young personality, and as her personal publicist Fru Josephine thought it would be best for Malou's public image if she carried charitable sweets.

Dawila was buzzing in the sun with the rest of the kids playing tag, her hair flowing behind her. She was almost Baldomero's height, which made her the tallest girl in the class. She was a striking girl. She wasn't unintelligent, by Malou's standards, but she wasn't a distinguished scholar either. Malou could under-stand why Eliseo would be attracted to her. In so many ways she was an ideal candidate for young male posturing and Eliseo was nothing if not a bantam. Clearly. Because he began crooning as Dawila broke away from the honking gaggle and walked toward them.

"Eliseo! ¿What're you doing over there?" Dawila asked, half-shouting.

"Aquí sentao con Malou."

"¿Malou?" She seemed genuinely vexed, as though she'd never heard of Malou.

Eliseo pointed to Malou beside him.

"Malou." He said again flatly introducing her presence.

"¿La negra?" Dawila responded incredulously. "¡Pero coño morena! I didn't see you there in the darkness."

Dawila broke into affected laughter and stopped when she realized neither of them found it funny. She turned her attention exclusively upon Eliseo.

"¿What are you doing over here wasting your time in the dark? Come play with us!"

"Malou's not feeling well so I'm just going to sit here with her for a while."

Dawila sat down beside Eliseo slipping her arm in beneath his and whispered into his ear, loud enough for Malou to hear:

"She's always sick. Don't waste your time."

He untangled himself from her tightly locked arm and sidled closer to Malou. Dawila leered dramatically in Malou's direction, as though she were searching a void for purpose, and this Malou recognized as the first taste of another's romantic envy, romantic insecurity. All of the novels seemed to come alive in that moment. *Put out the light.* Crimes of passion, erotic ennui, adultery. She didn't mind this kind of attention at all. Being the dark envy of another's unacknowledged desire. Less than a minute later and discouraged by their silence, Dawila hopped up and ran back into the throng of initiated youth.

"Don't listen to her," Eliseo said ruefully.
She shrugged.

"¿Can you tell me a story?" he asked.
    "¿What kind of story?"
    "A good one."

She thought for a moment and started on the first story she could think of.

"There once was a girl who lived at the bottom of the sea. ¿She was very beautiful Can you imagine what she looked like?"
    "She must have had long legs, long hair," he paused, "a nice figure. Light-skinned . . ." He smiled impishly.
    "You know, you're absolutely right, that's exactly what she looked like," she responded half-amused by his cheek, "except for one small detail . . ."
    "¿What?"
    "She didn't have legs. She had fins!"
    "¿Fins?"
    "Not only fins. She had the whole tail of a fish from the waist down. Half-girl, half-fish, but truly one of the most beautiful creatures on God's earth. And she lived under the sea with her father the King. He was a very big man who commanded all the fish and sharks of the sea. The turtles. The octopi. Even the whales. But not the bacalao."

He smiled.

She continued, "This girl had a lot of sisters. And every year after a certain age, like fifteen or something, each one was allowed to come up to the surface and peek at the human world. When it was the girl's turn she peeked into the human world and on the surface she found a ship. ¿Guess what—or I mean, guess who she saw on the ship?"

"¿Who?"

"A handsome young prince. The most handsome. ¿What do you think he looked like?"

"Prieto," he said gallantly.

"¡Exactly! She fell in love immediately. He was so handsome. I mean, she didn't know he was a prince at first, but she could tell he was a cut above the rest—standing there on the prow of the ship, a regal young captain. She wanted to know him, who he was, what his name could be. Floating behind the ship as it sailed along she imagined all kinds of stories about his origins. And while she was imagining who he was and where he came from the sky turned grossly pale, then heavy with clouds. An unexpected storm had rolled in against the tide, hastening the current and stirring the crew into alert. Thunder crashed overhead before a streak of red lightning parted the immense and sudden darkness and cracked the hull of the ship in twain. Torrential rain fell and water rushed into the hull. They were sinking fast. And there was the little girl, witness to it all. Witness as bodies were flung overboard."

His face became grave.

She continued, "Since the little girl was half-fish she had nothing to fear from the brutality of the storm. She could always go back home. Right?"

"¿What about the prince?"

"Exactly!" Her finger shot up in eureka-exclamation. "She

couldn't leave him to drown! Of all the names listed on the ship's manifest, only one survived."

"The prince?"

"Precisamente. She swam him back to shore, depositing him at the entrance to the shrine of a sea goddess where she breathed life back into his singing lungs."

Just then the cowbell was rung to announce the end of lunch and recess. Malou and Eliseo watched as the kids went trouncing, all sweat and curious vitality, back into the schoolhouse.

"I'll finish telling you the story tomorrow," she said.

Eliseo got up first, extending his hand to assist the lady's ascent. Side by side, sometimes touching shoulders, they walked toward the belling. They were the last to enter and they entered, up the steps, together.

Inside they took their respective seats, both a bit distracted and glancing. Malou felt tangibly his sincerity when she was telling him the story of the Little Mermaid. The way he looked at her, as though she was the only person worth any attention in the world, as though she was the most fascinating and enlightening person in Santurce. He was so open. So boy.

He couldn't stop thinking about her story, the way she signified without saying, which kept him interested. He wanted to— he should have sung to her. "Torna a Surriento". That would have really impressed her. It was a song he reserved only for the good days, in moments of transcendental beauty, when without thought it came out as clearly and perfectly as the world laid bright before him. Maybe it was the way she looked at him, eyes dark and half open, half-grinning with intelligent reservation. How she would pass her fingers over the neat bun of her hair, just to check, just to announce and re-announce its perfection.

Nothing seemed to faze her. Not even Dawila's witchy intonations. She was cooler than the other side of the pillow.

So the day came and went. The sun sliding across the transoms with an afternoon breeze to accompany each of the children on their way home. As usual Herr William was waiting for Malou outside. She only managed to look back twice before her father, smiling, grabbed her by the hand and they began to walk home.

///Λ•Λ\\\

There was a cow in the field with whom she felt very comfortable. She wore a brown cowl in the field there beside her cow. There was a cow in the field with whom she made love and it felt familiar and without desire but for nourishment. There was a cow in the field with a bell on its neck and the wind that came down made its cast-iron bell jingle and sing. There was a cow in the field at the foot of a hill that rolled up to the sky it was gray and got grayer. There the cow chewed cud with a fistula in its left hide from which sprung a field at the foot of a hill which rolled up to the sky it was gray and got grayer. There the cow opened its left hide to speak and from it sprung forth a gray cloud over the field at the foot of a hill which rolled at the ankles and fell a soft body familiar and uncanned. There was a cow in the field with a bell on its neck and the wind that came down made its cast-iron cackle and cackle and grayer then black as all air vacated the space.

She woke weeping. She woke to her mother beside her gently wiping the sweat from her shoulders and forehead, wiping the remnants of a vision perhaps they shared. She looked at her mother, half-crying, and knew. Josephine sat at the edge of the bed and pulled her daughter nearer. Malou put her head in Josephine's lap and wrapped her arms indelicately around her mother's waist. Malou could smell Herr William in the kitchen frying up salchichas and eggs for breakfast. Josephine kissed Malou on the forehead and got up from the bed, presumably to join Herr William in the kitchen.

Malou's clothes for school were laid out on the armchair opposite the bed, pressed and ready. She peeled herself, sweating and slightly disoriented, from the sheets and walked to the bathroom basin where she washed her face and rinsed her neck. Her nightgown, drenched in sweat, clung uncomfortably to her back and chest. She grabbed it by its hem and lifted, unpeeling it from her torso, tearing it off up high over her head. She began to towel the sweat from her body and paused for a moment in front of the mirror. Her thighs were getting bigger it seemed, every day. In profile those thighs rose into a blooming convexity that, if she stood with good posture, seemed somehow more palatable. Looking in the mirror she felt almost as if she could mold herself, and daily the tragedy that this was not possible compounded in her some entirely new grief. Her breasts weren't developing the way the other girls' breasts were developing. They were small, almost overwhelmed by the wideness of her aureole. She tried to squeeze them together and give them some weight, but there wasn't much to squeeze at all. In any case she thought this might have been her gift and her curse. Fru Josephine was not a top-heavy woman, but she had something decent there. And the girls with breasts were actually attracting the kind of attention Malou found offensive. She finished toweling off and powdered. Then she dressed rather quickly, remembering that she had to finish telling Eliseo the story of the little mermaid. It was something to look forward to.

Breakfast was waiting for her at the kitchen table. Fru Josephine was looking through *El Mundo* and Herr William was putting the finishing touches on a batido of bananas and sweetened milk over the sink. Pirouetting on one foot from the sink to the table Herr William planted the batido beside Malou's plate, then dipped to kiss her forehead and dipped to kiss Josephine's forehead. Then without much ado he dismissed himself from the ladies to get dressed for the day's work. Fru Josephine shook her head and smiled to herself.

The sun was up and pouring in at a sharp angle through the window, bending around two red-winged blackbirds that sat as still as statuary on the window's ledge. The kitchen was cozy, pastel yellow with a gas-lit stove and a basin. At center was a small round table, surrounded by four foldable wooden chairs, for casual meals like breakfast and lunch. It doubled as a prep station for larger meals when entertaining guests.

Malou always assisted her mother with some of the heavy lifting that accompanied banquet-style meals—rare potlatch occasions usually in celebration or on holiday. Malou always assisted, that is, unless the cousins arrived from Fajardo, at which point she was entrusted to keep them entertained and out of trouble. Those meals were taken in the adjoining dining room where, when company was expected, place settings were made up neatly. The table could accommodate six guests, which sometimes meant the children ate in the kitchen. There were hand-crocheted doilies beneath every pot, every plate, and every vase. From the ceiling hung a basket full of ripening fruit, maduros and piña, usually surrounded by a small cloud of fruit flies.

Scattered throughout the house were tiny fetishes, almost indiscernible to the uninitiated. For those more conventional, a large cross hung on the wall in the living room. Malou always had the sense growing up that despite all dignity theirs was a culture of paying unaccountable debts.

Fru Josephine licked the tip of her index finger, turned the page to the international section in *El Mundo*. Malou could see her mother's interrogative face over the top of the paper.

Even over the smell of breakfast she knew her mother's scent, which played always like needle on wax, floral print, garlic, and menthe salve. Like nocturne through the fullness of her being.

Josephine tapped her foot against the nearest leg of the table, signaling her daughter to finish up breakfast. Herr William would be out and dressed in any moment, ready to escort her to school. Fru Josephine put down the paper and went to fix her daughter's school lunch while Malou finished breakfast. She glanced at her mother's ankles, swollen, the skin burnished like semi-precious stone.

Taking two biased cuts of salchicha on the tines of her fork she peeked at the exposed pages of *El Mundo*, the nearest headlining an article on Ana Roqué de Duprey. Malou swallowed the salchicha followed closely with a gulp of the batido. Today the batido was a bit thicker and sweeter than usual. She gathered almost all of the eggs onto her fork and crammed them into her mouth, hardly chewing at all. Josephine, with eyes in the back of her head, turned around and shot Malou a chastising look. She wasn't one to tolerate nonsense, which included unladylike manners at the table. Even when no one was around to witness. Malou took the hint and remembered to pace herself. She finished the rest of the batido in a few delicate sips and immediately washed the kitchenware in the basin, beside her mother. Herr William emerged from the master bedroom, where almost ten years earlier he delivered his own daughter. He was ready to walk her to school. Fru Josephine handed her the bagged lunch and her books and hand in hand the big man and the little girl departed the mother.

With the sun on their necks it was already warm. It would likely be a hot and sticky day. People were up and on their way to work or sitting idly on their patios or attending to house chores. Walking there Malou noticed an old man with a sleeveless undershirt pulled up over a tanned brown, unusually smooth potbelly. Passing on her father's side Malou was just close enough to witness a mosquito land on the perfect smoothness of the man's paunch and pierce through it, beginning to engorge itself. She half-expected his stomach to deflate like a hot-air balloon. He looked neither contented nor displeased and his eyes seemed fixed in a sun-glazed squint. His head rested quietly on an ample second chin. He was chest napping, browning through noon. They turned onto the avenue.

Everywhere down Ponce de León were palm trees, tall and bent over the powerlines toward the sun, which washed over the entirety of the neighborhood as it climbed to its zenith. Malou smiled remembering how, once upon a time, she anxiously awaited the quick transit of the sun, its rise and slow descent that meant the nearness of dismissal and home. School was so tedious, but now, in some real way, all of her knowledge and reading could be applied to the actualization of something tender and true. She had someone to share it with. She had a little prince in the palm of her hand, which she knew was wide and strong enough to carry him and his curiosity. Trolley 40 passed on their left ringing its bell on the way to clear foot traffic from the track of a game of stickball being conducted further down and in the middle of Ponce de León. The trolley's striped curtains were drawn at various lengths to shade passengers, faithful commuters, tourists, and factory workers, from the heat of the sun. These were rather impressive American manufactured models. A single-end and streamlined design outshining the handful of worn down jaulas still in circulation.

Herr William gazed at his daughter, who gazed reactively back at him—his features illuminated in morning, prominent cheekbones and a distinguished jaw, pug-nosed, his eyebrows heavy copper bars over wide oriental eyes. The weight of his gaze made her feel slightly self-conscious, her palms warmed, as though he could see through her. But his gaze lifted in a blink, transfixed again somewhere in the distance as the trolley passed completely, rolling along the avenue. He was wearing his white short-sleeved guayabera over pressed khakis and shiny brown loafers with no socks. No hat today, although he often donned a panama with a little red feather in it for warm open days like this. His hair was conked, slick and lustrous, but beginning to kink again in the back. He carried a tortoise-shell comb and a small pair of shears in his left breast pocket, like a barber. Reading glasses and measuring tape on the right. He covered his mouth to cough once, cleared his throat, then hawked his phlegm which landed viscous white on black tar. Her mind wandered.

She imagined humanity in space and thought of Daedalus and Icarus. She imagined inhabiting space and melting back to earth from its vacuum. She imagined the sun made deity and herself its prophet—a sentience which would allow or disallow humanity's arrival and departure from the world, driving all motion and harmony with the sun's immense gravitational pull. Moving from star to star on a solar barque, fugitive and new, she would become the foundation of a civilization beyond the failure of the old world.

Some nights, from the patio, she traced the constellations against the diagrams of her astronomy guide. Ursa Minor, which contained the North Star, was always her means of orientation and the astral object of her affection. She'd developed an interest in the stars from the small incantations and lunar observations of a neighborhood bruja, La Negra. She was what the adults called an original Lucumí. When Fru Josephine took Malou to see her, the old woman, whose eyes were clouded completely, felt for Malou's face and immediately assessed that her guardian orisha was Yemaya. Mother of Waters. With her unsteady hands La Negra placed around Malou's shoulders an eleke of hand-hewn beads. The beads alternating between azurite and a soft translucent white stone she couldn't recognize—some sort of quartz perhaps. It had a faint, very faint, pink hue to it. She wondered about La Negra's actual blindness as she examined each polished and smoothed bead. How did she manage to make each bead so perfect, she wondered. And in that moment without any sign or warning, La Negra grabbed Malou's small left hand and made her feel.

Herr William gazed at his daughter once more as they neared the schoolhouse. Ms. Panaini stood outside waiting, a smile plastered on her face, as the students, one by one, climbed the stairs behind her. Malou could see against her father's eyes the last dark expression her mother wore while reading the paper, half chastising. Age fanned from the corners of Josephine's eyes. She left the fullness of her lips undisturbed, save her directive and her kiss. She was entirely the embodiment of water in motion, at mercies capable of stirring her immensity, but mercies wholly incapable of containing her. While quietly reading she often stroked the fine hair that grew beneath her chin.

A cool breeze licked the sweat along Malou's brow, passing a cool wave of relief through her anxious frame. The nearer the schoolhouse, the faster her heartbeat, thinking of concluding the tale of the little mermaid with Eliseo. Would she have his full attention again? She could see Dawila hopping up the stairs into the schoolhouse.

Ms. Panaini sounded the cowbell. Herr William gave her a little pinch on the shoulder. She didn't look back. Instead she fixed her gaze on the steps, on the door to the schoolhouse, where she'd sit uncomfortably warm until recess. She was the last to enter, taking each step slowly. Ms. Panaini put her hand on the small of Malou's back as she followed her inside.

Immediately, and trying her best to look inconspicuous, Malou scanned the room for some sign of Eliseo. She took her seat, between Carmelina and Josef, feeling her heart beat faster to the point where she began to worry about passing out again. She closed her eyes and took deep steadying breaths and thought about her mother sitting at the kitchen table staring darkly at *El Mundo* as her breasts hung slightly in her smock and how she never seemed to sweat even in the most insipid summer heat. She tried to focus on the lesson, the reading, going through the motions with little interest, with one eye trained on the door, until the sun crested for recess and still no sign. She went out with the rest of the kids, sharing ajonjolí among those now accustomed to her generosity, a sort of schoolyard philanthropist whose palms the kids grew accustomed to licking. She sat in the shade, feeling on edge, a ghost on the precipice of having its body back, Miguel and Baldo playing round as though they hadn't noticed the absence of their fearless leader.

The cowbell rang and the kids scampered inside, Malou of course the last to enter. It was possible that he was feeling mal and his mother decided to keep him for the day, perhaps to feed him her onion-heavy sancocho with chorizo. She began to feel the absence of all music, the music present in his presence. Then she stopped herself and wondered if the heat of the island made her so foolishly amorous that she would forget herself. She thought of her mother singing in the evening at the basin with her back to all light, washing glasses and plates of their residue. She thought of the way light blued against her mother at dusk and how she wanted this power for her own. She thought of how this may have been her blood inheritance, the eventuality of her back to all light witnessed in awe one day by her own daughter.

And the entire afternoon passed across the window mullion. The lesson felt like it went on forever and the classroom was unbearably hot.

When class was dismissed Malou took her time packing her books and things. The class had funneled out and she was left with Ms. Panaini.

"Ms. Panaini, was Eliseo sick today?"
"Oh! No, Mathilde. That reminds me—"

Ms. Panaini scribbled something on her desktop planner, which was filled with all sorts of intertwining chicken-scratch notes in American.

She continued, "No, Mathilde. Eliseo has been withdrawn from classes. His mother wanted him working to support the family."
"Oh."

Malou didn't really know what to say. She stood there, increasingly uncomfortable, wanting to dismiss herself from the conversation and find her father.

"Did you like him, dear?" Ms. Panaini asked.

Ms. Panaini's face was open and sincere, her eyebrows raised in a sort of curious empathy, almost nostalgia. Malou didn't know how to respond.

"You know I taught him a few songs. His favorite that I taught him was "Torna a Surriento"—an old Italian number. He learned it so quickly. Truly a bright boy. He lives on calle Pesante."

Ms. Panaini paused, grinning, then raised her finger as though she'd gotten an idea.

"Mathilde, I notice your boredom. It's clear that you're an advanced student and I want to encourage that talent and curiosity." She reached into her desk and pulled out a tome with a gray and red dust jacket. "I want you to have this."

On the cover was what looked like a white marble statue grappling with the ghostly, vaguely human figure of a black wraith behind it. It intrigued her, this Manichean agon. Good and Evil. Light and Dark. Material and Immaterial. She let the book fall open in her hands. It fell open to the title page, which was signed in a modest, unadorned cursive and inscribed. Among the superficial characteristics by which Malou measured the potential quality of a book, weight was important, and this book was heavy. Not excessively heavy, but it had a weight to it that seemed unique, the kind of weight that comes with being entrusted to care for a rare treasure, an object animistically imbued, a fetish from the U.S.

"This is a special book," Ms. Panaini began to explain, as though she were conducting a lesson. "I met the author at a bakery in Mississippi." She looked up as if querying the ceiling, then looked sharply back at Malou. "Back when I was your age. I was dark and skinny. My hair, if you could believe it, was patent-leather black, like a pair of your father's shoes, and always pulled into pig-tails. I remember it like yesterday. He was quite small, I thought, for an older man and I was lost. I had no idea where I was going or which stop I was supposed to get off at and I had no idea who he was, at the time. My family had just moved from New York City. I remember him being dapper. You know what that means? Like a southern gentleman with a little moustache over his top lip and a mop of dark hair. He really wasn't much older than me, although he seemed really old. Just a couple of years ago, at a reading for his new novel, I approached him and he recognized me. And he signed and inscribed my copy." She gazed down at the book in Malou's hands.

"I want you to have it. And more than that I want you to read it. You have the intelligence and reading comprehension of someone much older and more mature. Unusual for a bilingual. We shall meet once a month, at the end of the month, after class for discussion. Is that clear?"

Malou thought at first that this was some ridiculous form of punishment. It seemed harsh and unusual. But something in Ms. Panaini's face seemed earnest, bordering on jubilant. It occurred to Malou that the woman who smoked slims during recess in the quiet emptiness of the classroom may have been dealing with an intense boredom. Perhaps she made a habit of encouraging her students outside of the classroom as a means of combating ennui, reasserting her purpose and perhaps a latent ambition to touch young lives in profound ways.

Malou weighed the book in her hands again and gazed up at Ms. Panaini, then at the switch in the corner. Then she nodded her confirmation.

"Excellent!" Ms. Panaini exclaimed. "I will see you in two months to discuss the novel. It's a difficult one, but I think, of all my students, you're the only one capable of breaking it open. I can't even take credit for that. You came into my class with a gift beyond my comprehension."

Malou nodded her thanks, looking into Ms. Panaini's face as if for the first time. She delicately piled her new book atop her other books and made a quick exit.

Outside her father was waiting for her, standing with arms

crossed at the foot of the steps, impatient and agitated. They joined hands for the walk home. He offered to carry her books, but she respectfully declined. She wouldn't let go. She had been entrusted with a signed edition of a new American novel. God forbid it slipped and fell and came apart.

The sun was midway through its full descent, the air still warm and thick. Herr William was wearing his Panama, which cast shadow over the prominence of his features. His eyes were drowned in sockets of darkness and from his cheekbones fell a gray heaviness. He looked ancient and ominous.

Across the street was an old man hunched, alarmed, and hobbling after two hens escaped from a chicken coop. With his arms outstretched before him he looked absolutely hopeless. It was almost as if the hens took turns making his life difficult. It wouldn't be long before his back shattered into a million pieces, if he kept on after them hunched in that way. One hen broke away entirely and ran off into the street where the old man wouldn't venture. He straightened up slowly with hands on hips, the sun in his brown face, staring down at the remaining hen sitting on the curb before him.

Herr William clutched her hand tighter as they continued their walk, his eyes fixed ahead and her eyes on the unusual tension in his gait. He looked like he was sweating under his Panama hat. She could not recall a moment in her life where she had seen her father sweat. Even in the cruelest heat and humidity Herr William maintained an even cool.

So little traffic was passing on the street. For the moment the world seemed abandoned and the road open only for two. A soft sweet breeze seemed every few seconds to thread itself between the tall old man and the short young woman. When his palms began to sweat he let go of Malou's hand and placed his hand on her near shoulder. Something was wrong. His silence suddenly made him alien to her. For the first time in her life Herr William appeared fragile.

Eliseo was taken out of school and put to work. The thought of it made her stomach sink. It made her slightly nauseous to imagine him and his family struggle through poverty, like so many other families in the neighborhood. She couldn't figure out if it was better or worse for him that he was talented. He could only be one of three foreseeable things—a hero, a tragedy, or ghost. A lot of talented young boys in the neighborhood disappeared under the weight of familial obligation. Hopelessness grew through the vigor of their youth, which quickly became age and resignation. She considered the Parable of the Talents, and the idea that a man, if he was talented, could harvest his talents and succeed in life. But this took a concerted effort, and so many of the boys, fatherless, never had enough encouragement to excel. A talent, after all, is a gift from God manifested wholly, for a child, through the blessings of their sires. Malou couldn't figure it out. There were too many variables to account for—Eliseo's intrinsic desire to succeed (or not), his Mother's influence on him, his extra-familial support systems. She had to see him. She had to know where he was going.

An old woman passed with a piragua cart, all of her bottles near empty and no block of ice. Perhaps she was also headed home. She was an old creole woman with her hair up in a hat. Her lower lip was crooked and hung to the left. She smiled at Malou as she passed. Malou smiled back as the cart rumbled on its way past, down the sidewalk, glass clinking, an old woman humming.

With no classes for the weekend she figured she'd sit for a while with the new book. Herr William jingled keys in his pocket as they reached the front gate of the house. Fru Josephine had prepared a nice little meal, bacalao salad, and left it covered on the patio table. Malou could hear her inside singing along to Antonio Machín—his record playing on the phonograph.

Herr William left her at the gate with a warm pinch on her shoulder and a tall, toothy smile. She could see his face fully in the shade of the near tree, bloated and strangely luminescent. He went on his way back to the sastreria. She watched as he walked off, stepping out of the shade and into the sunlight, crossing from one dark world into another made of fire.

The house felt eerily empty. Wind swept in beneath the linen curtains.

Her mother in the kitchen sat fanning herself. Malou stood there staring at her. She reached out for Malou to come nearer.

Malou stepped into her mother's seated embrace. Josephine pulled her onto her lap and caressed her daughter's cheek. Malou could feel her mother fanning her from behind and it felt good. She was still singing Machín's pregón with warm affection. She was loose. Her breath like Cane. And Malou, too old to be there and young enough to draw the last nurturing from her mother's breast, rested her head on Josephine's shoulder and wrapped her arms loosely around her waist and closed her eyes until the side came to conclusion, spinning vinyl static against maternal cloth. She tucked her fingers in beneath her mother's blouse to knead the soft smooth skin of her back and they sat there in the afternoon haze, Josephine's chin to the top of Malou's head, cradled against her collarbone. Josephine humming against the temple of her first and only daughter while the record turned, neither too pressed to get up and lift the needle. Half aware that the other side of their pleasure as one body signified separation. The sweeter the tenderness the nearer their separation and it couldn't have felt any sweeter for Malou, who began to cry.

Until Josephine could hear Herr William enter at the gate and remembered the food left on the patio table untouched. She patted her daughter once on the back to get up, abiding the world which stood at the gate ready to enter, always ready to enter. A world which Malou didn't yet understand. Josephine knew the day would come like a fearsome angel sent to test the resilience of her daughter's spirit. But not today. With a smile Josephine wiped the tears from her daughter's little cheeks.

Herr William came into the kitchen holding plates of food from the patio. He put them down on the kitchen counter. He kissed Malou on the forehead, then Josephine, and began picking at the bacalao salad. Sweat through his shirt crested along the high ridge of his shoulder, tapering like the tail of a bird down the center of his back. Josephine crept up behind him and authoritatively slapped his hand from the salad. She took the plates from him and began readying the meal to be reheated for a proper dinner.

Malou took a chair at the kitchen table, leafing through her new book and its density while her parents bantered over dinner prep. The text was composed of four narratives, each presumably occurring on four separate dates. She began to wonder where and under what conditions culture thrived and what, in America, constituted a public offering of its production.

While the thought of reading the new book and meeting intimately with Ms. Panaini seemed promising, Malou was looking forward to the centering simplicity of mending seams. She spent Saturdays helping her father and mother at the sastreria. She needed something to take her mind off of *things*. Something of the air was entirely fugitive, a pall on the day which no longer felt like Friday, but some monstrous hole in the fabric of the universe. She watched as her parents slid around each other at the kitchen counter preparing the meal. Malou sat still, observing, trying to salvage a wholeness from the blue mundanity of the moment.

From the window came a cool gust and the smell of rain. Josephine grabbed the plates and walked them back out to the patio, where, in so doing, she decided they would be taking their dinner. Herr William picked up the warmed rice and three plates in his left and with his right gently pinched the back of Malou's neck. She was left in the kitchen, in the blue mundanity of the moment and before it felt like something she should get used to she got up and walked toward the patio.

Herr William and Fru Josephine were already seated and waiting for their daughter before they could eat. Malou sat (always) in the chair facing the street because her parents knew she liked to people-watch. She noticed that it was only raining on one side of the street. How the white light of day died bent and refracted through the rhythmic falling of water was a marvel to her. A prismatic rainbow approaching her private rainbow shrinking as the sound became local over the patio and the rainbow disappeared.

////\•/\\\\

The shirt, a white collar shirt, hand-stitched, Italian, had come apart at the right armpit. She laced her needle with white thread and turned the shirt inside out. She imagined coming through the eye of a needle, passing through the hold, and how it mattered if who lay beside her was a child or an adult. Who then she would have had to become? She imagined hearing through the eye of a needle the vertiginous echo of her mother.

It was a small hole and took no time to mend and when she finished she stitched a small blackbird into the hem at the end of the fly front, just beneath the last button. This was her signature, her stamp of approval for the work she had done. It was a small, but noticeable blackbird with its tail in the air leaning forward slightly in preparation for flight. Fru Josephine and Herr William hadn't noticed her signature on any of the garments, or at least they never mentioned it, and Malou hadn't heard any complaints from patrons, so she assumed it was fine.

She recognized the shirt as that of the Richter boy. Tall and lanky. Pasty, freckled, and blue-eyed. He always left her feeling strange. Half discomfort, half fascination. She heard rumors that he'd been caught giving himself a quick little fist in the last pew of the church. Supposedly the father caught him and dragged him by the ear to the front of the church, where he was made to kneel and finish. It seemed fantastical. But he looked the type, a bit slick, slackjawed, and wet in places where most were dry. Still, she noticed at moments in the elusive boy an absolutely gentlemanly poise—really by no elegance of his own. This she attributed to his rearing. The Richters were decent people with poor accents and sense enough to teach their son etiquette and manners, which included the proper posture for a young man. He would have been a lech otherwise.

She sat at the table for a while, having finished the shirt, having finished signing it, and stared out the window behind the painted sign announcing backwards *Sastreria Cornejas*. There was easy Saturday morning foot traffic. Old women with carts heading step by pained step to the market were followed often and closely by grandchildren. Young men strolled in delinquent packs with their chests exposed, their shirts unbuttoned at the top, laughing and carrying on, discussing conquests and conquests. Model A Fords with muddy runner boards kicking up dust and exhaust scattered light across the storefront. Occasionally a new Model B would pass slowly down the street, its tall louvered grill between two large cowl lamps inspiring admiration and envy in passersby.

A party of palomas were gathering awkwardly on the awnings along the avenue, as though they were meeting to discuss the weather and gossip, each turning a disinterested gaze at people while preening their feathers.

The grocer across the street, Theophilio, seemed to suffer the worst of their congregation and cooing, which grew louder as, minute by minute, it seemed, another paloma arrived. Today while attending to his morning chores, which he usually completed with placid resolve by 9 a.m., it appeared Theophilio lost his temper. He emerged from his shop with a broom, the one he swept the sidewalk with, and began harassing the mangy cluster, poking and prodding them off with the tip of the handle. One flew away. Then another. Until finally the flock in a cloud of small feathers and panicked wings departed in one large gray-black mass for a more amenable awning—power lines, or perhaps a monument in the capital. He stood there shaking his fist for a while before coming back to his senses, looking suspiciously from left to right just to make sure no one had seen him behave in such an embarrassing way.

Despite the outburst Malou knew him as a gentle old man, a dark criollo with a son in his twenties living in New York. His wife had already passed. He took his coffee black and strong with a small piece of buttered bread seated in front of the grocery always at sunrise, with a mendicant mien, appearing to passersby and commuters as though he'd been sitting there all night sipping his drink from a tin mug. He lived alone and read often and because of this he treasured Malou's occasional visitation, during which he'd decompress current events and the random books he could get his hands on. He'd just finished, per her recommendation, a collection by Berceo, although, by his own admission, Poetry was not something to be read. Poetry was intended, in his understanding, to be the object of one's life. To read Poetry, he reasoned, was the least poetic thing one could do. Nonetheless, he was grateful and excited for her recommendation. She was looking forward to hearing his opinion on it.

The one time she broached the subject of independence literature (which she would thereafter cease recommending as light reading material) he scowled at her and followed with the acerbic interjection "¿Do you want us to be like Haiti? Poor and destitute?" He paused to formulate a new thought. "Haiti confirms the fate of the modern maroon republic. Infighting and servility." She just shook her head in resignation, unable to elocute the possibility of a nation becoming, and he went back to inventorying bananas, immediately dismissing her green-black noise from his mind.

She liked to watch him stock the shelves, loading and unloading crates, which engorged the veins on his arms beneath fine blonde hairs. In his prime he was a strong man, a bodybuilder who reveled in his own might and physical appearance. There was grace in the raw labor of his movement, lifting from the legs, sparing as best he could the muscles of his lower back, which were, in his age, prone to injury. One crate at a time. He was methodical in his procedure, stacking emptied crates one by one in a corner of the small grocery store to arrange the produce in neat rows outside on the stand—as neatly as possible, walking back and forth, in and out of the store all while folding and unfolding his lips against each other, as if kissing himself. It was the routine he grew accustomed to, the routine that kept him grounded firmly in the realm of the living.

Her eyes turned to Herr William sitting at the table opposite her peddling the family Singer, it seemed, through three shirts and two pants at once. She watched as he stitched without wincing his own shadow into the lapel or the cuff of the garment or garments. He was fast and precise, which is exactly why he was such a trusted tailor. When at work Herr William recognized nothing but his fingers, the fabric, and his tools—the whole world disappeared. Even if Malou were to get up on her workstation bare to the world and do an inappropriate dance, he wouldn't have noticed. In a way she envied her father's ability to tune out the noise of the world. Unfortunately her expectation was that sewing through Saturday morning would settle her state of mind, but she was emotionally hungover, still swollen with Friday's melancholia.

The peddle kept time. Fru Josephine shuffled between the racks, carrying wooden hangers and arranging the clothes, finished and pressed, ready for pickup. The walls were lined with ribbons of measuring tape, spindles of thread and shears. There were newspaper clippings of articles regarding their success as a small and reliable business along with a few family photos—the most prominent of these taken by Jens. It was a fairly small space, large enough to accommodate racks, two workstations, and the reception counter. On the counter was a small bowl of plastic-wrapped peppermints and other assorted dulces beside the account book, which held the names and articles of each patron in her mother's cursive, as well as the cash register. There were three chairs arranged by the door, in front of the glass, for patrons to sit and wait if needed. There was a fern at the front of the sastreria beside the three patron chairs, visible through the glass front, and a ceiling fan which, when hot, was left to spin what air would come through the wedged-open front door. In the fern lived a small black spider, which Malou could see dangling against the window's light. The only serviceable windows were in the back, above a wooden desk that Herr William used after hours to balance the day's budget. There, in the back, was also room enough for a tall file cabinet and the vault, which contained cash, important documents, and heirlooms. It was a beautiful, lived-in space. Always clean. Always inviting, from 7 a.m. to 6 p.m., Monday through Saturday. For Malou the shop was never more beautiful than on those Saturday mornings, quietly following her father, who keyed into the store and flipped open the lights. He'd motion her, if it was going to be hot, to kick the wedge in beneath the door and leave it propped open. Then he'd look through the accounts and call out numbers which Fru Josephine would pluck from the rack and lay gently on one of the work tables, depending on whose task it was and whether it could be hand-stitched or needed the Singer.

Malou made note of the ways light fell on her father's needle. How his needle stitched light itself into fabric or how light slid from the tip reflected or how light swung fast and hip if his hand came up too quickly and high between the angle of incidence and the surface of the needle within the sound of the treadle lockstitching at some thousands of revolutions per minute. She followed his movement, from treadle to ankle, from knee to thigh, back hunched over the station wearing spectacles and following closely the opened inseam of a boy's pants.

For years privy to the closest things people allowed with regularity to touch their bodies, one never noticed color fade. The tailor could only acknowledge that the garments did fade, that they had faded, that they were gradually unwoven and damaged, and in this way stained by time.

The colors were fading where an egret hung in flight over the grocer. Its long glide relative to her distance appeared slow and dreamlike. A wide wind swept in a cloud of yellow dust and Theophilio, sweeping the sidewalk, threw his broom down in marked frustration. The broom's sharp crack against the concrete and Theophilio's expletive startled the sensibilities of a middle-aged woman passing on the opposite side of the street. Malou could see her, as she passed the sastreria, grab her young son's hand and walk faster away from the seemingly deranged old man who fell to one knee and shook his fist in frustration up at heaven. Then one paloma arrived, hovering just above the awning before perching—still on his knee he looked up at the bird, which looked down dispassionately down at him.

As the middle-aged woman and her young son passed across the glass of the window and out of her line of sight, Malou fixed her attention on the fern. Therein the spider began to climb toward the full body of its web ornately constructed between two of the largest leaves and settled there patiently waiting for the arrival of a gnat, a fly, a mosquito, some sustenance. The web was small, adequate for a small black spider, almost imperceptible without light which illuminated each silken fibril into crystalline radiance. A black body poised in laqueus abyss, its own construction for subsistence. The spider was still and disappeared briefly into pentiment under the close shadow of a passerby.

Josephine laid a darling skirt in front of Malou, breaking her reverie. To be hemmed according to these measurements, taking in the waist with two pleats at each hip, and adorned with a bow at the waist-back to conceal its buttons. The skirt must have been passed down from mother to young daughter. Its fabric was noticeably worn, light cotton stretched and thinned from usage and age. She wondered to what extent it pleased or agitated the mother that her daughter was slimmer.

An itch at her right ankle called her quick attention to look down, but it was nothing. Not, as she feared, a flea or gnat or blood-sucker. It was just an itch. She reached for her ankle, stretching her right arm and extending her middle finger to get at the remoteness of the itchy sensation when suddenly she had to stop, her right cheek at the edge of the table. She heard a faint and familiar sound which grew louder.

Coming slowly into view from the storefront window was a jíbaro leading a brown cow down the middle of the street with the heavy tintinnabulation of its bell growing louder as it lumbered nowhere rhythmically nowhere. The jíbaro's face was completely obscured under the shadow cast by his pava, his right arm guying a jute rope tied around the beast's neck. He wore a sweat-soaked earth-stained white shirt with sleeves rolled up past his elbows and pants with tattered cuffs that sat just inches above nondescript mud-caked shoes. His arms were black.

Fru Josephine, sifting through the account book by the register, looked up at the unusual sight, her brow furrowed and lips pursed in consternation. Malou saw Theophilio step out of his shop with one hand on his hip and the other atop his head gawking at the ambling mountain man and his ambling cow. The vexation in Theophilio's face was priceless. Malou would have laughed if it wasn't for the seriousness in her mother's face, which gave her pause.

Business was fairly steady, fortunately due to the Cornejas' reputation for fine and dependable work, but the economy was showing signs of decline. Competing tailors were making paltry sums. Needleworkers were floundering and shops closing. She looked again at her father, whose hands could turn and chew failure into success, whose spirit affirmed her belief in the possibility of the impossible becoming. He hadn't looked up once, not even at the sound of the cowbell. Nothing ever seemed to surprise him anyway. She looked then to her mother, who'd quietly disappeared into the backroom. The jíbaro and his cow were moving so slowly across the vista of the storefront, down the street, that Malou started to wonder if they were moving backward.

While regarding the mountain man and his cow from the corner of her eye, she reached again for the itch at her ankle, which felt against the tip of her index finger like a mosquito bite. She started lightly to scratch and play with the bite, careful not to break skin, alternating between the use of her cuticle and the softer padded flesh of her fingertip.

The cow began to shit as they both, bovine and jíbaro, passed from sight of the shop. All that was left in the street was Theophilio, still vexed and leaning over a mound of dung, and the dopplering of the cowbell, which rang down the avenue with an eerie, tinny clarity.

There was talk, according to Theophilio, of riots and mobilized strikes to the south and west. Violent skirmishes between needle workers on strike and police in Mayagüez were mestastisizing a climate of socio-political inquietude. Of the needle workers in Santurce Herr William was among the few, being independently owned and locally operated, who remained impartial—neither in solidarity with strikers, nor dependent on American subsidies.

«216 Pesante» She thought as she returned to an upright position in her seat and began to prepare her needle for work on the skirt. She had to see him, somehow. She hunched over again to scratch. The itch this time more pronounced.

////\•/\\\\

She began by torquing in half-sleep the spread of her bedsheets
into a helical mass. She half-woke to the mildness of honeyed
oatmeal, coughing dramatically. «Go» «It's ok» She reassured her
parents. «Go» «Pray for me» «I'll be here when you get back» She
locked herself in the bathroom, a spectacle of feigned comor-
bidity and martyrdom. «It's just my stomach» «Don't worry»
«cough» «¡Go on!» Until it seemed her parents had gone. Until
the house was silent.

She'd never known the silence and full solitude of the house, its
breathing memory left unguarded. She opened the bathroom
door slowly and, straining her ears to hear any familiar sound
from within the house, stepped out into the fruit of her guile.
In the absence of her parents the house had been transformed.

She walked on tiptoes to the master bedroom, peeking in around
the doorway. She'd never experienced its emptiness. From the
bed on which she was born, neatly fixed, drifted an adult scent—
warmth in proximity, Cane and prolixity, full of the mystery of
having lost all mystery to age and marriage. Something tangible,
maybe the scent, which inspired reverence or fear, kept her from
crossing the threshold into their room. It seemed too burden-
some, the air too dense, too private a space to profane with her
curiosity when already she'd lied to them—for the first time in
her life.

She stepped back slowly from their bedroom and walked toward
the kitchen, where, out of the corner of her eye, she thought
she saw her mother. She turned her head lightning-fast to find
that it was just a frond swaying in the window. The bowl of
oatmeal Herr William left for Malou was still warm. She uncovered the oatmeal, which Herr William had drizzled with honey
and finished with a dab of salted butter, and sat down to eat it.

The morning sun sat crisply against the siding of the neighbor's house as she took her first spoonful and listened to the day's first chorus of Aves chirping.

The neighbors had a daughter. She was a real Indian. Small teeth, small eyes, sharp bones, and oro-skinned Indian always with the boys and there she passed beside her home, a specter in broad daylight, stranger with a cigarette tucked between her lips navigating her way through the bushes and flowers. Malou could see her creeping on through the window and she wondered if, eating her oatmeal in the kitchen, she was equally exposed. Josephine both pitied and distrusted the neighbors' girl, who was in her teens. Amélia Grau had been deemed by most, including her parents, as one well on her way nowhere. She was thin and careless, macho at moments in front of the house jangueando with two or three boys at once to the chagrin of her mother and father. She seemed to Malou unafraid and vibrant. She'd creep home Sunday mornings after long Saturday nights, makeup untouched, barefoot and carrying her pumps. In fact, she was unusually punctual, arriving home every Sunday morning at 11:30, plus or minus ten minutes, when her folks were on their way to church.

The neighbors attended the same Pentecostal church as Herr William and Fru Josephine. Refugio Eterno in St. Just, Carolina conducted service from noon to 7 p.m. These were all-day affairs punctuated by a meal of empanadas or pollo guisao cooked in the basement kitchen by the elder wives. It was a ramshackle Spanish colonial building with a façade coated in an unadorned layer of stucco. The walls inside were unpainted sheetrock which, in the basement, had been marked by heavy water damage and lent most of the building a dank and musty odor. As a result, black mold grew unchecked in the recesses of the building. Of course, during offrenda, the congregation was encouraged to contribute to the building fund, and of course the Pastor, whether or not the donation was significant, would divvy it up according to his moral and spiritual imperative. So it didn't matter. If there was one dollar in the basket he'd take it to the bodega and break it one hundred ways. Elders of the congregation would arrive on Sunday afternoons to find a set of new potted plants or a new armchair on the dais and with a small nod of approval hail Jehova Jireh in humbled gratitude for the abundance and pecuniary grace of the Pastor—this to say the least of his exploits.

It was humid at home alone. Malou felt sticky, but not uncomfortable. The skin on her forearms opened into a sheen of cooling sweat as she lifted to her lips another warm spoonful of oatmeal coated in golden honey and melted butter.

There was something glamorously tragic about the comings and goings of trigueña Amélia, to which Malou was often and secretly privy. She snuck in a boy once and later that evening Malou could hear her sobbing. She was caught and then beaten by her father. Her father was an alcoholic. The complete tragedy of this happening, and it happened more often than anyone in the neighborhood or church cared to admit, was how much Amélia loved her father.

As Amélia disappeared from sight and mind Malou began to realize her own anxiety for the planned events of a Sunday unfurling itself quickly before her. She needed the guidance of the bruja before undertaking to find, and this she felt incredibly unsure of, the home of Eliseo Sánchez. She lost her appetite in a sudden swell of self-consciousness, but felt compelled, per custom, to take another spoonful of the oatmeal prepared for her by Herr William. She was taught to waste nothing, because nothing was promised, and the blessing of abundance should not be taken for granted. As well, and also per custom, if a guest or guests were to arrive unexpectedly the host would be expected to share what food had been or would be prepared. Of course there were those in the neighborhood who abused the privilege, but the consequence of such abuse, even if motivated by poverty, was a sort of social ostracizing by way of bochinche. So meals were meant to be eaten to completion and satisfaction, sometimes to the uncomfortable point of overeating, but never as a matter of careless gluttony. Puerto Rican logic. It was a gift economy within a communal system wrapped in bourgeois ideology. Xenia to a fault. Perhaps a manifestation of the deep and unacknowledged belief that God(s) or angels walked among them disguised as the wretched of the barrios.

Today, Malou reasoned, she was off the moral clock. It was her moment to step out, and this meant acknowledging the fact that she wasn't hungry, despite custom and courtesy. This meant defiance, but defiance with reasonable purpose. Still, disposing of the food of course would have to remain a secret. She left the plate uncovered on the table and went to her room to gather her things before departing to see La Negra. She dressed and grabbed her purse, a few dollars and change she had saved in her drawer. Her eleke of Yemaya. A banana from the kitchen. Then she peed.

She decided to dump the oatmeal on Amélia's side of the fence, in a bush. She crept through the backdoor with the bowl of oatmeal and, looking around first to confirm that no person was in sight, she dumped the contents out over the fence. Then she stopped, with the empty bowl in her hand, and looked at the Grau home. There was Amélia, on the other side of the window, watching with a vacant expression as Malou snuck away from the scene. Malou turned and went back inside, careful not to engage Amélia's gaze for too long, careful not to feel too guilty.

What she was feeling then, before departure, she interpreted as her entry into the cooler depth of adulthood. She had her things, what things she needed and since she didn't have the keys to the house she left the backdoor unlocked. She decided to leave through the front, with all dignity, the door locked behind her, taking her first step off of the patio into the benthos of Santurce.

Humidity made the air thick and with the sun more or less at zenith she felt as though she were passing through the heat of a glasshouse. Then came the noise of midday traffic. Trucks and pretty Fords, roadsters and coupes, smothering a distant trolley's bell in exhaust, fume pouring black from their mufflers under the futurist gurgling of the V-8 engine. Runner boards from which men dressed in night made machine gun fire. The wistfulness of the cosmopolitan. Three teenage girls, blanquita, all dressed in white walking together in the direction of Ponce de León. Their giggling, secretive shivering and the shuffled language between them. As if on cue they all turned to look at the dark young girl idling at the precipice, then just as quickly looked away, resuming their bird talk. Palomas from the powerlines high-walking their judgment of the lesser going on foot nowhere. This, the world laid bare and its machinations obtusely aware and leering for her entrance into the transit of things, into the economy of a port city stillborn to the touch of modernity. This, amid stirrings of dissension from heavy heads hung and low-slung brows stretched thin from labor, searching for restitution among others among the streets.

La Negra was only a few blocks away so the trip itself wasn't too risky. Even if she were spotted by a familiar it wouldn't look so conspicuous. She was just going for a walk in the neighborhood. She kept to the shade, when and where she could, so as not to feel burdened by the high light of the sun. There was a certain cool with which she needed to enter the physical and spiritual space of La Negra's brujeria and the shade, what shade she could find on her walk, offered her some protection.

She thought about her parents singing along with the choir, the Pastor on the dais, the old women in the back, her mother included, wearing a long puritanical skirt. Her mother was treasurer of the church. She was trusted with money and tallied the offering. Her father sat stoically in the second row. He stood when instructed and sat when instructed, bowed his head when instructed, and never sang. Sometimes Malou sat with her father. Sometimes she sat in the back with her mother, staring occasionally at the severity of her father's stillness which was often more intriguing than the sermon itself.

She crossed at the corner through a break in traffic, now only a block and a half away and still feeling fairly cool. The contents of her purse, a handful of change, jingled as she bounced along the street. It was fairly empty, few passersby and fortunately none that she recognized or that seemed to recognize her. In fact nobody seemed to notice her at all, walking down calle Loíza in slivers of shade.

She needed some affirmation from the old mystic to know that what she found in Eliseo was worth pursuing. In a sense she was consulting a spiritual compass for direction. Surety she'd find on the way, along with her knees.

On her right she passed an old deli, situated beside a new American-owned and operated corner tavern called Ransom's. Up until a year ago, when the Americans had bought the lot and built Ransom's, that corner space was an unused eyesore. It was home to a few drunken squatters who reeked of piss and Cane. They were quickly evicted by the authorities, but only after the

Americans arrived. Ransom's featured live music, mostly Puerto Rican artists, but on special occasions they'd have an American performer come in. Recently, Rafael Hernandez, just in from abroad. For a few days in March, Juan Tizol just in from New York, performing "Mood Indigo" and "Sophisticated Lady." The owners were wealthy American expatriates from Memphis, Tennessee. Music lovers, jazz especially. They were both middle-aged, white, both diminutive in stature, and both warm and cordial in their demeanor. They did their best to cultivate a healthy working relationship with their neighbors, despite poor Spanish. For the most part they remained jovially uninvolved, aloof, in the subclime of their new environs. Clearly, despite their manner, they were there to assay a certain freedom denied them in the States. There had been some speculation regarding what brought about their relocation to the island, but it was clear that they'd found in Santurce some security, judging by a year's worth of fixity and good business.

The deli, family-owned and operated, had been there for fifteen years and with the arrival of the tavern they were making good business selling sandwiches to a late night crowd of expat hipsters. The business managed to stay afloat solely on loyal local patronage before the Americans showed up and started bringing in an entirely new customer base. These late night sandwiches, called Tío Sam's, were made on freshly baked soft-buttered bread with pickled peppers, pernil, jamón, queso blanco or Swiss, maduros, and a house-special mojo. All pressed with a side of yucca fries and often ordered with home-brewed mavi. Americans were going ape for these sandwiches, which allowed the owners to raise prices. The logic behind their pricing followed basic rules of supply and demand—hence the name Tío Sam. These Americans were young and liberal and they'd spend anything for the purpose of their pleasure in the island of enchantment.

Malou crossed the street, traffic still lean, and neared La Negra's, which was a hole in the wall wedged between two buildings in the middle of Loíza. The front door was nothing more than a gate, black cast-iron bars that reminded Malou of a prison. Behind the gate a beaded curtain hung from the doorway. The sound of the beads being parted, jostling and clicking against each other, was enough to alert the old mystic, whose eyes were clouded with age. From the sort of astral displacement one attains from staring long into the sun, La Negra was near complete blindness, but she could assess by the sound of entry the spiritual shape of the visitor. The entry was among the first of the tests La Negra employed to determine the individual's character.

Malou was aware of all of this when she slowly pulled open the gate, which squealed with rust at its hinges, and she passed like a breeze through the beaded curtain to find herself face to face with the seer. La Negra sat rocking back and forth at the center of the shrine in the dimness of three large candles, two on small shelves, each above her left and right shoulder, and one at center between them, all in a space no larger than a water closet. Above her head mounted in the wall behind her was a small slotted vent which let fall three shafts of natural white light on the face of the young querent. The air was almost completely still and clotted with musk and dust, urine and feces, incense and cigar smoke, which transformed what small light into hanging tangibility. All along the floor surrounding the room stood small fetishes with their mouths closed and arms stretched high in supplication, with gaping eyes and asymmetrical limbs, breasts held forever at attention against gravity, tricksters with erect members staggering among fashioned reeds and bits of molded metal woven together into chainlink. From the ceiling, mobiles of feathers and beaded apostrophe hung in memoriam, spinning slowly above what light flickered quietly from the candles and what light poured in through the vent, shuttered on occasion by quick and unmappable nubivagance and second by second, with the passage of time, angled more acutely over the plane of La Negra's nepheline gaze. There were spirits among them shuttling beyond the knowable.

La Negra sat among these moving texts wrapped in a dirty coral-colored silk robe on a small stack of carpets with her back to the wall. Propped up against the back wall to her right was a sheathed saber and kora beside a mephitic wastebucket. Her eyes were like jade in the dark, fixed on the space above them, unflinching orbs within the obsidian architecture of her face, framed in a shock of white hair exposed beneath the hood. To her left were three mugs of what looked and smelled like potent spiced rum. Beside the mugs were three brown eggs in rusted servers and several pieces of jerky. All of this neatly cut up, arranged, and within reach of the high priestess, who made her way in the dark space haptically.

La Negra extended her right hand toward Malou and motioned her inside. She was standing at the entrance with the beaded curtain draped still over her shoulders and along the delicate curve of her back, waiting for this moment of acknowledgment. She knelt before the seer.

Flies were swarming en masse in the curdled atmosphere of the chamber. Malou could feel them and hear them, the high humming of their wings, as they flew up against her temples and cheeks, her neck. Despite an intense hatred of flies and the bacteria they carried she knew not to swat them in the presence of La Negra who could sense the slightest movements of her querent and might interpret her swatting as a gesture of disgust and discomfort. Instead she reached slowly into her purse to remove the eleke of Yemaya. She held it in her hand for a moment, examining the small bundle of polished stones in the faintness of the glim and intruding light. Then she wrapped it loosely like a rosary around her left wrist without bothering to close her purse. Her gaze returned to the seer, whose clouded eyes remained fixed on the space above them.

Both hands now, palms facing upward and ghostly white over the candle, were extended toward Malou, who reached forward timidly, sliding her hands flat over La Negra's. She began to feel warm and uncertain, gradually becoming unnerved as they sat together, hands submitted to the will of the future.

Without warning La Negra clutched Malou's hands tightly within her own, wrapping her bony fingers around Malou's small hands. Hot and cold the high priestess's skin like leather, cracked and weathered. La Negra began to examine the girl, digging her fingers into and out of Malou's flesh, climbing her vice-grip spastically from Malou's hands to her wrist and back. La Negra was sensing and developing an image of the girl who'd grown since last she made her feel. She settled on the beads around Malou's left wrist with her fingers less forcefully examining them, their familiarity, acquiring the history of each bead in the memory of her stone fashioning, each composed of a distinct poetic origin wholly accessible by the high priestess. Still strung around her wrist, the beads came loose against the prying fingers of La Negra.

Malou felt the weight of the ocean lifted by the susurration of a stream and three hundred voices as broken and jagged as the voiceless and hungry in the hold. It was making her nervous, the hold and to be held by the feral and know then, or believe in, the deliberateness of her wilderness, which spread through her totally and left her lip feeling split and mouth brackish. Her language cut open not by the sea, but in the sea and, spared the indignity of submitting to death and its calcification, became the music of the new world. Opening variously and for some never at all, held forever there, voices turned current of the deep. Vacillating between origin and elocution. Vacillating between silence and execution until she could let go and she would let go of the hold and like a nova emerge from the world with the same unseeable magnetic force that bore their connection. How the intelligence of a being can only be discerned from a distance sufficient to gauge the proficiency of its act, the grace of its act, against the arc of others and things and the shadows they cast, is what is given to her leaving the hold, letting away time and space at a point precisely where there is no common language. No necessity for common language.

Loosening her hold and withdrawing her arms, which were as dark as the limbs of an ash in the sleeve of her robe, the high priestess fixed her cold gaze on Malou. Wrapped around her right hand was Malou's eleke of Yemaya, which quickly disappeared into the immensity of her robe.

Malou was sweating, just beginning to realize that she had tread the deep and what waited beneath her was any single eventuality willing to potentiate its form against her small light. She reached into her open purse to pull out the seer's tribute. Before they could proceed she'd need the offering, one dollar and eighty-three cents she'd earned and saved from work, and the banana.

Both hands emerged slowly from the hooded robe guided by the exchanged currents of their breathing toward Malou's humble offering. La Negra stowed the money in her robe, but the banana she examined with her fingertips. She lifted it to her nose, inhaling the scent along the convex arch of its dim and ripening yellowness. Then again with the same glacial composure she trained her cool gaze upon Malou, gently placing the banana at her left beside the spiced rum, jerky, and eggs. She withdrew her arms into her robe once again so that she looked like she had no arms and this time emerged with sixteen cowry shells, eight shells in each cupped palm. La Negra spilled the shells on the soft sand in front of the candle. They lay scattered there for a moment before the high priestess with her right hand attempted to gather them again in one clean pass, like jacks. There were left two shells and with her left hand she drew two lines in the sand.

This was repeated fifteen more times, each time yielding a different result. Then spoke the high priestess in a voice like glass blown over the roar and crackling of a kiln.

Within Yemaya is a deep current, a river run through the middle of her spirit where time sounds differently. Where time is measured in air that escapes toward the surface like jewels. The old turtle moves by this current moving so quickly through Yemaya that she can no longer carry old turtle or call its name. It is carried by Ochun and will be called by Ochun to shore where it finds its mate, where it sires its young. Where Ochun is beloved, on the banks of the river, in life-giving streams, around which the people gather to cup their hands within her breast. She is loved by Orunla, taught his divination, but finds a partner in Chango and begets the twins. Ibeji. Ochun is blessed then, mother and prosperous, given richness, given life in the brass palace of Chango with whom she begets the twins. Ibeyi. She fans Chango's flames waking in him the sound of thunder and the stave of lightning which falls silent and reflected over the surface of her riverain power. Ocha of beauty and attraction.

Ochun chose quickly and wisely between which of her lovers would best stimulate her prowess and invoke her impressive power. Many Ocha are desirous of her, but only Chango can stir in her the mad beauty that is her true nature. And only by Chango can she sire the destined Twins. Only Chango can stir in her the mad beauty that is her truest nature. Hers, which is intimacy, tenderness, quickness of wit, healing, divinity, prosperity, vengeance.

Power.

Ibeyi is born to the coupling of Chango and Ochun. Taiyo, born first in red, and Kehinde, born second in blue. Taiyo, born first to excel, and Kehinde, born second and sage. While the blessing of twins in her life yields great fruit, it also brings upon her house much envy. The great fortune of birthing the first twins of the universe comes at great cost when the Ocha, witnessing her prosperity, begin to consider her an evil sorceress. A hoarder of privilege and power. Once again she is forced to choose, this time between the blessing of her twins or the legacy and good standing of her house. This is the dangerous side of Ochun's divine grace. Ochun's prosperity brings with it many detractors, those jealous of her beauty and profound success. Because of this Ochun must remember always to be generous. With generosity Ochun protects herself and others against the jealousy of those lesser.

A rare few, highborn with tremendous wisdom, destined to live life backwards, acquire youth in old age. Your wrists are young and do not yet know what music is for death made. When these currents meet will there be war and Ochun its mother and arbiter.

The road you take will be one of Ochun closely guarded by Echu at each important crossroads. Choices will be made for you. You are marked by a certain predestination. Choices must also be made. Your road may not be straight, it may indeed be painful and marked by years of poverty and detour, but with patience the road will yield great freedom, beautiful union, and unexpected riches.

She withdrew from her robe a brass bangle and motioned for Malou's wrist. Malou raised her left arm slowly and the high priestess, reaching for it, slapped the bangle on quickly. It fit loosely around Malou's wrist.

La Negra reached again into her robe and pulled out a new set of beads, alternating red and blue. These are yours too, said La Negra. But these are not for you. These are to be given to the one you choose.

The beads were rough, hand hewn and strung together on a leather rope. Malou put the beads in her bag and before she could ask the high priestess a question she was instructed to leave. She gathered her things, her new knowledge, and backed out of La Negra's chamber, stumbling in the dark through the beaded curtain, backing into the heavy gate, which squealed open. And all she could see departing the chamber was the soft light of the high priestess's gaze which fell quiet, two dim crescents narrowing as she closed her old glowing eyes.

Malou closed the gate behind her and took a deep breath of fresh air, which rushed cool relief into her lungs. She felt as though she'd surfaced from the sea floor, starved of her natural atmosphere.

She had more questions than answers, brought on by the vaguest shape of things to come. In fact she was starting to feel a little dizzy. Lightheaded, she leaned against the wall of a cobbler's shop, clinging to what shade it provided from the high sun just behind it. Some troubadour on the corner began playing his trumpet, plateauing his notes against the heavy tide of traffic. She turned to look. He'd just unpacked. In his case was a meal's worth of change. Young and lithe. Negro. Maybe hoping that the owners at Ransom's would pick up on the quality of his tunes, which she'd never heard before. Unlikely that they were original compositions, but his sound was certainly new, jarringly up-tempo and played just off of and around a vaguely familiar melody.

Trying to orient herself anew against the relative stability of the wall she was startled by a hand on her shoulder. In panicked quickness she turned to see first the hand on her shoulder, white with long fingers, attached to the slender arm of the Richter boy. He looked taller than usual. So pale and parked in the sun he looked as though he were happily toasting, his forehead red with what would ostensibly become sunburn. Squinting his blue eyes made the freckles on his cheeks gather at the bridge of his nose. He was wearing a white short-sleeved shirt and blue trousers with a brown leather belt and loafers. No socks.

"Hi Malou. ¿Are you ok?" His voice quavered.

"¡Oh! Hello, Jens. Yes. I'm fine. Thank you for asking. Have a good day."

She tried to inflect a finality that would tactfully suggest that she was not in peril, that she did not need his help, and that he should take leave.

"You just look a little fatigued. I was passing by and saw you lean up against the wall . . ."

He obviously didn't get the hint.

"¿Where are you headed?"

"¿Shouldn't you be in church, Jens?!"

"I could ask you the same thing . . . But no, my family doesn't go to church. Not since they left Germany."

She flushed, like she'd been caught. He continued.

"¿So do you mind if I walk with you?"

«extortionist»

She stared at him incredulously in the hope that her discomfort
would translate somehow, but his spirit was illiterate. He stood
there smiling at her with his hands clasped behind his back like
a mad Buddhist, waiting for an answer. How could she explain
to him, dumb interloper, that she was stalking like prey the boy
that would become her destiny?
"Sure," she heard herself say.

«shit»

They began walking in no direction at all. He followed her
aimless lead, looking over at her every few steps, almost ready to
say something, until he did say something, after two full blocks
of awkward silence.

"Nice bracelet."
    "Thanks."
    "¿Is it new?"
    "I've had it for a long time."

She clutched it nervously, trying to hide it in her palm. He continued, suddenly loquacious.

"So if you had to choose between your senses, just one, which
would you choose?"
    "¿Huh?"
    "I mean if—"
    "Maybe taste."

"¿Really? . . . Not sight? Or sound?"

"Well, you never specified what the choice entailed. I chose to *lose* my sense of taste because taste, in any case, is intrinsic."

"Oh. I hadn't thought of that."

"Yes."

"I think it would be a strange world without taste. Sad."

"It was a strange question. Strange questions only get strange answers."

"Yes. I guess you're right."

"¿So what about you?"

"¿What sense would I choose? To lose?" He looked surprised.

"Yes . . ."

"¿You know when I asked the question I meant, if you could only preserve one of your senses which would it be?"

"I thought that's what you meant, but that's a cruel question."

"Ok. Ok. So wait, what was it? If I were—"

"¿If you were to lose one sense, which would it be?"

He looked amused, furrowing his brow contemplatively and stroking the pale bareness of his chin.

"Smell," he said after a moment of deliberation.

"That tells me a lot about you," she responded quickly.

"¿Oh? Like what?"

"I don't think you want to hear this. You're not ready for this."

"No, no. I'm ready for it. Give it to me."

"It would hurt your feelings. It's ok, let's forget it. Smell. Yes. Understood."

"No. Now you have to tell me."

"¿You sure?"

He looked at her with unusual frankness and expectation. He was getting comfortable.

"Smell you said, yes?"

"Yes."

"¿You sure you don't want to change that answer?"

"Yes I'm sure. Smell."

"Well. This tells me you're a coward . . ."

"¿What?"

". . . A noseless freak out of some Russian short story."

She grinned and flicked her wrist at him in mock dismissal, the oversized brass bangle given to her by La Negra nearly flying off.

"¿How does that make me a coward?"

"Think about it. If you deprive yourself of sight, then you deprive yourself of color, light, and you severely interrupt the ability to perceive objects in space. You begin to rely on your hearing to determine proximity. Your relationship to wind changes. It becomes personal. Touching." She blinked at him dramatically, then continued. "If you deprive yourself of sound you lose aural language and song, ambient noise, the sound of the coquis. You rely on the interplay of light and the absence of light. You begin to experience music as it exists infrasonically, bass in your chest, percussion in your teeth." She turned and flashed him a toothy smile. "If you deprive yourself of touch, you lose pleasure and pain, you lose texture, you lose a sense of groundedness. You rely instead on reaction, sound and language, to determine the significance of what physical pressures you exert on objects. Surface is distorted insofar as you cannot experience surface. No threshold. No limit case. If you deprive yourself of taste, you lose what distinguishes your person, your likes and dislikes, your appetite for life. Of course, *some of us* are born characters." She smiled and demured with a quick shrug of her right shoulder. "And then, finally, if you deprive yourself of the ability to smell, you lose your most intimate memory of people. You forget. You gradually lose meaningful connection. You slip away. You lose territory. You forget your mother. You forget the sensual significance of home. You forget the smell of color and love. Because to have a broken heart means knowing you'll never be close enough again to that person or place to be able to recognize their scent."

He wore an incredulous smile, his eyebrows high on his forehead. "You're exactly how I imagined you."

"¿Excuse me?"

He said nothing. They walked in silence for some time. Then she began.

"You know I've always wanted to experience what a horse experiences when its haunches are being brushed. You know what I mean? Do they experience pleasure? Does the brush stimulate them?"

"¿Am I making you uncomfortable, Malou?"

His frankness took her by surprise. "No." She almost laughed. "I'm sincerely curious. ¿Why do you ask?"

"I don't know."

"¿So what're your plans for today?"

"Oh I'm not sure. I wanted to go for a walk. I passed by the shop on my way down the avenue. Which reminds me—"

He untucked the fly front of his shirt from his trousers, which startled her into defensiveness.

"¿What are you doing?" she asked.

"¿This is you, right? You did this."

He motioned for her to look down at the shirt in his hand, just over his crotch. With equal parts reservation and curiosity she looked down and noticed the small blackbird stitched into the hem. She immediately flushed and said nothing. She wouldn't risk incriminating herself further.

"I love your lines," he said. Smiling. "If this is actually your handiwork. It looks like it's about to take off and fly away. My father likes the little birds too."

She suddenly felt self-conscious that they'd both stopped in the middle of the street to stare at his crotch. She disengaged and kept walking. He stuffed his shirt into his trousers and hurried to catch up with her.

"¿How is your family?" she asked indifferently.
    "They're well."

He followed up. "My father's been a little tired lately, which is putting stress on my mother."

They stopped at an intersection. A pack of strays lay together in shade under the near awning of an abandoned building. The bitch, a mangy old dog with large tufts of fur missing, lay beside a larger male, also old. The butch, its body swarmed by flies, lay on its side whimpering under its breath. Malou watched as the butch began to move, exhaling in exhaustion as it lifted its sclerotic leg and curled inward to lap at its own groin. The sound of its wet tongue slurping its own genitals, commingled with the odor of rotting animal flesh, flustered her. She had the urge to beat the dog, beat it out of its misery, as it lapped faster and faster at its own parts until the dog stretched out again on its belly, beside itself with the briefness of its satisfaction. The bitch, staring back, blinked once slowly, never taking her bleary black eyes off of Malou, meeting with equal awareness the intercession of her curiously malign gaze.

"¿Malou?"

"¿Yes?"
"Are you alright?"

"¿Yes?" she responded, irritated.
"Okay. You looked like—"
"¿Tired, you said? Something about your father being tired?"

She turned to meet his eyes, to greet his alacrity with the full
breadth of her attention. Sweat beaded on his upper lip and his
cheeks flushed bright red. A tepid sheen spread from temple to
temple across the pale arc of his brow. Her patience was wearing.

"I don't—"

He was uncomfortable again.

"Jens, I have things to do. I hope you don't mind if we part ways
now. It was nice walking and talking with you."

Jens stopped, red-faced and his collar drenched in sweat, and
shrank as Malou rounded the corner without looking back.
She'd allowed him to drag her and her attention too far in the
opposite direction, too near El Fanguito, north-west toward old
San Juan. By now she reasoned it must have been two, or past.
The sun, following them west, was in its descent.

The unpleasant odor of the mud slum wafted eastward on bay-
wind and with it the image of them walking one dirty foot in
front of the other across a narrow plank of wood to keep from
falling into the bleak morass. The slum was built over uninhab-
itable swamp lands. Children passed hookworms, dying slowly
with their stomachs distended and limbs like twigs, skeletal and
emaciated for which their mothers had nothing, empty-handed
and sorry swaying together in their shoddy homes of corrugated

zinc and rotten wood. It was not uncommon to witness a child playing in feces beside the corpse of its cousin left to insects over black water. And to later witness the same child drinking discharge to slake thirst then suck the salt from engorged drift-wood. The men in the dark what they did to their sons and the animals while their wives if they were wives savored what water weeping left in the family cloth.

It was a place Malou was forbidden from. She was forbidden even from looking by Herr William, who taught her not to en-tertain its decay or conversely the prospect of its redemption as a community. To witness its abjection was to ingest the virulence of pathos that bred poverty in the mud slum. It could only end in one of two ways. It would end in fire, burned to the ground, or it would consume the stability of its surroundings within the disease of its own stagnation. All who ever lived there written off.

The smell tarried in her throat and nose like infection, like clam and fever, even as she walked farther and farther away. She took another right, doubling back on Ponce de León to make the walk to Pesante.

The street was congested and soon drowned the lingering fla-grance of the mud slum in exhaust smoke and noise. Even on Sunday the avenue was alive with people engaged in the mouth to mouth exchange of news and weighty gossip. A few major vendors stayed open for business and necessities, but most shops were closed and most people either at church or at home. Still, something this Sunday was in the air—not a smell per se or any unusual fluctuation in weather and temperature. It seemed something other hung in the air like the early tremors of a seismic happening. Midday heat and humidity had subsided just enough to make it a comfortable walk. A crisp breeze picked up.

Walking in her Sunday shoes she was reminded of the beads rattling in her purse. That she had to make a choice seemed an absurd and obvious statement. In the life of Ochun there could only be one Chango. She looked at the large brass bangle hanging loosely around her left wrist and it made her feel lithe and feminine. She was blocks away from the family shop and not too far from Pesante. Whispers of a new government-operated Lottery system were floating with new money through the neighborhood and the construction of several modern theaters—The Teatro Paramount, for example, which was being renovated from the old Olimpo in grand art deco fashion.

```
            *

      *     *     *

      *     P     *

      *     A     *

      *     R     *

      *     A     *

      *     M     *

      *     O     *

      *     U     *

      *     N     *

      *     T     *

      *     *     *

            *
```

At night along Ponce de León the running lights of the Paramount's marquis stood out as an exemplar of the gilded potential American developers found in San Juan's outlying neighborhoods. The architects had chosen for the façade a Greek revival style which smacked of bald newness, but fit neatly within the larger modernity of the avenue. A three-story, first-run, movie theater. Paramount Pictures loaned the owner, R. R. Cobián, money to rebuild the theater marquis after the catastrophic passage of Huracán San Felipe II in 1928 and San Ciprián the year before. The only condition was that the owner change the name from Olimpo to Paramount. Eventually the theater was ceded to his wife pending their divorce. Or so the story went.

She remembered being taken by her father to a matinee there before it became the Paramount. She could hardly remember the film itself, only that it was an escapist picture and a talkie and that this was a label of some import. What she did remember was the grandiosity of the experience. She always remembered, before anything else, the smell of the popcorn, which she tasted for the first time. Popcorn, she was delighted to discover, was delicious. The sweetness of corn drenched in salty drawn butter. She fed one little popped kernel after another into her mouth between bright black and white frames. What flashed loudly across the silver screen was secondary to the sumptuous treat she had eaten until all that remained at the bottom of the box were small, unpopped black-brown kernels.

Then she invariably remembered the faces behind the counter at the concession stand, the man who, smiling, handed her the popcorn—the face of the ticket taker, the usher, the bathroom attendant, the janitor—and the experience became bittersweet, all quickly flooded by a sort of swimmingness which dislocated the centrality of her pleasure—her pleasure mired in the first realizations that they were the bread and bane of an entire economy.

She remembered descending the spiral staircase from the balcony and the pop of her white Mary Janes against the red carpet—her father held her hand at turns too tightly or not tightly enough. She remembered her hand uncomfortably greasy in his own, worrying whether his unsteady grip meant that he thought her disgusting. She remembered the greeter smiling, thanking them for their patronage as they stepped like aliens back into the natural madness of Ponce de León.

Even if the building under renovation wasn't made larger, it seemed larger, with its new marquis, its new American feel, and it would undoubtedly attract a larger box office draw.

Today there were a few vendors still haunting the avenue with their songs. On Monday the avenue would be rife again with vendors wearing tall straw hats, selling their cocos, piraguas, candies and sugared fritters, pastelillos and alcapurrias, lottery tickets, fruits and vegetables, peanuts. *¡Mani! ¡Mani! ¡Aquí! ¡Tengo Mani!* Anything one would need of goods and services was available right on the avenue. Vendors ranged in age from children of six up to the elderly in the autumn of their lives, many from the country, but most from the slums and working class neighborhoods of the surrounding areas. Some of them were accompanied by their own beast of burden, or livestock, much to the dismay, amusement, and chagrin of the sharply dressed twentieth-century cosmopolitans on foot in their polished oxfords and heels or drawn in their exhaust-spouting V-8 carriages. People established a rapport with their vendors and knew their hours of operation and paid regular patronage. There was a durable sense of community in this unregulated osmosis of bodies and capital, a natural circuitry for direct transaction and the dissemination of news and ideas.

She could no longer discern if what necessitated the meeting of so heterogeneous a group of people was love or capital. More sinister and haunting was the idea that there on the avenue happened the conflation of both so that neither had a defined shape—so that neither love nor capital could be accepted or declined without undue confusion and self-abnegation.

What bound most communities was ritual and a cohesive worldview. Was this market gathering an intimate cultural ritual? She wondered what, apart from a bastard language, bound them in exile. Not a national identity per se, but a culture—a derivative. Music, sure. Food, sure. An ethos, maybe. But what did a Puerto Rican worldview look like? Some slow breed of Catholic colonialism. Was the cultural memory of a Puerto Rican exile intimately tied to the land itself?

What bound them, exiles in the monster of a northern nation where it hails, where people are employed in factories and hardly see the light of day? What bound them together when separated from the land—the memory of the land as it was when they left it? It seemed too carnal, too frail a connection to be of adequate use in the agency of a people. This labor, maybe.

As a new gentry imposed itself upon the infrastructure of the city something like ennui was spreading among pre-industrial Santurceños, the rural vendors who relied on the city's paved avenues for market, the laborers and working class families— ennui among a functioning caste which was racially and economically animated—phenotype and socio-economic status being directly correlated.

There was across from the cowbell of cultural memory the prospect of a national memory which wilted from a cry into a whimpering. These things existed apart from the other, inversely correlated so that cultural consumption meant the disintegration of national memory—a dying shout half-remembered in another language as the embarrassment of a bygone moment, as the exhaustion of an untenable dream. Half-remembered as a brand of failure. No more music she sometimes wished and it seemed always and only a wish made mid-Sunday.

La Le Lo Lai. Lo Le Lo Lai.

She was walking quickly—faster than she had even realized, rushing by her own reflection in the window of a local barbershop. The sun in the sky was at middle descent and the avenue had become more intimate as she left in her wake the grandiosity of the marquis and neared the humble glass storefront of the family shop. The buildings as they shrank to no more than one story slowed against her pace making room for the clear vista of afternoon—crossed in maroon shadow cast by the wide wings of a Colirrojo hanging in the ether.

She felt at home standing in front of the red painted calligraphy, trimmed in gold, which announced Sastreria Cornejas.

A trolley passed ringing its bell to clear the street—*¡Mani! ¡Mani! ¡Aqui! ¡Tengo Mani!*—a boy emerged a block away chanting gleefully his pregón. Three birds before her leapt into flight at the sound of police sirens and another unrecognizable sound, more vibration than sound, more tremor than vibration, as though the street itself were surging under the force and din of three hundred marching feet. She had to look down at her own body to confirm by sight what it was not—that it was not a somatic reaction—a nervous involuntary trembling of the knees or a lightness in bone and breath—but something beyond the ken of her prescience, something loud and heavy approaching. Standing under the architrave of the entrance to the family shop, the glass around her vibrating.

Theophilio emerged from the dark door of his grocery store across the street holding his broom, scanning the avenue for some sign of a happening. His eyes quickly made contact with Malou's.

Then came hundreds of feet marching, hundreds of bodies

turning as one body onto the avenue enraged and carrying signs in protest. Their faces at the front of the phalanx were glistening with sweat, their bodies so densely packed together that their shoulders were wet with the sweat of their neighbors. They poured into the emptiness of the avenue, arms pumping up and down in unison to the cadence of their marching rhythm. Arms on the fringe thrashing against the current. The last trolley had passed and there were no cars or vendors within sight.

Malou, trying to hide in the slim shade provided by the architrave, reached for her purse, wishing she had a copy of the key to the store. Then she could hide herself in the back room. Someone in the crowd shouted above the general din, which startled her and made her fumble her purse. It fell to the ground with a loudness that made her tense immediately, holding her body in a fixed position like she'd been caught doing something wrong. And she stayed there leering at the contents of her purse, which spilled out onto the sunlit sidewalk as the mouth of the marching throng neared. No keys, loose change, and La Negra's beads.

All of it trampled within seconds by the marching mass and drowned in the sound of approaching police sirens. She lost sight of Theophilio. She pressed herself nearer to the door amidst swelling cries for liberty and justice, hoping not to be seen by any among them. They were as awesome as they were grotesque—a carnival of characters whose collective smell was of must and displacement. She was so close to the mass and so near the ground that she could see the sweat drip from their bodies as they pressed to within feet of the family shop. Their legs together moved like the undulating legs of a centipede, a circumrotation of knees, ankles, and heels—uncanny when each pair of legs observed in isolation was attached to the slenderness of youth, or aged and familiar, or negro among criollo, or stuttering on the heels of those before and behind it.

Some of the faces in the marching crowd she recognized. Mostly women, some men, all of them distance tailors beholden to American demand for their product. All crippled momentarily by the sudden lapse of new money in circulation. The crowd halted in front of the shop and began, from the front, to still and quiet. Vexation spread from the back as the protesters began to inquire why they'd so suddenly stopped. Leading the march were two young women, neither of whom Malou recognized. She could see them, their chests heaving, their legs planted squarely, shoulder-width apart. Their expressions were grave and fixed on the intersection ahead. Both were dressed in flared skirts and heels. The one closer carried a bullhorn. The other carried a cowbell which she began to ring in the air. Its heavy trilling caught the attention of the ralliers, making nearly everyone among them fall silent.

Three police vehicles and four times as many officers cordoned off the intersection, impeding the path of the protesting crowd. Malou could see them through the glass, armed and prepared for confrontation.

The woman carrying the bullhorn, her eyes seething and face full of brutal vitality, with surreal surety raised the amplifier's conic aluminum to her lips. Sunlight gleamed on its dented surface. The woman holding the bell looked to her in anticipation. Her voice boomed through the horn, a short declarative statement— *¡WE WILL BE RECOGNIZED!*—which was followed by a ringing of the cowbell and a collective shout of support from the ralliers.

Malou was beginning to feel trapped looking into the throng crowding the avenue, effectively pinning her into the architrave of her own family's shop. Their shouting more than suggested the potential destructive power they had—that if they wanted to they could train that gaze on her family's independently owned and operated shop and destroy its front. Despite the claustral hellishness of feeling trapped she couldn't close her eyes to the happening. It felt like a movie—like what would happen next was scripted. Three bodies into the crowd, right in front of her, she recognized a narrow pair of trigueña legs—those of Amélia Grau. She was standing on tiptoes trying to get a glimpse of the police barricade and shouting along with the ralliers at the end of every bullhorned declarative ¡WE WILL NOT BE MOVED! FORWARD!—the last of these command-demands before the cowbell was rung, before two flat pops—which whipped warm across Malou's face—and then a hush like the hush of bewildered animals under the hush of enacted mourning.

Coming through the tail of its echo, a tall shriek and the sirens again and a chopping of feet. The ralliers scattered, some resisting and throwing objects at police, most running in the opposite direction. Like tissue an old black woman's body taken under the hysterical stampede, trampled, two successive boot heels in flight, which tore for footing into her back. She cried.

Malou reached for her own face where it had been touched by the sound of the gun, spattered from her lower lip across her right cheekbone to the corner of her eye, ferric on her tongue, viscous witness between her thumb and index finger, red, and she was young and once warm and announced her last laid there on the avenue as the mass of bodies dispersed leaving what was full of fire and promise—a beautiful corpse, shot clean through the neck and once in the stomach, still regarded as dangerous by the police who approached in pairs with their guns drawn and sirens blaring.

She wiped the martyr's blood from her lips with her sleeve and a young man, chased by two police officers, stumbled into the architrave beside her. One of the two police officers caught up, grabbing him by his arm, pulling him into a barrage of clubbed blows which landed hard against his skull before he could even reach up to protect himself. The other officer arrived close behind, engaging Malou with his predatory gaze, ready to pounce and yank her into violent submission. She braced herself as best she could, balling her hands instinctively into

fists, concentrating all of her weight and density into muscle, bone, and nerve.

In the split second before they would collide old Theophilio strode in between Malou and the officer, tall and imposing in a white t-shirt, his muscles on display and his broomstick readied to absorb the blow. The officer was startled and reached for his sidearm, but before he could draw it Theophilio tackled him to the ground. *¡Malou Run!*

The glass around her bent. She felt suddenly light and climbed to her feet, which felt like they weren't there at all, neither stationary nor moving, but she ran, nearly crashing into a woman frantic for escape over two or three bodies fallen, trampled, but breathing and injured, over several pamphlets and hand-drawn protest signs discarded in fear and panic, down the avenue and around the bodies and around the block, out of sight from police and away from the sirens.

People were running crazed in all directions. Some were walking slowly and curiously toward the commotion, eyeing her suspiciously for some clue as to what happened. Startled again by something loud popping once over the din. Gunshot. An ambulance parted the madness swerving around, honking at addled onlookers as it made its way to the scene of the protest, the scene of a killing, through the scene of unrest. Things were blanching. She was close now.

Past the two sunbent palms and the neighbor's sacred mother, through the front gate, which she carefully shut behind her, along the side of the house brushed at her side by the branches of the bushes, into her own backyard, where she left the door unlocked—just in case. She jiggled the handle delicately and stepped left foot first, almost sideways, through the door.

The house was warm and full of a sacred stillness. Late afternoon light through the louvered windows illuminated the dust that hung in the air and it was like sugar in her eyes. She shut the door behind her and realized finally that she was trembling, that she couldn't lift her hand without feeling a terrible nervous exhaustion. Her stomach contracted in fits involuntarily, her diaphragm jerking the air from the bottom of her lungs like she was crying. Then a brief and piercing pain, like she'd been stabbed. Blood brayed in the bones of her ears and nose.

She stumbled into the bathroom and rid herself of all clothes in disgust and in frustration threw Ochun's brass bangle against the tile. Its largeness was irritating her, sliding capriciously up and down her forearm, chafing her wrist to rawness. She washed her hands in the sink, washed the dry blood from her cheeks which colored the basin a diluted red and trickled down its sides as she washed her neck, buffing with a bar of soap everything that had accumulated under her skin and she washed her breast, splashing water against her chest until her knees gave out and she collapsed onto the floor with eyes bleary and feet weary. Too light-headed to stand, too heavy-hearted to fall unconscious.

The sun was in its way primitive over what happened itself into the human chronology of events. Like a kind of twine which unraveled itself from her neck bright red, ejected at such a speed and across such distance that it suggested alterity, profanity, abjection, and a spare music like the tapping of a pen almost so that it seemed all at once to spurt from her neck, rob her of her iron, and lay her flat, before the sound itself was registered. Between the cowbell and the bullhorn, which fell after everything had already fallen and the softness of its commonly durable material was bent, only the sound of the cowbell escaped.

Sweat on the officer's brow had caught light like fire, a kind of lustful viscera. His lips had parted to reveal teeth grit bright white against the sun. She could see herself, small and black and afraid, in the lenses of his sunglasses.

The sheer force of the officer's club against the skull of the protester flooded Malou with electricity—the image of the protester's body limp and twisted and held up by the left arm. His head cracked open and bleeding, hung so low over his chest that she couldn't see his face, but his knees just touching the sidewalk and his toes exposed in open sandals dragging along the concrete. There existed between life and death no tragedy as great as that escaped. Life was no tragedy. Death less tragic. What escaped—a thread of saliva hanging from the mouth of the protester like an unanswered question.

She was gradually regrouping between swatches of white space a sense of what had happened. The floor was covered in water. It was getting late.

She got up and grabbed a dark towel from the back of the adjoining linen closet and covered her body. She walked into the quietness of her bedroom and from her dresser pulled the nightgown she wore to sleep. She went back to the bathroom and clothed herself, then took the towel and began to clean up the excess water. She was careful to wipe away any trace of blood. She wiped scuffs marks from her Sunday shoes. She picked up the bangle.

When she finished cleaning the bathroom she took the towel to her bedroom and draped it over the foot of the bed. To give it a vaguely medicinal odor she daubed the towel in rubbing alcohol, then she hid the brass bangle behind the bottom drawer of her dresser and began finally to feel and embrace her exhaustion. Ms. Panaini's novel sat precariously at the edge of the dresser. It must have been wedged loose from the other books when she opened the bottom drawer in the dresser. She tipped the spine squarely into her palm, eyeing the deckled edge of the text block. She let gravity pull the pages apart so not to crack the spine too severely.

June Second, 1910

When the shadow of the sash appeared on the curtails

   curtains it was between seven and seven and

seven and eight o'clock and then it was in time

  ***I was in time** again, hearing the watch.*

Wedged between the pages was a small nondescript receipt for $14.32. Scribbled at the bottom of the receipt was what looked like a phone number and the name Raul. She closed the book gently and placed it neatly atop the stack on her dresser.

As she lay down in bed, in the sacred stillness of her mother and father's home, all she could hear was the enigma of the cowbell escaping, escaped—as her eyes grew heavy, each of her thoughts terminating, terminated in a tinny gong . . .

////\•/\\\\

In the zavana of the hogplum trees there was a dog. The trees were arranged in long allées, as far as the eye could see and each bore two fruits. The sun hung at a low angle. Its light entered the eye sharply and threw spareness over the plain. The dog was long-nosed and muscular. The dog was albino and took her forward toward the sound of a shore where it was likely she would find her mother eating fruit. There was orange dust on the horizon of the island rising upward into the sky, which was bright white. The dog looked up at her and suggested she go this way. The sound of the shore grew louder and she could smell the pleasure in her mother singing to the rind of the fruit. It was cold and the wind picked up and whistled on its way there through the branches, which jingled like irons. Now and again the dog would growl and threaten and fear climbed her. Then the dog would stop and rejoin her and she remembered not to stay long. Her bones began to rattle. Then a bell.

It was dark by the time her parents arrived. She woke to the sound of the front door being opened and one, two, three bodies crossing the rickety threshold. She could hear them in their hushed voices asking about the day's events—the protest and its players, the police, and the aftermath. They were in the living room, gradually making their way in stuttering steps toward her bedroom.

The first face she saw, to her surprise, was Theophilio, grinning and well dressed in a clean long-sleeved shirt. Not a mark on his body, like nothing had happened. Herr William and Fru Josephine stood in the doorway behind him, dressed in their Sunday best, looking in sympathetically. Herr William loosened his tie.

Malou was careful to keep up the façade of her illness. She was prepared to disavow any story Theophilio might have told her parents with bile, if need be. But neither of her parents seemed particularly perturbed and Theophilio was a lot of things, but snitch wasn't one of them.

The old man was holding something behind his back.

"You left this in my shop yesterday. I thought you might want it. It looks like there are some special things in there."

She propped herself up, half alarmed, half grateful, as he placed the purse at the foot of the bed. She nodded her thanks. The purse was open and inside she could see her Ocha beads and recovered change. None of her things had been destroyed in the organized chaos of the protest. It seemed miraculous.

He continued. "I was just telling your parents about a protest which turned into a riot on the avenue. It was a good thing the shops weren't harmed. You must have slept through it, Malou." His grin turned into a knowing smile. "¿Poor dear, are you not feeling well?"

He leaned over and put his palm to her forehead as though he were checking her temperature, then turned back to address her parents.

"She's still a little warm, but she should be fine and ready for school by morning." He righted himself. "Well, I'll be going now. I'm glad you're all well. See you tomorrow, si Dios quiere."

He turned and with a slight limp walked out of the room. She heard the front door opened and closed behind him. Herr William and Fru Josephine left her to rest. Things were returning to equilibrium. They hadn't discovered her dishonesty and it seemed Theophilio, for some reason, hadn't told them about finding her at the site of the protest. She was grateful and drowsy and a little achy from the day's events.

Her stomach was still doing nervous little flips and her muscles were still twitchy with the waning weight of her anxious energy. She sat up and listened closely for what sounded like a cowbell and realized it was nothing more than the distant jingle of a wind chime. She wiped the mucus from her eyes with her index finger and thumb. The sound of the bell, the memory of the sound of the bell, brought her to the early blueness of nausea. Her stomach grumbled. She hadn't eaten since breakfast.

She rolled out of bed and crept to the bathroom, passing her mother on the way. Fru Josephine sat solemnly at the kitchen table. She gave her daughter a circumspect glance. Herr William was in the bedroom, perhaps asleep or preparing for sleep. It was still early in the night, but on Sundays the family retired relatively early. Church services were often exhausting and they performed best the following Monday when they were each prepared—Herr William and Fru Josephine at the tailor's and Malou at school. Fru Josephine watched as her daughter hobbled through bluish moonlight toward the outhouse and latched the door behind her.

Inside the outhouse Malou lifted her nightgown, bunching it between her armpits, and sat on the toilet, tensing immediately on the cold wood beneath her. She had a terrible stomach ache. Pressure descended on her abdomen like a block of cement. Everything in her head was throbbing. Her vision was unstable, bleary and unfocused. Her ears felt feverish. She felt like she was full of gas, but nothing was moving. She doubled over on the toilet, trying to negotiate her discomfort into a posture more agreeable, more amenable for a bowel movement. Then she looked down, casting her eyes between her thighs, and whitened with shock and fear at the unusual dark color and viscosity of what could only have been el castigo de Dios.

///Λ•Λ\\\

1947 [SANTURCE] Protests had spread from the west to Santurce by September of '33 and continued well into the early hours of the new year when sugar workers declared a full labor strike. Things worsened. American General Blanton Winship was appointed by Roosevelt's administration Governor of the island in 1934, ushering in a period of violence and turmoil unrivaled in the history of the nation.

The nation in these years would find itself politically and ideologically divided in its efforts to find a singular voice, to assert its identity. Confrontations between police and protesters more frequently resulted in massacres. The murder of Police Commissioner Francis E. Riggs by two radical nationalists further divided people and powers. The Commissioner made bold promises that he would prevent any and all nationalist militancy, by force if necessary. Nationalists reacted in kind. It all seemed to reach a climax with the Ponce Massacre in '37—the bloodiest massacre of the decade.

Nationalism rose in reaction to the imposed violence of militaristic American oppression, but it rose with the head of a ram, in the mode of a bellwether, and only made it logistically as far as fortune would have it. Ideologically it sailed loudly, but slowly and darkly, along its own meridian, chasing its tail. Nationalists appeared like fata morgana on the horizon as heirs to a revolution enacted and seemingly quashed in September of 1868. And they were—proper heirs to failure, tragically reactionary and dying a slow and painful death. Lead by the enigmatic and hard-working political visionary Pedro Albizu Campos, nationalists lit a new patriotic fire in the imagination of a people, the terms of which ran contrary to the true culture of the island. Staunchly Catholic, Campos failed to recognize that Catholicism itself was among the first of the island's colonial impositions. It was a mask they all wore as a provision of protection against the wrath and punishment of the colonizers. And while he famously inspired women Nacionalistas for the cause, he still held certain staid views on marriage and gender equality. His bourgeois noblesse discouraged women and students from engaging in armed revolution.

Campos was arrested and deported in June of '37. Found guilty by a jury comprised of ten Americans and two Puerto Ricans for conspiracy and accessory regarding the murder of Commissioner Riggs the year before. Word spread that he was in New York, having been freed in '43. Quiet as a dormouse. There was talk of torture.

As reality converged with dream and the politics of sovereignty were again on the table, things were looking strangely narrow. Opinions were divided between two symbols of Puerto Rican actualization—the Rebel Wonderwaif (Campos) and the Progressive Patrician Dandy.

Luis Muñnoz Marín, son of Luis Muñoz Rivera, had since risen to political power—a poetaster who married and sired children with American poet Muna Lee, lived and studied in America, and returned to the island with a sense of socialist reformation and the promise of a new national direction. His brand of idealism, half-studied in Marxism and half-studied in populist American poetics, was moving aggressively toward modernity by way of compromised assimilation.

Malou, now twenty-three, soon to be twenty-four, was busy arranging the bouquet. She sat on her knees adjusting and readjusting each stalk between small clouds of light filler to her aesthetic satisfaction. Lady tulips, Waxflower, and St. John's wort berry. An arrangement of whites and pinks offset by lustrous green leaves and the maroon of the berries.

It was a strange time to entertain love. She was weary of the lies being told by men less intelligent than they were touted to be. Journalism was just as guilty of partisanship, depending on where the funding came from. In those days funding could be traced, with some diligence, to a few well-fed, opinionated patrons who sat ideologically on one side of the pond or the other. Things were changing. Lines were blurring and the moment for radical change was being submerged in fascistic singularity once again. It seemed that the people wanted it this way.

She shooed a fly that flew too close, then quickly withdrew her hand when she realized it was a honeybee. It swooped in from the sun, circled her head once in wide orbit, then landed in the bouquet, on the petal of a lady tulip. It danced closer to the pistil to collect on its goldenrod body the pastel yellow dust of the flower's pollen.

She'd grown into one of the most beautiful young women in Santurce. She had her father's height and gait, and her mother's dignity and shape. Her skin was smooth and of an even brown complexion, and the features of her round face appeared pinched with an easy joyfulness. Lips half-pout, half-grin, beneath a slightly bulbous and upturned nose. Her eyes were wide and dark, gitana black, and her gaze haunting and perspicacious. She kept her hair pulled back in a neat no-nonsense bun that tapered into a crown of soft black curls. She spoke with royal refinement, well versed in the literature of several cultures and languages, and she was going to be the first in her family to attend university—the first in her family to join la Asociación de Mujeres Graduadas. She never spoke out of turn and she certainly never felt compelled to speak with anyone she felt unworthy of her time. Darling of Santurce.

"¿Mami? What was it like for you with Papi? Because right now with Jens everything feels so familiar. Of course I love him, but I'm not excited by him like I used to be. ¿Is that normal? I don't feel 'in love' anymore."

She paused as the bee, laden with pollen, hovered in front of her nose, then hummed off into the sun behind her.

"Sometimes I just want to cut and run. Lately it feels so fraternal. I don't know. He's so pale."

She looked at the brass bangle around her wrist, marveling at how perfectly it sat between the heel of her palm and her forearm, how she'd grown into it. People were leaving the island in droves, buying plane tickets to settle in El Barrio. Harlem, U.S.A. Leaving one island for another island. Leaving one poverty for another. Leaving one language for the loss of language. The poets she loved were gone too. Emilio Delgado, the soft-spoken *noísta*, and Julia de Burgos, the riverain conscience of the people.

Eliseo was one among them, who left to follow his dream of being a pop singer. After he was taken out of school he started making money for his family by singing the pregones of a peanut vendor in the old city, handing out paperbags of picked nuts to tourists. As he got older he sang at the popular haunts chasing fame along the circuit, paid paltry sums or paid in alcohol. He sang now on weekends at the Park Plaza, West 110th St, with a group called Alfarona X. She kept a black and white photograph of him, which he'd signed, sharpest among the ten other members all matching in gray double-breasted suits with wide peak lapels and white pocket handkerchiefs—a striking and handsome juxtaposition to their panchromatic blackness. They all wore their handkerchiefs differently. Most were worn loosely, haphazardly stuffed into the front pocket. A few were folded.

Eliseo's was folded. He stood in the back row, fourth from the left after Sabu, Pucho, and Mon, wearing the same easy expression that she fell in love with so many years ago as a girl. His eyes were still smiling, his mien relaxed.

Luis Cruz, the director, sat front row center bringing their number to eleven. He wore a lighter, looser suit with a rounded shawl lapel and a narrow black bowtie to distinguish himself as leader. Luis moved to Santurce in the early thirties. He was older than the rest, a man about town, a carpenter by day, poet by night, an aspiring guitarist and vocalist. That was then.

Most of the other members, whose names escaped her, were lost or losing themselves, drunkards and junkies dead to history, scrounging the circuit for their last electric moments of recognition, trolling the streets after midnight for strange. They often shared batches of their homebrew Cane and fashioned themselves fast-living, wood-drinking, sporting men. They were carriers of a rare righteousness—the affective labor of a convivial spirit keeping the people aloft in affirmation and celebration. They were the sufferers. They were lightning-rods of collective grief. Mártires, unwittingly. Sundry saints.

Eliseo left behind two illegitimate sons by two different women. He did his best to care for them, outside of marrying one or the other mother, but ultimately he made the decision to leave them in Santurce and pursue his dream, find his fortune in Harlem, where musicians were paid thrice as much and still hardly anything. He was a chauffeur by day, lounge singer at night.

Amélia Grau, born on the Fourth of July, also left for New York City, and with legitimate cause to forget the island. Her father died from cirrhosis, which drew her into a period of depression. She was often seen walking home alone from work, chain-smoking Parliaments with her eyes down and vacant. She was careful not to acknowledge passersby and in this way preserved what little joy and hope remained bundled privately within her being.

On occasion Malou could hear their fighting next door. Her father was an abusive man. He would sometimes throw bottles at Amélia and her mother, the caustic thrill of shattered glass echoing through the night. Or he would come home late, presumably from whoring, drunk, with a heavy hand and Malou could hear Amélia begging him, in a high pathetic wail, not to. He was a big man, intimidating in his seriousness, black, and never missed Church with his passing white wife on Sunday. To confront him would have been a breach of social decorum, but most of the congregants knew and it seemed all they could do, would do, was pray for the family in crisis.

Amélia loved her father despite his addiction because she knew him also to be a tender man who cared for his family, feared God, and believed in redemption. She'd seen him cry, seen him humbled to tears by his own incapacity. She was the last living witness to his humanity, even after her mother had given up, after her mother was worn thin by prayer, after stress colored an impermeable darkness beneath her eyes.

Amélia's experience was a near tragedy of faith—to have been witness to her father's ultimate failure. Dead still drunk, flammable and waiting on Heaven for one last healing—and when Heaven was silent, said nothing, as his life whined to inflamed end—

She left to live with an aunt in New York City. Rumor spread through the neighborhood that Amélia met a young chanteur from Santurce with a high forehead and an easy demeanor at an uptown nightclub. They were engaged to wed.

Malou was having second thoughts about the waxflower, at what might have been too much pink in the bouquet. She pulled some from the stem and paused, dilating her pupils to envision a bouquet without the waxflower. As filler it was necessary for the spatial arrangement of the bouquet and how it would be perceived by the eye. Although it hardly mattered. The lady tulips would wilt within two days and who would remember the bouquet anyway?

It was quiet. She laid the bouquet over her mother, on the grass of the yet unmarked grave where she was buried. Herr William paid for a humble marker, a bronze plate on stone with her name, dates, and from Proverbs:

No tiene temor de la nieve por los de su casa
porque todos los de su casa llevan ropa escarlata.

So loved by the community was Fru Josephine that the verse from Proverbs was inscribed free of charge. The plot beside her was reserved for Herr William, for his day yet to come. Across town she imagined the old man was dutifully tending to garments at the sastreria, one less employee, but no less dedicated to his craft.

In memoriam he daily tended at the shop an orchid potted in soil taken from her grave. Beneath it, two small segments of sugarcane. This he left in place of her former workstation, directly across from his own. He hung the family photo above it.

He cried only once at the viewing, after everyone had left. He pulled Malou into embrace, his right hand kneading the nape of her neck, his left hand clutching tightly her back, finding some comfort in his daughter and in what she still carried of her mother. Malou held him tightly, her arms wrapped firmly around his back, feeling less affected and charged to be his rock, his keeper. He was an independent man, a stoic in good health, but one now separated from the tenderness that kept him grounded. He wasn't in need of a caretaker per se. What he needed now was buoyancy, what Josephine had been for him, the conduit for his nightly dreaming. For now he contented his days by diligently working at the shop.

The grocery across the way had fallen into disarray. Theophilio too had passed away and his son was unwilling to care for the shop. His father left instructions that it should not be sold. So it sat in limbo. The fruit crates were emptied, their fruits stolen, the appliances inside vacated, stolen or repossessed. Malou managed to sneak into the grocery store one afternoon and found its emptiness eerie. Light filtered in from boarded windows illuminating each mote of dust, each forgotten wish of an old man. There were a few rotting heads of lettuce still on the counter. The register was taken. There now lingered a square-shaped discoloration where it once sat, where its drawer once opened and closed. Behind the counter were several newspaper clippings chronicling political happenings and the rise of radical reforms, stacked on top of each other, yellowing in their own tabloid acid. The building itself and all of its furniture, those things that had not been taken, finally fell to passing hands, light, and the general dynamics of erosion. But in his lifetime he had given her the impression that there existed such a thing as invincible.

Malou looked down at the plot of land that now held the

carnal remains of her mother, marked now by the presence of flowers. Without her noticing, a brown recluse had settled into the bouquet. Still seated on her knees, she leaned over, stretching slightly to grab with the tips of her fingers a twig. The sun was setting between the trees throwing its last warmth over the marbled heads of hundreds of tombstones arranged in rows before her and her mother and the sky began its quick transition from lavendered twilight into the colder depths of night.

She stuck the twig into the bouquet between two lady tulips, angling it beneath the spider so that it would climb on, and with so little space to maneuver the spider climbed on, attaching each long leg to the twig, almost hesitantly, one at a time. She slowly pulled it out of the bouquet to examine it, the reticent angularity of its eight legs like black steel supporting a dark, carapaced body.

It began slipping silver from its spinnerets, dangling from the tip of the twig, and before it could land she decided to fling it. With a flick of her wrist the spider's legs tensed around its own spun wire and it swung from the twig in a high arc. It snapped off exactly at the crest of the arc with the grace of a diver flying three rows of tombstones ahead and disappeared behind the nearest holy mother.

Malou leaned forward to kiss the earth at her knees then stood and walked along the dirt path leading to the gates of the cemetery, where she made a left to enter again the electric hum of the city and its common time and carried with her the anxious desire to wash when she made it home also feeling half-worried that her father had not eaten though he usually around this time if he was still hungry prepared a simple caldo to quell his hunger so she traced the lights from window to window as they flickered open along the avenue intervention against night and the cool air that began to slip beneath her skirt and up along her thighs inciting thoughts of hot water and the water boiler which made it more convenient to luxuriate in that way and while it seemed sometimes too convenient like a concession to modernity which signified a kind of submission she had to admit she enjoyed it and in fact felt powerful with her legs sprawled in the perfectly adjustable temperatures of water made fragrant by a secret concoction she'd purchased on the avenue only a week ago and that was mostly because and she hated to admit this she felt sorry for the old vendor who barely had breath enough for a pregón but shared freely her impeccable smile as it was the kind of smile which brought sincere joy to small children and adults afflicted by adulthood when they could not so easily humble themselves before the immensity of their troubles and needed to know that there was joy in the act of surviving and more than that thriving so she absolved herself with the knowledge that it wasn't pity she felt for the woman so much as a desire to support her saintly good works and anyway the concoction which was an oil mixture left her feeling softer than cotton and smelling lovelier than the pharaoh's daughter at equinox but this evening in the cool darkness of the night the old curio vendor was nowhere to be found not croaking not smiling as a reminder that even those we rely on for the sustenance of happiness must retreat to recenter their souls and the breeze picked up a frigid gust of air which came off the water and carried in it the salted scent of the ocean then she saw the manchildren in their hats grouped in three in the distance swaying like black algae under the lamp where they twittered like birds with affected bass in their voices about women and parties and bullshit well into the night each scaffolding the other to be more adequately masculine and in that way more honestly invested in the act and nomenclature of manhood so that as she passed she could hear them snigger and spit that hey nigger bitch how much you'll take it for free at least three times but she wasn't afraid because they knew who she was

the tailor's beautiful daughter and the architect's wife-to-be and
they'd be damned to harm her in any way aside from the feeble
attempt to shame a woman who so painfully symbolized in her
freedom their own global insolvency and political impotence
but at least they were cool staying up late in their little feathered
hats which was a shame really when the diaspora was grouping
itself on another island and the thought that what united them
could have been this outdated machismo inherited from the last
colonizer which would undoubtedly meet and mingle with the
cultural offal of their new colonizers to breed more narcissistic
young minds contorted to fit the fantasy mold of those in power
with their hands extended and mouths open and starved to the
point that they would eat their own children like animals or
individuals in the purest painful sense of alien solipsism only
concerned with their next and blind to long-term collective ad-
vancement which she imagined left them vulnerable to the more
insidious colonization of perennial consumerism perpetually
promising a more adequate self-image and in this way served to
divide and conquer a people successfully and without bloodshed
and all of this colored her dark vision of the cosmos which was
blurred by the lights of the avenue but she could just make out
the long tail of the scorpion and Antares the bright center and
the lonely heart of the constellation made her feel vertiginous
looking up so long and squinting through lamplight to glimpse
the ancient fires that drew them all into last call in the perfect
blackness of space where something of her mother's essential
spirit must have been traveling in astral orbit collecting the necessary particles scattered and lost of her now lifeless and vacated
form before she could *be* again but it seemed absurd and oriental to think that in passing the site of a centuries-old burial plot
she might have also been passing the last manifestation of herself
and more than that it was presumptuous to assume that she
could have been anything more than a weed or mosquito or
banana in the dim astrology of a bygone civilization when in fact
she was walking through the inhabited remains of a little under-

stood civilization being rebuilt to look like a pleasure paradise
to the kitschy satisfaction of Americans obsessed with theft and
ghosts and soon they would attempt the colonization of the
cosmos traveling with intentions and microbes certain to demol-
ish ecosystems capable of equilibrium in atmospheres without
oxygen and no more than a trace of water that would be invisible to the naked eye and beyond detection by the most advanced
imaging technology because there is without a doubt some uni-
versal order which varies beyond any singular constant or
measure but holds its own discernible shape and every replicable
object within it bound to a calculus which evades logic like an
ungraspable piece in the human puzzle depicting a curious insistence on opacity and how these paradoxes always found
economy in the first world trouble-tempered and valued and
displayed at market was the captive spectacle of its madness
giving her cause to believe that if anything she was once an unforgettable sound which it seemed after becoming human she'd
forgotten and it hardly bothered her that she could be on earth
also in search of what was lost in becoming like the notes of a
song if her sound was a song she was careful not to rush through
before hearing its last notes and departing likely and hopefully
not for another eighty years when and where and because these
pieces-before-departure were scattered across the orb of the
globe in places so remote and beautiful that they would require
a caravan of elephants and pilgrims whose origins could be
traced to the same tribe all searching and all enlivened by the
prospect that some semblance of zion sat over the next high
heat-distorted dune which brought her back to the avenue and
her brief reorientation passing the dark glass of the shop which
was now closed meaning two more blocks and a left a little ways
before home then looking across the street at the gaping emptiness of what used to be old Theophilio's place she realized she
was hungry and her stomach gurgled loudly so loudly that she
felt slightly embarrassed though the avenue there and then was
unusually empty save the light from the lamps and passing cars

the trolley line was flying or had flown its last and the papers
were full of pseudo-wistful headlines that told the story again of
a bygone moment in the history of the island's infrastructure
and most people could see it was time for them to be respectfully retired as they'd fallen into disrepair and with privately owned
automobiles on the upswing traffic along the avenues was unbearable by midday a miasma of so many bodies being shuffled
through the city just for work and then vacating the city for
sleep in their humble homes on the outskirts of town where the
powerlines streaked the sky like any inappropriate joke and a
familiar face was received in the eye like a kind of water in the
desert she supposed and picked up a little speed as she neared
home because her bladder felt bloated and itched for relief
against the waistband of her skirt and she was cold and beginning to shiver and her father, whom she wasn't prepared to care
for could have collapsed in a state of illness and neglect which
was unlikely but not beyond the realm of possibility and if an
atom could be split in half and take with it several thousand it
felt more real when she unlatched the gate and no lights were on
and the patio was empty of any sign of lunch or dinner no plates
there and the door was left unlocked so she locked it behind her
in a haze of white noise coming from the master bedroom which
grew louder as she approached and where she found him asleep
with his head against the radio box and his mouth wide open.

She shut the radio and leaned him back in his chair. From the
bed she grabbed a blanket and threw it over his lap. The blanket
still smelled like her mother, gave her brief pause as it swelled
in her frontal lobe. Then she ran to the outhouse, plunged back
into cold night, which had settled fully and finally, and relieved
herself under the vast plangency of the stars.

Now she felt she could slow her pace and perhaps make herself
a little dinner. The day's work was complete and she could rest
now and steep in something like a dreamstate before dream-

ing. School would be starting soon and she felt prepared for its challenges—some challenges she anticipated and some she was certain would come with the territory of being there, dealt with through patience and a touch of improvised thinking.

She came back in from the cold through the kitchen feeling more at ease and opened the light. She hadn't noticed on the way to the outhouse a small bowl covered and waiting on the kitchen table, presumably for her and presumably left there by Herr William. She lifted the saucer covering the bowl and took a peek at what looked like a congealed carne guisa'. It made her smile.

Everything was left neatly in the kitchen. The dishes were washed and the adjoining living room was tidy and still. She grabbed a spoon and sat at the table to pick at the lukewarm stew. She angled a cubed chunk of beef-round into her mouth and let it bounce from her tongue to her molars. The meat was tender and well seasoned. He must've left it simmering for hours so that the starch of the potato broke down and thickened the stew for a savory gravy which dressed the vegetables—yuca, yautía, onions, all a tender mouthfeel. Then something moved unusually out of the corner of her eye. Her body contracted.

Suddenly Malou jumped in her seat, startled by the presence of Herr William, who came shuffling up behind her draped in the blanket like a ghost, like the specter of death reflected in the glass over the sink. He put his large, wrinkled hands on her shoulders.

"¿Tod' 'tá bien?" he asked in crackling Danish.
"Yeah." She responded without looking back. "Bendición."
"Que Dios te bendiga mija."

He nodded once and shuffled back into the bedroom. She wasn't as hungry as she thought so she put the spoon down and sat

there in silence while her heart slowed to its resting rate, while
Herr William fumbled around his room making the noises of a
man passively alien to his own surroundings, and when finally it
settled that so much had been lost she drew a bath and idled for
what seemed like hours, emptying into another emptiness in its
convenient warmth until it cooled and she began to prune, until
her mother decided it was enough and stepped fully clothed
into the tub and smiling opposite her first and only daughter
began to sing

mi negrita linda tiene
chiquitito los ojitos
si me tira una guiñada
se va conmigo pa' Puerto Rico

¡Mai!

v. Orations [Redacted]

The Hon. Arjún J. Joglar
Former Resident Commissioner of Puerto Rico
Former President of the New Progressive Party
Declared Adjutant General
Prepared Statement
U.N. Special Committee on Decolonization
17 JUNE, XXOI

WE, THE PUERTO RICAN PEOPLE, AND ALL OF THE OPPRESSED, SURVIVALISTS WHOSE LIVES HAVE BEEN ENSNARED IN THE BOOT-STRAPS OF STATE-SPONSORED TERROR AND VIOLENCE, MUST NOW AWAKEN WITHOUT FEAR TO OUR ULTIMATE RECOURSE FOR NA-TIONAL EMANCIPATION. IMPERIAL NORTH AMERICA PERSISTS IN ITS OCCUPATION OF OUR COUNTRY AND PROVOKES US, DAY BY DAY, AND NIGHT BY NIGHT, TO DEFEND OUR NATIONAL DIGNITY. [1]

////\•/\\\\

I ASKED TO PARTICIPATE BECAUSE AN EVENT HAS TAKEN PLACE THAT FUNDAMENTALLY CHANGES THE TERMS OF THE DEBATE ON PUERTO RICO'S POLITICAL STATUS.

ON NOVEMBER 6ᵀᴴ, XXXX, PUERTO RICO EXERCISED ITS RIGHT, UNDER THE AUSPICES OF THE U.S. CONSTITUTION, TO SELF-DE-TERMINATION BY FREE AND FAIR VOTE ON THE STATUS QUES-TION. THE RESULTS DEMONSTRATED THAT 54 PERCENT OF VOTERS

DID NOT WISH TO MAINTAIN THE SO-CALLED COMMONWEALTH STATUS. TO THE EXTENT THAT THE PEOPLE OF PUERTO RICO EVER GAVE THEIR CONSENT TO A COLONIAL STATUS, THAT CONSENT HAS NOW BEEN WITHDRAWN.

THE RESULTS FURTHER DEMONSTRATED THAT, AMONG THE THREE INTERNATIONALLY RECOGNIZED ALTERNATIVES TO COMMON-WEALTH STATUS, 61 PERCENT OF VOTERS SUPPORTED STATEHOOD.

I AM HERE TO TELL YOU THAT WE ARE NO LONGER VICTIMS OF SPONSORED TERROR AND VIOLENCE AT THE INVISIBLE HAND OF A COLONIZING AGENT. THIS SORT OF THINKING HAS CRIPPLED US AS A PEOPLE AND AS A NATION FOR CENTURIES. WE ARE NO LONGER PLEADING FOR INTERVENTION. THESE U.N. SANCTIONS, HOWEVER APPRECIATED, HAVE FALLEN ON DEAF EARS AND TIED HANDS IN THESE FIRST DECADES OF THE 21ST CENTURY. CLEARLY NEGOTIATION HAS FAILED AND THIS DENIAL [OF STATEHOOD] [OF RECOGNITION] HAS INSTILLED WITHIN OUR COLLECTIVE IMAGI-NATION A NEWLY INVIGORATED SENSE OF NATIONAL PRIDE AND NATIONAL DUTY.

WE, THE PUERTO RICAN PEOPLE, NOW OCCUPY A FREE AND SOV-EREIGN STATE WHOSE RECOGNITION BY THESE UNITED NATIONS WE SEEK. BUT LET ME BE CLEAR THAT OUR SOVEREIGNTY IS BY NO MEANS CONTINGENT ON THE TENDER OF SUCH RECOGNITION.

I WANT TO CLARIFY AN IMPORTANT POINT. ON THE SURFACE, THOSE WHO WANT PUERTO RICO TO BECOME A STATE AND THOSE WHO WANT PUERTO RICO TO BECOME A SOVEREIGN NATION APPEAR TO HAVE LITTLE IN COMMON, GIVEN OUR DIFFERENT VISIONS FOR PUERTO RICO'S FUTURE, BUT WE ACTUALLY AGREE IN FUNDAMENTAL RESPECTS.

WE ARE THE REALITY-BASED MOVEMENT OF PUERTO RICO.

WE NO LONGER RECOGNIZE PUERTO RICO AS AN UNINCORPORAT-
ED TERRITORY OF THE UNITED STATES.

WE WILL NO LONGER STAND FOR THE PARADOX THAT, ALTHOUGH
THE UNITED STATES APPROVED A CONSTITUTION FOR PUERTO
RICO IN 1952 AND WAS RELEASED FROM ITS REPORTING RE-
QUIREMENT UNDER ARTICLE 73 OF THE U.N. CHARTER IN 1953,
PUERTO RICO WAS DEFINED A "NON-SELF-GOVERNING TERRITO-
RY." IT IS A MEANINGLESS APPELLATION INTENDED TO OBSCURE
MORE THAN A DECADE OF COLONIAL RULE.

WE NO LONGER RECOGNIZE THAT, UNDER U.S. LAW AND INTER-
NATIONAL LAW, AS ENSHRINED IN U.N. GENERAL ASSEMBLY RES-
OLUTION XXXX, THERE ARE THREE STATUS OPTIONS THAT WOULD
PROVIDE PUERTO RICO WITH A "FULL MEASURE OF SELF-GOV-
ERNMENT": INDEPENDENCE, NATIONHOOD IN FREE ASSOCIATION
WITH ANOTHER NATION, AND INTEGRATION THROUGH STATE-
HOOD. WE DO NOT MISREPRESENT WHAT PUERTO RICO IS, OR
WHAT IT MIGHT BECOME, FOR THE SAKE OF POLITICAL ADVAN-
TAGE.

WE RECOGNIZE WHAT PUERTO RICO USED TO BE: AN UNINCOR-
PORATED TERRITORY OF THE UNITED STATES. WE LIKEWISE REC-
OGNIZE THAT THE U.S. CONGRESS COULD HAVE UNILATERALLY
RESCINDED THE POWERS IT HAD DELEGATED TO PUERTO RICO IF
IT SAW FIT TO DO SO.

WE RECOGNIZE AS SELF-EVIDENT THAT PUERTO RICO DID NOT
HAVE DEMOCRACY AT THE NATIONAL LEVEL. THE UNITED STATES
GOVERNMENT MADE AND IMPLEMENTED LAWS FOR PUERTO RICO.
WITH FEARS ROOTED IN THE DESTABILIZATION OF THE ELECTOR-
AL COLLEGE, ISLAND RESIDENTS WERE NOT ALLOWED TO VOTE
FOR THE U.S. PRESIDENT, WERE NOT REPRESENTED IN THE U.S.

SENATE, AND THEN EXPECTED TO ELECT ONE MEMBER TO THE U.S. HOUSE OF REPRESENTATIVES—THE RESIDENT COMMISSIONER—WHO COULD VOTE IN COMMITTEES, BUT WAS EXCLUDED FROM THE FULL HOUSE. I SERVED AS RESIDENT COMMISSIONER AND COULD NO LONGER DO SO WITHOUT SEVERELY DENYING MY AND MY OWN NATION'S SOVEREIGNTY.

As RESIDENT COMMISSIONER I REGULARLY EXPERIENCED FIRST-HAND THE INJUSTICE OF OUR PREVIOUS STATUS. I WAS EFFECTIVE-LY SILENCED IN MY FIGHT TO ENSURE THAT PUERTO RICO WAS NOT EXCLUDED FROM JOB CREATION, HEALTH CARE, OR BORDER SECURITY BILLS THAT AUTOMATICALLY INCLUDED THE STATES. AS MY FELLOW REPRESENTATIVES IN THE U.S. HOUSE VOTED ON LEGISLATION THAT AFFECTED EVERY ASPECT OF LIFE IN PUERTO RICO, I COULD ONLY WATCH, EVEN THOUGH I REPRESENTED AP-PROXIMATELY FIVE TIMES AS MANY U.S. CITIZENS AS ANY OF MY COLLEAGUES. I RELIED ON THE GOODWILL OF U.S. SENATORS WHO WERE ELECTED TO PROTECT THE INTERESTS OF THEIR CON-STITUENTS, NOT MINE—AND, NATURALLY, SUCH GOODWILL WAS NOT ALWAYS FORTHCOMING. AND I REQUESTED ASSISTANCE FROM A PRESIDENT WHO, HOWEVER STRONG HIS AFFINITY FOR PUERTO RICO MIGHT HAVE BEEN, WAS NOT REQUIRED TO SEEK OR EARN OUR VOTE. TO EXPECT THAT HIS ADMINISTRATION WOULD FEEL THE SAME URGENCY TO PRODUCE POSITIVE RESULTS FOR PUERTO RICO AS IT DOES FOR THE STATES IS, FRANKLY, TO SUBSTITUTE HOPE FOR EXPERIENCE.

And now, those who wanted Puerto Rico to become A STATE AND THOSE WHO WANTED PUERTO RICO TO BECOME A SOVER-EIGN NATION—WHETHER IN FREE ASSOCIATION WITH OR FULLY INDEPENDENT FROM THE UNITED STATES—ALL RECOGNIZE THAT PUERTO RICO'S TERRITORY STATUS IS THE ROOT CAUSE OF THE ECONOMIC AND SOCIAL PROBLEMS THAT IMPAIR QUALITY OF LIFE ON THE ISLAND. WE CATEGORICALLY REJECT THE BACKWARDS

VIEW, EMBRACED BY CERTAIN POLITICAL LEADERS IN PUERTO
RICO, THAT THE STATUS DEBATE IS SOMEHOW A DISTRACTION
FROM EFFORTS TO ADDRESS THESE CHALLENGES.

FINALLY, AND ABOVE ALL, ESTADISTAS, SOBERANISTAS, AND IN-
DEPENDENTISTAS NOW SHARE A DEEP CONVICTION THAT THE
PEOPLE OF PUERTO RICO, 3.7 MILLION STRONG, DESERVE A FULLY
DEMOCRATIC AND DIGNIFIED STATUS.

IN NOVEMBER, PUERTO RICO TOOK THE INITIATIVE, EXERCISED
ITS RIGHT TO SELF-DETERMINATION, AND UNEQUIVOCALLY WITH-
DREW ITS CONSENT TO TERRITORY STATUS.

THE ONLY PATH FORWARD IS SOVEREIGNTY. THE PEOPLE OF
PUERTO RICO, BY PEACEFULLY PROTESTING, HAVE VOICED THEIR
AGENCY, POWER, AND POLITICAL POSITION.

IT IS NOW INCUMBENT UPON THE UNITED STATES GOVERNMENT
TO RESPOND BY KEEPING OPEN CHANNELS OF DIPLOMACY AND
TRADE. I HAVE EMPHASIZED THAT ACTION IS NECESSARY FOR
BOTH LEGAL AND MORAL REASONS.

AS A LEGAL MATTER, FOR PUERTO RICO TO EVOLVE AND BECOME
A SOVEREIGN NATION, IT IS NOT ENOUGH TO JUST PROCLAIM
OUR INDEPENDENCE; WE MUST BE VIABLE AND RESPONSIBLE
PARTICIPANTS IN ALL SPHERES OF INTERNATIONAL AFFAIRS. WE
HAVE OPENED DIRECT TRADE, IMPORT AND EXPORT, WITH OTHER
NATIONS.

AS A MORAL MATTER, OUR NEW GOVERNMENT RIGHTFULLY
PRIDES ITSELF AS A CHAMPION OF DEMOCRACY AND SELF-DETER-
MINATION AT HOME AND AROUND THE WORLD. OUR BRAND OF
DEMOCRACY IS NOT IN OPPOSITION TO OUR ECONOMIC POLICIES
AS REGULATED BY OUR GOVERNING BODY—THE VOICE OF THE

PEOPLE. THEREFORE WE SHOULD, INDEED WE MUST, ADHERE TO OUR PRINCIPLES WITH RESPECT TO OUR CITIZENS OR WE WILL LOSE CREDIBILITY AT HOME AND ABROAD.

I HAVE FAITH THAT OUR PEOPLE, THE PEOPLE OF PUERTO RICO, THE PEOPLE WHO CONSTITUTE THE BODY OF OUR NEW NATION, WILL FULFILL OUR LEGAL AND MORAL OBLIGATION TO FACILITATE OUR SELF-SUFFICIENT SOVEREIGNTY. BUT MY FAITH IS NOT BLIND. WE WILL DEFEND OUR NATION, WITH ARMED OPPOSITION IF NEED BE, AGAINST THOSE OPPOSED TO THE TRUE DEVELOPMENT OF INDEPENDENCE, DEMOCRACY, AND NATIONAL DIGNITY.

I AM FULLY COGNIZANT THAT THE WHEELS OF GOVERNMENT OFTEN TAKE LONGER TO TURN THAN ONE MIGHT PREFER, AND I THEREFORE APPRECIATE THAT A DEGREE OF PATIENCE IS IN ORDER. BUT I ALSO KNOW THAT JUSTICE TOO LONG DELAYED IS JUSTICE DENIED. AND AFTER XXX YEARS AS A TERRITORY PUERTO RICO'S PATIENCE HAS RUN OUT.

LET ME BE CLEAR. IN THE ABSENCE OF CONCRETE AND TIMELY ACTION FROM THE U.S. GOVERNMENT, WE HAVE TAKEN RESPONSIBILITY FOR OUR OWN FUTURE. AS THE REPRESENTATIVE OF OUR NEW NATION I HAVE NO DESIRE TO PUBLICLY CRITICIZE OUR FORMER COLONIZERS. BUT IT IS MORE IMPORTANT FOR ME TO SECURE JUSTICE FOR MY PEOPLE THAN IT IS FOR ME TO BE POLITE.

THAT SAID, I HAVE NOT BEEN ENCOURAGED BY THEIR RESPONSE TO DATE. THE PRESIDENT HAS SAT TOO LONG ON HIS HANDS AND THE HANDS OF CONGRESS TO ENACT A FEDERALLY SPONSORED VOTE FOR PUERTO RICO'S STATUS. THEY HAVE THREATENED US WITH MILITARY FORCE. I AM HERE TO SAY, WE ARE UNAFRAID.

LAST MONTH WE INTRODUCED LEGISLATION, THE *LABORER'S PROVISIONARY ACT*, WHICH PROCEEDS FROM THE INDISPUT-

ABLE PREMISE THAT LABORERS WORKING IN AMERICAN-OWNED PLANTS AND FACTORIES DESERVE BETTER TREATMENT. THE ACT, WHICH ALREADY HAS AN OVERWHELMING MAJORITY 72 COSPON-SORS AMONG THE MUNICIPALITIES FROM ALL SIX ESTABLISHED PROVINCES, OUTLINES THE RIGHTS AND RESPONSIBILITIES OF THE LABORER IN A DECENT AND SAFE WORKING ENVIRONMENT. THE ACT HAS ALSO ESTABLISHED, VIA ADJUSTED NATIONAL TAX, A PROVISIONARY WAGE AND ADEQUATE HEALTH BENEFITS FOR OUR LABORERS, LARGELY COMPRISED OF PHARMACEUTICAL WORKERS, WHILE WE NEGOTIATE WITH AMERICAN INVESTORS THEIR PRAC-TICAL ECONOMIC ALLOWANCES AT RATES COMPETITIVE OR SUPE-RIOR TO NATIONS LIKE IRELAND. THEY ARE BEHOLDEN TO OUR DIRECTIVES WHILE THEIR FACTORIES REMAIN UNSTAFFED. I AM HERE TO SAY WE WILL BE FAIR. WE WISH TO MAINTAIN A DIPLO-MATIC RELATIONSHIP WITH OUR FORMER COLONIZERS.

I WANT TO EXPRESS MY BELIEF THAT THE INTERNATIONAL COM-MUNITY, LIKE THE U.S. GOVERNMENT, SHOULD HONOR THE GOODWILL OF OUR NEW NATION. CONSISTENT WITH THE U.N. CHARTER AND RESOLUTION 1541, THE INTERNATIONAL COMMU-NITY SHOULD SUPPORT A PROCESS OF SELF-DETERMINATION THAT WILL RESULT IN A FULLY DEMOCRATIC AND DIGNIFIED NATION. THE PRINCIPLE OF SELF-DETERMINATION SO REQUIRES.[2]

////\•/\\\\

I WILL DO MY BEST TO BE BRIEF IN THESE FINAL DELINEATIONS. AGAIN, LET ME BE CLEAR, THIS IS NO DESPOTIC DECLARATION—THIS IS A STAND FOR HUMAN RIGHTS, OUR RIGHTS. THE STATE OF THIS OR ANY NATION DIRECTLY CORRELATES TO THE GENERAL WELL-BEING OF ITS INDIVIDUALS. PUERTO RICO WAS SUFFER-ING A PROTRACTED ECONOMIC DEATH MARKED BY CONSISTENT CONTRACTION, BECAUSE IT WAS WILLFULLY MISMANAGED BY THE SUZERAIN SINCE THE 1970S—THE DECADE MARKING OUR IN-

CREASED DEPENDENCE ON U.S. FEDERAL TRANSFER PROGRAMS AND THE SUBSEQUENT FAILURE OF A PREVAILING NATIONAL IMAGINATION.

THE UNITED STATES GOVERNMENT IN UNION WITH OUR FORMER GOVERNING BODY FROM THE EARLY AUGHTS ONWARD HAD QUIETLY INVESTED IN THE PRIVATIZATION OF THE ISLAND'S GREATEST ASSESTS IN WHAT BECAME A PROLONGED SEQUESTRATION OF THE NATION QUA TERRITORIAL PROPERTY. THE RESULT HAS BEEN A SUCCESSFUL AND INSIDIOUS MEANS OF SECLUDING LARGE SEGMENTS OF THE POPULATION WHO WERE THEN LEFT WITHOUT ACCESS TO HEALTH CARE, EDUCATION, AND A FIGHTING CHANCE AT A PIECE OF THE PIE, SO TO SPEAK. WHERE ONCE PUERTO RICO SERVED AS AN ECONOMIC MODEL FOR DEVELOPING COUNTRIES, IT IS NOW ALL BUT FORGOTTEN AND DISMISSED AS NOTHING MORE THAN A VACATION DESTINATION.

THE MODERN WORLD IS BEING BUILT AND DETERMINED NOT BY A SINGLE ENTITY OR NATION, BUT BY THE MECHANISMS OF HUMAN CAPITAL AS THEY'VE EVOLVED TO MEET DEMAND AND BY THE DREAMS AND DREAMERS THAT BIND THIS CAPITAL. OUR CAPITAL HAS BEEN—OUR *PEOPLE* HAVE BEEN—CRIPPLED BY THE NEO-MERCANTILIST PROFITEERING OF SUZERAIN GOVERNANCES AND NOW WE STAND UNITED IN ANNOUNCING OUR PLACE AMONG THE FAMILY OF NATIONS.

INFORMATION TECHNOLOGY WILL BE THE SAVING GRACE OF THIS NATION'S GROSS DOMESTIC PRODUCT. AN OPEN INFRASTRUCTURE PROVIDING EQUAL ACCESS TO INFORMATION FOR ALL OF ITS CITIZENS CAN ALLOW EQUAL FAVOR, EQUAL COMPETITION, AND IN THIS WAY, WE MAY ENSURE THAT OUR MARKET REMAINS EFFICIENTLY BALANCED AND SKEWED IN FAVOR OF NO SINGLE BENEFICIARY. WHERE THE U.S. HAS SO FAR FAILED IS IN THE ASSUMPTION THAT MARKET EFFICIENCY EXISTS, IN STRONG-FORM,

REFLECTED IN SHARE PRICES WHEN AND WHERE INFORMATION, BOTH PUBLIC AND PRIVATE, IS AVAILABLE—THE EARLY GIFT AND LATE CURSE OF AMERICAN CAPITALISM. FREEDOM IS INTEGRAL TO THE FORMULA AND THE FAILURE OF THIS HYPOTHESIS IS THE PRESUPPOSITION THAT INFORMATION IS FREE. WHEN IN FACT INFORMATION IS VIOLENTLY HOARDED BY THOSE IN POWER. THIS MONOPOLIZES AVENUES OF GROWTH FOR POTENTIAL COMPETITORS IN THE MARKET. EFFICIENCY HAS FAILED. ADAPTATION IS THE FUTURE. NOW IS THE TIME TO ADAPT TO THE DEMANDS AND POSSIBILITIES OF A NEW EPOCH.

IN UNDOING THE COLONIAL HOLD WE HAVE STEPPED, RESPECTFULLY, INTO THE INTERNATIONAL ARENA, BROKERING IN THE LAST TWO MONTHS TENATIVE TRADE AGREEMENTS AND TREATIES WITH SIX NATIONS IN BOTH HEMISPHERES. WE INTEND TO ATTRACT THE BRIGHTEST MINDS IN ECONOMICS IN A BID TO DIVERSIFY.

U.S. CABOTAGE STRICTURES IN PLACE SINCE THE EARLY 20TH CENTURY SHALL NO LONGER LIMIT OUR ABILITY TO CONDUCT TRADE FOR THE ECONOMIC WELL-BEING OF THE NATION. THE EFFECTS OF WHICH HAVE PARALYZED OUR ECONOMIC AGILITY AND SILENCED TRADE DIPLOMACY. OUR BORDERS ARE OUR OWN AND WE ARE PREPARED TO DEFEND THEM IF NEED BE AGAINST INTERVENING AGENTS. WE WILL NO LONGER TOLERATE THE EXTORTIONARY SERVICE OF THE U.S. MERCHANT MARINE—THE MOST COST-INEFFECTIVE MEDIUM FOR TRADE IN THE WORLD.

WE ARE ENACTING RIGOROUS NEW FISCAL POLICIES AND COUNTERCYCLICAL MEASURES WHICH PRESENTLY INCLUDE BROADENING THE TAX BASE AND RETURNING INCENTIVES LIKE A TEN-YEAR EXEMPTION FROM PROPERTY AND INSULAR INCOME TAX, MUNICIPAL TAX, AND EXCISE TAX FOR PRIVATE INVESTORS INTERESTED IN OUR CAPITAL OR OUR PORTS AS A MEANS OF ACCESS TO OTHER CAPITAL AND MARKETS, SUBSIDIES FOR CORPORATIONS THAT

ADHERE TO A THOUGHTFUL MANAGEMENT PROGRAM WHICH
MITIGATES REDUNDANCIES, MEETS AND EXCEEDS PRODUCTION
GOALS, AND STIMULATES EMPLOYEE DEVELOPMENT. I HAVE PER-
SONALLY REACHED OUT TO THE GENIUSES OF SILICON VALLEY
AND SILICON ALLEY. WITH NEW RESEARCH AND DEVELOPMENT
FACILITIES AS WELL AS FULL PRODUCTION FACTORIES WE CAN
SALVAGE OUR ECONOMY FROM INSOLVENCY. WE CAN MANAGE THE
PUBLIC DEBT BY INVESTING IN THE CREATION OF A 21ST-CENTURY
NATION, THEREBY LOWERING UNEMPLOYMENT TO SINGLE-DIGIT,
FRICTIONAL LEVELS.

PUERTO RICO'S 78 MUNICIPALITIES WILL REMAIN INTACT WITH
THE REGIONAL ADDITION AND DEMARCATION OF SIX UNIFYING
PROVINCES TO ESTABLISH A NEW UNICAMERAL LEGISLATURE. OUR
CONGRESS WILL OPERATE UNDER A SELECTED SOVEREIGN AU-
THORITY UNTIL ELECTIONS CAN BE SAFELY HELD. PARTY LINES
ARE BEING NEWLY DRAWN BASED ON THE SOVEREIGNTY OF OUR
PREVAILING GOVERNMENT. WE WILL APPOINT OUR OWN CHIEF
JUSTICES, SIX TO TRAVEL THE CIRCUIT BETWEEN EACH OF THE
NEWLY ESTABLISHED PROVINCES WITH ADDITIONAL APPEALS CON-
VENED IN THE CAPITAL. THE VAST MAJORITY OF LEGAL DECISIONS
WILL BE OFFICIATED BY THE BODY POLITIC BEYOND THE POWERS
OF OUR SOVEREIGN WHOSE SOLE TASK IN THESE COMING YEARS
WILL BE TO DEFEND OUR NATION AND PROCURE ALLIES, TRADING
PARTNERS, AND CULTURAL LIAISONS.

SEVERAL OF OUR CITIZENS HAVE DUAL CITIZENSHIP—THEY HAVE
BEEN ASKED TO MAKE A CHOICE.

FINALLY, WE HAVE TAKEN THE RIGHT TO EXPLORE AND DRILL OFF-
SHORE. WE HAVE KNOWN SINCE THE 1970S[3] THAT OUR SHORES
ARE POTENTIALLY OIL RICH. WE ARE ALSO PRESENTLY NEGOTI-
ATING TERMS WITH RESEARCHERS AND INVESTORS ABROAD RE-
GARDING THE FOUNDATION OF NUCLEAR ENERGY ON THE ISLAND.

WE HAVE THE RESOURCES AND INFRASTRUCTURE NECESSARY TO PURSUE ECOLOGICAL EQUILIBRIUM IN THE HOLOCENIC AGE. OUR UNIVERSITY SYSTEM IS MAKING GREAT STRIDES IN WATER PURIFICATION RESEARCH, DESALINIZING SEAWATER FOR CONSUMPTION AND ERADICATING DANGEROUS LEVELS OF MERCURY AND NUCLEAR WASTE.

IT IS CLEAR THAT WE MUST INVEST IN ALTERNATIVE ENERGY, WHETHER IN THE FORM OF SOLAR FIELDS OR WIND FARMS OFFSHORE, ON THE PLAINS, OR ON THE WINDWARD SIDES OF OUR MOUNTAIN RANGES. WE ARE AN ISLAND WITH FAVORABLE CONDITIONS FOR SUSTAINABLE ALTERNATIVE ENERGY. AND WE WILL SET THE EXAMPLE BY STANDING IN HONOR AND REVERENCE OF THE LAND WHICH NURTURES US.

I SHALL CONCLUDE WITH HISTORY. THE YEAR WAS 1901. THE CASE WAS *DOWNES VS. BIDWELL* (182 U.S.244). JUSTICE EDWARD DOUGLASS WHITE RULED THAT *PORTO RICO* WAS "FOREIGN IN A DOMESTIC SENSE." THIS RULING HAS COME TO DEFINE OUR RELATION TO THE SUZERAIN FOR THE PAST CENTURY AND HAS NOT SHOWN SIGNS OF CHANGING. POLITICAL SOVEREIGNTY IS THE FIRST STEP TOWARD REBUILDING WHAT HAS BEEN CONCEALED, CONCEDED, AND CONDEMNED. AS OF THIS MOMENT WE ARE NO LONGER CITIZENS OF THE UNITED STATES. ON THIS DAY THE WORLD WILL HEAR AND RECORD: WE ARE NO LONGER SUBJECT TO THE MISTREATMENT OF THE SUZERAIN. WE ARE A FREE AND INDEPENDENT STATE. WE ARE THE LAST POETS OF THESE AMERICAS—FIRST POETS OF THE NEW UNIVERSE.[4]

////\•/\\\\

8 OCTOBER XXOI
FROM NSA TRANSCRIPT   <T=00.01.56_00.06.43>

1.   CIA;   # alone.
2.   COLONEL;   This is coming. It's unavoidable. So let
me make you an offer. I can't stay here. I know what's coming.
American sympathizers and multiple citizenship holders are
being exiled. You've already lost. Paramilitary forces are mobilized. Plants and factories across the island have been evacuated
workers on strike. The people from top to bottom they
want this so I'll give you the time and place of our last move
provided I'm granted asylum. I'll give you the time and place.
3.   CIA;   Why^
4.   COLONEL;   Because. (.8) I'm American.
5.   CIA;   What exactly are you prepared to sacrifice for asylum^
6.   COLONEL;   The Adjutant General [will] be there.
7.   CIA;   [We]
8.   COLONEL;   He's gonna make things hard for us
moving forward # # gonna wanna shut him down quickly.
9.   CIA;   We don't make martyrs ~Colonel=
10.   COLONEL;   =@No @you @make @effigies
      @_<DUR=4.1>
11.   COLONEL;   And what else. (2.7) You don't negotiate with terrorists^ Let's be serious. I # mince words.
12.   CIA;   I fail to see how you can call yourself
American [more ab]surd that you would expect asylum.
13.   COLONEL;   [Because]
14.   CIA;   Conspiring against this country is a
criminal offense prosecuted on a federal level and punishable
[by death.]
15.   COLONEL;   [I am Am]erican. From
birth. And because it behooves you to accept this information #
the only lead you have.

16.   COLONEL;   America cannot afford to be internationally embarrassed as the last colonial power . . . @well . . .
the last colonial <u>entity</u> in the world. It would destroy an already
ailing public image and ruin international relations. I'm giving
you uh uh chance to salvage what little you have left of the great
white glory. Consider me your friend here.

17.   CIA;   What do you have for us^

18.   COLONEL;   The Adjutant General. What I can give
you is the time and place where you can find him. I feel like I'm
repeating myself.

19.   CIA;   And why are his whereabouts of any
importance to us^

20.   COLONEL;   Are you serious^ Try him. Hang him.
You'll need someone to answer for the things that have been
done and for the shit show you and I both <u>sus</u>:pect is going
down.

21.   CIA;   Suspect^ What do you think is stopping us from locating you now and taking your life^ And I
don't mean murder here. I mean your life in a matter of minutes
can be ours and however tough you think you are (1.6) you'll
be wishing your pissant father pulled out and your whore of a
mother never gave birth to you.

22.   COLONEL;   Easy now ~Agent Smith. My mother
isn't a whore per se. She wasn't paid for her work. She was more
like an intern in the industry. But I'm honored that you'd think
so highly of her.

23.   CIA;   We know who you are ~Colonel. And
now that we know what you want we can do this the easy way
or the hard way. You're going to give us what we want and if it is
to our satisfaction then we may grant your request for asylum.
Is that clear^

24.   COLONEL;   So kind. So American.

25.   CIA;   Your provisionary budget must be
running low by now. I'm sure you know. And this blockade

can't be good for trade. We've got you locked down so tight
you're gonna have to ask our permission to pass wind. You're in
no position to be making demands °friend.

    (4.3)

26.   CIA;   We've frozen your assets and I imagine
Millie isn't very happy about that.

    (7.7)

27.   CIA;   Yes we're very familiar with Millie.
Such a won::derful artist. And your eldest son. Ason. He's going
to be a great architect one day. Maybe. Who knows. Maybe not.
Who can say really. We managed to make it out to one of his
swim meets at Stuyvesant. He took second in the individual
medley. And Ridgely Torrence. He looks just like you. Has your
nose.

    (6.9)

28.   CIA;   And correct me if I'm wrong but there's
another little ⌐Colonel on the way. Right^

29.   COLONEL;   [·hhhhh]

30.   CIA;   [In fact I] [saw t]he sonogram:. I bet
you'd like to know if it's a boy or if it's a girl.

31.   COLONEL;   [₂hhhh]

**** BEGIN LOGGING AT Wed **Oct 07 07:05:11** xx01

Oct 07 07:05:11 sabu what you niggas been doing without me
Oct 07 07:05:20 storm owning 2600.net
Oct 07 07:05:21 storm about it
Oct 07 07:05:39 sabu jEa
Oct 07 07:05:51 * Sabu gives channel operator status to [redacted] value Topiary lol

**** ENDING LOGGING AT Wed **Oct 07 07:05:51** xx01

**** BEGIN LOGGING AT Thu **Oct 08 13:24:31** xx01

Oct 08 13:24:31 sabu get your boxes ready
Oct 08 13:24:35 sabu I want you to hit them
Oct 08 13:24:59 sabu storm hit their ircds again
Oct 08 13:25:04 sabu take out collection
Oct 08 13:25:05 sabu and madjack
Oct 08 13:25:44 joepie92 - madjack.2600.net ------------------
--------------- | Users: 104 (19.6%)
Oct 08 13:25:44 joepie92 - '- blackbeard.2600.net -------------
------------- | Users: 0 (0.0%)
Oct 08 13:25:44 joepie92 - |- collective.2600.net --------------
-------- | Users: 252 (47.5%)
Oct 08 13:25:44 joepie92 - |- djslocker.2600.net ---------------
-------- | Users: 166 (31.3%)
Oct 08 13:25:44 joepie92 - '- services.2600.net ---------------
-------- | Users: 9 (1.7%)

**** ENDING LOGGING AT Thu **Oct 08 13:25:44** xx01

**** BEGIN LOGGING AT Thu **Oct 08 16:23:01** xx01

Oct 08 16:23:01 <neuron_> is Fox trustable?
Oct 08 16:23:02 pwnsauce Sabu - as far as he knows im some random
Oct 08 16:23:04 sabu consider yourselves lucky no one really gets to see me work in action
Oct 08 16:23:14 sabu no one is trustable outside out crew
Oct 08 16:23:17 sabu remember that neuron
Oct 08 16:23:20 sabu our*
Oct 08 16:25:11 trollpoll well, is clear that in #lulzsec channel the half part of them are feds . . .
Oct 08 16:25:26 sabu yup
Oct 08 16:25:45 trollpoll btw who is nakomis?
Oct 08 16:25:48 trollpoll lol?
Oct 08 16:25:57 Topiary some Anonfag
Oct 08 16:25:58 sabu hes some airforce guy thats "anon"
Oct 08 16:26:00 sabu you know
Oct 08 16:26:05 <neuron_> ahh
Oct 08 16:26:06 sabu hes airforce intelligence right topiary?
Oct 08 16:26:08 sabu thats what he told me
Oct 08 16:26:11 sabu airforce
Oct 08 16:26:16 Topiary not sure, seen him on TinyChat
Oct 08 16:26:22 Topiary the person who made that Anon wiki thinks he's with us
Oct 08 16:26:29 sabu who made that
Oct 08 16:26:34 Topiary nonynews
Oct 08 16:26:40 Topiary we got IPs
Oct 08 16:26:48 Topiary they listed you and nakomis as my "associates"
Oct 08 16:27:13 trollpoll ok
Oct 08 16:28:41 Topiary we're gonna be using that 2600 chan as a way of correlating data from AnonOps' past/wikis
Oct 08 16:28:44 Topiary to assess spies

Oct 08 16:28:52 **Topiary** it's a front really
Oct 08 16:28:42 trollpoll nakomis is the name of a novel character of Katherine Neville
Oct 08 16:28:46 trollpoll Nakomis Key
Oct 08 16:28:49 trollpoll and . . . is a girl.
Oct 08 16:30:01 **sabu** this guy fox
Oct 08 16:30:04 **sabu** might be bullshit
Oct 08 16:30:11 **sabu** may even better jester himself
Oct 08 16:30:26 **Topiary** mm
Oct 08 16:30:28 **Topiary** crossed my mind
Oct 08 16:30:33 **[redacted]** netjester
Oct 08 16:31:02 pwnsauce I'm being nice to hom
Oct 08 16:31:08 pwnsauce *him
Oct 08 16:31:16 pwnsauce going to get ALL his goodies
Oct 08 16:31:22 **Topiary** by all means sap shit out of him
Oct 08 16:31:29 **Topiary** if he is a spy, he'll do that to gain trust
Oct 08 16:31:53 pwnsauce exactly
Oct 08 16:31:57 pwnsauce TBH
Oct 08 16:32:09 pwnsauce im just goodierping
Oct 08 16:34:18 **sabu** HAHAHHAAHA
Oct 08 16:34:20 **sabu** I JUST FIGUREDO UT
Oct 08 16:34:21 **sabu** WHO HE IS
Oct 08 16:34:22 **sabu** AHAHAHAH
Oct 08 16:34:26 **sabu** Faggot.s
Oct 08 16:35:07 **sabu** dude
Oct 08 16:35:09 **sabu** he fucked up
Oct 08 16:35:15 pwnsauce yeag I know
Oct 08 16:35:18 **sabu** <@Fox> xxxx@SECRETFUCKING-LAIR # ~$cat nmapawesomeness
Oct 08 16:35:18 pwnsauce "xxxx"
Oct 08 16:35:18 **sabu** <@Fox> nmap -P0 -sS -sV -O -A --defeat-rst-ratelimit -F ip_address
Oct 08 16:35:18 **sabu** <@Fox> The other one is a xerobank VPN set

Oct 08 16:35:18 sabu <brazil> all I see is a nmap line

Oct 08 16:35:18 sabu <@Fox> I'll package up the VPN information here in a few

Oct 08 16:35:18 sabu <@also-cocks> this is a superfast nmap string . . .

Oct 08 16:35:18 sabu <@also-cocks> by the looks of it

Oct 08 16:35:18 sabu <@Fox> I <3 that string.

Oct 08 16:35:18 sabu <@also-cocks> it rm-s the RST limit so it scans faster

Oct 08 16:35:18 sabu <@also-cocks> hmmmm

Oct 08 16:35:18 sabu <brazil> xxxx you still got access to xxxxxxxxx?

Oct 08 16:35:18 sabu <@Fox> lol, I can, but not at this second.

Oct 08 16:35:18 sabu <@Fox> por que?

Oct 08 16:35:18 sabu <brazil> they have a few targets I'd like to own :)

Oct 08 16:35:21 pwnsauce florida

Oct 08 16:35:22 sabu ROFL

Oct 08 16:35:34 sabu he just admitted oh man

Oct 08 16:35:36 pwnsauce Sabu - xxxx, Florida, Smokes,

Oct 08 16:35:36 sabu oh so bad

Oct 08 16:35:45 pwnsauce 53rd ewg

Oct 08 16:35:48 pwnsauce who is he?

Oct 08 16:35:59 sabu xxxxx xx xxxx

Oct 08 16:36:00 sabu lol

Oct 08 16:36:06 joepie91 wat

Oct 08 16:36:22 sabu hahahahahah

Oct 08 16:36:26 sabu if this is the real xxx x

Oct 08 16:36:29 sabu we have a gold mind

Oct 08 16:36:31 sabu mine

Oct 08 16:36:48 pwnsauce :O

Oct 08 16:36:49 joepie91 wait

Oct 08 16:36:49 joepie91 so

Oct 08 16:36:52 joepie91 you are talking

Oct 08 16:36:53 joepie91 to xxxxx xx xxxx
Oct 08 16:36:54 joepie91 ?
Oct 08 16:36:57 trollpoll creech afb? omg
Oct 08 16:36:57 sabu I know he's starting to regret coming in here
Oct 08 16:36:58 sabu or rather
Oct 08 16:36:58 sabu hes regretting
Oct 08 16:37:02 sabu that I even fucking logged on that irc
Oct 08 16:37:07 sabu I figured his whole shit out
Oct 08 16:37:08 sabu rofl
Oct 08 16:37:18 * joepie91 palmfaces
Oct 08 16:40:23 * Disconnected (Remote host closed socket).

**** ENDING LOGGING AT Thu **Oct 8 16:40:23** xx01

**** BEGIN LOGGING AT Thu **Oct 8 16:56:21** xx01

Oct 08 16:56:21 sabu make sure we take advantage of that
Oct 08 16:56:25 sabu see what n1ggers got access to
Oct 08 16:56:27 sabu that we can use
Oct 08 16:56:49 joepie92 #xxxx has passed the point where it's better to simply scorch the earth and create a new system from scratch.
Oct 08 16:56:53 kl0ps unvalidated reports that xxxxxx has hacked into #xxxx Nice trick to gain notoriety.
Oct 08 16:56:54 kl0ps wtf does that mean?
Oct 08 16:56:54 storm i just read the twitter
Oct 08 16:56:59 kl0ps WUR FAMOUZ

**** ENDING LOGGING AT Thu **Oct 8 16:56:59** xx01

Alden Pyle
@Alden_Pyle25 FOLLOWS YOU

Alden Pyle (@Alden_Pyle25). "I wishe d there existed someone
to whom I could say that I was sorry"
18 JUNE XXOI, 3:42 a.m. Tweet

Alden Pyle (@Alden_Pyle25). "How coul d one explain the
dreariness of the whole business:"
18 JUNE XXOI, 3:50 a.m. Tweet

Alden Pyle (@Alden_Pyle25). ". . . the private a rmy of
twenty-five thousand men, armed with mortars made
out of the exhaust-pipes of old cars . . ."
18 JUNE XXOI, 3:53 a.m. Tweet

Alden Pyle (@Alden_Pyle25). "From ch ildhood I had never
believed in permanence, and yet I had longed for it."
18 JUNE XXOI, 3:57 a.m. Tweet

Alden Pyle (@Alden_Pyle25). "Always I was afraid o f losing
happiness."
18 JUNE XXOI, 4:12 a.m. Tweet

Alden Pyle (@Alden_Pyle25). "one for gets so quickly one's own
youth"
18 JUNE XXOI, 4:30 a.m. Tweet

Thomas Fowler (@Fowler_Thom58). "Why . . . tea se the
innocent?"
2 JULY XXOI, 2:01 p.m. Reply

Alden Pyle (@Alden_Pyle25). "absorbe d already in the
dilemmas of Democracy"
6 JULY XXOI, 2:04 p.m. Tweet

Thomas Fowler (@Fowler_Thom58). "and the responsibilities of the West?"
8 JULY XXOI, 2:02 p.m. Reply

Alden Pyle (@Alden_Pyle25). "'Between six and ten.'"
8 JULY XXOI, 9:46 p.m. Tweet

Alden Pyle (@Alden_Pyle25). "determi ned . . . to do good, not to any individual person but to a country"
8 JULY XXOI, 10:07 p.m. Tweet

Thomas Fowler (@Fowler_Thom58). "a continent, a world—I learnt that very soon"
9 JULY XXOI, 8:43 a.m. Reply

Thomas Fowler (@Fowler_Thom58). "I got u p and went to the bookshelf."
9 july xx01, 8:50 a.m. Reply

Alden Pyle (@Alden_Pyle25). "'I had a drink at the Continental at six.'"
11 JULY XXOI, 9:09 p.m. Tweet

Alden Pyle (@Alden_Pyle25). "'The wai ters will remember.'"
12 JULY XXOI, 12:34 p.m. Tweet

Thomas Fowler (@Fowler_Thom58). "'Would you mind ident ifying him? I'm sorry. It's a routine, not a very nice routine.'"
15 JULY XXOI, 1:12 p.m. Reply

Alden Pyle (@Alden_Pyle25). "'Not at all.'"
15 JULY XXOI, 2:00 p.m. Reply

Alden Pyle (@Alden_Pyle25). "I suppo se you arrived about
eight thirty—"
24 JULY XXOI, 10:05 a.m. Tweet

Thomas Fowler (@Fowler_Thom58). "'At six forty-five I walked
down to the quay to watch the American planes
unloaded.'"
24 JULY XXOI, 12:56 p.m. Reply

Thomas Fowler (@Fowler_Thom58). "I must have dined within
fifty yards of his body"
24 JULY XXOI, 1:01 p.m. Reply

Alden Pyle (@Alden_Pyle25). "'God save us a lways,' I said,
'from the innocent and the good.'"
10 AUGUST XXOI, 4:30 a.m. Tweet

Alden Pyle (@Alden_Pyle25). "We went out behind the church
in single file, th e lieutenant leading"
10 AUGUST XXOI, 4:32 a.m. Tweet

Alden Pyle (@Alden_Pyle25). "halted for a moment on a canal
bank for the soldier with the walkietalkie to get contact
with the patrols on either flank"
10 AUGUST XXOI, 4:34 a.m. Tweet

Thomas Fowler (@Fowler_Thom58). "'Where is Pyle?'"
11 AUGUST XXOI, 7:30 p.m. Reply

Thomas Fowler (@Fowler_Thom58). "Didn't Pyle always go his
own way?"
12 AUGUST XXOI, 10:10 a.m. Reply

Phuong (@KhmerMon). "Well, h e was in his element now with the whole universe to improve."
14 AUGUST XXOI, 10:45 a.m. Reply

Phuong (@KhmerMon). "the opi um reasoned within me."
18 AUGUST XXOI, 8:08 p.m. Reply

Phuong (@KhmerMon). "Aren't we all better dead?"
18 AUGUST XXOI, 8:11 p.m. Reply

Phuong (@KhmerMon). "in adva nce of the Far East and the problems of China."
18 AUGUST XXOI, 8:16 p.m. Reply

Alden Pyle (@Alden_Pyle25). "My pape r would get the news first under a Paris date-line."
25 AUGUST XXOI, 6:21 a.m. Tweet

Thomas Fowler (@Fowler_Thom58). "'Come h ome,' I said."
25 AUGUST XXOI, 9:04 a.m. Reply

Phuong (@KhmerMon). "'Trop f atigué.'"
25 AUGUST XXOI, 9:07 a.m. Reply

Alden Pyle (@Alden_Pyle25). "'No, D ominguez. Just leave me alone tonight.'"
25 AUGUST XXOI, 9:10 p.m. Tweet

Alden Pyle (@Alden_Pyle25). "the best in Indo-Chin a, flown over the late battlefield at a height of 3,000 feet"
31 AUGUST XXOI, 7:58 a.m. Tweet

Alden Pyle (@Alden_Pyle25). "'Three hundred have been reported in this village here."
1 SEPTEMBER XXOI, 8:12 a.m. Tweet

Thomas Fowler (@Fowler_Thom58). "'Murder and sudden death?'"
1 SEPTEMBER XXOI, 9:14 a.m. Reply

Alden Pyle (@Alden_Pyle25). "'No. Petty the fts. And a few suicides.'"
4 SEPTEMBER XXOI, 3:33 p.m. Tweet

Alden Pyle (@Alden_Pyle25). "Harding wrote about a third force."
4 SEPTEMBER XXOI, 3:59 p.m. Tweet

Thomas Fowler (@Fowler_Thom58). "a shodd y little bandit with two thousand men and a couple of tame tigers. He got mixed up."
5 SEPTEMBER XXOI, 7:20 p.m. Reply

Alden Pyle (@Alden_Pyle25). "'It was at five to seven that you walked to Wilkins.'"
7 SEPTEMBER XXOI, 6:43 a.m. Tweet

Alden Pyle (@Alden_Pyle25). "'Anothe r ten minutes.'"
7 SEPTEMBER XXOI, 7:00 a.m. Tweet

Alden Pyle (@Alden_Pyle25). "'And it had only just struck six when you arrived at the Continental.'"
7 SEPTEMBER XXOI, 7:10 a.m. Tweet

Thomas Fowler (@Fowler_Thom58). "'What t ime do you make it now?'"
7 SEPTEMBER XXOI, 8:00 a.m. Reply

Alden Pyle (@Alden_Pyle25). "'Ten ei ght.'"
7 SEPTEMBER XXOI, 8:34 a.m. Tweet

Thomas Fowler (@Fowler_Thom58). "'Perhap s we'd better cancel that dinner.'"
15 SEPTEMBER XXOI, 7:02 p.m. Reply

Alden Pyle (@Alden_Pyle25). "'No, do n't do that.'"
16 SEPTEMBER XXOI, 7:13 p.m. Tweet

Alden Pyle (@Alden_Pyle25). "'In a way you could say they died for democracy,'"
16 SEPTEMBER XXOI, 7:25 p.m. Tweet

Alden Pyle (@Alden_Pyle25). "'You kept it up all r ight, even after your leg was smashed you stayed neutral.'"
19 SEPTEMBER XXOI, 2:09 a.m. Tweet

Thomas Fowler (@Fowler_Thom58). "'There' s always a point of change,'"
19 SEPTEMBER XXOI, 3:00 a.m. Reply

Thomas Fowler (@Fowler_Thom58). "'Some m oment of emotion . . .'"
19 SEPTEMBER XXOI, 3:06 a.m. Reply

Alden Pyle (@Alden_Pyle25). "'You ha ven't reached it yet. I doubt if you ever will.'"
21 SEPTEMBER XXOI, 4:37 a.m. Tweet

Alden Pyle (@Alden_Pyle25). "'And I' m not likely to change either—except with death,' he added merrily."
21 SEPTEMBER XXOI, 4:40 a.m. Tweet

Thomas Fowler (@Fowler_Thom58). "'It was a pity, but you can't always hit your target.'"
22 SEPTEMBER XXOI, 3:30 p.m. Reply

Thomas Fowler (@Fowler_Thom58). "'Anyway they died in the right cause.'"
30 SEPTEMBER XXOI, 4:12 p.m. Reply

Thomas Fowler (@Fowler_Thom58). "'I left it to Dominguez.'"
2 OCTOBER XXOI, 3:09 p.m. Reply

Thomas Fowler (@Fowler_Thom58). "I walke d down to the Majestic and stood awhile watching the unloading of the American bombers."
6 OCTOBER XXOI, 2:00 a.m. Reply

Thomas Fowler (@Fowler_Thom58). "Against   my will I listened:"
6 OCTOBER XXOI, 2:02 a.m. Reply

Alden Pyle (@Alden_Pyle25). "a shot?"
7 OCTOBER XXOI, 5:54 a.m. Tweet

Alden Pyle (@Alden_Pyle25). "some mo vement"
7 OCTOBER XXOI, 6:00 a.m. Tweet

Thomas Fowler (@Fowler_Thom58). "'I got   a cable this morning from my wife.'"
8 OCTOBER XXOI, 10:23 p.m. Reply

Alden Pyle (@Alden_Pyle25). "'Yes?'"
8 OCTOBER XXOI, 11:00 p.m. Tweet

Thomas Fowler (@Fowler_Thom58). "'My son' s got polio. He's bad.'"
8 OCTOBER XXOI, 11:09 p.m. Reply

Alden Pyle (@Alden_Pyle25). "'Has Mo nsieur Vigot been to see you?'"
8 OCTOBER XXOI, 11:46 p.m. Tweet

Thomas Fowler (@Fowler_Thom58). "'Yes. He left a quarter of an hour ago.'"
9 OCTOBER XXOI, 12:02 a.m. Reply

Alden Pyle (@Alden_Pyle25). "'Was the film good?'"
9 OCTOBER XXOI, 12:13 a.m. Tweet

Thomas Fowler (@Fowler_Thom58). "'It was very sad,' she said, 'but the colors were lovely.'"
9 OCTOBER XXOI, 12:20 a.m. Reply

Alden Pyle (@Alden_Pyle25). "'Are you ready to smoke?'"
9 OCTOBER XXOI, 12:24 a.m. Tweet

Thomas Fowler (@Fowler_Thom58). "'Yes.'"
9 OCTOBER XXOI, 12:30 a.m. Reply

Thomas Fowler (@Fowler_Thom58). "Christ and Buddha looking down from the roof of the Cathedral on a Walt Disney fantasia of the East, dragons and snakes in technicolor"
9 OCTOBER XXOI, 12:34 a.m. Reply

Thomas Fowler (@Fowler_Thom58). "A mosquito droned to the attack and I watched Phuong"
9 OCTOBER XXOI, 12:38 a.m. Reply

Thomas Fowler (@Fowler_Thom58). "'Pyle est Mort. Assassiné.'"
9 OCTOBER XXOI, 12:40 a.m. Reply

Thomas Fowler (@Fowler_Thom58). "The canal was full of
bodies:"
9 OCTOBER XXOI, 12:41 a.m. Reply

vi. Poshlost

14 OCTOBER XXOI [TRANSIT] Waxing crescent, it fluttered between the black boughs of the trees as she drove through the mountains. Pitched toward the evening star like a cuticle, setting brightly behind the peaks to an invention of blue neither rightly of night nor day.

She slowed to take another blind curve on PR-14, north-westward bound for the Arecibo Observatory, highbeams flooding the fore.

The jeep she was driving, a red Willy's, belonged to her father. It was a refurbished military model that needed considerable attention and a new paint job, but which served its purpose, getting her safely from point A to point B along the narrow winding thoroughfares of the mountain. And not without trailing a noxious haze of exhaust in its wake. In the passenger seat sat her sidearm and a brown weekender the Colonel advised her not to open until she reached Arecibo. The bag weighed next to nothing. It was to be transferred confidentially to her contact.

The jeep itself was an object charged with memory. She could remember sitting in the passenger seat while her father drove them to the Festival de las flores, hardly nervous that she'd fall out of the jeep as they passed within inches of the steep cliffs of the mountain. It was their day together. No nanny. Just the two of them. She could remember looking up at him in the driver's seat, steely-eyed with the window down, his dark hair caught in the wind. His right hand at twelve on the wheel, manicured. His right arm abar between them. My baby, he'd say looking over lovingly. Her father was a capable driver. He was confident, vigilant without being overly cautious, and he knew the roads well. He took each turn and hill so smoothly and quickly that as a child she might have believed they were on a track, on some sort of auto-pilot which took them without fail to their destination. The notion of her mortality, trundling those verdant high-wire passages, never crossed her mind.

They drove in relative silence. He with his eyes on the road and she absorbing as much of the vista as she could with her own wide green eyes. Vines hung between palisades of bamboo and mangos fell strewn across the roads. If they managed radio reception it was Ismael Rivera or Lucecita Benítez's voice that broke through the static—the two voices she most remembered from childhood. Rivera was for them what Marvin Gaye was for Americans. He was remembered as an archetype of the artist, a walking contradiction of moral conscience often tempted by temptation. Lustful and tender. Soulful and synthetic. Lucecita was another artist-archetype, a kind of marvelous shape-shifter. She vaguely remembered seeing Lucecita on the tube sporting a natural. Hers was a powerful almost masculine voice. In the seventies she had undertaken the national question and the music she produced in that period survived as a high-water mark of cultural consciousness.

Frances could remember the music and its place in her early childhood fondly. The last years of the sixties in America birthed the Black Power movement. How much of that newfound race consciousness had to do with the marketability of American influence and how much of it was authentically born of the island? She couldn't tell anymore. Where one started and the other stopped.

She was coming up on the turn. A tight bend left. The jeep lurched forward as she leaned on the brake, grabbed the stick, then popped the clutch to shift gear. But she timed it poorly, overeager perhaps, her mind and body still bathed in the heavy levity of laudanum—*Krzzzzt*—then the tussive scrape of mishandled manual transmission. The engine stalled and the car rolled of its own accord quickly toward the turn, propelled now by God and gravity.

She was strapped into the machine trying to engage the clutch, trying to pull the engine out of its stall. The machine rattled. Panicked, her arms and legs in damp freefall from the tincture of opium, she was at once acutely aware of impending death and physically laggard, incapable—dread palpitations in her chest as she struggled to decide whether her right hand should remain on the stick or move to free her from the seat so she could jump to safety. There was no guardrail, just what looked like a small row of stones beyond which radiated the last light of the moon.

The buckle was jammed. The rattle of the machine happening in real time registered as if not. Its sound slowed and bending. She was overwhelmed by a kind of familiar fallow surging through her nasal passage, settling on her palate like the yellow currency of confessing her sins as a girl to her father. She could barely remember what sins—cursing at a classmate, lusting for her cousin's attention, stealing jewelry from her mother's belongings—only that feelings of guilt kept her up at night anxious and weeping. She remembered feeling like a disappointment to her father, who she thought could sense even the slightest defilement of her innocence. She remembered holding the immensity of that feeling for days before she could answer for it.

No matter the gravity of the sin she would walk to the chicken coope, running her fingers along the wire, to claim from the nests a small yellow chick, soft and fragile, and hold its docile warmth in her palms until she found audience with her father. Standing before him, a giant of a man, she'd uncup her palms and present with doleful eyes her penance. A little yellow chick to say I'm sorry. She couldn't remember the logic of her doing so, or even if there was a logic behind it, or the origin of the thought in her imagination. She could only remember that the embodiment of this kind of yellow signified for her, and then for her father, an entreatment to forgive. The same kind of yellow that adorned the façade of La Casa.

La Casa was a gift from her father for her quinceañera, 1990. It was renovated from the old slave quarter, painted yellow, and modestly decorated for her blind-folded arrival following the ceremony. It was the only part of the family estate left. She spent the best days of her teenage years in the little house, which grew into her home. As a child the small house on the outskirts of the estate scared her, but her father somehow managed to exorcise its demons and make it a new and habitable place. She liked to believe her father chose that hue of yellow as a reminder that she, as an adult, had nothing to apologize for. She built a life over all of that penance.

Looking at it before leaving for the Observatory, even in the darkness, filled her with an odd wistfulness like she'd never see it again. The house faded to black in her mirrors as she drove away down the gravel path to the main road on orders.

How she felt there in those days before the revolution, swaddled in blankets and candlelight on the carpet beside Sam, watching volutes of smoke curl from a filtered cigarette. The air was thick with Parliament and body odor, a bright and bitter smell that filled them both beneath the smoke with electricity.

Let's have a baby

Dr. Ruth says that if the man comes first it'll be a girl and if the woman comes first it'll be a boy Or vice versa Ya no recuerdo.

Who

Dr. Ruth La judía vieja esa que habla de sex y quéséyo She's old and funny and little Has an accent

Oh right I know her I love the diagrams in her books The women are drawn so confident and toned and it's like they look a little impish and their breasts are perky

Graciosa

Breasts like we used to have

Sam pushed her breasts together, mashing them to pornographic pertness. Then she let go and laughed at the sight of them falling to the side. Frances didn't laugh. To her, Sam's breasts had the enviable buoyancy of a woman half her age. Candlelight, yellow and clipping, elongated Sam's nose in profile and threw her dossed shadow to dance against the wall. Like the projection of a map. Her body, a nation with a name, with borders and law. Her culture, an underbite. What imaginations sleep unhasped from her lips.

Sam had just moved in. She was everything Frances felt she could never be. Devil-may-care, almost gothic, Sam was foil to Frances' practiced manner. She was a graphic designer and fashion photographer born and raised in the States, based out of New York City, well-regarded with moderate fame. She was, by one editor's estimation in Elle magazine, ". . . the best-kept

secret in Manhattan fashion . . . a consummate professional . . .
a taste-maker with the Midas touch whose work, in her lifetime, will garner all of the praise her genius deserves." All of her
recognition was won under the working name Doris N. Vian,
born 1996.

To those who knew her well, she was born in New York City,
1979, Samantha Martinez Viguié. Her family held passports
from the United States, Spain, and France, though she, only in
the United States and France. Her father was a French national,
her mother a veterinarian from Ponce.

That they had grown up so near each other, entirely oblivious,
made for hours of talk in awe of serendipity. She spent much
of her childhood summering at the family ranch in Aibonito,
where her mother bred and raised Paso Fino horses. Sam liked
to say that she learned everything about feminine politesse from
those "prancing pansy" horses, and in saying so let silence settle
in the conversation like the ghost of her mother. She never spoke
Spanish. Not with Frances.

Sam tossed the blankets off and sat upright, taking slow drags of
her cigarette. Slowly she rose from the carpet and tiptoed over to
the stove top. She ashed the cigarette in a red earthenware tray
between the back burners. She opened the cabinet above the
stove and grabbed her usual mug. The cabinets were lined with
canned meats, tuna, spam, beans, soups. There were packets of
oatmeal and vacuum-sealed bags of crackers. From the floor
Frances lay in full view of her back, the dramatic curvature of
her shoulders, the hillock of her ass which descended into her
thighs, her calves, the cushion of her heels, while her arms remained busy over the counter. Her skin looked like velvet in the
light. Frances listened for the naked clink of glass on glass as Sam
let the spout of her laudanum dropper touch the rim of the mug.

Want coffee

Frances hesitated thinking of the laudanum, how it would slide down the inside of the mug, circle the base, then diffuse—how Sam would add another drop. She looked at Frances over her left shoulder and asked again, this time impatiently.

Want coffee

No Not now

Frances, feeling understood, closed her eyes to the smell of coffee and smoke and hid in the eigenlicht, absconding with her treasures into the last private corner of a seamlessly integrated world. They were lovers among a generation grown accustomed to cold-war cuisine and the sweet smell of gasoline. In the morning they planned on driving into Ponce for a portable generator.

Do you still want to meet my father tomorrow

Of course baby

The coffee was percolating. Sam turned to face Frances lying with her eyes still closed on the carpet, her head resting on her elbow in a thrill of quietude.

After every fourth breath Frances inhaled deeply and released an inaudible sigh, being neither asleep nor awake. She lay curled in fetal position beneath the blankets. Her dark hair on the floor above her head spilled over the edge of the carpet, each loose strand winding almost into the grain. Fine hair like peach fuzz along the soft swoop of her jaw trapped light, giving her cheek a feyish glow.

They met at Hunter College, Manhattan, in the early aughts. Professors Juan Flores and Edgardo Rodríguez Juliá were reading from a newly published bilingual edition of *El entierro de Cortijo*. Professor Miriam Jiménez Román sat in the front row wearing a thoughtful expression. She was flanked on her right by students buzzing with small talk or gossip. At her left sat Juliá with his legs crossed and arms folded over his lap, holding a frayed and bookmarked proof of the original. Beside Juliá, at his left, was an empty chair presumably saved for Flores.

The gray walls of the library conference room, where the reading was held, were decorated with handsomely framed mid-century ICP sponsored works by Lorenzo Homar and Rafael Tufiño. Beneath one of Homar's works, a soulful wood-cut portrait of Betances, was a table arranged with an assortment of finger foods, plastic cutlery, plates, napkins, cocktail cups, and various canned soft drinks. The room was relatively cool, sweater weather, and was everywhere lit by white fluorescent light. It must have been around six p.m.

Frances sat third chair from the left in the third row. It was a modest audience, with one or two empty seats between attendees. In her row, three seats to her right, was an older woman wearing thick prescription lenses in tortoise-shell frames and an authentic Hermes scarf. In the row in front of her were three students. None of them seemed friendly. The row behind her was empty. The reading started a few minutes later than scheduled, making room for those unfortunate few "delayed by traffic" to arrive without significantly distracting the readers and audience. In fact most of the people in attendance had arrived and settled into the audience during this grace period. A handful of students holding notepads sat on the carpeted floor with their backs against the walls. Their open bookbags were tossed casually beside them.

Flores was already minutes into an introduction of Juliá. He spoke quickly, but precisely, evidence of a mind always at work, and shared the warm joy of his character by making eye contact with members of the audience. Flores was an engaging speaker, methodical, analytical, and always, it seemed, on the verge of laughing his distinctly hearty laugh.

When he finished the introduction, which was followed by a round of applause for Juliá and his esteemed presence, Flores felt ready to begin reading directly from his translation. He considered some exposition, but decided to leave it for the Q&A session following the reading. The audience would then have an opportunity to ask them both about their collaborative effort in translation, and about the man himself, Rafael Cortijo.

Flores was about to begin reading from his translation when she walked in. She could remember Sam, so fashionably late and clad entirely in black, gliding into the room unhurried, as if they were all waiting on her. He paused for a moment, distracted by her presence, which seemed to command the attention of everyone in the room. Possessed with grave beauty. Six feet tall in boots with the piercing gaze of a supermodel and the obnoxious self-assurance of an athlete, Sam had inspired a palpable breathlessness.

After scanning the room for her seat, Sam sat one chair behind and to the left of Frances, who sat in the wake of her scent, musk, leather, smoke. Attentions returned to Flores, who was tempted to say something clever about the latecomer, but chose not to. Instead, he commenced reading.

She could remember him standing in front of the room, reading at the podium, and reading not quickly, but at an unusually quick pace.

She could remember at some point feeling Sam's breath behind her when the leggy stranger released a sigh, so near she could almost taste it.

She could remember the view from Sam's apartment, overlooking the Manhattan Bridge, and waking up to the smell of Bustelo and breakfast.

That was then. It still felt surreal to have her so near, nude, so tangibly new in the new year, preparing her coffee. Stranger still, the lithe fantasy that walked into the reading room dressed in black leather pants and salt-streaked boots, four years later, remained a revelation. The actualization of a yearning which went nameless until it announced its presence in her life.

Sam shut the stove, careful not to overbrew. She took the percolator from the stove. Frances could hear the hot rush of coffee poured as Sam filled her mug. Frances could set her watch to the ritual, blinking one two three times for each spoonful of sugar, then the twelve full revolutions the teaspoon made around the bowl of the mug.

Sam turned to face Frances. She held the steaming mug in both hands against her bottom lip. She blew lightly over its surface.

Frances sat at attention, letting go of the blanket. It fell from her breast, the fabric brushing her nipples. She watched as Sam blew steam from her mug, her legs crossed, her ass perched on the edge of the counter. Her eyes drifted down Sam's torso, over her stomach, into light glancing over the soft hair of her mons. Warmth spread.

Sam's sexual appetite was impressive. Everything ranging from trashy passions to decadent and formal evenings, Sam seemed always in the mood. Frances, no stranger to sex, initially felt challenged by Sam's apparent insatiability. She felt sloppy and overindulgent, sometimes inferior, having sex so often and at the whim of another woman. Not typically a position she enjoyed. On occasion she felt intimidated by Sam's forward behavior. Intimidation gave way to feelings of violation. A kind of baseness. Dirtiness. Being fingered sub-rosa, for example, in the passenger's seat. En route. That kind of tawdry arrogance went against her breeding, but the thrill was marvelous. A verboten feeling Frances wasn't quite used to which functioned for her as insurance against boredom.

She watched Sam curl and uncurl her toes, feline, as the silly weep of the opiate's slow onset grid in her a giddy muscular dissociation. The shutters were still. The air, curious, came in to trouble the lit wicks of the candles.

Sam put her coffee aside. Her body flushed as she approached Frances. The weight of her heels against the wood sent chills up Frances' spine; the bass of each gamine footfall rummaging her thighs. Tall and cool, Sam stopped and stood inches from Frances's lips.

Frances sat between Sam's long legs appraising her body, her knees ashy and forelegs dotted with bruise marks like cigarette burns. Likely scabs that weren't allowed to heal. She marveled at Sam's figure. How her skin stretched like canvas over the bone frame of her pelvis. The pale and precise curvature of her underbreast. Discolored skin that formed a thundercloud on her right hip. Sam hung slightly long and flared. Slick. Swelling.

Frances felt the beginnings like an ache, then a swell of pressure between her thighs, her nipples puffed and erect. She could taste the scent of Sam's pussy, radiating heat, bilirubinic excess.

Peering up at Sam, at the excited peaks of her breasts, feeling their fullness against the convexity of her pupil, her mouth began to water.

She slid Sam's fingers into her mouth. The nails were soiled, a dark ridge beneath each. She passed her tongue across the tips and under each nail, sucking from them oil and residue.

She slipped them from her mouth like warm nothing, a cord of spit dangling from her bottom lip. When it snapped she brushed the tip of her nose against Sam's engorged clit—perfectly smooth, dark pink, waiting to be touched.

Frances took the woman on her tongue, balancing the pubic bone on the delicate protrusion of her chin. She forced her tongue inside, thrusting in and out, tonguing the walls. Sam's knees bent as she began to roll her hips against Frances' lips, willing the tongue deeper inside, their borders collapsing, sliding further, pressing further into breathlessness.

Frances grabbed Sam by the waist to steady her as she began to tease the pink nerve beneath its hood. She locked her lips over Sam's clit, sucking blood into the flesh around it, cradling softly with the middle of her tongue. She slid an arm in between Sam's thighs and grabbed what she could of the tall woman's ass, pulling her in closer while reaching blindly for her own sex. The taste made her want to touch herself. To burst.

Sam's knees buckled and Frances, holding onto Sam's ass, sank backward slowly. Sam followed her downward, knees crashing to the floor with a hollow wooden thud, still grinding to the tempo of her pleasure.

There was something immensely powerful about the way Sam

worked the world and it titillated Frances to put her lips to her like a wind instrument and make her sing. It was hard for her to say why really without feeling shameful. But even her shame, when pleasing Sam, only heightened the arousal. She felt her entire body electrified. She wanted to exceed and consume it all in one ecstatic orgasm. Frances slid her index and middle finger inside, prying herself apart, hooking in beneath the bone, chasing from her lips a sound that startled them both. She was so close now. She pushed her ring finger inside, further spreading her swollen box, brief pain chasing blueshifting pleasure. Slowly at first, curling her fingers up and in. Then faster.

Sam leaned backward, grinding harder and spastically against Frances's face. For leverage she dug the heels of her palms into Frances's stomach. Frances gasped. The added weight over her mons pressing into her hooked fingertips pushed Frances to the cusp of orgasm. She was loud and the sound of her so near excited Sam to climax.

Sam arched her back at the height of her pleasure, contractions sweeping in waves through her body. And Frances, flushed beneath her own voice dying down from ecstatic ululation, released into her own palm a rush of fluid. Her mouth agape and covered in Sam's wet excess. She slowed her stroke and pulled out, trembling.

They collapsed, wet and entwined, serpentine and panting for air. Smiling and settling tenderly against each other's body, shaking off their last spasmodic tremors while a cool breeze carried the heat from their sweat-covered skins. Then Sam, so full of curious energy, took Frances's hand, still wet from sex, and began to examine her ejaculate.

You see this

The cottage industry surrounding this stuff

It's frightening

Sam yawned, plying the viscous remains of Frances' orgasm between her fingers.

Why

What comes out of a pussy that's not a child

And comes strictly for pleasure

Money shots

They want to see that they can do to us what we can do to them

They think making a woman piss and moan is a badge of honor

You know that's what they do right In the movies

It's piss The squirting

We're failing the Bechdel test right now

I know

Que sé yo

She yawned again

Que sé yo

You were wonderful

It's you You bring it out of me

Are you tired

Let's sleep

I'm tired but still awake

Relax

Just

Lie with me

Listen to my body

Frances began to drift. An unusual thing for her, night owl and chronic insomniac that she was. She could remember in the somnolence of the moment Sam whispering a charm, as though she were plucking the petals from a daisy while lying perfectly still.

A cache of colors to give me sleep

A cache of colors to make me water

A cache of colors to wake me up

A cache of colors to make me holler

The air was crisp when they woke. Sunlight poured in through the windows, golden over the wooden floor, over her cheek. She could remember Sam stretching across the floor like a cat, one leg under the blanket, the other exposed, both arms extended over her head and her fingers interlocked. She cracked her knuckles, the discs of her spine. The sun lay pale yellow and warm across her stomach. Stretchmarks ran through her like the vessels of a leaf.

Frances, having fallen asleep on her back, woke with a stiff neck and a sore right hip, but she felt young, comfortably situated in what she knew would have been an unbearable transitional period. Had it not been for Sam, Frances, so near a kind of spiritual and mental precipice, knew she would have suffered a breakdown. This realization in retrospect lent the experience a divine and bittersweet significance.

You're my angel you know

Sam lay on her side between Frances and the window. She grinned and clasped Frances' hand in her own. Their joined hands pulsed with gracious weight. They lay there for an hour more with heavy eyes, then Sam rose. She opened the door to the balcony and stepped out against the blueness of the sky and the sun that inched toward noon.

Frances lay for a moment more observing with contentment the perfect plainness of the room. There was her Steinway, the paintings, the bookshelves. There was the 10-gallon aquarium, still empty, that Sam bought for her. She had promised to fill it with an unusual assortment of creatures and there was that one oddity in particular she was excited to put in the tank, but the promise was made a month prior and perhaps since forgotten by Sam. Owing to her love of Cortázar, Frances thought the promised oddity might have been an axolotl, a pinkish albino or a grinning sable. Nearly extinct, they looked like creatures lost in time and space and, in an admittedly strange way, Frances felt she could identify with them. The axolotl, to be named Julio, settled into the lockbox full of empty promises Frances kept stowed away.

Their clothes were strewn across the piano. Lingerie draped the keys and trouser legs hung from the hammers and strings. She rose slowly, massaging her left shoulder, which was sore. She grabbed a ripened banana from the fruit bowl on the counter, peeling it and pulling from it soft chunks which she chewed with bovine lethargy.

Sam came back in from the balcony, smiling from ear to ear. She winked at Frances before floating into the bathroom. The clock on the wall read 11:50. Frances called out to Sam.

Use the Lemisol

No bitch

Are you hungry

We'll eat in the city

Are you sure I can make you a banana

No baby Thank you though

Through her late teens and twenties Frances cultivated a studied uselessness, the sole purpose of which was the attempted preservation of her individuality. She found herself perpetually dissenting, disinvested. Nothing conceived of in the neo-classical halls of the university or attainable in an economy of men and women seemed to her worthwhile. She dropped out. She spent much of her time in melancholic self-absorption, reading, writing, tinkering. Abstaining. She was satisfied in those years to be composed in solitude, spinning silk around her ankles, regularly visiting her father. She entertained brief affairs, enough to sate a perennial. They were each dimissed within two weeks.

She knew herself truly in service to those who sought their own purpose, those wounded and in need. The wanderers, the searchers, the roads they took often led them to her counsel—the counsel of one admitted against her will to the edge of abyss and brought back. She was the hermit. Their high priestess. She had enjoyed this.

Nearing her thirties, by then the sole heir and executor of the family estate, she began a philanthropic campaign—a charitable foundation for children suffering from leukemia and large donations to various oncology wards across the island. All of her donations were given anonymously, as though she were returning something stolen or borrowed.

She profited from the sale of the estate, save the two acres of land on which she lived. It was smaller, more manageable, all she needed. She had no attachment to the land as it was or the idea of land ownership. She considered it all damned, the uncultivated vestiges of a sad history and a long outmoded system. She paid off the family debt and invested in another kind of infrastructure, a largesse that never managed to close the gap between her and the rest of the world.

She remembered those years fit between the dark walls of an echo chamber, the smallest sounds amplified to crippling cacophonies and every memory augmented to humiliating proportion. How she could become auto-cannibalistic with shame, friendless and philanthropic. The vacated spaces in her adult life trembled with urgency and feelings of helplessness prolonged and at their darkest, how they slipped into delusions of suicide or madness, confusion, crying because she lost the chicken coop. Driving out in the darkness to find it vacant, in disrepair. She could remember alternating states of anger and depression, exaggerated self-importance and violent self-pity. Only Frances could say when it was that her solitude became potlatch silence or when it was that her persona became indistinguishable from her reality. She never sought counsel. She didn't speak often of those years.

Sam knew not to ask about the jagged seam across the flesh of her bottom lip.

Sam's arrival was a significant departure from the quiet mysticism of her early twenties and the approaching vacuity of her thirties. For the first time she could turn to another for sustenance, for life and vitality.

Sam stepped out of the bathroom smelling fresh and minty, and went straight for her clothes. Frances too began to dress.

What will we name our daughter

Daughter Not son

Daughter

Léontine

Léontine

Lucie for short

After her panties, her bra, Sam put on her linen trousers right leg first, then her blouse, which she buttoned top-down so that the last thing Frances saw was her downward pointed, ovoid navel. She liked the way Sam's bony fingers twisted around each small, mother-of-pearl button.

In their first year together Frances found herself overwhelmed by their relationship. Sam was not her first woman, but the first woman who had elicited such a strong emotional response. She felt a desire to remain with Sam, a desire to taste her imperfection in the unforeseeable arc of her life thereafter. She was attached and it was wholly new and frightening, especially since Sam could travel for months at a time for shoots.

She knew attachment, felt it like fire once, and knew never to touch it again. Implicit in the concept of attachment was separation. It was a viral *something* she had avoided for most of her adult life. Her relationships were conditional and never without a cost-benefit analysis. For one troubled by casual goodbyes, the notion of being vulnerable and then violated seemed more than illogical. It seemed to her masochistic, suicidal. But the alternative wasn't any better. She had, at some point, come to the painful realization that she was hiding—hiding behind charity, wallowing in grief and fear and loss. She came unbound.

It was lost to her, how or what changed. It existed in a haze, in the distinctness of that sublime color which had no name. She could remember the music. Certain songs when queued, cued certain of those tepid days. Music, because it was still magical enough to elude the law, hinted at actualization and healing and carried with it its own history of resilience and triumph.

The lost experience music differently. That experience is neither a hearing nor a listening. The lost surrender to the sound and allow the sound to carry the burden, mitigating for a moment the gravity of a life riven from its principal paradigm. It is temporary escape to savor the signified potential of harmonic and rhythmic organization. And then one comes into her own music.

In that first year she regularly entertained darkly arousing variations of the same cuckold fantasy. She was prone to paranoia and deliberate distancing from Sam when she felt uncertain and distrustful. She managed to balance her fits of insecurity with grand gestures, unusual gifts or financial assistance, which Sam seemed to appreciate. There were days when the trajectory of the relationship lay before her with such convincing lucidity that she would panic and sit alone in the dark until it passed or until she passed out. From these dark and all-consuming breaks she woke feeling humbled, broken, and vacated, and the first thing she could think to do was reach out to Sam, who still lived and worked then across the pond.

The clearness of her voice on the other end of the line, unaffected and bright, signaled for Frances the strange submission of the person she was, the vacancy she no longer wanted to live with. For a full year it was this cycle of gratitude, distrust, frustration, breakdown, and vacancy. Lust complicated the honest communication of their emotions. Still, at the end of their first year together Sam was there, no less beautiful, no less hardy or interested or committed. So Frances was confronted with a choice: protect her already fragile being from the painful inevitability of separation, or take the risk of breaking the cycle by becoming a new person.

She chose ultimately to suffer through the renegotiation of her being and in Sam she allowed her bodhisattva. Sam was strong enough to endure the violence within Frances that manifested itself outwardly in fits of rage, in paranoia, in desperation. Not only had Sam endured this period in Frances' life, but she acted as a mirror for Frances so that she could see herself, writhing on occasion in her own frailty. Sometimes, on those days when she felt the fallow orb of her failing, all Sam could do to keep Frances from shattering was hold her hand. To avoid pain is to never know joy, said Sam. And a tabulation of nights spent wishing she could cry because the emotional weight and noise of feeling forced to stand on so narrow a strip of earth where nothing and no one could speak into her being three years later survived only as an abstraction of the personhood she once experienced. The world can break you, said Sam.

Let it

It was an hour's drive from La Casa in the mountains to Ponce. Sam was driving, her left hand at ten on the wheel. In the States she had grown accustomed to the automatic responsiveness of a leased Audi coupe. Driving stick through the mountains in an old military jeep was unusual for her, but a challenge she was willing to accept. She leaned into every turn. Her legs were so long she had to pull the seat back to its farthest setting. She drove with her right hand on Frances' knee. She knew Frances enjoyed the view and Sam, who never seemed to feel too threatened by her quietude, could accept this with a degree of comfort that trued them both.

Did you register for that bartending class

Yes I sent in the dues last week

Are we going to pick up the generator first or see your father

Generator first

For the rest of the ride she did little more than belch quietly and observe the light in the trees as they neared their destination.

////\•/\\\

The generator was loaded onto the Jeep by two burly men. She could remember then feeling uncomfortably warm. A dread weight settled in the pit of her stomach. A spider sat stationary on a small web spun between the windshield and dashboard. It didn't move until they arrived.

Daddy this is Sam

Who

Sam She's my friend I wanted you to meet her

He said nothing He played with the straps

Daddy how are you feeling

What

How are you feeling

Who is that

This is Sam My friend I wanted you to meet her

Hello Mister Villegas

She's a photographer

I photograph models and artists yes

He said nothing He shifted his gaze back and forth between them His eyes were jaundiced

Look at you You look good They take good care of you here
Shave you nice

She put her palm to his cheek He was cold He winced

You think I don't know what this is

She felt empty-handed

Your mother would be ashamed

If she lived to see you

Let go, whispered Sam. It's the lithium. It's the lithium, Sam
repeated, grabbing her arm before she could do permanent
damage. She hadn't realized that she was clutching her father's
neck. A squat and stern-looking nurse approached.

Is everything alright

Yes thank you said Sam

And they left. She could remember having let go—an unburdening the likes of which she hadn't experienced even in ecstasy
with Sam. It was as though for the first time she could see,
she could feel, she could breathe. All sense of threat seemed
pulled from the air. She was at ease. She hadn't realized until that
moment how much of her adult life she'd spent in fear, moved
by the yellow knot of a chick in her chest that made it hard to
breathe. How it dawned on her, the revelation that her only
responsibility was to the cultivation of her own spirit.

Frances wanted Sam to see the tarn.

They made the trip to Adjuntas a week later, climbing down an unkempt path through a grove full of wild flowers, flocked on all sides by fluttering butterflies and darting dragonflies, to the banks of a clear blue-green tarn. The tarn was fed by a small waterfall on its opposite side, which poured out from the river Yahuecas over a large rockface. The tarn itself sat recessed and surrounded by a dense greenery of ferns, willows, and hibiscus in bloom. Locals called the watering hole El Mangó. It was a cool day, too cool to swim, but the sun was up and the sky bright blue. Not a cloud for miles. Beside the fall on the far side of the tarn was a tall narrow tree. The tree with its light bark stood out against the gray-green backdrop of the mountain. From the tree hung a rope tied at the end with a wooden handle to make a swing capable of vaulting a young spirit twenty feet into the air before it would come splashing down over the middle of the tarn. Against the trunk of the tree was a long, free-standing stalk of bamboo used by visitors to pull the rope near.

From the banks of the tarn the rope-swing was nothing more than a charming piece of the milieu, a mystery. To access the rope-swing was another thing entirely. One had to swim to the other side of the tarn, climb the steep and slippery hill, reach the rope, and take the dive. The tarn itself was deep enough to allow for diving, but to let go too soon would cause serious injury, perhaps even death. The arc of the swing had to be long enough and high enough to clear a ten-foot protruding rock that sat just beneath the surface of the water.

Frances never took that dive, that leap of faith over the charco. On two occasions in her youth she managed to swim to the other side, ford the algae-covered rock, climb the steep hill, grab the rope and, both times, in that final moment rational sense bucked against desire. She was an inheritor. If she let go too soon, if she slipped, she would mangle herself on that stone.

It was too much a liability. There was too much at stake, too much responsibility. She thought of herself in that disembodied way then—the scion, the prodigal, an object insured at a price greater than she could even fathom. She never knew the satisfaction of clearing the stone in one spectacular arc.

This is beautiful I've never been here

Charco El Mangó The locals treasure this place They keep it clean they respect it

I can't believe how beautiful this is Such an idyll Unreal Who hung that rope there

I don't know Some intrepid mountain boy Boricua Huckleberry

Have you swung from it before

No Honestly I never had the courage

Frances picked up a stone and examined it. Like a river rock it was smooth and round, flat. She skipped it, four hops, over the tarn.

I love you Frances

I love you Sam

We've been together for a long time

What four years now

Yes

Wow

Does it bother you when I leave for sessions

I get lonely sometimes sure but I know you'll be back Distance makes the heart grow fond As they say Why

Just asking

I'd be happy to go with you sometime You still have the apartment

True

Frances began to take off her clothes.

Baby what are you doing It's a little chilly for that

I'm going to do it

Do what Swim to the rope

More than that I'm going to swing across

But we don't have towels You'll catch a cold

No no no I have you here to keep me warm

Oh your faith in me is sweet, but

I have to do this

Fine but you're driving us home

Frances stripped entirely. She ran to the lip of the tarn and dove in, the sun sliding across her back as she dove into the blue-green water. She surfaced some yards ahead, already at the middle of the small tarn, and turned to look back at Sam with a smile. She waded past the waterfall to the high wall where the tree stood waiting. She climbed onto the slick algae-covered stone beneath the tree and for a moment it looked like she was walking on water. She grabbed a low root and used it to stabilize herself as she climbed from the stone up the earthen wall. Once at the top, clinging to the trunk of the tree, she grabbed the loose stalk of bamboo and reached for the rope. She stretched her torso over the water and caught the rope on the very tip of the stalk, but it slipped off. She was nervous she'd slip and fall headfirst into the water, cracking her skull on the stone. The balls of her feet were firmly planted between the curling roots of the tree and her left arm hugged the trunk. She had to tiptoe just to reach the line. She brought the long stalk around again. This time she caught the rope and it wriggled down the stalk toward her. Once securely back on her feet, she took the rope in her left and dropped the stalk at her right.

She got a firm grip on the handle, which was nothing more than a thick piece of wood fastened to the line in a loose knot. She bent her knees and decided that the trick was not to look. Instead she would swing as fast and far as she could until gravity found her at the crest and there she would let go and come flying down. Like jumping off of a playground swing. The trick was not to look.

So she looked. The stone beneath her looked like the massive gray head of a whale ready to surface. She hesitated. Her eyes in the light struggled to adjust. She started shivering. She looked at Sam, who smiled and waved from the banks.

The small gesture of support, familiar and comforting, gave her courage enough to push beyond her rational limitation. Over the threshold of her own cautiousness she jumped into the electric uncertainty of the air, swinging high over the blue-green tarn, past the head of the whale-stone, and when she could go no higher across the verdant majesty of the mountainface she let go.

She felt weightless. She could hear the cascading waterfall, the silvery rush of air around her, the rustle of leaves, a snapping sound, the marvelous immediacy of her destination. She spread her arms and flailed the whole way down, splashing into the blue-green belly of the tarn unharmed and thrilled beyond her wildest imaginations. She swam eagerly back to the banks, where Sam stood waiting for her with arms wide open.

Come here you

Frances managed to smile despite chattering teeth, shivering like a wet cat in Sam's long arms, her head against Sam's chest. Sam kissed her on the forehead.

Let's get you dressed

They had an early dinner in town and drove home. She could remember two months later Sam leaving for a shoot in the States. One week. One month. Two months. One year. Two years without a word.

Quiet engine.

////\•/\\\\

It was slow going and the light low red over the booth; Tuesday in an American tavern tucked between the cobblestone alleys of the old city. The tavern catered to a young professional crowd. On weekends the place was packed with smart trust-fund babies sporting handle-bar moustaches and unkempt locks flexing an international network of eccentric half-educated effetes, self-styled revolutionaries in the early hours of a new millienium. On this Tuesday it was relatively empty. Only an odd handful of non-descript bourgeoisie looking to unwind.

Have you ever walked through Llorens Torres?

No.

Of course not. Why would you?

She sipped her beer. An IPA.

It's the smell I mean. Walking through projects. They all have a smell.

His affect was flat. He was nervous, depressed, or disinterested. His hands lay flat on his lap under the table.

I went to visit a cousin in the south Bronx. He must have thought I was a come-mierda because I couldn't hide my distaste for the place. We haven't spoken since. That was like three years ago. I like New York, pero ahora ya 'tá como—

He grimaced searching for the word.

Decrepit. So yes I know what you mean about the smell.

No. No. Don't get me wrong. It's not disgusting to me. It's just intriguing. It's proximal. It's sultry and perfumed and violent. It's guarded. It's unfair. It's infirm. It sings. It's dizzying, that smell. I met someone today whose sense of in and out was severely destabilized, though not entirely. And for some reason I thought of those times after a birthday when or during a birthday when an elder would ask how it felt to be whatever age. The way they would ask. I'm thinking of someone specifically, a specific instance, but they all wore the same grin now that I think about it—like there was a correct answer and it puzzled the shit out of me. So today, when I met this stranger who seemed to float in and out of everything simulatenously, I realized the irony. Getting older, it feels like nothing, like a lukewarm drip that goes suddenly hot. You don't realize it's hot because its such a localized sensation, but when you do—then you have to pull your hand back. But that's something entirely other.

She paused to gather her thoughts into one satisfactory expression.

It's like being intimate with someone, being close enough to smell their breath whether you want to or not, regardless of context. As soon as you smell it and feel it, how heavy it is, you know you've entered a different kind of place with a different kind of energy and it engenders a different kind of relational knowledge. I grew up in the sticks behind privileged gates where there was always enough space for play. It was just so different for me. You grew up where? Ocean Park?

Yes.

See, so you were close to that. I dated a boy from Llorens Torres. Ecuatoriano. He took me to meet his family and I stayed for dinner. The relationship didn't last long, but I'll never forget being in that small apartment with his mother, his sister, his grandmother. Him. We all ate in front of the TV on little foldable tables. I think we were watching the premiere of *El Derecho de Nacer*. Remember that?

Mami loved it.

This was the remake I think?

2001.

I was too young to see the original. And someone told me that it was even older than that. A radio show. Anyway. What was I saying?

About being in Llorens Torres with an ex-boyfriend's family.

Right. He wasn't really a boyfriend by the way. We came from vastly different worlds so it was doomed from the outset. Anyway I'm talking too much. I'm going to ask you a strange question. Are you ready?

He grinned slightly, unable to suppress his amusement.

I'm ready.

Ok. So tell me. What was it like growing up with Doña Malou as your mother. What was she like?

He took a deep breath, disappointed, while he composed his thoughts. An elegant red and blue beaded necklace, wound twice around his neck, was just visible beneath his collar. The beads looked like small aged river stones, or dyed bone, sanded to smoothness. It seemed to be wound too tightly around his neck, distracting an already distracted man. He readjusted the necklace so that it sat comfortably around his neck.

My mother, believe it or not, wanted me to become an oncologist. Needless to say, I didn't quite meet her expectations. But my mother is nothing if not dignified. She was like Phylicia Rashaad before Phylicia Rashaad and just as beautiful.

You know, for a few months in my teenage years I had a Clair Huxtable thing.

He forced a grin.

It's ok, dear. It was a long time ago. I was just trying to get a rise out of you. Tell me more about your mother. She's such an intriguing and knowledgeable individual.

She was the first in her family to attend college. She was incredibly nurturing, sometimes doting. She was an advanced child, the way she tells it, and an only child.

Go on.

Well, she's incredibly creative as you may know. It was always Mami I could turn to and she would have some encouragement or some inspiration that would lift me up when I was feeling down. One thing you probably don't know is that she's cultivated a library since she was nine.

Oh I've seen it! Full walls, floor to ceiling bookshelves and a ladder that wraps around it.

Did you see the industrial dehumidifier?

Yes! The room is practically vacuum sealed.

Exactly. She really loves those books—to the point where my brother and I were only allowed to handle them in her presence. She watched us as we read.

Can I get you two more drinks? Something to eat? The fries are good.

Oh, I'm fine.

You sure?

Yes, thank you. Nothing for me.

And you, Sir?

I'm good. Still working on my beer.

Ok. Nothing for now. I'll come back a little later.

Great, thanks.

So you were saying?

She took another sip of her beer.

So my brother and I knew she was a character and beloved from
one side of the island to the other. It didn't quite make sense
to either of us until we got older. She was a fixture in her own
right, even before she married our father. The family shop was a
cornerstone of style and service. You know the signature brand,
the small black bird? She started doing that when she was a girl
and it took off. She really made it a thing when our grandfather
entrusted her with the shop. Much of its success was due to its
location. The shop was wedged conveniently between worlds. It
was rooted in Santurce, frequented by settlers from Ocean Park
and Condado, and by people from municipalities all over the
island. The rich especially loved it. People came from everywhere
which, as she tells it, was unusual at the time because the island
was a much bigger place.

I've known her obliquely for years.

How do you know her?

My father used to frequent the shop when he was in the city on business. He liked her. Her manner. Sometimes he took me with him on his errands and I liked her because she gave me candy. She's nurturing.

She is.

Tell me more about her.

Um.

Like how she got to be so political.

You know it's funny because a few people have asked me about this. I feel like the child of a celebrity or something. Me and my brother just grew up with that, with her ideas. So we just thought it was normal. There was nothing unusual about it. And to tell you the truth I'm not sure where her ideas came from. I think my grandparents encouraged her with books and things. They could read. But they had just come out of slavery, more or less. Short answer: I'm not sure. She taught for a few years after her degree. That was before grampa died. Then she took over the shop. Then Papi died. Heart failure. That was almost ten years ago. He died a month before the turn of the millenium. He was 81. I remember because I had just bought him a portable DVD player for Christmas. And I had a collection of his favorite films on DVD. And the *Dean Martin Roast* collection. I was going to give him those on Noche Buena or Three Kings. I hadn't decided.

His face under so much red light became ancient, hardened to stone. He sat just inches away from her, but couldn't have been more distant. Walking a lightyear's worth of memories that came to him in disappointed color. A livid ruin. She had the sense that if she were to touch him he might crumble and the wild animal which he worked so hard to keep captive, thrashing behind his red eyes, might leap forward and make a noise.

////\•/\\\\

She cut the wheel, half turn left and threw her weight as hard as she could against the driver's side door forcing the car into a screeching drift.

The back tires skidded out toward the cliff, crashing against a low row of stones as Frances whipped and willed the jeep left around the bend in the last possible second. Inertia pushed the back right tire with a thud over the stones. The car bounced up throwing her head like a ragdoll against the driver's side window. The chassis buckled and groaned. Pain swelled through the back of her skull, through her shoulders and collarbone. Dizzy, she felt gravity rattle all the fluid between the bones of her ear as the vehicle tilted backward and began to slide. She saw the tip of the moon in her rearview as it set over the range in a flash of white. Momentary stillness. The vehicle froze.

She closed her eyes and tried to still her trembling. She felt like she'd been mauled. Her head was pounding, sinking under laudanum, coffee, adrenaline, and sleeplessness. Her vision was cloudy. Her right arm was loose and retained feeling. Delicately she touched the place on her head where it cracked against the glass. She winced at her own touch, which, despite her best effort, felt brutish. It was swelling and open, throbbing with feverish heat. She could feel blood or sweat, something viscous and wet on the tips of her fingers.

Her left arm from the shoulder down felt numb, bruised into a kind of superficial paralysis. She could move her fingers. Her legs felt heavy, but otherwise unharmed. Slowly it dawned on her, the violent realization; she was teetering on a very thin line.

It was a front-wheel drive vehicle. She could see the front left tire elevated slightly off the ground while the back-right hung precariously over the edge of the cliff. The headlights lit the trunk of a tree a few feet in front of the bumper. The road ahead curved into an incline. Even if she could get the engine going she still risked rolling backward off the cliff.

She set her feet on the clutch and brake, depressing simultaneously. She shifted into neutral. The car lurched backward a few inches, then froze. Her vision began to blur. She shut her eyes and gripped the key and felt her lucky rabbit's foot brush against the heel of her palm. She took a deep breath and turned the key. The engine cranked into a bronchial stutter, a series of false starts, a succession of trying breaths flooded and immobile. A legato chuffing, *ChChChChCh*—She let go. The car was still. The night sky filled with stars came into focus in her rearview. She could see the Milky Way spread like a gash across the belly of the night. She could feel the stars together in entropy, pulling her, inches and seconds away from being consumed by their stellar vastness. With her feet firmly planted on both clutch and break, she tried again. The engine stuttered for a full minute, but failed to spark.

She could shut the headlights. She wouldn't see any of it, any of the mountains or trees turning over in the air. All she would see were the stars as she fell backward—simple, brutal, elegant. It wouldn't hurt. Like being pushed from behind. Then fade to black. She took a deep, stationary breath.

Turning the key again the engine broke into emphysemic laughter, a hollow and damning loop which seemed to echo abyss, hacking impossibly as if to confirm she could let go then, because what else was there after all? What else was there after wanting it more than what willed otherwise? She'd come so far and finally, like a shot to the heart, fateful and awaited relief, the machine started into full ignition! She wanted to vomit.

Immediately the new liveliness of the engine trembled through the chassis, endangering her tenuous equilibrium on the brink. She let go of the brake, put the jeep in first. The jeep jerked backward. Her heart leapt. Cold sweat clung to her skin and clothes. Slowly she eased her left foot off the clutch and pressed the gas. The engine revved responsively, deliciously, followed by the screech of the front right tire catching asphalt. The jeep jerked forward. She too lurched her body forward, willing the vehicle ahead. Then the screech and smell of burning rubber as the front left tire caught the road and the jeep made full efforts to pull its hind over the row of stones. RPMs were climbing into the red. Her body tensed. With her hands wrapped tightly at ten and two she threw her weight forward again, her chin nearly crashing against the top of the wheel.

She gave the engine a final rev and the jeep cleared the ridge with a satisfactory hop. She cut the wheel hard left and swerved just inches clear of the palm tree in front of her, steering herself back onto the road. She let out a sigh of relief and made the slow, surreal climb up the incline. She pulled over safely onto a narrow shoulder at the top of the hill and put the car in park. She shut the headlights. Left flickering the hazards.

Something in her stomach twisted water from her eyes, nausea, and a weakness in her arms from the shoulders down, as if she'd carried the vehicle on her back uphill. Her fingers, pale and ghostly, coming in and out of focus, trembled uncontrollably when she let go of the wheel. She dry heaved twice, then clutched the wheel again. Began to nod.

The weekender and sidearm had fallen from the passenger seat onto the floor of the jeep. The soft luster of the gunmetal caught her eye caught her eye. The bag was open. Something small and angular laid exposed in its dark maw.

She forced the rusty seatbelt latch until it came unhinged and leaned over to pick up both the gun and the bag. She checked the safety, then laid the gun between her thighs and opened the bag. Inside was a paperback. She searched the bag for any remaining items. Aside from the book, the bag was empty. She opened the light and examined the cover. It was a well-worn edition of *The Quiet American*. She flipped through flipped through pages dog-eared, stained, and highlighted. A loose page, folded in half in half, fell out of the book and into her lap. She unfolded the page and found it addressed to First Lieutenant. She had difficulty reading the handwritten letter. She struggled even holding the flaccid sheet of paper in her trembling hands. Bleeding and her vision blurred she felt sedated, etherized, and spread against her will. If she could just rest her eyes—

First Lieutenant,

I trust you have in **Arecibo.** *Your contact* *terminal* *I suspect I* **no** *longer be here.* *myself slipping.* *that* **my being** *disintegrating* **under** *the weight of knowing.* *I am* **lost then** *after* *bury me here with* *What I* *need you* to do is understand that it had to happen this way in order for us to win our freedom. In our time together I know **you did not trust** me. You had no reason to. I know we come from different worlds, but we are from one people. We need each other. Our people have suffered in the diaspora *and* **we continue to suffer** for lack of home. When **this battle is won and** the war is over you will lead them. You have everything you need and you have everything this nation needs to build a new and sustainable future. Please believe in yourself. **Believe in the strength** and righteousness of our **people. Establish Ponce** as our new capital. Of ports north and south it will have sustained the least damage. It remains most available and profitable for trade. On the *verso you* **will find instructions.** The character key to my correspondence with Arjun. Lines are **highlighted and annotated in the book.** Pages correspond to dates and coordinates. Once you *decode* **the correspondence** you will have some insight into this plan—which could not be revealed to *you* in **medias res for fear** *of compromise.* **Please understand** it had to be this way. You among us are the only one capable of leading the people. You among us are the only one strong enough to steer this nation into the future. Do not let *them* **all die in vain.** The stage has been set for you. Now you must do *what* **you were born to** do

Colonel

ps. find **Theophilio** you will need each other

Pounding in her skull. Trembling and geodic with delusions infested by a kind of yellow neither in nor out but through the breastplate. Nervous exhaustion. Bleeding. If she could just rest her eyes in the house against the house—

////\•/\\\\

13 OCTOBER XXOI [AIBONITO; CASA VILLEGAS] It was almost
midnight. The laudanum had already begun to take hold of her
body. Colonel sat opposite in the wing chair fighting fatigue
between songs on Miguel Zenón's *Ceremonial*. She had to stay
occupied and she had to keep him from falling asleep. In order
to preserve what little energy was left in the room, she set up
a chessboard on a small wooden table beside the armchair. She
pulled up a folding chair on the black side of the chessboard.

Your move.

He looked at her out of the corner of his eye, sitting with his
elbows on the armrests and his hands clasped into a steeple over
his chest.

Your move, she repeated. White first.

She reached into her pocket and pulled out a brass cigarette
case and matchbook. She opened the case and pulled one from
among a file of seven white cigarettes with tawny golden filters.
She closed the case and tapped the cigarette six times lightly
against the cover, packing the tobacco to her satisfaction. With
the cigarette between her lips she replaced the case in her pocket,
struck a match, and brought the flame carefully to the tip. She
pulled on the flame, the cherry aglow with first combustion.
With a flick of the wrist she put out the light and threw the dead
match over her shoulder. Thin smoke expelled quietly from her
nostrils, dissipating over the chessboard.

Colonel turned in the armchair to face the Lieutenant and the
chessboard, noting the smell of her smoke, a blondish blend
tobacco. Vaguely industrial. The recognizable red insignia.

Double Happiness. Where'd you get them? He asked, his voice
hoarse, his eyes beginning to show signs of life.

They were a gift, she said, taking another drag.

[white: e2 – e4]

The chessboard, cherry-lit. With each long drag she donned the ignibarbative mask of one between worlds, her brow plastered into an orange scowl, her mouth a frown—what he saw across the board in the dark, half-awake. The severest contours of her face.

The glim was dying and neither felt compelled to get up and search for and light a new candle. I know about you and Theo, he said, regaining his voice.

You know about what?

He said nothing.

[black: e7 – e5]

"Great Is Thy Faithfulness" began to play. It felt prematurely Yule and Poinsettia, but the raw energy of Zenón's sax unwittingly energized them both. Colonel tightened his left hand into a fist over the armrest, scanning the board for the right move among several possible moves. His body tensed, straining as he had earlier for breath. A man perpetually bracing himself against all probability.

[white: Ng1 – f3]

You know, I was never interested in being interesting. She said quietly, as Zenón launched into his final solo. The glim flickered out as the album approached its restrained conclusion. Frances ashed the butt of her cigarette on the windowsill and lit another.

The moon glowed softly through new silence, pale blue through the muslin drapes. There was just enough light to see the pieces clearly. The room around them grew dim and made no assertion of its history, suggesting in darkness its non-future. He ignored her.

Status report on evacuation, Lieutenant.

[black: Nb8 – c6]

Surveys indicate that most, if not all sympathizers, have made it out of the city. What's more, we've raised no noticeable alarm. The exodus occurred over this past week with individual barrios and families moving at allocated times. They were instructed to pack light and only bother to take valuables. Doña Malou has distributed most of the uniforms to members of the tercios. Several orders were anonymously delivered to undisclosed distribution centers. Malou has volunteered to help en cualquier manera.

[white: Bf1 – b5]

He could smell the coffee on her breath, she was so close. Warm and dizzying under the smoke. The Lieutenant continued. Families left behind are either out of our network, remain on the fence about the cause, or simply reject our ideas. They constitute a majority of the city, which is probably why we managed to evacuate without alarm, but our numbers are nonetheless substantial.

And the factories?

Cleared. Is there something else you'd like to listen to Colonel? A new album? Something upbeat? She pulled long on her cigarette, gaze fixed on the board.

[black: Bf8 – c5]

What time do you have? he asked.

11:02 by my watch.

Arjún should be arriving any minute now.

[white: Qd1 – e2]

Colonel was awake. His voice again carried the ingaled urgency of the gangster he was looking for.

Catholicism has ruined this country for centuries.

He spoke slowly. Deliberately.

And it's led the people of the diaspora to vote against their own interest. These are registered democrats in the poorest congressional districts, nationwide, who side ideologically with the conservative right. Our people have never been convinced that a national project, a national family, could work or be worthwhile. Until now. And whoever's left standing after the smoke clears will make the foundation of our future. I want you to know Lieutenant, there's been a change in plans. New choreography. You were originally stationed for the sniper's station atop Banco Popular with Theophilio, yes? He didn't wait for her response— Baldomero will be going instead, to be stationed atop the department store farther up the hill. *Marshall's* on Calle Cordero. Arjún will be stationed atop the Institute, Antiguo Asilo. I'm not sure that Theophilio will arrive in time for our departure. We'll have to leave without him. Once Arjún arrives, we're gone.

The air was still. He turned to the window, the moon in the muslin illuminating the lines of his face. For a moment she couldn't recognize him. His face had grown suddenly alien and ossified in the cold glow. He looked older and crueler, carved like a gargoyle into the high-relief of his every intention. He turned back to the Lieutenant and the chessboard over the armrest, light shunted from his face.

You'll be taking the jeep to our contact at the Arecibo Observatory. It's a relatively safe location. You'll be acting as our intel liaison. You'll also be transporting an important piece of information. It's presently strapped into the passenger seat of the jeep. Not to be opened until you arrive. It's crucial that you get it there safely. Is that clear? Do you know the way to the observatory?

[black: Ng8 – e7]

Of course. She responded, propelling as she spoke a cloud of smoke and a cool unburdening sigh, which echoed in her head against immediate recall. The laudanum had laid hands on her with a welcome heaviness that made her feel colossal. She leaned backward and sank slightly in her chair, receding almost entirely into the dark, scattering the embers of a canoeing cigarette across her chest. The smoke in her throat felt like velvet and unfolded in her lungs like the cure. She ashed her cigarette on the underside of her seat and lit a third.

I don't envy you, she said. Wife to hope.

[white: O – O]

And you? he managed. Husband to power? He glanced at the bandaid over her throat.

[black: O – O]

I don't think you understand. There's no explaining harmony.
There's no explaining things as they are.

She rose slowly from her seat and staggered toward the bookshelf behind her. She gave her eyes little time to adjust, moving
instead by muscle memory, a kind of faith in familiar darkness;
the silhouette of a person reaching through smoke slowly for
things across her body, barely distinguishable from the black
space around her. She sparked a match and brought its flame
trembling to the wicks of three tea lights, which sat gathering
dust on an empty eye-level shelf.

And there's hardly any changing things as they are. You think.
You do. And it's all an illusion. What you think this island needs,
it already has, she said without looking back.

She took down the three tea lights and placed them on top of
the piano. With her back to the Colonel she returned to the
bookshelf, scanning each of the top three shelves casually with
her index finger. She stood loose, hip cocked and shoulders depressed. She wore her jeans tucked into black military boots and
a brown leather bomber over a white linen blouse which hung
just inches below her waist, accentuating the athletic pertness
of her behind. Her roving finger settled on the third shelf where
sat the aquarium and from beside it, wedged in shadow, she
removed a stack of cards bundled together by a double-wrapped
rubber band. She turned slowly and returned in no hurry to the
table. She stood before him like a titan with cards in her left
hand and the cigarette half-smoked between her lips. She bent
forward, her hair falling across her face, to reach between her
legs for the edge of the chair which she dragged in beneath her.
She fell slowly and landed loudly against the backrest, all muscle
and bone. She sighed and held up the deck.

Do you know what these are?

There was nothing to read in his face. She ashed her cigarette on the windowsill then unbound the deck. The rubberband snapped off, sprung overhead, and landed somewhere behind him.

[white: Qe2 – c4]

She spread the cards between her palms and held them over the table. They were adorned with clubs, cups, swords, coins or discs—Greco-Roman or Galician iconography. There was the tip of what looked like a knight on horseback exposed between a three of clubs and a three of swords. There was an unmistakable queen. The cards by face looked like Tarot, but they were small like playing cards and laminated like a Bicycle deck. Colonel didn't respond immediately. His face gradually engorged with concern, uncertainty, and distaste for a question that felt leading and unfair. They both knew he couldn't answer in the affirmative. His brow furrowed and eyes squinted like something of it survived on the tip of his tongue, trying to piece together the vague familiarity of the cards. In fact the cards were familiar to him, but the name of the game and its object were lost to memory. She closed the deck in her right hand. Her nails, he noticed, were chewed to the quick.

[black: d7 – d6]

She asked again. Do you know what this is?

No, he responded. I remember seeing them as a boy, maybe, but I don't remember what they're called or how they're used.

Leaning back in her seat she crossed her legs, the toe of her right boot dangerously close to toppling the chessboard.

This is Brisca, Colonel. She began to shuffle the cards casually against her stomach. Forty cards in a deck. She paused. They're playing cards. A game, maybe derived from Tarot. Italian or some say Dutch in origin. But we here on the island love this game. In fact it's a tradition. Part of the culture, one might say. Is it coming back to you now? You starting to remember?

[white: Nb1 – c3]

Something in the stillness of the room smelled like dead vermin, like a rat resigned to death behind the stove or the bookshelf. A ghost of a thing, rotting and anonymous. The smell crept in between them, between the smoke and tea lights.

I remember.

[black: Nc6 – b4]

My brother tried to teach me once. How to play. He spread the cards out on his bed and explained each one and their value. I was frustrated. I was always frustrated by the things he tried to teach me because I thought I was smarter than him. But he was always teaching me. He was so good and patient. He was my heart, you know.

Study left his eyes for the lay vacancy of looking.

I don't remember how to play.

Something quietly taken from the muscles of his face. Wrinkles from the corners of his eyes like spiders stretching their legs.

I'm sorry.

His fist, the whole time clenched, came loose over the arm of the chair. Not a peacefulness, but the shame of incontinence which reveals in evacuation the hollowness of the vessel.

A sound outside at first like stiff wind grew into the uncanny staccato cadence of hooves. Baldomero's voice came deep and low and elided over the radio.

Ya él 'tá quí.

////\•/\\\\

14 OCTOBER XX01 [OUTSIDE VALPARAISO, FLORIDA; EGLIN AIR FORCE BASE] The hula girl dancing on the dash of his Ram pulled him apart, made him wonder, bouncing on her spring, about the arc of his life. Plastic banana leaves at her brown waist worn away from kelly green to weathered white. And his reflection in the rearview. Clean-shaven. Showing signs of age. Son of Susan Sussilleaux and Orestes Huit. His mother, a creole from the bayous of Louisiana. His father, a guitarist from Guayanilla. Wanderers who met in the late seventies and settled in Miami. Both now in their late sixties. And his reflection in the rearview. Major T. P. Huit, son of Susan Sussilleuax and Orestes Huit, parted momentarily from his own body to see everything unspeakably from the verso. The emblem of the 53rd. A winged saber upward bound along a white stripe parting air and space, breaking at its foible two bolts of red lightning. Sprites in the upper atmosphere. The same prescription he wore since fourth grade. The numbers and tags. The boots—still covered in dust from Creech. The hula girl dancing on the dash of his Ram. In the front seat where he lost his virginity. The Clash on the radio.

He could've been a surfer.

California was a kind of heaven or hades to which his young loves let go were lost and sometimes from which reappeared, always and only before receding again to the red light of the west. But, as Susan Sussilleaux often reminded her boy, this was an unchristian sentiment, which merited no further thought, which could therefore be transcended.

There was Maia, first among his loves possessed by California, from Salinas, whom he'd mistaken for Persian. She was Mexican-American, in fact. They were young and eager students together at M.I.T., sharpening their teeth on the mechanics of the universe, Terry Gilliam, shrooms, and orange juice. She was as tender as she was intelligent. Sensible. Bicurious or bisexual or just splintered and sensual. How quickly the veneer of freshman year faded into sophomoric disillusionment, weeded and spinning on the finer sounds of *Stadium Arcadium*, favoring the emotional vulnerability of Mars to the tender bravado of Jupiter. Tracks like "Tell Me Baby," synthetic and angular, which came to him in blocks of primary color. And "Hard to Concentrate." The fantasy of family in California.

Maia couldn't afford to stay in school. Her scholarship was paltry, barely enough to cover the cost of room and board. She had realized, after a year of listless study, that what she sought was conceptually simpler than four years of required courses toward ceremonious institutional discharge. Love and a life well lived. The only two things still cheaper than water and cleaner than air.

She had encouraged him, before dropping out, to hop on a cross-country train and be with her in California. There she would teach him how to surf. How to really surf. How to be a real surfer. And up until that point they had agreed, in eyes and smiles, that they were both in the gentle throes of what could have been worth a lifetime of shared exploration. So they made love and found it appropriately dull. Then she was gone.

He stayed in school designing cascading style sheets for more enterprising classmates, accruing academic language and debt, farming experience for two rogue night elves (Drizzt and Cattie) on his *World of Warcraft* account, illegally downloading albums, and frequenting porn sites—the full history of which, he would find out much later, was documented in his classified dossiers. He wondered if a posthumous biography could be based on one's porn history. He wondered what one's erotic tastes, one's fetishes, could illustrate about one's dark side.

In his senior year before graduating from M.I.T. he was tapped on the shoulder and asked by Uncle Sam to attend the most exclusive house party in the world. His country needed him.

He was transferred from 53rd Test and Evaluation Group, stationed on Creech AFB in Nevada, to 53rd Electronic Warfare Group at Eglin AFB in Florida. He was one of the Air Force's foremost experts on MQ-9 long-range operations. His was a particular brand of nerdiness the military deemed too dangerous to dismiss.

The staff psychologist noted in his dossiers that this dangerous nerdiness may have been piqued by an early obsession with Nintendo's Game Boy. Miguel, his best friend growing up, owned an original Game Boy—a gray plastic brick of a machine with a black directional pad [+] and operational buttons, **A** and **B**, which looked like shiny raspberry-colored candies. There was also **start** and **select** which looked like gray tictacs arranged beside each other at a bias on the face of the machine. Miguel had on his Game Boy a sticker of the Kool Aid Man between the directional pad and candy-coated buttons. For several months the young Major thought all Game Boys came with a Kool Aid Man totem, and was disappointed to find out that this wasn't the case.

He feigned a curiosity in the contents of Miguel's games—*Tetris*, *Super Mario Land*—but his actual interest was in how Miguel played the games, how he could assimilate the hardware of the machine to the functions of his own body. In short, he was interested in the Game Boy as an instrument. He liked to read the secret language his friend's thumbs made while playing. To watch Miguel play was something like watching a nervous portrait or a score to the music of his friend's mind. His tempo and interpolations. Improvisations.

A year later, when the young Major was gifted by his mother and father a Game Boy of his own—one with a neat transparent shell, but no Kool Aid Man totem—he absconded with the machine and took it apart. He wanted what was inside.

Decades later he still found himself ogling people as they played with their smartphones, sliding and sweeping and arranging dream stuff across their retina-display multi-touch screen LCDs—gleaning their reflections from a mosaic of downloadable applications. Inputting magic into little black boxes. Their thumbs like prone asps spitting back and forth across the glass. He checked the lock screen on his phone. Twenty minutes until briefing.

The MQ-9 is a Remotely Piloted Aircraft—an unmanned aerial vehicle popularly referred to as a drone, designated the Reaper, operated by a two-person crew consisting of a pilot and sensor operator with an additional intelligence analyst. The Reaper is classified by the Air Force as a Tier II MALE (medium altitude, long endurance) hunter-killer. Effective use of the Reaper is contingent upon their corporate performance. From ergonomic leather chairs in a ground control station no larger than a shipping container, not unlike a dorm room, they were given seraphic power. The Reaper was quickly and internationally proving itself worthy of its name. Compared to Grumman's fine F-14 Tomcat, immortalized in the 1980's film *Top Gun*, General Atomic's Reaper was quicker, smarter, deadlier, and safer for our troops who more and more seemed to resemble civilians.

His life wasn't anything like *Top Gun*. He was still single. No prospects. Now and again vignettes came to him of a brooding Tom Cruise in bluish profile over the ravished and ravishing broad-shouldered body of Kelly McGillis. Without realizing it he would start to hum "Take My Breath Away," as performed by Berlin, mouthing Giorgio Moroder's heavy sex synths before shaking off the indulgence of his latently homosexual fantasy.

Almost all of his military hours were logged under I.S.R. (Intelligence, Surveillance, Reconnaissance). An accomplished sensor operator, the Major was instrumental in early development of the nine-camera sensor they called the Gorgon Stare. His earliest missions were startlingly mundane. What seemed like violations of privacy, verging on the pornographic. Patrolling the border for cows and aliens. Watching two women suspected of conspiracy bathe together in the mountains of an island he had never been to, even as a civilian. Their bodies like ants intertwined in the kill box.

He started feeling buck. Pulse and temperature rising. Sweat.

It was nothing like *Top Gun*. It never quite felt like sex, masturbating after a mission where nothing happened. Tense because nothing was happening and because anything could happen. Tense because it wasn't much different from reality television, or *Jane's Combat Simulations*. Nothing in real-time could be so inconsequential or convenient.

Only two days earlier had he asked Carruthers what it felt like for him not only operating the bird, but, you know, just being as like a person who walks and talks and feels. Carruthers looked at him and said flatly, it feels like a video game. Like *Grand Theft Auto*.

What maybe saved them from complete monotony was the inextinguishable unknown that made gamblers of sound men—a slight delay in transmission between operator and RPA. Somewhere between a one and two second delay. It was never as immediate, never as synchronized as one assumed in the middle of operations. They were always operating on the back end of real-time, which is often how they grew to will the machine, meld with it in some fetishistic way. When the machine stalled, if the feed froze, the crew (pilots especially) took pride in the resuscitation of the RPA. Aware of the machine as an extension of self, each of the crew imbued the Reaper with something human, something wholesome and alive. *Come on baby*, the pilot would sometimes say under his breath, off mic, like pillow talk or prayer. Like talking back to the dot matrix screen, stereo speakers, and candy-coated buttons on the face of a Game Boy. Inputting magic into little black boxes.

He thought he knew he could still fuck if the opportunity presented itself, but he couldn't remember the last time he'd won a fist fight.

vii. Music for *The Law of Club and Fang* by Jack London [Studio Sessions]

14 OCTOBER XX01 [CONCERTO FOR ORCHESTRA, Sz. 116, BB 123, MVT. 1] A boy sat at the northbound bus stop on Calle Luna wearing headphones, tapping his foot to the sound of a private familiarity, unaware of the mendicant down the block, beneath the overpass evacuating a kind of private urinal—a styrofoam cup from Bebo's which he carried among his things for waste. In the predawn dark a sheet of hot liquid flung from his cup hung like black glass beneath the sodium lamps before smacking loudly against the concrete. Piss trickled steaming toward the road.

The mendicant down the block with his cup and his jacket sat down beside everything and over everything saw the primacy of his origin. A meandering mass of rags and odor so dissociated he could hardly be called human. A primitive living unenviably without language.

An infant crying mistaken for a cat in heat. Nobody was listening. Nobody walked down Calle Luna in the direction of the overpass holding in his left hand a 9 mm gun. Across his right shoulder: the black strap of a duffel bag.

14 OCTOBER xx01 [THE BARTOK COMPROVISATION; LAWRENCE
D. "BUTCH" MORRIS] They came humming over the horizon,
bent by fata morgana into one rapturous tidal plane, while
beneath them the old city imploded. The sky remained clear
through the night and by noon had become a cloudless and
achingly bright blue. He adjusted his sights and tried to steady
his hands, which hummed with the nearness of death beyond
reason. Treason. Trembling, he reached for the beaded necklace
his mother gave him, force of habit, and remembered it was
gone, given over. He felt for the first time in years as airy and
vulnerable as he had when he was a boy. Left in the woods tied
to a tree. It felt fair. He thought of his mother, but whispered
his brother's name.

Arjún lay beside him on the roof of the old sanctuary, one eye
fixed in the sights of his rifle, the other shut tight, still as statuary
while everything about them shook. He was at least the same
height as Baldomero, tall but emaciated. His clothes were in
tatters and he smelled like the insides of a dead and decaying
beast. The regular doorman of the building, a middle-aged man
who lived in Carolina, was an Evangelist sympathizer who left
the entrance unlocked for their early morning arrival. Baldo
practically had to carry Arjún's weakened body inside and up the
stairs. He weighed next to nothing. Arjún, ailing, asked Baldo
to stay with him on the roof. They made it to the top of the
building, where before dawn they set up and watched as the
Evangelists, all dressed as officers or armed guards, filed casually
into the old city and went to work. First on a list of sites to
infiltrate was a mobile police command center overlooking La
Perla. It took a team of four. Baldo watched and waited from the
roof of the sanctuary for the first sign that everything following
would go as planned.

In the nineteenth century the old sanctuary was a home for the poor. Now it was home to the Institute of Puerto Rican Culture—a place rarely visited with intention, even by tourists who came en masse with Nikon and Canon digital cameras hanging from their pale throats on the first day of good weather in December. A human zafra. Tourists and strangers who wandered into the old sanctuary often left or lingered trying to decipher its purposelessness. It was seemingly empty save one or two smiling so and so's presiding over the bookstore in the lobby and the left-handed doorman who appeared to them the sole proprietor of an inside joke that involved their casual visitation and subsequent vexation. Even so, it was a beautifully kept building with shutters on its windows, an open courtyard with garden, gallery space, all stuccoed pastel in the Spanish colonial style. The thought occurred on his last melancholy walk through the old city, brushing through the color and confluence of language and culture, that the sanctuary would make a significant outpost. It was a building sturdy enough to withstand the implosion of the old city surrounding it. And the roof, which was also commonly accessible to the public, provided them with a clear view of the bay and La Fortaleza. Its centrality was of strategic significance.

Today the roof was not accessible to the public. The doors were locked. The halls were empty of visitors. Only the doorman remained. He was sitting in the lobby behind the hospitality desk with his duffel bag and three 9x19 mm parabellum clips when they came droning over the horizon, soft as a sigh. And outside the earth shook and the streets unraveled and the two revolutionaries on the roof bided time.

Baldomero's mother, Malou, was ill when she gave him the necklace. Her hair was dry, thin and white and curled like stripped birch. Skin tags peppered the sides of her eyes and cheekbones. Little black dots like tribal cicatrices. She lost a lot of weight. He knelt by her bedside and she, holding the necklace like a rosary, laid it tenderly over his salt and pepper crew cut and looped it twice around his neck. It hung there between the tattoo of an adder on his left pectoral and a lion on his right. Hazme un favor mijo. Nunca apartas de ti este collar. He nodded solemnly and took her hand. Doctors forecasted her imminent demise. He and Theo prepared for the worst. But it was Baldo who stood by her side every day for three months while she lay delirious and agonizing on what was expected to be her deathbed.

After three months, to everyone's surprise and relief, doctors reported a miraculous change in her health. Malou survived. In fact she was thriving, alive and well and likely on course to become a centenarian. She tailored the imposter officer suits that several of the Evangelists donned for the Fourteenth. To distinguish them from officers of the state black armbands were administered to all Evangelists. Malou was also responsible for tailoring these. The armbands were a discreet way of visually identifying each other. It was feared and very possible that friendly fire casualities would occur in the confusion.

He rubbed his bare neck aware of his mortality, listening through dust and debris and smoke for a field of broken bodies trapped within collapsed streets. Some he imagined caught in the blast radius, not dead and more than dying. He surpressed a smile. The Kevlar made him sweat. He wanted to take off his vest.

Kites were still being flown on the main green of El Morro. The sky remained clear through the night and by noon had become a cloudless and achingly bright blue. Children for the most part remained aloof, running and laughing on the citadel green. Strings tied to strings. But one by one the adults, tourists and insouciant islanders alike, turned toward the sound and smoke rising from the heart of the old city. Their faces were full of a concern that poorly masked their excitation, while behind them four came riding quietly over the horizon.

A colirrojo circled overhead.

Air-raid sirens were triggered, slightly behind schedule, and all eyes turned to the sky. There began a slow and suspicious descent of kites. Strings tied to strings. Box and bowed kites. Kites with elaborate tails. Flags over the rails of the sunken cemetery and the sun-touched white vertices of obelisks just visible among vestiges of Catholic privilege. All beneath a web of kite strings. Parents implored their children to hurry or let go of their kites altogether. Two diamond-shaped kites trailed off into space over the bay. A Chinese dragon fell from the sky, dragged with an occasional easterly wind across the citadel green toward the cemetery. A few families ran toward the old stone safety of the citadel, ducking inside its old walls. Older flyers took their time reeling in their kites, perhaps recognizing the absurdity of their position, their backs to the bay with no viable route for escape. Or perhaps they hadn't realized the gravity of the situation and had yet to panic. Overall there was no trend in their migration. They each went, it seemed, where the wind took them.

The first rifle fire came echoing in three shots from the old city. A likely sign that American military forces had touched down, although it was just as likely that they had encountered domestic resistance. It wasn't specified over radio.

They were outnumbered. Two to four. Baldo announced range and wind. Soon they would fire their first disabling shot at the approaching aircraft. Arjún had his index finger firmly on the rifle trigger, one eye fixed in the scope of his rifle and the other shut tight, still as statuary while everything about them shook.

He liked to think of his study as palmistry. Arjún's were the clubbed fingers of a laborer attached to a large and imposing palm. Malou on the other hand had long thin fingers and relatively small palms. She said she had her father's fingers and her mother's palms. As a boy his mother's dismembered hands often crept through his sleep. For three years night terrors shook him awake and the thought of being held and comforted by his mother and her hands kept him awake through the night. Frances had short bony fingers. Funny little digits, which probably accounted for her consistent mediocrity on the piano. He recalled her hands in fragments culled from one eidetic mosaic. Whenever he could, he stole a furtive glance at her hands, looking for the way she polished her nails or at the smooth stretch of skin over her knuckles. He often tried to extrapolate the breadth of her person by the shape of her hands. He assumed that the boniness of her fingers was indication of capriciousness, although he couldn't say which preceded which. He imagined her nude and he imagined the shape of her toes in dim light. He wondered if she was shy about her body or earthy and tender or one of those magnificently carnal individuals. He wondered what he would have felt like and looked like in her hands. He tried to piece together her lineage and what traits made favorable their survival. He imagined finally that he would never understand Frances. He understood at least that she couldn't have understood him. He looked at his own left hand, then back at Arjún, whose sights had lowered some thirty degrees.

Humming now like hundreds of vuvuzelas four faceless Reapers visibly armed and ready for combat flew low and fast overhead.

The colirrojo came diving in the wake of the aircraft to snatch a kingbird midflight. The kingbird, caught momentarily in the powerful talons of the colirrojo, quickly flapped free. In the struggle to free itself the bird appeared to have been wounded across the belly. It fled bleeding.

The aircraft would make another pass. Baldo prepared to change position on the roof of the sanctuary, but Arjún's sights remained fixed on the citadel green.

Baldo had difficulty recognizing whether he first registered the sound or the sight of the shot exploding from Arjún's rifle barrel. And into the slightness of that moment torn in part he slipped and froze.

Arjún had already sent a bullet whistling through the skull of a five or six-year-old boy. Pink mist spurted from the back of the boy's head and like a ragdoll he went limp. The boy's father, still holding his hand, paused from the sudden dead weight and turned slowly to face his now faceless son. He fell to his knees aghast, cradling the boy's body in disbelief, blood and matter spattered on the stone wall of the citadel behind them.

From the roof, under the din of the city imploding, Baldo couldn't hear the sound that came from the mouth of the boy's father. He thought to stop Arjún, then thought against it. Within seconds the man fell dead atop his son, shot through the chest as if touched there mercifully by the angel of death. Son como cucarachas, said Arjún pulling away from his scope. He laid the rifle down against the ledge of the roof. He looked up, searching the sky for returning Reapers.

This was American policy in action, comestible for an international audience—if the U.S. could not control Puerto Rico, they would see to it that no one would. But how and why would the U.S. destroy what was already in disrepair? Baldo felt some joy in imagining their confusion. U.S. forces arrived expecting to capture a handful of resistance leaders and found instead strange calamity, implicating themselves in the bombing of the old city. It was a facilitated declaration of war and grounds for secession. American politicians would deny their hand in the tragic destruction of the old city, but the sheer damage and the "coincidental" presence of American military aircraft and para-military forces would be too much to refute in international court. American media would go immediately on the offensive, claiming that a radical sect of Puerto Ricans have declared war on the island nation and that by extension they have declared war on the U.S. But they will not have anticipated the under-ground agency, which finally reached its tipping point.

Arjún fixed his mad gaze on a point in the sky behind Baldo, who spun around quickly to the sight of two Reapers speeding down toward them. Baldo pulled his firearm and Arjún dove for his rifle. He rolled into a ready position on one knee and opened fire, piercing the left airfoil and fuselage of one aircraft. It spun out of control, winding hard right while losing altitude. The other aircraft released a Hellfire missile. Baldo had only seconds to dive out of the way before impact.

The roof blew apart like it was papercraft and beneath the sonic weight of the explosion Baldo could hear Arjún shrieking. Baldo turned on his side to see Arjún running across the roof con-sumed from head to toe in fire, trying to rip off clothing that burned before he could strip loose and then trying to rip free from the skin that plagued him. He ran to the ledge overlooking the bay and stood there ablaze with his arms to the sky. Then he dove off.

Baldo twisted onto his stomach. He felt himself burned or burning. The sky was saturated with black smoke. Wind coming in through the gape in the roof fanned flames higher. He felt in his chest a rhythmic and familiar bass like the sui generis resonance an adult calcaneus makes, surrounded by soft and sturdy tissue, coming down in march or trot or stroll against something like tile. He thought of the sound of her walking barefoot across the

14 OCTOBER xx01 ["FOREST TEMPLE"; COMPOSED BY KOJI
KONDO] It got caught suddenly on a protruding root and yoked
him backward by the throat.

His father was fond of humming in the earliest hours of morning,
visiting the bathroom beside the bedroom he shared with his
brother. The sound always woke him and left him feeling torn
through breakfast, sometimes all the way until noon when the
children were allowed recess and all ills were forgotten. He felt
torn because how dare the old man disturb his sleep, but also
because his father, a pauciloquent man, seemed to genuinely
enjoy humming. He hummed with a vim and vigor invisible in
the quiet economy of his diurnal person. Tone-deaf and com-
pensating for his lack of ear by modulating volume, he sounded
often like a cow giving birth or being put to pasture. There was
something *young* about his humming. The humming seemed,
through the thinness of the bedroom wall, a pipeline into his
father's most precious and innocent sense of self. And for Theophilio, then too old to know awe in the making of myth and too
young to know what was good for him, this was a strange thing.
After imbibing Freud in college he was obliged to consider his
father's love of music repressed within the silent hum of his adult
life as a smoker.

The sound that came out of his throat because it had nowhere to
go fell dead and dull in the chemiluminescent glow.

Beyond the coke-induced invasiveness of Freudian psychoanaly-
sis, which was then unpopular in the Academy due in part to the
ascendence of deconstruction theory and third-wave feminisim,
he was obliged to accept that age and maturation in life required
a palatable kind of opacity. He left psychology immediately after
the introductory course and focused on his Eng.D. His father
instilled in him the importance of being a practical man and
psychology as a career choice was impractical and suffocating.

But his father, the amateur photographer and trained drafts-man, loved music in unmusical chambers. It was his first love every morning—a levity tempered immediately afterward by his first lit pipe, his first full-bodied breath of blonde tobacco. Such uncomplicated pleasures he never indulged in the pres-ence of family, stealing away to the den and his drafting table where within minutes his hardy perfume slipped through the door, always left ajar. The boys knew not to disturb him when at work, assuming he was at work, but they did anyway, risking his various moods. He in his leather armchair seated with his long right leg across his left, his smoking jacket, his hunting rifles hanging on the walls.

Using his elbows and shoulders, his toes and knees, he shimmied backward slowly, loosening its tight hold around his neck. The necklace was caught on a simple root, fortunately untangled, but caught nonetheless. He tried to pull it free reaching across his body with his right hand, but the space was too tight. He twisted over, core first followed by torso, a quarter turn left. Now on his side he could better leverage his reach, but the AR-15 pressed sharply into the discs of his spine.

His throat, coated in dust and mucus, felt raw in the subterra-nean clime. The node beneath his jaw felt swollen and sore, the first inklings of infection and a sharp pain like a rib pressed into his left lung. What sustained thought-objects held back panic were beginning to crack. His breath became shallow, swept away suddenly by the sensation of being buried alive in an unmarked tomb which would first suffocate him, then erode his flesh in a cilice of scavenging vermin.

Theophilio was his father's son chosen above his brother to excel and it took him forty years to understand the vast privilege this afforded him. His father taught him and his brother how to hunt, but he favored Theo. Sunday afternoon on the hills of Vieques, rifles in tow, their bodies laid low downwind of game. They listened together in quiet competition for their father's whispered instructions. The grass was tall, golden, and dry and broke in a rustle beneath the weight of their prostrate bodies. They were both leery of insects, the kind that puttered quietly and had venom enough to kill grown men. They were particularly cautious of ticks, centipedes, and spiders. The grass dried in July where they hunted, passed over by a warm inland breeze and long exposure to the sun. The grass was a proper home for those solitary, malign insects.

Their father did not tolerate complaints, but they both felt each blade of grass, sharp and fragile against the green sensitivity of their bodies like the bite of a black widow or the wrath of an army of red ants. The experience was often uncomfortable, especially and always at first. But within hours they began to feel themselves a part of nature, then apart from nature, then given dominion over nature. And too, they were young enough to believe sincerely that whatever was in the grass could not match the strength and wisdom of their father. Fortunately he was never put to the test. They were comforted by his presence, by his tacit vigilance of the clouds, the shape of the horizon. He taught them to account for wind, which blew easterly on the island. He taught them to recognize the relationship between light and distance. Certain optical distortions which contributed to the mismeasure of one's relative distance from the target. The angle and position of their bodies relative to the target. They hunted twice a year through their adolescence until it became unsafe to do so.

Their last day hunting together, as brothers, as sons, set a strange precedent. Much of the afternoon was spent in silence observing two white egrets. It was a warm day, humid and overcast. By two p.m. they found and chose their game. By three p.m. the clouds parted to reveal slivers of sunlight, which lit upon the lowveld. One egret stood still only sixty yards away digesting a small rodent, which protruded limp and round from the bird's gullet. The other egret stalked through the grass nearby in search of its own meal.

Air stood still on the back of his right hand. His right hand was mounted with confidence on the butt of his rifle. His index finger on the trigger. He and his brother breathed slowly and deeply on their bellies, from the diaphragm, from the bottom of the lungs per their father's instructions. He learned to quiet the noise of the city, which always followed him on his way out. The hum of traffic and the salience of conversations overheard. Wandering lust and a rush of blood. Hiding. In search of anonymity and gratification. With so little wind the sounds of their chosen grounds carried clearly and brightly. From the solitary cooing of a red-necked pigeon to the sound of the shore pulled on by the tide.

After their first hour of observation, like a molting of urban sprawl, he settled into a meditative state which gave him steadiness and clarity. He felt his body sink into the harmony of things that his presence would typically bend or disturb. Everything became proximal then, and unthreatening.

Baldo, the inferior marksman, was asked to take the digesting egret. The stationary egret. Theo was told to fire upon the second bird only once it had lifted into flight. A test of his skill and a test of his father's tutelage. They readied themselves for the moment. The timing had to be perfect. Baldo fired on the first egret. Its legs went limp and it fell flapping as its last few nervous impulses shot through its body. At the sound of Baldo's shot the second egret, only thirty feet away from the first, took off in one, two, three great flaps of its long wings. Theo could feel his father's eyes on him. The egret was climbing quickly, ten, twenty, thirty feet into the air and he still hadn't fired his shot. A cloud drew suddenly over the lowveld, further distorting Theo's sight of the egret as it fled. He began to panic. His breath became shallow and his palms sweaty. Then in his ear an unexpected eruption. Left him deaf and ringing. The egret stopped mid-flight and hung in the air for what seemed like a full minute before falling dead to the ground, a streak of red across its snow white body. In that split second Baldo had reloaded and fired. One dead shot.

Both he and his father looked in awe and vexation at Baldo, whose gaze was trained on the second kill when suddenly something flashed in the sky to the east like lightning, followed closely by a thunderous boom. Like a skyrocket. Just one at first, loud and jarring. Then a succession of Roman candles. Explosions, one after another, sent caustic wind westward and grew louder and brighter. Theo felt the sheer bass and proximity of each explosion in his chest, blowing out the hammer and anvil, the drum and stirrup of his inner ear. It was both frightening and exciting. A shell fell through the branches of a nearby coconut palm.

His father grabbed them both by their collars and they fled together down the hill toward the main road where the Volkswagen was parked. Nimbus clouds rolled in, streaked red-orange as the bombastic tumult, one explosion after another, shook the leaves in the trees. Baldo looked back with a wistful glint in his eye as his kill disappeared behind the hill and he stumbled running toward the road.

The car was in sight just over one final grassy incline. His father grabbed him by the arm. Rushed into the back of the car, his father practically throwing him inside with his rifle right behind him, he caught sight of something he'd only read about. It was the first time he had ever seen snow. It wasn't particularly cold, but there it was, flurrying over the windows and windshield. He tilted his head backward to look up at the sky and count as best he could each flake as they fell and drifted across the glass. His father started the car as the firmament parted on fire and full of snow.

That night when Theo was sure everyone was asleep, when Baldo's nose began to whistle and no sound came from the master bedroom, he crept into his father's den and turned the lamp on. The light was soft yellow and warm over the wainscoting and woodgrain furnishing. All of the framed photos hung on the walls and the memories captured therein were obscured under a hoary layer of dust. All except one. There was an 8x10 photo of his mother as a girl, dressed up with her mother and father in front of a bookshelf.

His father was said to have taken the photo and his father was fond of saying it was love at first sight. Above the door inside the room hung a stuffed hawk. Its wings were open and talons bared as though it were swooping down on imaginary prey. Oil portraits of the Richter men hung in succession behind the desk, so that they looked over his father's shoulder as he worked.

He always felt dutiful in his father's den. He took a seat in his father's catty-cornered armchair and remained there with his eyes fixed on a portrait of his great-grandfather. He was an official-looking gentleman, bald pate with a handlebar moustache, epaulettes, and several military badges on his lapel. The little brass plaque beneath the portrait was engraved with his great-grandfather's name, his date of birth and his date of death.

MAX LUKAS RICHTER
1. MÄRZ 1840 – 11. OKTOBER 1912

Six years shy of his grandson's birth. He wondered what life
had been like for old Max. He wondered what kind of father he
was to his father's father. The portrait captured his great-grandfather's torso, shoulders turned slightly to the right, his head a
quarter turn left to face the artist. There wasn't much to deduce
about the man's personality from his expression. Nothing in the
indistinct light painted into his black pupils. He looked like a
general, or an equestrian with epaulettes. He stared so long at
the portrait he thought it might speak. But after a while it was
apparent that his great-grandfather had nothing to say. So Theo
spent the rest of the night with his legs crossed in his father's
armchair, trying to recover the incalculable light of a day long
gone. He woke up in his own bed in his own room after noon
to the smell of rain.

The earth was becoming damp and could give way above or
beneath him at any moment. He could hear it falling like a
muffled drum on the surface three feet above. His edges pressed
too comfortably into the isotropic dissolution of quick mud.
The glowsticks radiated enough light for him to see the necklace
caught between the dendritic tips of a thick hanging root. He
reached across his body to tug it loose. With little resistance the
necklace came free. He took a deep breath with his eyes closed
and clutched it in his palm, against his chest. He exhaled slowly,
felt himself briefly light-headed, then tucked it into his vest. He
began to quiet the noise, breathing slowly from the bottom of
his lungs just as his father had taught him. He could feel a draft
pouring in from the surface. He was close to la Casa.

["Come Clean" (Instrumental); produced by DJ Premier]
He hadn't spoken intimately with his brother in several months.
Their interactions were curt, neither familiar nor alien, but
damming an unsettled matter that would likely come pouring
out when it gathered enough mass. That's how it went with

them. Baldo held things in. Theo let things out. It was no big secret what, or who, had come between them.

On that final hunting trip, when his brother shot both birds in one breath and Armageddon had finally arrived, he realized that his brother thrived under the lights of the live show and that he himself lived his life like a studio artist, a retreat artist. He composed the happening of his life in privacy to be consumed publicly. Baldo on the other hand was a sleeping natural, one whose life spilled out before him in one long improvisation. Neither personality projected honestly the underlying capability and capacity of their character. Theo studied for things that came natural to Baldo. And while Theo was generally considered the charming and effortlessly brilliant brother, his father's son, he had difficulty making lasting connections with people. Baldo, outwardly reserved, sometimes to the point of standoffish and cruel, always cut to the heart of an individual. He had their mother's intuition. He was the shepherd—the consummate protector intolerant of bullying or anything violent in the guise of nicety. He offended as many as he befriended, but the ones he befriended were unerringly loyal.

They grew together and apart on tracks that ran parallel and sometimes converged. Almost every night they would convene, inheritors genetically identical and compelled to share the day's events with each other well past bedtime in hushed voices, only to be parted with the coming of the sun. Each assuming his public persona.

As boys they were spared the early disillusionment of their father's mereness. It wasn't until their twenties that they learned of his fondness for superficialities, self-destructive displays of machismo driven by nagging insecurity, and high society ridicule—an incestuous cabal on a small island—of his negress wife and the big mule twins whom he loved, but dutifully, and often it seemed without happiness. He drank heavily. Rum. He became distant through their teenage years and unaffectionate. Twice at least he stepped out on their mother for strange. Only, according to their mother, because he suspected her of committing the same sin. His joys were muddled through middle age. A period of crisis in his life to which his sons remained oblivious. In this way Jens had not failed them.

In their twenties they understood fatherhood, and manhood in general, as the consistent and successful performance of his character against the notion of a perilous world. Part and parcel of this performance of manhood was the recognition that no man could be perfect, and that what defined the man was his ability to salvage himself from the inevitable wreckage of his own hubris.

So when Jens had become, in their eyes, only a man fromwith flagging age; when he was sufficiently pressed against his breaking point and suffering from delirium tremens, the old man checked into a private rehabilitation program.

He surrendered his life for a second time to Malou, who guarded him for a time against his own addiction, locked him in the back room on days when he was belligerent, coddled him when he suffered through second childhood, and cared for him in his final infancy. She saved his life and he, to his credit, made efforts to salvage what he could of his dignity and purpose. He blossomed in old age. His sons, even Malou, could attest that he was at his best in those days, having rediscovered his humanity within the now recognizable boundaries of his own limitation. Reacquainted with faith, fatherly and uxorious, sometimes truckling.

The rain was falling steady. The farther he crawled the damper the earth became. Warmer too and the air that reached him tinged with a severe chemical odor like that of gasoline. He was unsure of its source. More than anything he was anxious to surface. The crawl space, after nearly two hours, was becoming unbearable.

Before leaving for the perimeter check Baldo grabbed him by the shoulder. He couldn't remember the last time Baldo had touched him in such a way, with the full weight of his hand coming down almost against his neck. He felt sucker-punched, unable to gauge the ambiguity of his brother's intention, which could have been anywhere. He turned to face his brother enswathed in shadow in the doorway, uncertain of what to expect, and remembered involuntarily Frances saying that he came like all pious men—in breathless revelation, quickly and gratefully and smiling like a happy little thief. Theo surpressed a smile.

Baldo wasn't smiling. Sleeplessness had worn itself into and around his eyes and tension trembled in his lips and jaw. He was starting to look like their father. Theo braced himself for whatever was coming. He knew in his bones that he wouldn't and couldn't retaliate. He would take it squarely.

Baldo pulled Theo into an embrace so quickly and quietly it took him a moment to recognize what was happening. Baldo held his brother tightly, as though he were restraining him, both arms wrapped across his shoulders with his face buried in Theo's neck. It was an unwarranted and certainly unexpected show of affection. Theo didn't know how to react, let alone respond. He couldn't quite read the situation and he couldn't quite place where it came from, or why. But he felt in his brother's stifling embrace an appropriate weightiness. He felt fastened secure. Re-lieved. Still loved. Before Theo could return the gesture, trying to slide his restrained arms behind his brother's back, Baldo let go. And just like that Theo was a ghost again, so suddenly light and transparent. Naked and vulnerable.

Baldo stood only inches away staring at him with bleary red eyes. Strange candor wringing its hands. Even though they were identical twins, the person staring sin vergüenza at Theo was hard to recognize. They couldn't have been more different.

Baldo bowed his head, both hands reaching for the nape of his neck. Beneath his vest were beads, blue and red, which he lifted gingerly and removed from his person. He gathered the beads into a compact mass in the palm of his hand and extended it out into the sunlight before him.

"Take these. Put them on."

Theo reached for the beaded necklace.

"They're yours now. Don't take them off."

They were weighty in his hand, weightier than they looked. The beads were rough and fashioned out of some composite ore. It certainly wasn't the usual cheap plastic. He thought to ask Baldo where he got the necklace from and why he wanted him to wear it, but the look in Baldo's eyes suggested urgency and insistence—an imploring gaze Baldo wore only when language seemed to fail him and the beast he kept caged came unbound.

Theo put on the necklace, wrapping it twice around his neck. He tucked the beads into his vest and said thank you.

Baldo shrank as Theo adjusted to the necklace. His eyes went flat and his formidable posture went slack, as though he were holding his breath for years and now found himself relieved of a burden, bowed suddenly instead by the weight of his age, the cruel passage of time. Thank you, Theo repeated. He moved in to hug his brother again, but Baldo stopped him.

"Promise me."

Of course, replied Theo. Of course. I promise. He was sincere and happy to be on speaking terms with his brother at such a fragile moment, when one or the other or both could lose their life without notice. From the corners of Baldo's mouth curled what could have been a smile. A strange mirage that gave way to characteristic impassivity.

"She—" Baldo started to speak then paused as though something were caught in his throat. With a wince he swallowed what invisible obstruction had lodged itself there and continued. "She could have stayed, you know. And she would have been happy. But I couldn't—" He stopped again. "I knew I wouldn't have been enough. For her. And eventually she would go out sniffing. Because that's what beauty does. Or it dies." He looked down dolefully, then leered into Theophilio with the intensity of a small star. "We surrender our lives to the sovereign." And without pivoting he swung a hard right hook, connecting with Theo's chin. The sheer force of the blow was enough to knock Theo backwards, off his feet. More than anything it was the shock of being sucker punched that stung.

Baldo spit into the sun and turned on his felled brother, receding into the cool darkness of la Casa.

That was the last time he spoke with his brother before leaving for the perimeter check. It was unlikely that Baldo was still waiting at la Casa with Arjún and the Colonel. They were probably well on their way, preparing for the arrival of American forces and the coordinated implosion of the old city.

The foxhole was fast becoming a muddy quagmire and the chemical stench, like nail-polish remover over a camp fire, came pouring in with rain and faint light and seared his eyes and nostrils. Mud had crept into his nose and into his mouth and his body ached from crawling through the morass. The rain, cold and inspiriting, came in over his head. He had finally reached the foxhole opening. Fifty yards away from the house he was presumably ahead of the two others in the crew conducting the perimeter check. Though he received no signal from either of them. Something must have gone wrong. He felt a mechanized hum like an air conditioner through the ground beneath the serein and the whisper of wind as it passed over the hollowed earth, which began to cave in around him.

He managed to look up and out into the world above. He could feel the weight of the earth like a kind of heavy comforter interring him as it slowly gave way. There was smoke, heavy smoke, drifting through the air. He could see the skeletal shadow of the flamboyant copse thrown flickering against the black bark of a tall maga. The light from a fire large enough to throw the full shape of trees through darkness, competing with the light of the moon which made what little sky visible a bluish color. A color neither rightly of night nor of day. He gathered what energy he could not to be buried, pulling himself up through fen which dissolved in his hands, pushing upward with his legs, extending his body outward in efforts to grab the nearest root and pull himself free.

The trench wasn't so deep that he couldn't escape. It was only a matter of time. Terra firma within reach, he couldn't remember the last time he had a decent plate of fresh fish. When the white flags were flown, for good or bad, he would make it a point to enjoy a nice hake fillet or empanada de cetí in Arecibo. Hell, he would open his own seafood place if the future allowed. And maybe Baldo would join him, somewhere on the coast. Maybe Piñones. But first he had to get free.

A root from the maga tree was within reach. Because it was so thick he couldn't get a firm grip, but it was sturdy enough to leverage his slow lift from the mire. As air was pushed from the collapsing crawl space it formed a vacuum around his legs. He dragged his knees through mud near hardened to cement using the root to anchor his ascent. It took all of his upper-body strength to free himself, but he managed to climb onto tenable earth.

A migraine beating the back of his skull blurred his vision further and radiated through his neck and shoulders a feverish ache. Firelight throbbed against the sopping black mass of his body huddled on hands and knees in a kind of child pose beneath the maga. He lifted his head to face the fire. La Casa was ablaze and billowing chemical black smoke. Something went wrong. The Lieutenant's little yellow house, from what he could see, was twice its size in flame, bright orange wisps floating through the flamboyant copse that surrounded it.

He began to lift himself slowly, the muscles and bones of his back and breast bracing and groaning against each other like the aged beams of a galleon on choppy water. An audible pop between the discs of his spine relieved some lumbar stiffness, but pain surged up and down his left side like cold fire. His shoulders were sore and his arms heavy, hard to lift, but it wasn't his time yet to give in to gravity or give up to entropy. He got to one knee, his eyes fixed on the burning house. He dropped his left hand over his raised knee for balance and threw his right against the trunk of the tree, lifting himself onto both feet. Standing, he leaned for a moment against the tree, resting his cheek against its cool bark as circulation returned to his extremities under the full weight of his armor, the rifle, and tools he'd carried through the tunnels on his back. The visor. The beaded necklace. He watched as the foxhole collapsed entirely at his feet, swallowing the last green light of the glowsticks used to illuminate his way through the tunnel.

Upright and regaining balance he turned to face the fire and started slogging waterlogged and caked in mud across the sod toward it. Branches smoldered like tinder in the blaze. He walked slowly and surely to a hum beneath the rain. Then he froze.

His vision was blurred, but he could see something moving behind the copse. Its strange shape between the trees seemed to float a few feet above ground. Smoke curled around its extremities, as though the thing had emerged from its own cloud of hellfire—Bayamanaco come to settle some ancient score.

Theo stood still, trying to gauge its movements. He unslung the rifle from his shoulder and readied himself, crouched and approaching the target. The copse opened into a clearing only thirty yards ahead and the house some ten yards beyond that. All of his training had come to this one decisive moment. All of his father's instruction. He had the undeniable advantage of a superior position, hidden as he was in the copse, watching his game. Slowly he made his way toward the target, taking cover behind the flamboyants. His heart palpitating and a cold sweat over his body. Rain thinned between the trees and nearer the untamed blaze of the house, which only seemed to grow more threatening. An explosion, a violent plume of fire ejected like a solar flare from the second-floor balcony over the entrance sent one of its supporting cantilevers smoldering to the ground. It was only a matter of time before the whole balcony fell, reduced to tinder in the crackling distortion. The cache of explosives likely left in the house would begin to ignite, sending fragments of the house

like fireballs hurtling through air. Keep to the copse, he thought.
He fixed his gaze on the dark figure unfazed in front of the
house. The ghost humming above ground in bent light began
to take shape. It wasn't humanoid. In fact it looked more like a
UFO from the *Twilight Zone*. It was an aircraft of some sort with
small canted vertical stabilizers in what he assumed to be the
hind part of the fuselage. It was oblong and dark, coated in ra-
dar-absorbant material. Sleek, like Yeager's Glamorous Glennis,
with one recessed air intake duct over the fuselage. Mid-mount-
ed and relatively short wings tapered on both sides. At its wing-
tips were large ducted turbines tilting at self-adjusting angles to
keep the bird lifted. He looked through the scope of his rifle for
some identification and a closer view. Printed atop the fuselage
was US national signage, one white star flanked by stripes in
low-visibility gray. There were no other identifying marks or
serial numbers. Obviously it was reconnaissance, judging by
the large bulb of camera equipment housed beneath the nose
of the craft, rotating left and right as it surveyed the landscape,
presumably for signs of life. But if it was a recon craft why was it
so near the site? And was it also responsible for the catastrophe?
He couldn't see any payload armaments housed beneath the
wings or fuselage and they were just out of range of the E.M.P.

There were whispers that American Dynamics had designed
a new unmanned vertical takeoff and landing craft for quick
support and surveillance missions, touted for its maneuverabil-
ity and potential access to remote locations. There were always
whispers of a new machine.

Just then the aircraft spun around, one hundred-eighty degrees,
to face the copse. It must have caught wind of Theo watching
behind the trees. Theo tensed up in position, ready to fire if need
be. The craft hovered over to the edge of the wooded area, thirty
yards ahead. It was possible that the craft had sighted him via

night-vision or infrared. Or radar. There was no gun mounted in the fuselage, and it didn't look like it was equipped for any particular payload. The question was whether the aircraft would call in reinforcements or a coordinated strike on the position. Its eyes seemed to fix a red quartz gaze on his position and it hovered perfectly still, its propellers humming over the wild hiss of the fire. Then, from the very tip of its nose combusted a small spark.

The trees at the edge of the copse blew up in violent flame and a sudden backdraft seared his cheek. The trunk of the tree was too narrow to protect him from what seemed to be the long destructive reach of a military grade flamethrower. He tucked his weapon and somersaulted for cover behind the nearest tree, tucking and rolling across soft sod to get clear of its range and find a better position. Then the aircraft lifted twenty, thirty, forty feet above ground. Its sudden lift fanned flames dangerously close to his position. The machine was taking the elevated position, moving to ignite the red tops of the trees and smoke the rat from its hiding place.

He looked up just in time to see the aircraft spit a jet of fire above him, a rapturous saber of light shooting across the black night. Terror at the sight of such conflagration sweeping across the canopy, a bright orange wave scattering ash and ember like rain above his small black body leaving no place to hide. Flames sucked oxygen from the air, making it hard to breathe. He ducked into a prone position and began to crawl toward the clearing with red leaves aflame falling around him, twigs and small branches landing like hot whips across his back, against his calves, on his bare neck. The trees were beginning to lose structural integrity. Soon he would have to worry about whole limbs coming apart and falling across his body. The weight of one full branch might pin him, or worse, impale him. The air was thick with chemical smoke, even so low to the ground, and if he didn't make it out soon he'd be baked alive. Twenty yards and closing until he made the clearing. There he could engage the target.

He could hear the hum of the aircraft above and the roar of its flamethrower spraying the canopy with impunity, lighting the mountainface with a golden fury one could see for miles. He was starting to feel lightheaded from the heat, the lack of oxygen, and he couldn't tell if it was still raining. He'd give anything to be back in the foxhole, drenched in sweat and mud and rain, cold and sick and safe. Funny how things worked, he thought. One minute you're digging your way out of the earth, the next you're digging your way back in. Head down and fatalistic.

His father in a tux stood with arms crossed in the clearing, untouched by flame, ten yards and closing. He spoke in the deep and recognizably faulty voice of his forties. It's only when the heat is on that we're tempted to run, tempted to fold. Looking away is no small prayer. Like this travesty, this hurdle, is beneath what you're wont to engage. It won't go away. It won't ease up. This, what lies ahead of you, is everything, son. You have to face it. You have to face it and breathe through it and conquer it, even if only by being the last man standing. You conquer it. Even if it kills you. You—his father stopped to pull an apple from his pocket. He took a crisp bite and continued. When I was a boy my father beat me for playing with my infant sister. You didn't know her. She died before we left Germany. I didn't even know her. Your grandparents, they must've known she was doomed. I couldn't see it coming. And when she died my father kissed me, an unusual thing in itself, and told me life would change. I couldn't understand how. Until things changed. That last time we went hunting. Remember? Your brother's not here now. Don't miss this time. The bird, he added while chewing a mouthful of apple.

Five yards and closing and the sound grew louder like a vacuum on the inside of a turbine and a hot wind ripped across his face as the aircraft descended before him bent like a mirage in the clearing, a match-sized flame ready in its mouth.

Instinctively Theo buried his face in the mud and tucked his hands in beneath his waist. He tried as best he could to keep his exposed skin from what was coming. The nomex fiber woven into his armor might stave off third-degree burns. At least it was designed to. He lay flat and still, holding his breath, willing his body into the earth, in his mind imagining he could be as dense and unencumbered as the mud around him.

Then the bird fired into the copse, a pillar of flame passing just inches over his body. He grit his teeth to keep from screaming as it tore violently across his back. His hair, the back of his neck, his armor, the metal of his rifle heated to unbearable temperature. It felt as though hot knives were shoved into his ears and a burn at the extremities not unlike a feeling of extreme cold, severe frostbite. He could feel the skin of his neck literally begin to crisp and peel away entirely, scorching deep tissue to indelible trauma. The hairs on his head were singed from tip to root like sparklers and sent his skull to boil in the mud, until finally he realized he was screaming for breath, for relief and salvation, for the last narrow fibers of consciousness.

His father lay face up in the mud beside him and began to explain. I cheated on your mother because I loved her. When a man loves a woman the way I loved your mother he stands to lose his wildness. So I stepped outside of our vows. He paused to take another bite of his apple. You must be wondering why. I'm not sure, in retrospect. I felt like I submitted myself entirely to your mother and I felt like I had no control over my life, public and private. I mean, I loved your mother in every way. It's unthinkable to do what I did to a woman whose box always

tasted like black truffle oil. Even in old age. There was royalty
in her veins. But my dreams every night, no exaggeration, were
reinventions of teenage anxiety. Twisted deliriums. The firm was
floundering. Dullness settled into our marriage. The sex cooled.
He turned on his side to face Theo. I was insecure, to say the
least. I was depressed. I needed to know I was still a man. So I
stepped out for strange pussy. For a while I was riding high. I
felt like I found something lost. Youth. But when she found out,
your mother, she was hurt. Neither you nor your brother knew,
because she was taught to keep up appearances. She was hurt
anyway. And seeing her like that made me sick, made me more
self-loathing. I hit the bottle hard. Believe me, I never wanted to
hurt you boys or your mother. But, and I don't know how, she
was strong enough to save us both. Save us all really. You ever
have your heart broken, Theophilio? he asked, resting his head
on his elbow. Get up.

The bird-machine stopped breathing fire. He rolled on the
ground like manic swine, trying to extinguish his agony in the
mud. But the ground around him was scorched, as dry and
cracked as the skin of his neck and head. He tried to rise quickly
and take cover, but only managed to get to one knee. With every
movement he felt his skin pulled taut, near tearing and charred.
He held his spine as straight as he could to keep from the searing
pain of sudden movement. Each shallow breath tested his mettle,
the subtle rise and fall of respiration made more difficult by a
dearth of oxygen, the sharp pain in his left side, and the damage
done to his skin. His vision was considerably blurred, but he
could still see the dark shadow of the fire-breathing bird floating
before the house engulfed in flame.

He moved quickly against injury and the phantom pain of a
skin carapace formed to the back of his skull and neck, reaching for the hot metal of his rifle. Slowing and deepening his

breath he fixed his sights on the bird-shadow, fit the butt of his rifle between his shoulder and armpit, and squeezed the trigger. But he heard no sound pop from the barrel. He felt no recoil against his shoulder. The rifle hadn't fired. The bird-shadow was unfazed, a match-sized flame flickering at the ready in its mouth. His hands began to tremble. He pulled the trigger this time, spastic and imprecise, and when it got stuck, when the mechanism had sucked its teeth in denial, he realized that the rifle had jammed. A white wave of terror and panic swept over him, evacuating his last sense of self-preservation. He tried checking the rifle for its malfunction, fumbling over the chamber and safety, but he could barely see. It was only a matter of time before the bird-shadow unleashed another jet of lacerating flame. And then what?

He wanted to cry, like a child exhausted of all options. It felt strange not to have his brother there behind him, shepherd over the sheepfold. He could hardly feel Baldo's beaded necklace beneath his vest, but he knew they were there, still safe and unharmed by the fire. He clutched them between trembling fingers.

At the sound he flinched and shut his eyes. He saw, in the split second before the sound, fire erupt from the shadow-machine.

But he felt nothing. You've never had your heart broken, have you son? His father whispered in his ear. I knew you were never really in love with your wife. It was all superego. You let her go because you didn't really want her and she knew it. I wanted your mother from adolescence. When I saw her I knew. She was someone special, someone I should know. It was divine. She thought I was strange. I think she sensed I had an inferiority complex, then. But I'm not without my charms. I loved your mother like no other woman. She was truly the one for me. I was hers. I was her man. And it took me years and having twins to realize that my heart and soul belonged to that woman. I was responsible to her and for her. You understand? But how could you. You've never had your heart broken. Open your eyes.

The last of the cantilevers had collapsed and with it the balcony. The inferno must have detonated another cache of explosives in the house. What he heard before closing his eyes was the explosion and the sound of debris landing on one of the bird-machine's ducted turbines, causing it to hover erratically in the clearing. It was now or never.

He rose to his feet and ran with rifle in hand toward the blurred figure of the bird-machine. Surrounded on all sides by unchecked volatility, the canopy on fire above him raining ember and ash, numb to the charred inflexibility of his skin, he scrambled toward the bird-shadow flailing in the clearing. He met the creature at eye level, squinting through its nine-eyed gorgon stare at the ghost of a crew miles away. A mud-covered golem, half-dead and grimacing. The bird-machine kindled its flame in preparation.

He only had one chance. He ducked quickly under the port-side wing. The bird-machine spun around to engage the assailant, unleashing a violent jet of bright orange flame, but it was too late. Theophilio leapt up behind it latching onto the wing and jammed his rifle into the turbine. He only had moments before the compromised propeller blew and sent the machine flying out of control. He let go and fell hard on the ground as the bird attempted full lift. With one prop down and its starboard wing damaged the bird-machine spun out of control and crashed into the copse, triggering an explosive dead-man switch intended to prevent tech recovery by the enemy.

Theo sat there. Drifting. It was still raining. He could feel it
now falling cool and steady in the clearing. He let himself sink
in exhaustion, careful not to sink too near a sense of relief. The
cars were gone. The Lieutenant's red jeep gone. Both levels of
La Casa and the cellar reduced to nothing in the fire. A dying
candle adorning the side of the mountain. He was startled by his
own reflection in a small puddle, its glassy surface rippled by rain
beside him. For a moment he couldn't recognize his reflection.
He was afraid to see what deformed monster he had become
under the shadow-machine's flamethrower. He turned his head
slowly to examine the back of his skull, studying the area gingerly with the tips of his fingers. He felt his brother's beaded necklace at the nape of his neck and worked his fingers slowly upward
from there. He felt his neck where it was burned and the back of
his head. He felt hair beneath his probing fingers, still sensitive
to his own light touch. The air was that rarified density which
reminded him of childhood and the scent of refined hemp in his
mother's hair. All of the possibilities that came with not knowing
what happened or what would happen next.

15 OCTOBER XX01 [COLORMINUTE 15; EMPRESS OF] Alma woke painfully stiff and hungover to the sound of her sister already awake and washing dishes, shifting her weight back and forth between the bunioned balls of her bare feet, amplified and echoic and so like a hymn she knew she knew, but couldn't remember.

¿Alma? ¿Quieres un chispito d'ajoz?

viii. 5CREENSTARS

I remember as a boy falling asleep beside Solomon. His bed, its smell, like the inmost layer of fur on a wild dog—warm, natural, beyond me. How we lay together. My small body beside his, sometimes awake enough to feel him touch me, feel his hot breath on my neck. He'd find my right ear in the blue hours of morning, kneading its cartilage between his thumb and index finger like a priest with prayer beads. Sometimes he'd whisper in my ear a wish for the day. Because he wanted wisdom for his little brother, he'd say when asked why in the afternoon. Always the same answer.

With his spare change he bought me pens, pencils, paper, color. He bought me comic books, Marvel and D.C. canon, which inspired me to pen my own contributions to the well-established mythos of my favorite heroes. Nothing ever came of these experiments in story-telling. No grand discovery by Stan Lee. And they're all lost now, thankfully. But I remember drafting an alternative origin story for the character of Peter Parker—a young man bit by a spider irradiated after an incident at Indian Point.

Drunk with newfound power and guilt over having let escape the man who murdered his dear uncle Ben, Parker decides to pursue the killer. The killer, the reader discovers, flees the scene on foot with no more than forty dollars. A dirty take. NYPD is dragging ass, so Parker follows the killer. He finds him holed up in an abandoned tenement on what was then Stone Ave, now Mother Gaston, in Brownsville. Parker doesn't tell the police.

Instead he chooses to observe him for six days from the roof of a neighboring project building, sometimes leaving him food. An apple is foregrounded. On the seventh day the killer is gone. The apple left to rot in a single, final frame.

Neither boy nor man, Parker wanders the city at night, despondent over the loss of his uncle. He wants to disappear, press his nose into the extinguished shoulder of what used to feel like consolation. For lack of refuge, he hides, hanging upside down for days on end without food or water until, finger by finger, his grasp on reality slips. His senses radically compartmentalized, he experiences the world in parallel phenomenological threads, a simultaneity of occurrences in time and space processed as if happening independently. In one story arc he follows a man walking in drag from Fourteenth to Twenty-third concurrently rapt in the break-up spat of a young couple newly graduated from a high school in Battery Park, all the while pining after the sweet scent of Magnolia's on Bleecker carrying across the general barometric trend, which seems to indicate rain. A four in seven chance of being catcalled follows the man in drag. The young lovers stand a one in three chance of getting back together (only to break up again for good).

He spends weeks apart from his grieving Aunt May, calling her exclusively from pay phones. No longer the resilient woman that raised him, she is in his eyes reduced to an unbearable fragility. The cubistic abstraction of a person he once felt strongly for. A responsibility he is unready to assume.

At his most vulnerable he loses the desire for language and dissociates entirely from his body. On days flooded with sensory noise he encounters, almost accidentally, his estranged body elsewhere in the city, aloof and muttering about the singularity of a sensation. The sound of the train beneath Sixth Ave. The urgent odor of Staten Island present in traces for miles and miles.

Despite these difficulties he manages to hold it together, navigating the vagaries of normalcy by subsisting in shadow, on theft.

He dreams of walking the snow-covered streets of East New York after sunset. In these dreams he is lost and trying to get back to Church where the community has gathered to discuss education reform. Eventually he finds the Church and proceeds to trudge toward it through an ever deeper and more impenetrable darkness, unable to see more than three feet in front of him. He's abandoned hope, frozen in snow beside the chain link fence of an abandoned playground, calling out for help, ready to cry out for Guidance, when, suddenly, he is startled by a pair of hands, long thin fingers like the bare limbs of a tree reaching through the fence. He falls backward startled and panicked to witness Mungo, six feet tall with the enlarged and hairless head of a man, glowing red eyes, a naked body the color of Mars, four or more legs, and those long unseemly fingers reaching ominously toward him. He dreams nightly of Mungo, who leaves him with the impression that he is there to collect a debt.

Then, one day on Fifth Ave, he encounters the man who killed his uncle. The killer's eyes are worn considerably in his gaunt face. He looks ill and desperate. He's walking fast. He's wearing threat. They lock eyes in a moment of recognition. Then the killer steps into traffic at the crosswalk and is hit by a cab barreling down the avenue. His body is dragged half a block before the car comes to a screeching halt.

Peter becomes a cabbie. Providing financial security and relative solitude, the job allows him to operate comfortably on the fringes of society, witness to its microcosmic fiber. He sends remittances to Aunt May hoping she'll use them to pay for the removal of black mold from her basement and bathrooms. With

the rest, he rents a studio in Queens where he begins adjusting
to the dissolution of his former life and the genesis of another:
six times as strong as an adult male in peak condition, twice as
agile, and three times as quick. His metabolism allows him to
go for a full week without food.

He drives afternoon routes between Brooklyn and Manhattan,
making occasional trips to the airports. Even with his newfound
power the unseen world, a world that could allow such a fantastical metamorphosis, escapes his grasp. Curious how even in a
city as large as New York he can encounter the man who killed
his uncle on the street and, in the same second, watch him get
dragged to his death. Unlike Marvel's hero, justice as an ideal is
not something that keeps my Peter awake at night. What keeps
him awake is his inability to forget the pathetic sound of Ben's
heel scraping the sidewalk on the night of his murder. That slip
into the ether of unforeseen circumstance from which Ben could
have escaped if he were quicker or smarter or more prescient.
The sound of his heel scraping the sidewalk; or, the casual vertigo
of a man approaching eighty-seven, leaning ever so slightly into
irretrievability. Like a child learning to walk, his uncle seemed
worthy of a kind of protective affection reserved only for the in-
defatigable. The ones who daily defy the odds and live to remind
us that it's possible.

Afternoons on duty come and go for young Peter Parker. Nightly
he cruises New York City's underworld with his off-duty lights
on or no lights at all looking to scratch a persistent itch. He
lingers among the prostitutes, observing them with their pimps,
the johns they service, and the law-enforcement officials who
take their bribes. He observes them for months, learning their
behaviors and routines, marveling at slight variations in deci-
sion-making that surprise and reveal character. One bird, for
example, refusing twice the pay to perform an act she is uncom-

fortable with, despite the risk. One john having second thoughts about cheating on his partner.

In retrospect, my take on the character was decidedly mature, postmodern, and, perhaps, dull. Too passive to rival the cult status of Spidey's pulp origins. The regular gimmick of my vision for your friendly neighborhood Spider-Man was not a gallant, high-flying quest to protect the city from colorful villains, but the thoughtful and sometimes gritty illustration of how delicately intertwined people are in the web of life. Some would argue that Marvel's web-slinger, with his everyman origin story, already achieves this. Maybe so. My Peter's greatest difficulty was not asserting authority over a slew of campy villains, but learning to assert authority over the circumstances of his own life. My Peter was learning how to manage emotional and mental well-being and how to love despite loss and a history of violence. Looking back, it bothers me to think of the psychic trauma I must have internalized as a child. I couldn't imagine an artist bold enough to try penciling my Peter. Frank Miller, maybe? Maleev? Mack? Mignola? Pichelli? Chris Ware.

And I can't remember where I left my copy of *Amazing Spider-Man*, vol. II, no. 36. The all-black cover on the memorial 9/11 issue. It's not the most valuable comic in my collection, but it's my favorite. Number 36, despite its historical import, wasn't a particularly well-written issue. It felt rushed, melodramatic, incomplete. John Romita Jr.'s penciled iconography bordered on facile chauvinism. But there was something beautiful about its address of real-time, its attempt to draw the solidarity necessary to overcome catastrophic trauma and how that solidarity, that brief American undressing of the individual, correlated with a kind of heroism.

Volume II represented an exciting rebirth for Stan Lee and

Steve Ditko's Spider-Man. I liked JRJR as penciller. It seemed only natural for him to succeed his father, John Romita Sr. Jack Kirby or George Pérez he's not, but for Spidey I liked JRJR's angular lines, his magnificent spreads, and thereafter imagined Spider-Man penciled intermittently by inheritors of the Romita name. My attachment to the old-made-new ethos of *Amazing*, vol. II had much to do with the zeitgeist, the imminent release of the Sam Raimi film, and my rekindled love affair with things extraordinary.

I can't tell if it's still raining. I'd rather walk tbh, how much I abhor car service, but sometimes, late and desperate to get anywhere in this city, you do strange things, make questionable decisions. Gideon Schwartz, *son of Ham*, has the radio on low, music spilling faint over the glass. It's funny. You give up on certain things, on certain places and people, until the *unfinished* finds its way back to you—as unprepared to deal with it now as you were then. I didn't plan on calling Gideon, but between Millie still groggy from the birth and the baby, it only made sense to phone it in, take a risk on a stranger. "We hanged our harps upon poplars in the midst thereof," he recites to himself in the driver's seat. How like an old man, humming to dam up the weight of the world, he assumes the vague shape of a familiar Psalm. Wearing a red knit cap high and tight on his head like the unpinched tip of a condom, Gideon glances in the rearview at the backseat imbrication of our bodies. My back angled against the door, cradling my wife in my arms. My wife, her feet up, half-awake against my chest. Our newborn girl asleep against her mother's breast, asleep against the post-diluvial light of a city at night. Being escorted home gratis, at ease with a world passing wet and electric outside.

The barely audible voice present over the radio is masculine, crooning in Spanish, and the instrumental accompaniment hearkens to another bygone *NuYor*. Héctor Lavoe is crying, post-orgasmic tremolo and vibrato, through the second verse of "El Cantante." The song's been stuck in my head since I got off the train.

"We lost him in Kirkuk," says Gideon out of the blue. "Couldn't find him. Not dead. Just deserted. Last I heard he was doing merc work in northeast Iraq. On the border."

Gideon makes a smooth left turn onto Second Ave, cutting through Stuy Square.

"Sol used to get letters," he said. "You never wrote?"

I pretend not to hear Gideon's question. Outside I catch sight of a young man, Slav-looking in a bright red Spyder jacket. He's a long way from Brighton Beach, only a few dark hairs out of boyhood, hanging around Union Square with head down and hands in pockets. Like so many of the goons I grew up with, all Buddha-smoke, body spray, and affected machismo.

My eyes drift back inside to the warmth breathing in sync between my arms. To the bundle of quiet cradled between her arms. *Black Ice* hangs from the rearview filling the cab's solemn atmosphere with an artificially cool scent. But I just want my wife. I want to be home with my wife. I press my nose as softly as I can into the top of her head, let her birth-labored scent fill my nostrils.

A new silence settles. Gideon, it seems, has abandoned his curiosity regarding my brother. Lavoe is still singing.

The song was written for Lavoe by Rubén Blades. Performed to beautiful effect with acoustic accompaniment by Blades himself in Jennifer Lopez and Leon Ichaso's 2007 biopic, *El Cantante*, we are treated to a glimpse of the song as it was intended to be performed—that is, as the lament of a sad and resilient clown. The song debuted on Lavoe's 1978 Fania album, *Comedia*, the cover of which features him dressed as a Chaplin-esque tramp with toothbrush moustache, bowler hat, and cane.

What makes Lavoe and his performance rare, nigh operatic (clocking in at over ten minutes), is the sincere struggle which combusts marvelously within his own voice. At once a declaration and waging of war. His voice is simultaneously composed of and distorted by a melodious tremolo. This undercurrent of tension lends it a distinct sublimity, impressing upon the ear an urgency and tenderness which inhabit the same auditory space. The song is about the affective labor of the performer, in this case a singer, and Lavoe is clearly working in this song, showcasing the affective endurance that made him a star.

A tonal preoccupation and struggle with affective labor mark his work as he became a transnational phenomenon. Lavoe was a quintessential product of the diaspora. A boy from a small island transplanted to the Moloch that was and is New York City searching for success and stability in adulthood. His popular success came only after the wholly American experience of having his name changed (from Héctor Juan Pérez Martínez) to sound more marketable and sophisticated. More European. The name Lavoe, an ironically unsophisticated portmanteau of La Voz, marked our young, gifted, and ambitious Héctor Martínez.

The narrative of exile (political and socio-economic) that commonly frames the Latin and Caribbean diaspora is entrenched in this loss and labor. Asked constantly to submit and assimilate, the exile must suppress, if not lose wholly, language and memory. The exile is stripped of identity, cautioned toward liminality, and shamed for cultural visibility. Moreover, the exile, thrust again into the mechanized hold of capitalism, must find work. What does this look like in a post-employment economy?

Where affective labor has adapted to the demands of an increasingly wired world by operating on-call, the laborer must be ready
at all times, even during sleep, to respond to a happening of necessity. Affective labor varies across the board, but a general lack
of recognition and understanding for those who labor discreetly
to provide a needed service reminds us of an ethical and meta-
physical quandary as old as history itself. Sports, art, religion,
sex, entertainment, education (public, private, and hard-knock),
law enforcement, legal and judicial systems, politics, the health
care industry, psychiatric services, hospice and visiting nurse
services, child care services, nannies, the death care industry,
the hospitality industry, human resources. These are only a few
examples of extant industries and occupations that have as their
focal point practices of affective labor. These affective industries
exist in service to a humanity that happens irrespective of all
thinkable mores and socio-systemic apparatuses. Why? Because
the body has its needs and its needs have so far eluded absolute
control. Even for the oncologist, the sudden disappearance of
certain cancers can only be explained as an act of God.

So the question is posed to the arriving exile: what service can
you provide for the betterment of our union? Lavoe could sing.

"For there they that carried us away captive required of us a
song; and they that wasted us required of us mirth, saying, 'Sing
us one of the songs of Zion.'" Gideon's voice startles me again
out of reverie. He's still reciting the Psalm, pulling lines from
memory. I hope he's not reading. I can't tell from the backseat.
The drive has been smooth sailing so far, cruising downtown
in that imperceptible seam between night and day where city
residents dissolve like so much ground glass back into the architecture. The baby is awake in Millie's arms. That, I can see. Her
eyes puffy and open. Her skin a tissue colored the muted bark of
an ash. Wrapped in a pink cotton blanket. Wisps of hair peeking
out of a pink cotton cap. Seven pounds even. Her eyes are open.

"How shall we sing the Lord's song in a strange land?" mutters Gideon, suddenly recalling the next line of the Psalm.

The song shifts dramatically in the second half from epic recitation to antiphon. Like a Greek tragedian, Lavoe makes the song his own in a call-and-response with a backing chorus, inviting a discourse that extends well beyond the borders of his performance. With his eyes shut tight behind aviator shades, feeling and responding to the sound of his band, he reaches in excess of their canny consonance. Ecstatic, running over, calling attention to his greatness above and beyond all those bygone performers. Daring any and all critics to challenge his assertion. Typical posturing. But for his contemporaries he reserves a reverence...

Lavoe's choice to conclude the song with a roll call, *una descarga*, is a curiosity. *Mis saludos a* Celia, Rivera, Feliciano. His esteemed contemporaries. Celia Cruz. Ismael Rivera. José Luis 'Cheo' Feliciano.

Celia Cruz, of the three, garnered by far the most international success. She is perhaps the most significant icon of Latin-Carribean music and culture. Ismael Rivera was a man of the people. A mid-century pillar of afro-latinidad. Born and raised in Santurce, he bridged the gap between folk traditions like Bomba with modern Salsa. Rivera's phrasing alone is notable for its inventive vitality and playfulness. He had the righteous bravado and swagger of a homegrown, hometown hero and worshipped only at the feet of black Christ. Cheo Feliciano, like Lavoe, was another product of the diaspora and a founding father of Salsa. A rehabilitated addict, both original and prolific, with a Prussian blue voice, Feliciano reinvented the romance of the bolero.

Lavoe's improvised acknowledgment of these artists at the very end of this operatic song is an attempt to absolve a debt owed.

With a kind of hipster savvy, Lavoe bows to a tradition which is African, Indigenous, European. A syncretic tradition from which he borrows and to which he contributes. This was, in a sense, the ethos of Salsa. An aural manifestation and representation of the island's creolization. A rhythmically engaged account of history chronicling the triumph of love over encomienda, genocide, slavery, colonialism, imperialism, and exile.

Perhaps more importantly in this acknowledgment, or deference, is a concession to the idea that Lavoe has moved beyond entertainment. He is exposing the metaexigencies of being through the labor of his music, stepping from stage into audience. In Lavoe's voice, which is the voice within his voice, there's this unavoidable commingling of eros and thanatos—a transmigratory cycle wherein his desire for life (in carnal pleasure), when realized, hastens death. He was, as such, a tragic case. An addict, a catholic mystic who frequently consulted Babalaos, Lavoe died of AIDS-related complications in 1993.

His performance is a primitive calculus. He has nothing to say and everything is his tongue. He sings until he can no longer sing and if he has ceased to sing it is only because the highest authority in this universe shall have chosen finally to mute and reclaim what was divinely bestowed upon him at birth. His expression engenders both the actualization of his being and his inability to exist entirely within the imagined paradigm of his actualization. Shape and shapelessness, like a dream from which he wakes without language to describe what unspoken feeling lingers in the base of his skull, what temperature goes unabated in his palms.

One could even say that the same ethos which produced Salsa also produced Boogaloo, Uprock, the Hustle, all that and Hip Hop in the South Bronx. The context of Hip Hop's origins is, of course, different from what precedes it, but the ethos remains the same. Charlie Ahearn's 1983 film *Wild Style* is the most popular depiction of Hip Hop in its "Golden Era." But a more accurate film depiction of the origins of Hip Hop can be found in Gary Weis and Jon Bradshaw's 1979 documentary *80 Blocks from Tiffany's*. Both films are relatively poor attempts to cash in on the then-burgeoning fascination with the culture and condition of the inner city. But unlike *Wild Style*, *80 Blocks from Tiffany's* is negatively capable and projects a wildly prophetic and strangely lucid vision of Hip Hop's life cycle—from its miraculous inception to its sad and frequently contested death. The film's memorable opening montage features the uptempo second part of "Consuelate" by the Alegre All-Stars, precursors of Fania music. Weis and his crew follow, or try to follow, the exploits of the Savage Nomads and the Savage Skulls, two South Bronx gangs, as they go about their lives, giving brief and poignant testimonies of their experience. We glimpse the bombed-out ruin that was the South Bronx in the seventies. These are the conditions Grandmaster Flash and the Furious Five chronicle in "The Message": "Broken glass everywhere . . ." The Nomads and Skulls are clad in biker leather and punk garb, Alan Vega rockabilly fringe on a stroll, military surplus featuring memento mori and neo-nazi iconography. Swastikas, SS patches, and Kaiser helmets. Their rebellious sartorial choices were not meant necessarily to offend, but to provoke and suggest their eccentricity from bourgeois America. They were self-styled enemies of the state—an aesthetic frequently revisited in Hip Hop. Think of Kanye West and the appropriation of confederate flag iconography for his Yeezus tour merch. Or Capital STEEZ and his controversial Pro Era logo, an interlocking 47 designed to look provocatively like a swastika. All of this—prophetically contained in one documentary.

80 Blocks crescendoes at the block party with DJ Frankie Dee spinning behind the sweet *yes, yes, y'all / freak it to the beat y'all* of India, her eyes askew, sheepishly clutching the mic. Produc-

ers chose "Chic's" "Everybody Dance" to overdub the scene—
one impossible to forget. This was our wild west. Our frontier
America.

Elsewhere, a decade later, Panamanian General Edgardo
Armando Franco coolly proclaimed that the pum pum would
not be his undoing, inaugurating the movement el negro, Tego
Calderón, would initially dismiss as ". . . a carbon copy of
dancehall." Reggae en español was a cultural hybrid of West
Indian and Latin that went from local diversion to international
fame when a deadbeat (*por no decir caco*) ballplayer from Villa
Kennedy gave the world a gallon of his own high octane gasoline. By then, nothing of Shabba's toasting over Bobby Digital's
Dem Bow Riddim had survived the trip. It slipped from Patois
to Spanish (nigh faithfully) at the new-world crossroads of the
canal, making its way to New York and from New York to Puerto
Rico where Shabba's Dem Bow would arrive as *Dembow*, forever
transformed by the same manic languor of eros and thanatos
that marked Salsa a score in years prior.

I hadn't noticed the Lavoe hush into another music until,
I think, Herbie Hancock's "Mimosa" picks up on the radio.
Gideon's nodding along to Willie Bobo's steady time-keeping
timbales. The cab eases to stop at a red light before crossing East
Houston. Moving slowly from NoHo into SoHo. Millie's awake.
Our eyes meet in the rearview. Her gaze unflinching, full of her
mother's patrician unreadability. She closes her eyes again and
repositions herself against my chest, stretching her swollen legs
while holding the baby against her breast. I know she's tired. She
wants to be home. *Soon, my love.*

Bluish light from the backseat touchscreen lingers on her face.
Back-to-back advertisements flash for popular new haptic suits.
The advertisements segue into two news anchors mouthing
headlines on screen. I want to turn it off, but the most that pas-

sengers are allowed to do is mute the feed, so I lower the screen's brightness, letting the glow die down in the cab as we approach the Manhattan Bridge.

The streets are remarkably empty of traffic. Gideon turns onto Canal from Chrystie, then from Canal to the Bowery, winding our cab around the triumphal arch and onto the ramp for the Brooklyn bound upper level.

"I have a thing with heights," mumbles Gideon shaking his head as the car climbs quietly up the bridge, ascending into the sky over lower Manhattan. DSR is scrawled in fading white paint across the top of a tall and narrow tenement. It's been there for as long as I can remember, posted on the red façade of the tenement beside the city's first Chinese Presbyterian Church on Market Street. Seeing it always reminds me of *80 Blocks from Tiffany's*. DSR lives. A bittersweet thought considering that most of the original Skulls and Nomads are dead. And how one or two reformed Skulls gave their lives to the Lord, swinging wide right on the moral pendulum to make up for wilder days.

In the cab Millie kicks her clogs off, careful not to disturb the baby. They drop to the cab floor with a dull thud leaving her free to stretch her toes. She's still wearing the hospital socks with rubber treads, two or three pairs of which she forced into my jacket pocket. Her ankles are swollen from birthing, but her breathing is regular and comfortable. A caravan of cop cars go careening down the Manhattan bound side of the bridge flashing their berries. One train, then another, trundles along the tracks beneath them.

The cramped graff-bombed roofs of Chinatown pass quickly in the window as the cab drives onward—a bright blur of names and post-human personae claiming fame and heavens.

My last intimate memory of Chinatown is of having dinner with Millie, over a decade back, at a noodle restaurant on Doyers. She called it Chinatown's Bloody Bend—Doyers apparently famous for the early 20th century Tong wars. These were gangland wars frequently involving hatchets. The narrow winding strip of road just off of Chatham Square sits in lower Manhattan like a hole in the fabric of spacetime, a remarkable confluence of old and new.

When last we were on Doyers at the noodle spot Millie ordered the Fujianese Wonton with knife-pulled noodles and I had the pork and hand-pulled noodles. It was my first time there and I'd never had Fujianese wontons, so she let me try one and I loved it. Savory meat bundled in a silky dumpling, submerged in some sort of all-day-divine broth. Her bowl of wontons was clearly superior to my plain, old pork. When I went back for another wonton, casually dipping my sticks in her soup, she threw a spoon at me, a gesture I took to mean *I don't want to share*. Only after dinner would I understand what this meant. All tenderness aside, we talked about semi-weighty things, musing on post-war capital, the blaring faults of bipartisan politics, and why this may have been one of the reasons British astrologer Alan Leo believed the American national character to be Geminian, as opposed to the Spanish Sagittarian, French Leonine, or the entire continent of Africa in Cancer. We agreed that though no mention was made of the small Caribbean nation known as Puerto Rico, Leo most certainly would've deemed it Scorpion in nature—*an island possessed of a closeness the colour of a scorpion's carapace; the complexity of an entire hemisphere contained therein*. In the middle of our conversation Millie's face flushed. She swallowed the last of her last Fujianese wonton and announced with a coy, soup-sated smile that she was pregnant with our second son— my first—Ridgely Torrence. That was my postprandial notice.

The cab draws higher into the sky, doing seventy now on the way to Brooklyn. Chinatown tenements part revealing New York City's skyline between the trussed beams of the bridge, its dark, painted face wrung silent from millions of projected fantasies and dreams.

The expressway comes into view, a narrow strip of asphalt wedged and winding between the Brooklyn Bridge and Brooklyn Bridge Park, as the cab zooms over a baseball diamond and an almost empty FDR drive. Tired, but awake. The expressway looks uncongested. Only the intermittent red taillights of cars on their way home or to work on the graveyard shift. Gideon can take the BQE to the Prospect and drive straight there. Going home to the house the boys call St. James Infirmary—a centenarian Queen Anne style home so called for the wealth of stray pennies strewn about the foyer floor and the family of mixed-race squirrels nesting in the eaves. Its bold, triangular front gable covered in dark, near black shingles makes it one of the most impressive homes in Ditmas Park. The house sits on an elevated brick terrace, gained by low stone steps and enclosed by a vine-covered wall.

A gale force wind last week broke an entire branch from the Gingko tree that grows beside the house. The branch fell on the roof and made no sound. The first thing I noticed when finally I saw what happened was how hollow the branch had grown. To my astonishment, an active beehive had taken residence there, its fragile insides now exposed to the elements. I stood for a long time watching the bees scramble to recover order, hemorrhaging jelly and honey and young. It only seemed a matter of time. For all of their industriousness, the bees could not rebuild their broken tree.

The body was never recovered. And there was no interrogation regarding its disappearance.

III.
THIGMOTAXIS

////\•/\\\

She is awake beside him, her body half-covered in the down comforter gifted them at the bridal shower. A percale weave, almost twenty years in service now and still their most comfortable bedding. Everything in the bedroom is still, the air warmed by dayspring and draped in the scent of oil heat drifting in with dust from the vents. The stained glass window above the headboard, dated to the turn of the century and only slightly warped, was designed to face the sun at its earliest angle. This in winter makes for a kind of vernal light, caught like gold in the fine fuzz of her cheek. She looks young and speaks softly, her voice like dust on a vinyl record, still dressed in dreammatter, cresting in a half-yawn

this morning I watched a spider crawl- -the length of your shaft growing erect -undoing its shadow

2.2011 .:. 6.2014

18.9°F .:. 82.0°F

N40°39'24.4643", W-74°0'15.0561" .:. N40°38'38.713", W-73°58'9.93"

40.6567956, -74.00418225 .:. 40.644087, -73.969425

Brooklyn   NY

Providence RI

Carolina   PR

Providence RI

Brooklyn   NY

Marfa   TX

Brooklyn   NY

"Nothing good and worthwhile is ever done alone. So it is with this novel. The best parts of *The Sovereign* are due in part to the shaping hand of my greater angels. I hope you know who you are. I hope you know I am grateful. I owe you more than I can say and hope to repay this debt in person. While we are still here. Together.

And those unbearably tedious parts of *The Sovereign* consider a document of what wrongheaded loneliness a writer might mistakenly undertake. No good and worthwhile dream is ever achieved alone."

Andrew E. Colarusso was born and raised in Brooklyn. He graduated with a BA in Comparative Literature from New York University and received an MFA from Brown University. He is founder and editor-in-chief of *The Broome Street Review*, and Visiting Assistant Professor of Literary Arts at Brown. This is his first published novel.

MICHAL AJVAZ, *The Golden Age.*
The Other City.
PIERRE ALBERT-BIROT, *Grabinoulor.*
YUZ ALESHKOVSKY, *Kangaroo.*
FELIPE ALFAU, *Chromos.*
Locos.
JOE AMATO, *Samuel Taylor's Last Night.*
IVAN ÂNGELO, *The Celebration.*
The Tower of Glass.
ANTÓNIO LOBO ANTUNES, *Knowledge of Hell.*
The Splendor of Portugal.
ALAIN ARIAS-MISSON, *Theatre of Incest.*
JOHN ASHBERY & JAMES SCHUYLER, *A Nest of Ninnies.*
ROBERT ASHLEY, *Perfect Lives.*
GABRIELA AVIGUR-ROTEM, *Heatwave and Crazy Birds.*
DJUNA BARNES, *Ladies Almanack.*
Ryder.
JOHN BARTH, *Letters.*
Sabbatical.
DONALD BARTHELME, *The King.*
Paradise.
SVETISLAV BASARA, *Chinese Letter.*
MIQUEL BAUÇÀ, *The Siege in the Room.*
RENÉ BELLETTO, *Dying.*
MAREK BIENCZYK, *Transparency.*
ANDREI BITOV, *Pushkin House.*
ANDREJ BLATNIK, *You Do Understand.*
Law of Desire.
LOUIS PAUL BOON, *Chapel Road.*
My Little War.
Summer in Termuren.
ROGER BOYLAN, *Killoyle.*
IGNÁCIO DE LOYOLA BRANDÃO, *Anonymous Celebrity.*
Zero.
BONNIE BREMSER, *Troia: Mexican Memoirs.*
CHRISTINE BROOKE-ROSE, *Amalgamemnon.*
BRIGID BROPHY, *In Transit.*
The Prancing Novelist.

GERALD L. BRUNS, *Modern Poetry and the Idea of Language.*
GABRIELLE BURTON, *Heartbreak Hotel.*
MICHEL BUTOR, *Degrees.*
Mobile.
G. CABRERA INFANTE, *Infante's Inferno.*
Three Trapped Tigers.
JULIETA CAMPOS, *The Fear of Losing Eurydice.*
ANNE CARSON, *Eros the Bittersweet.*
ORLY CASTEL-BLOOM, *Dolly City.*
LOUIS-FERDINAND CÉLINE, *North.*
Conversations with Professor Y.
London Bridge.
MARIE CHAIX, *The Laurels of Lake Constance.*
HUGO CHARTERIS, *The Tide Is Right.*
ERIC CHEVILLARD, *Demolishing Nisard.*
The Author and Me.
MARC CHOLODENKO, *Mordechai Schamz.*
JOSHUA COHEN, *Witz.*
EMILY HOLMES COLEMAN, *The Shutter of Snow.*
ERIC CHEVILLARD, *The Author and Me.*
ROBERT COOVER, *A Night at the Movies.*
STANLEY CRAWFORD, *Log of the S.S. The Mrs Unguentine.*
Some Instructions to My Wife.
RENÉ CREVEL, *Putting My Foot in It.*
RALPH CUSACK, *Cadenza.*
NICHOLAS DELBANCO, *Sherbrookes.*
The Count of Concord.
NIGEL DENNIS, *Cards of Identity.*
PETER DIMOCK, *A Short Rhetoric for Leaving the Family.*
ARIEL DORFMAN, *Konfidenz.*
COLEMAN DOWELL, *Island People.*
Too Much Flesh and Jabez.
ARKADII DRAGOMOSHCHENKO, *Dust.*
RIKKI DUCORNET, *Phosphor in Dreamland.*
The Complete Butcher's Tales.

RIKKI DUCORNET (cont.), *The Jade Cabinet.*
The Fountains of Neptune.
WILLIAM EASTLAKE, *The Bamboo Bed.*
Castle Keep.
Lyric of the Circle Heart.
JEAN ECHENOZ, *Chopin's Move.*
STANLEY ELKIN, *A Bad Man.*
Criers and Kibitzers, Kibitzers and Criers.
The Dick Gibson Show.
The Franchiser.
The Living End.
Mrs. Ted Bliss.
FRANÇOIS EMMANUEL, *Invitation to a Voyage.*
PAUL EMOND, *The Dance of a Sham.*
SALVADOR ESPRIU, *Ariadne in the Grotesque Labyrinth.*
LESLIE A. FIEDLER, *Love and Death in the American Novel.*
JUAN FILLOY, *Op Oloop.*
ANDY FITCH, *Pop Poetics.*
GUSTAVE FLAUBERT, *Bouvard and Pécuchet.*
KASS FLEISHER, *Talking out of School.*
JON FOSSE, *Aliss at the Fire.*
Melancholy.
FORD MADOX FORD, *The March of Literature.*
MAX FRISCH, *I'm Not Stiller.*
Man in the Holocene.
CARLOS FUENTES, *Christopher Unborn.*
Distant Relations.
Terra Nostra.
Where the Air Is Clear.
TAKEHIKO FUKUNAGA, *Flowers of Grass.*
WILLIAM GADDIS, JR., *The Recognitions.*
JANICE GALLOWAY, *Foreign Parts.*
The Trick Is to Keep Breathing.
WILLIAM H. GASS, *Life Sentences.*
The Tunnel.
The World Within the Word.
Willie Masters' Lonesome Wife.
GÉRARD GAVARRY, *Hoppla! 1 2 3.*

ETIENNE GILSON, *The Arts of the Beautiful.*
Forms and Substances in the Arts.
C. S. GISCOMBE, *Giscome Road.*
Here.
DOUGLAS GLOVER, *Bad News of the Heart.*
WITOLD GOMBROWICZ, *A Kind of Testament.*
PAULO EMÍLIO SALES GOMES, *P's Three Women.*
GEORGI GOSPODINOV, *Natural Novel.*
JUAN GOYTISOLO, *Count Julian.*
Juan the Landless.
Makbara.
Marks of Identity.
HENRY GREEN, *Blindness.*
Concluding.
Doting.
Nothing.
JACK GREEN, *Fire the Bastards!*
JIŘÍ GRUŠA, *The Questionnaire.*
MELA HARTWIG, *Am I a Redundant Human Being?*
JOHN HAWKES, *The Passion Artist.*
Whistlejacket.
ELIZABETH HEIGHWAY, ED., *Contemporary Georgian Fiction.*
AIDAN HIGGINS, *Balcony of Europe.*
Blind Man's Bluff.
Bornholm Night-Ferry.
Langrishe, Go Down.
Scenes from a Receding Past.
KEIZO HINO, *Isle of Dreams.*
KAZUSHI HOSAKA, *Plainsong.*
ALDOUS HUXLEY, *Antic Hay.*
Point Counter Point.
Those Barren Leaves.
Time Must Have a Stop.
NAOYUKI II, *The Shadow of a Blue Cat.*
DRAGO JANČAR, *The Tree with No Name.*
MIKHEIL JAVAKHISHVILI, *Kvachi.*
GERT JONKE, *The Distant Sound.*
Homage to Czerny.
The System of Vienna.

FOR A FULL LIST OF PUBLICATIONS, VISIT: www.dalkeyarchive.com

JACQUES JOUET, *Mountain R.*
Savage.
Upstaged.
MIEKO KANAI, *The Word Book.*
YORAM KANIUK, *Life on Sandpaper.*
ZURAB KARUMIDZE, *Dagny.*
JOHN KELLY, *From Out of the City.*
HUGH KENNER, *Flaubert, Joyce and Beckett: The Stoic Comedians.*
Joyce's Voices.
DANILO KIŠ, *The Attic.*
The Lute and the Scars.
Psalm 44.
A Tomb for Boris Davidovich.
ANITA KONKKA, *A Fool's Paradise.*
GEORGE KONRÁD, *The City Builder.*
TADEUSZ KONWICKI, *A Minor Apocalypse.*
The Polish Complex.
ANNA KORDZAIA-SAMADASHVILI, *Me, Margarita.*
MENIS KOUMANDAREAS, *Koula.*
ELAINE KRAF, *The Princess of 72nd Street.*
JIM KRUSOE, *Iceland.*
AYSE KULIN, *Farewell: A Mansion in Occupied Istanbul.*
EMILIO LASCANO TEGUI, *On Elegance While Sleeping.*
ERIC LAURRENT, *Do Not Touch.*
VIOLETTE LEDUC, *La Bâtarde.*
EDOUARD LEVÉ, *Autoportrait.*
Newspaper.
Suicide.
Works.
MARIO LEVI, *Istanbul Was a Fairy Tale.*
DEBORAH LEVY, *Billy and Girl.*
JOSÉ LEZAMA LIMA, *Paradiso.*
ROSA LIKSOM, *Dark Paradise.*
OSMAN LINS, *Avalovara.*
The Queen of the Prisons of Greece.
FLORIAN LIPUŠ, *The Errors of Young Tjaž.*
GORDON LISH, *Peru.*
ALF MACLOCHLAINN, *Out of Focus.*
Past Habitual.

The Corpus in the Library.
RON LOEWINSOHN, *Magnetic Field(s).*
YURI LOTMAN, *Non-Memoirs.*
D. KEITH MANO, *Take Five.*
MINA LOY, *Stories and Essays of Mina Loy.*
MICHELINE AHARONIAN MARCOM, *A Brief History of Yes.*
The Mirror in the Well.
BEN MARCUS, *The Age of Wire and String.*
WALLACE MARKFIELD, *Teitlebaum's Window.*
DAVID MARKSON, *Reader's Block.*
Wittgenstein's Mistress.
CAROLE MASO, *AVA.*
HISAKI MATSUURA, *Triangle.*
LADISLAV MATEJKA & KRYSTYNA POMORSKA, EDS., *Readings in Russian Poetics: Formalist & Structuralist Views.*
HARRY MATHEWS, *Cigarettes.*
The Conversions.
The Human Country.
The Journalist.
My Life in CIA.
Singular Pleasures.
The Sinking of the Odradek Stadium.
Tlooth.
HISAKI MATSUURA, *Triangle.*
DONAL MCLAUGHLIN, *beheading the virgin mary, and other stories.*
JOSEPH MCELROY, *Night Soul and Other Stories.*
ABDELWAHAB MEDDEB, *Talismano.*
GERHARD MEIER, *Isle of the Dead.*
HERMAN MELVILLE, *The Confidence-Man.*
AMANDA MICHALOPOULOU, *I'd Like.*
STEVEN MILLHAUSER, *The Barnum Museum.*
In the Penny Arcade.
RALPH J. MILLS, JR., *Essays on Poetry.*
MOMUS, *The Book of Jokes.*
CHRISTINE MONTALBETTI, *The Origin of Man.*
Western.

NICHOLAS MOSLEY, *Accident.*
Assassins.
Catastrophe Practice.
A Garden of Trees.
Hopeful Monsters.
Imago Bird.
Inventing God.
Look at the Dark.
Metamorphosis.
Natalie Natalia.
Serpent.
WARREN MOTTE, *Fables of the Novel:*
French Fiction since 1990.
Fiction Now: The French Novel in the
21st Century.
Mirror Gazing.
Oulipo: A Primer of Potential Literature.
GERALD MURNANE, *Barley Patch.*
Inland.
YVES NAVARRE, *Our Share of Time.*
Sweet Tooth.
DOROTHY NELSON, *In Night's City.*
Tar and Feathers.
ESHKOL NEVO, *Homesick.*
WILFRIDO D. NOLLEDO, *But for*
the Lovers.
BORIS A. NOVAK, *The Master of*
Insomnia.
FLANN O'BRIEN, *At Swim-Two-Birds.*
The Best of Myles.
The Dalkey Archive.
The Hard Life.
The Poor Mouth.
The Third Policeman.
CLAUDE OLLIER, *The Mise-en-Scène.*
Wert and the Life Without End.
PATRIK OUŘEDNÍK, *Europeana.*
The Opportune Moment, 1855.
BORIS PAHOR, *Necropolis.*
FERNANDO DEL PASO, *News from*
the Empire.
Palinuro of Mexico.
ROBERT PINGET, *The Inquisitory.*
Mahu or The Material.
Trio.
MANUEL PUIG, *Betrayed by Rita*
Hayworth.

The Buenos Aires Affair.
Heartbreak Tango.
RAYMOND QUENEAU, *The Last Days.*
Odile.
Pierrot Mon Ami.
Saint Glinglin.
ANN QUIN, *Berg.*
Passages.
Three.
Tripticks.
ISHMAEL REED, *The Free-Lance*
Pallbearers.
The Last Days of Louisiana Red.
Ishmael Reed: The Plays.
Juice!
The Terrible Threes.
The Terrible Twos.
Yellow Back Radio Broke-Down.
JASIA REICHARDT, *15 Journeys Warsaw*
to London.
JOÃO UBALDO RIBEIRO, *House of the*
Fortunate Buddhas.
JEAN RICARDOU, *Place Names.*
RAINER MARIA RILKE,
The Notebooks of Malte Laurids Brigge.
JULIÁN RÍOS, *The House of Ulysses.*
Larva: A Midsummer Night's Babel.
Poundemonium.
ALAIN ROBBE-GRILLET, *Project for a*
Revolution in New York.
A Sentimental Novel.
AUGUSTO ROA BASTOS, *I the Supreme.*
DANIËL ROBBERECHTS, *Arriving in*
Avignon.
JEAN ROLIN, *The Explosion of the*
Radiator Hose.
OLIVIER ROLIN, *Hotel Crystal.*
ALIX CLEO ROUBAUD, *Alix's Journal.*
JACQUES ROUBAUD, *The Form of*
a City Changes Faster, Alas, Than the
Human Heart.
The Great Fire of London.
Hortense in Exile.
Hortense Is Abducted.
Mathematics: The Plurality of Worlds of
Lewis.
Some Thing Black.

FOR A FULL LIST OF PUBLICATIONS, VISIT: www.dalkeyarchive.com

RAYMOND ROUSSEL, *Impressions of Africa.*

VEDRANA RUDAN, *Night.*

PABLO M. RUIZ, *Four Cold Chapters on the Possibility of Literature.*

GERMAN SADULAEV, *The Maya Pill.*

TOMAŽ ŠALAMUN, *Soy Realidad.*

LYDIE SALVAYRE, *The Company of Ghosts.*
The Lecture.
The Power of Flies.

LUIS RAFAEL SÁNCHEZ, *Macho Camacho's Beat.*

SEVERO SARDUY, *Cobra & Maitreya.*

NATHALIE SARRAUTE, *Do You Hear Them?*
Martereau.
The Planetarium.

STIG SÆTERBAKKEN, *Siamese.*
Self-Control.
Through the Night.

ARNO SCHMIDT, *Collected Novellas.*
Collected Stories.
Nobodaddy's Children.
Two Novels.

ASAF SCHURR, *Motti.*

GAIL SCOTT, *My Paris.*

DAMION SEARLS, *What We Were Doing and Where We Were Going.*

JUNE AKERS SEESE,
Is This What Other Women Feel Too?

BERNARD SHARE, *Inish.*
Transit.

VIKTOR SHKLOVSKY, *Bowstring.*
Literature and Cinematography.
Theory of Prose.
Third Factory.
Zoo, or Letters Not about Love.

PIERRE SINIAC, *The Collaborators.*

KJERSTI A. SKOMSVOLD,
The Faster I Walk, the Smaller I Am.

JOSEF ŠKVORECKÝ, *The Engineer of Human Souls.*

GILBERT SORRENTINO, *Aberration of Starlight.*
Blue Pastoral.
Crystal Vision.

Imaginative Qualities of Actual Things.
Mulligan Stew. Red the Fiend.
Steelwork.
Under the Shadow.

MARKO SOSIČ, *Ballerina, Ballerina.*

ANDRZEJ STASIUK, *Dukla.*
Fado.

GERTRUDE STEIN, *The Making of Americans.*
A Novel of Thank You.

LARS SVENDSEN, *A Philosophy of Evil.*

PIOTR SZEWC, *Annihilation.*

GONÇALO M. TAVARES, *A Man: Klaus Klump.*
Jerusalem.
Learning to Pray in the Age of Technique.

LUCIAN DAN TEODOROVICI,
Our Circus Presents...

NIKANOR TERATOLOGEN, *Assisted Living.*

STEFAN THEMERSON, *Hobson's Island.*
The Mystery of the Sardine.
Tom Harris.

TAEKO TOMIOKA, *Building Waves.*

JOHN TOOMEY, *Sleepwalker.*

DUMITRU TSEPENEAG, *Hotel Europa.*
The Necessary Marriage.
Pigeon Post.
Vain Art of the Fugue.

ESTHER TUSQUETS, *Stranded.*

DUBRAVKA UGRESIC, *Lend Me Your Character.*
Thank You for Not Reading.

TOR ULVEN, *Replacement.*

MATI UNT, *Brecht at Night.*
Diary of a Blood Donor.
Things in the Night.

ÁLVARO URIBE & OLIVIA SEARS, EDS.,
Best of Contemporary Mexican Fiction.

ELOY URROZ, *Friction.*
The Obstacles.

LUISA VALENZUELA, *Dark Desires and the Others.*
He Who Searches.

PAUL VERHAEGHEN, *Omega Minor.*

BORIS VIAN, *Heartsnatcher.*

LLORENÇ VILLALONGA, *The Dolls' Room.*
TOOMAS VINT, *An Unending Landscape.*
ORNELA VORPSI, *The Country Where No One Ever Dies.*
AUSTRYN WAINHOUSE, *Hedyphagetica.*
CURTIS WHITE, *America's Magic Mountain.*
The Idea of Home.
Memories of My Father Watching TV.
Requiem.
DIANE WILLIAMS,
Excitability: Selected Stories.
Romancer Erector.
DOUGLAS WOOLF, *Wall to Wall.*
Ya! & John-Juan.
JAY WRIGHT, *Polynomials and Pollen.*
The Presentable Art of Reading Absence.
PHILIP WYLIE, *Generation of Vipers.*
MARGUERITE YOUNG, *Angel in the Forest.*
Miss MacIntosh, My Darling.
REYOUNG, *Unbabbling.*
VLADO ŽABOT, *The Succubus.*
ZORAN ŽIVKOVIĆ , *Hidden Camera.*
LOUIS ZUKOFSKY, *Collected Fiction.*
VITOMIL ZUPAN, *Minuet for Guitar.*
SCOTT ZWIREN, *God Head.*

AND MORE . . .